RAVES FOR JOSEPH WAMBAUGH AND . . .

THE NEW CENTURIONS

Books by Joseph Wambaugh

THE NEW CENTURIONS
THE BLUE KNIGHT
THE ONION FIELD
THE CHOIRBOYS
THE BLACK MARBLE
THE GLITTER DOME
THE DELTA STAR
LINES AND SHADOWS
THE SECRETS OF HARRY BRIGHT

The New Centurions

Joseph Wambaugh

A DELL BOOK

Published by
Dell Publishing Co., Inc.
1 Dag Hammarskjold Plaza
New York, New York 10017

Dell ® TM 681510, Dell Publishing Co., Inc.

ISBN: 0-440-16417-6

Reprinted by arrangement with Little, Brown and Company in association with The Atlantic Monthly Press.

Printed in the United States of America

Two Previous Dell Editions

April 1987

10 9 8 7 6 5 4 3 2 1

WFH

FOR DEE
And of course
FOR ALL THE CENTURIONS

The New
Centurions

EARLY SUMMER 1960

1. The Runner

Lying prostrate, Serge Duran gaped at Augustus Plebesly who was racing inexorably around the track. That's a ridiculous name, thought Serge—Augustus Plebesly. It's a ridiculous name for a puny runt who can run like a goddamn antelope.

Plebesly ran abreast of, and was matching strides with, the feared P.T. instructor, Officer Randolph. If Randolph took up the challenge he'd never stop. Twenty laps. Twenty-five. Until there was nothing left but forty-nine sweat-suit–covered corpses and forty-nine puddles of puke. Serge had already vomited once and knew another was coming up.

"Get up, Duran!" a voice thundered from above.

Serge's eyes focused on the massive blur standing over him.

"Get up! Get up!" roared Officer Randolph, who had halted the wretched weary group of cadets.

Serge staggered to his feet and limped after his classmates as Officer Randolph ran ahead to catch Plebesly. Porfirio Rodriguez dropped back and patted Serge on the shoulder. "Don't give up, Sergio," Rodriguez panted. "Stay with 'em, man."

Serge ignored him and lurched forward in anguish. That's just like a Texas Chicano, he thought. Afraid I'll disgrace him in front of the *gabachos*. If I wasn't a Mexican he'd let me lay until the crabgrass was growing out my ears.

If he could only remember how many laps they had run. Twenty was their record before today, and today was hot, ninety-five degrees at least. And sultry. It was only their fourth week in the police academy. They weren't in shape yet. Randolph wouldn't dare run them more than twenty laps today. Serge leaned forward and concentrated on placing one foot in front of the other.

After another half-lap the burning in his chest was no longer bearable. He tasted something strange and choked in panic; he was going to faint. But luckily, Roy Fehler picked that exact moment to fall on his face, causing the collapse of eight other police cadets. Serge gave silent thanks to Fehler who was bleeding from the nose. The class had lost its momentum and a minor mutiny occurred as one cadet after another dropped to his knees and retched. Only Plebesly and a few others remained standing.

"You want to be Los Angeles policemen!" shouted Randolph. "You aren't fit to *wash* police cars! And I guarantee you one thing, if you aren't on your feet in five seconds, you'll never ride in one!"

One by one the sullen cadets got to their feet and soon all were standing except Fehler who was unsuccessfully trying to stop the nosebleed by lying on his back, his handsome face tilted up to the white sun. Fehler's pale crew cut was streaked with dust and blood. Officer Randolph strode over to him.

"Okay, Fehler, go take a shower and report to the sergeant. We'll get you to Central Receiving Hospital for an X ray."

Serge glanced fearfully at Plebesly who was doing some knee bends to keep loose. Oh no, Serge thought; look tired, Plebesly! Be human! You stupid ass, you'll antagonize Randolph!

Serge saw Officer Randolph regarding Plebesly, but the instructor only said, "Okay, you weaklings. That's enough running for today. Get on your back and we'll do some sit-ups."

With relief the class began the less painful session of calisthenics and self-defense. Serge wished he wasn't so big. He'd like to get paired up with Plebesly so he could crush the little bastard when they were practicing the police holds.

After several minutes of sit-ups, leg-ups, and push-ups, Randolph shouted, "Okay, onesies on twosies! Let's go!"

The class formed a circle and Serge was again teamed with Andrews, the man who marched next to him in formation. Andrews was big, even bigger than Serge, and infinitely harder and stronger. Like Plebesly, Andrews seemed bent on doing his very best, and he had almost choked Serge into unconsciousness the day before when they were practicing the bar strangle. When Serge recovered, he blindly grabbed Andrews by the shirt front and whispered a violent threat that he couldn't clearly remember when his rage subsided. To his surprise, Andrews apologized, a frightened look on the broad flat face as he realized that Serge had been hurt. He apologized three times that same day and beamed when Serge finally assured him there were no hard feelings. He's just an overgrown Plebesly, Serge thought. These dedicated types are all alike. They're so damn serious you can't hate them like you should.

"Okay, switch around," shouted Randolph. "Twosies on onesies this time."

Each man changed with his partner. This time Andrews played the role of suspect and it was Serge's job to control him.

"Okay, let's try the come-along again," shouted Randolph. "And do it right, this time. Ready? One!"

Serge took Andrews' wide hand at the count of one but realized that the come-along hold had vanished in the intellectual darkness that fifteen or more laps temporarily brought about.

"Two!" shouted Randolph.

"Is this the come-along, Andrews?" whispered Serge, as he saw Randolph helping another cadet who was even more confused.

Andrews responded by twisting his own hand into the come-along position and wincing so that Randolph would think that Serge had him writhing in agony, hence, a "proper" come-along. When Randolph passed he nodded in satisfaction at the pain Serge was inflicting.

"I'm not hurting you, am I?" Serge whispered.

"No, I'm okay," smiled Andrews, baring his large gapped teeth.

You just can't hate these serious ones, Serge thought, and looked around the sweating ring of gray-clad cadets for Plebesly. You had to admire the control the squirt had over his slim little body. On their first physical qualification test Plebesly had done twenty-five perfect chins, a hundred sit-ups in eighty-five seconds, and threatened to break the academy record for running the obstacle course. It was that which Serge feared most. The obstacle course with the dreaded wall that defeated him at first glance.

It was inexplicable that he should fear that wall. He was an athlete, at least he had been, six years ago at

Chino High School. He had lettered in football three years, a lineman, but quick, and well-coordinated for his size. And his size was inexplicable, six feet three, large-boned, slightly freckled, with light brown hair and eyes —so that it was a family joke that he could not possibly be a Mexican boy, at least not of the Duran family who were especially small and dark—and if his mother had not been from the old country and not disposed to off-color *chistes* they might have teased her with remarks about the blond *gabacho* giant who owned the small grocery store where for years she bought *harina* and *maíz* for the tortillas which she made by hand. His mother had never put store-bought tortillas on the family table. And suddenly he wondered why he was thinking about his mother now, and what good it did to ever think of the dead.

"All right, sit down," shouted Randolph, who didn't have to repeat the command.

The class of forty-eight cadets, minus Roy Fehler, slumped to the grass happy in the knowledge that there was only relaxation ahead, unless you were chosen as Randolph's demonstration victim.

Serge was still tense. Randolph often chose the big men to demonstrate the holds on. The instructor was himself a medium-sized man, but muscular, and hard as a gun barrel. He invariably hurt you when applying the holds. It seemed to be part of the game to toss the cadet a little harder than necessary, or to make him cry out from a hand, arm, or leg hold. The class got a nervous laugh from the torture, but Serge vowed that the next time Randolph used him for a onesies on twosies demonstration, he was not going to stand for any rougher than necessary treatment. However he hadn't decided what to do about it. He wanted this job. Being a cop would be a fairly interesting way to make four hundred and eighty-nine dollars a month. He relaxed as Randolph chose Augustus Plebesly for his victim.

"Okay, you already learned the bar strangle," said Randolph. "It's a good hold when you apply it right. When you apply it wrong, it's not worth a damn. Now I'm going to show you a variation of that strangle."

Randolph took a position behind Plebesly, reached around his throat with a massive forearm, and hooked the small neck in the crook of his arm. "I'm now applying pressure to the carotid artery," Randolph announced. "My forearm and bicep are choking off the oxygen flow to his brain. He would pass out very quickly if I applied pressure." As he said it, he *did* apply pressure, and Plebesly's large blue eyes fluttered twice and bulged in terror. Randolph relaxed his hold, grinned, and slapped Plebesly on the back to indicate he was through with him.

"Okay, ones on twos," shouted Randolph. "We only got a few minutes left. Let's go! I want you to practice this one."

As each number one man got his arm around the waiting throat of number two, Randolph shouted, "Lift the elbow. You have to get his chin up. If he keeps his chin down, he'll beat you. Make him lift that chin and then put it on him. Easy, though. And just for a second."

Serge knew that Andrews would be very careful about hurting him after the outburst the other day. He could see that Andrews was trying not to, the big arm around his neck flexed only a little, and yet the pain was unbelievable. Serge instinctively grabbed Andrews' arm.

"Sorry, Duran," said Andrews with a worried look.

"'s allright," Serge gasped. "That's a hell of a hold!"

When it was twos on ones, Serge lifted Andrews' chin. He had never hurt Andrews in any of the prior P.T. sessions. He didn't think Andrews could be hurt. He squeezed the throat in the crook, pulling his wrist toward him, and held it several seconds. Andrews' hands did not come up as his had. He must be applying it wrong, he thought.

Serge raised the elbow and increased the pressure.

"Am I doing it right?" asked Serge trying to see Andrews' upturned face.

"Let him go, Duran!" screamed Randolph. Serge jumped back, startled, and released Andrews who thudded to the ground red-faced, eyes half open and glazed.

"For chrissake, Duran," said Randolph, raising the massive torso of Andrews in his arms.

"I didn't mean to," Serge sputtered.

"I told you guys, easy!" said Randolph, as Andrews lurched to his feet. "You can cause brain damage with that hold. You stop the oxygen flow to the brain for too long a period and you're really going to hurt somebody, maybe kill them."

"I'm sorry, Andrews," said Serge, vastly relieved when the big man gave him a weak smile. "Why didn't you tap my arm or kick me or something? I didn't know I was hurting you."

"I wanted you to get the hold right," said Andrews, "and after a few seconds, I just blacked out."

"You be damn careful with that hold," shouted Randolph. "I don't want nobody hurt before you even graduate from the academy. But maybe you'll learn something from this. When you guys leave here, you're going out where there's guys that aren't afraid of that badge and gun. In fact, they might try to stick that badge up your ass to say they did it, and that big oval shield would sure hurt coming out. This particular hold might save you. If you get it on right you can put anybody out, and it just might rescue your ass someday. Okay, ones on twos again!"

"Your turn to get even," said Serge to Andrews who was massaging the side of his throat and swallowing painfully.

"I'll be careful," said Andrews, putting his huge arm around Serge's neck. "Let's just pretend I'm choking you," said Andrews.

"That's okay by me," said Serge.

Officer Randolph moved from one pair of cadets to another, adjusting the choke hold, raising elbows, turning wrists, straightening torsos, until he had had enough. "Okay, sit down, you guys. We're just wasting our time today."

The class collapsed on the grass like a huge gray many-legged insect and each cadet waited for an outburst from Randolph who was pacing in a tight circle, formidable in his yellow polo shirt, blue shorts, and black high-topped gym shoes.

Serge was bigger than Randolph, Andrews much bigger. Yet they all seemed small beside him. It was the sweat suits, he thought, the ill-fitting baggy pants and gray sweat shirts always sweat-soaked and ugly. And it was the haircuts. The cadets wore short military style haircuts which made all the young men look smaller and younger.

"It's hard to put everything into the self-defense session," said Randolph, finally breaking silence, still pacing, arms folded as he watched the grass. "It's damn hot and I run you hard. Maybe sometimes I run you too hard. Well, I got my own theory on physical training for policemen and it's time I explained it to you."

That's very thoughtful, you bastard, thought Serge, rubbing his side, which still ached from the twenty laps around the track. He was just beginning to be able to take large breaths without coughing or without his lungs hurting.

"Most of you guys don't know what it's like to fight another guy," said Randolph. "I'm sure you all had your scraps in high school, maybe a scuffle or two somewhere else. A couple of you are Korean vets and think you seen it all, and Wilson here has been in the Golden Gloves. But none of you really knows what it's like to fight another man no holds barred and win. You're going to have to be ready to do it anytime. And you have to win. I'm going to show you something. Plebesly, come here!"

Serge smiled as Plebesly sprang to his feet and trotted into the center of the circle. The round blue eyes showed no fatigue and stared patiently at the instructor apparently ready for a painful, elbow-wrenching arm hold or any other punishment Officer Randolph cared to offer.

"Come closer, Plebesly," said Randolph, gripping the little man by the shoulder and whispering in his ear for several seconds.

Serge leaned back on his elbows, happy in the knowledge that Randolph was evidently going to use the remainder of the P.T. class for his demonstration. Serge's stomach muscles loosened and a sunny wave of relaxation swept over him. It was getting so he was having dreams of running the track. Suddenly he saw Randolph staring at him.

"You, Duran, and you, Andrews, come up here!"

Serge fought a momentary surge of anger, but then dejectedly plodded into the circle, remembering that the last time he had failed to master a complicated hold, he was given three laps around the track. He wanted to be a policeman, but he would not run that track again for anyone. Not this day. Not now.

"I picked Duran and Andrews because they're big," said Randolph. "Now, I want you two to put Plebesly's hands behind his back and handcuff him. Just simulate the cuffing, but get him in the cuffing position. He's the suspect, you two are the policemen. Okay, go ahead."

Serge looked at Andrews for a plan to take the retreating Plebesly, who backed in a circle, hands at his
sides, away from the two big men. Just like the Corps,
thought Serge. Always the games. First in boot camp,
then in I.T.R. at Camp Pendleton. The Korean War
had been over a year when he joined, and yet they
talked about the gooks like they would be waiting to
swarm over their ship the first moment they landed in
Pacific waters.

Andrews made a lunge for Plebesly, who almost
slithered away but was caught by the sleeve of his sweat
shirt. Serge jumped on Plebesly's back and the little man
went down under Serge's two hundred and fifteen pounds.
But then he wriggled and twisted, and suddenly Serge
was under Plebesly and Andrews was on Plebesly's back
forcing the combined weight of himself and Plebesly on
Serge's aching ribs.

"Pull him away, Andrews," Serge wheezed. "Get a
wristlock!"

Serge pushed himself up but Plebesly had locked his
arms and legs around Serge's body from the rear and
hung there leechlike with enough weight to topple Serge
over backward on the clinging Plebesly who gasped
but would not let go. Andrews managed to pry the little
man's fingers loose, but the sinewy legs held on and by
now Serge was beaten and sat there with the implacable
monkey clinging to his torso.

"Get a choke hold on him, damn it," Serge muttered.

"I'm trying. I'm too tired," Andrews whispered, as
Plebesly buried his face deeper into Serge's dripping
back.

"Okay, that's enough," Randolph commanded. Plebesly
instantly released Serge, bounded to his feet and trotted
to his place in the grassy circle.

Serge stood up and for a second the earth tilted. Then
he dropped to the ground next to Andrews.

"The reason for all that was to prove a point,"
shouted Randolph to the sprawling broken circle of
cadets. "I told Plebesly to resist. That's all. Just to resist
and not let them pin his arms. You'll notice he didn't
fight back. He just resisted. And Andrews and Duran are
both twice his size. They would never have got their

man handcuffed. They would have lost him eventually. The point is that they were expending twice the energy to overcome his resistance and they couldn't do it. Now, every one of you guys is going to run into this kind of problem lots of times. Maybe your man is going to decide you aren't going to handcuff him. Or maybe he'll even fight back. You saw the trouble little Plebesly gave the two big guys, and he wasn't even fighting back. What I'm trying to do is tell you that these fights out there in the streets are just endurance contests. The guy who can *endure* usually wins. That's why I'm running your asses off. When you leave here you'll have endurance. Now, if I can teach you an armlock and that choke hold, maybe that will be enough. You all saw what the choke can do. The trouble is getting the choke on the guy when he's struggling and fighting back. I can't teach you self-defense in thirteen weeks.

"All that Hollywood crap is just that—crap. You try throwing that haymaker at somebody's chin and you'll probably hit the top of his head and break your hand. Never use your fists. If someone uses his fists you use your stick and try to break a wrist or knee like we teach you. If he uses a knife you use a gun and cancel his ticket then and there. But if you find yourself without a stick and the situation doesn't permit deadly force, well then you better be able to out-endure the son of a bitch. That's why you see these newspaper pictures of six cops subduing one guy. *Any* guy or even any woman can wear out several policemen just by resisting. It's goddamn hard to take a man who doesn't want to be taken. But try explaining it to the jury or the neighbors who read in the papers how an arrestee was hurt by two or three cops twice his size. They'll want to know why you resorted to beating the guy's head in. Why didn't you just put a fancy judo hold on him and flip him on his ass. In the movies it's nothing.

"And while I'm on the subject, there's something else the movies have done for us—they created a legend about winging your man, shooting from the hip and all that bullshit. Well I'm not your shooting instructor but it all ties in with self-defense. You guys have been here long enough to know how hard it is to hit a still target, let alone a moving one. Those of you who make your twenty years will miss that goddamn paper man every time you come up here for your monthly pistol qualification. And he's only a paper man. He don't shoot back. The light's good and the adrenalin hasn't turned your arm into a licorice stick like it does in combat. And yet when you blow some asshole up and were lucky to even hit him you'll hear a member of the coroner's jury say, 'Why didn't you shoot to wound him? Did you have to kill him? Why didn't you shoot the gun out of his hand!'"

Randolph's face was crimson and two wide sweat streams ran down either side of his neck. When he was in uniform he wore three service stripes on his sleeve indicating at least fifteen years with the Department. Yet Serge could hardly believe he was more than thirty. He hadn't a gray hair and his physique was flawless.

"What I want you guys to take from my class is this: it's a bitch to subdue a man with a gun or a stick or a sap, let alone with your hands. Just keep yourself in half-assed condition and you'll *out-endure* him. Take the bastard any way you can. If you can use these two or three holds I teach you, then use them. If you can't, hit him with a brick or anything else. Just subdue your man and you'll be in one piece the day your twentieth anniversary rolls around and you sign those retirement papers. That's why I run your asses off."

"I don't know why I'm so nervous," said Gus Plebesly. "We've been told about the stress interview. It's just to shake us up."

"Relax, Gus," said Wilson, who leaned against the wall, smoking, careful not to drop ashes on the khaki cadet uniform.

Gus admired the luster of Wilson's black shoes. Wilson had been a marine. He knew how to spit-shine shoes, and he could drill troops and call cadence. He was Gus's squad leader and had many of the qualities which Gus believed men could only gain in military service. Gus wished he were a veteran and had been places, then perhaps he would have confidence. He should have. He was the number one man in his class in physical training, but at this moment he wasn't sure he would be able to speak during the stress interview. He had waited in dread so many times in high school when he had to give an oral report. In college he had once consumed almost a half pint of gin diluted with soda pop before he could give a three-minute speech in a public speaking class. And he had gotten away with it. He wished he could do it now. But these men were police officers. Professionals. They would detect the alcohol in his eyes, speech, or gait. He couldn't fool them with so cheap a trick.

"You sure look nervous," said Wilson, offering Gus a cigarette from the pack he kept in his sock, GI fashion.

"Thanks a lot, Wilson," Gus mumbled, refusing the cigarette.

"Look, these guys are just going to try to psyche you," said Wilson. "I talked to a guy who graduated in April. They just pick on you in these stress interviews. You know, about your P.T. or your shooting, or maybe your academic standing. But hell, Plebesly, you're okay in everything and tops in P.T. What can they say?"

"I don't know. Nothing, I guess."

"Take me," said Wilson. "My shooting is so shitty I might as well throw my gun at the goddamn target.

They'll probably rip me apart. Tell me how they're going to wash me out if I don't come to the pistol range during the lunch hour and practice extra. That kind of bullshit. But I'm not worried. You realize how bad they need cops in this town? And in the next five, six years it's going to get lots worse. All those guys that came on right after the war will have their twenty years. I tell you we'll all be captains before we finish our tours with the Department."

Gus studied Wilson, a short man, even a hair shorter than Gus. He must have stretched to meet the minimum five feet eight inches, Gus thought, but husky, big biceps and a fighter's shoulders, with a broken nose. He had wrestled Wilson in the self-defense classes and had found Wilson surprisingly easy to take down and control. Wilson was much stronger, but Gus was more agile and could persevere.

Gus understood what Officer Randolph had told them, and he believed that if he could outlast his opponents he needn't be afraid. He was surprised at how well it had worked so far in training. But what would a man like Wilson, an ex-fighter, do to him in a real fight? Gus had never hit a man, not with a fist, not with anything. What would happen to his splendid endurance when a man like Wilson buried a heavy fist in his stomach or crashed one to his jaw? He had been a varsity sprinter in high school, but had always avoided contact sports. He had never been an aggressive person. What in the hell had made him think he could be a policeman? Sure the pay was pretty good, what with the security and pension. He could never hope to do as well in the bank. He had hated that dreary low paying job and had almost laughed when the operations officer had assured him that in five more years he could expect to make what he, the operations officer, was making, which was less than a starting Los Angeles policeman. And so he had come this far. Eight weeks and they hadn't found him out yet. But they might at this stress interview.

"Only one thing worries me," said Wilson. "Know what that is?"

"What?" asked Gus, wiping his wet palms on the legs of the khaki uniform.

"Skeletons. I hear they sometimes rattle the bones in the stress interview. You know how they say the background investigation of all cadets goes on for weeks after we enter the academy."

"Yes?"

"Well, I hear they sometimes use the stress interview to tell a guy he's been washed out. You know, like, 'The background investigator discovered you were once a member of the Nazi Bund of Milwaukee. You're washed out, kid.' That kind of bullshit."

"I guess I don't have to worry about my background," Gus smiled feebly. "I've lived in Azusa my whole life."

"Come on, Plebesly, don't tell me there isn't something you've done. Every guy in this class has something in his background. Some little thing that he wouldn't want the Department to find out. I saw the faces that day when the instructor said, 'Mosley, report to the lieutenant.' And Mosley never came back to class. And then Ratcliffe left the same way. They found out something about them and they were washed out. Just like that, they disappeared. You ever read *Nineteen Eighty-Four?*"

"No, but I know about it," said Gus.

"It's the same principle here. They know none of us has told them everything. We all got a secret. Maybe they can stress it out of us. But just keep cool, and don't tell them anything. You'll be okay."

Gus's heart sank when the door to the captain's office opened and Cadet Roy Fehler strode out, tall, straight, and as confident as always. Gus envied him his assurance and hardly heard Fehler say, "Next man."

Then Wilson was shoving him toward the door and he looked at his reflection in the mirror on the cigarette machine and the milky blue eyes were his, but he hardly recognized the thin white face. The sparse sandy hair seemed familiar but the narrow white lips were not his, and he was through the door and facing the three inquisitors who looked at him from behind a conference table. He recognized Lieutenant Hartley and Sergeant Jacobs. He knew the third man must be the commander, Captain Smithson, who had addressed them the first day in the academy.

"Sit down, Plebesly," said unsmiling Lieutenant Hartley.

The three men whispered for a moment and reviewed a sheaf of papers before them. The lieutenant, a florid bald man with plum-colored lips, suddenly grinned broadly and said, "Well, so far you're doing fine here at the academy, Plebesly. You might work on your shooting a bit, but in the classroom you're excellent and on the P.T. field you're tops."

Gus became aware that the captain and Sergeant Jacobs were also smiling, but he suspected trickery when the captain said, "What shall we talk about? Would you like to tell us about yourself?"

"Yes sir," said Gus, trying to adjust to the unexpected friendliness.

"Well, go ahead then, Plebesly," said Sergeant Jacobs with an amused look. "Tell us all about yourself. We're listening."

"Tell us about your college training," said Captain Smithson after several silent seconds. "Your personnel folder says you attended junior college for two years. Were you an athlete?"

"No sir," croaked Gus. "I mean I tried out for track. I didn't have time, though."

"I'll bet you were a sprinter," smiled the lieutenant.

"Yes sir, and I tried hurdles," said Gus, trying to smile back. "I had to work and carry fifteen units, sir. I had to quit track."

"What was your major?" asked Captain Smithson.

"Business administration," said Gus, wishing he had added "sir," and thinking that a veteran like Wilson would never fail to throw a sir into every sentence, but he was not accustomed to this quasi-military situation.

"What kind of work did you do before coming on the Department?" asked Captain Smithson, leafing through the folder. "Post Office, wasn't it?"

"No sir. Bank. I worked at a bank. Four years. Ever since high school."

"What made you want to be a policeman?" asked the captain, touching the gaunt tanned cheek with a pencil.

"The pay and the security," Gus answered, and then quickly, "and it's a good career, a profession. And I like it so far."

"Policemen don't make very good pay," said Sergeant Jacobs.

"It's the most I ever made, sir," said Gus, deciding to be truthful. "I never made anywhere near four eighty-nine a month before, sir. And I have two children and one on the way."

"You're only twenty-two years old," Sergeant Jacobs whistled. "What a family you're making."

"We were married right after high school."

"Do you intend to finish college?" asked Lieutenant Hartley.

"Oh, yes sir," said Gus. "I'm going to switch my major to police science, sir."

"Business administration is a good field of study," said Captain Smithson. "If you like it, stay with it. The Department can find good use for business administration majors."

"Yes sir," said Gus.

"That's all, Plebesly," said Captain Smithson. "Keep working on your shooting. It could be better. And send in the next cadet, please."

3. The Scholar

Roy Fehler had to admit it pleased him when he overheard two of his classmates mention his name in a whispered conversation during a smoking break after class. He heard the cadet mutter "intellectual," reverently, he thought, just after he recorded the highest score in the report writing class conducted by Officer Willis. He found the academic portion of recruit training unchallenging and if it weren't for some difficulties on the pistol range and his lack of endurance on the P.T. field, he would probably be the top cadet in his class and win the Smith & Wesson always awarded to the top cadet at graduation. It would be a tragedy, he thought, if someone like Plebesly won the revolver merely because he could run faster or shoot better than Roy.

He was anxious for Sergeant Harris to come in the classroom for their three hours of criminal law. It was the most stimulating part of recruit training even though Harris was only an adequate teacher. Roy had bought a copy of Fricke's *California Criminal Law*, and had read it twice in the past two weeks. He had challenged Harris on several points of law and believed that Harris had become more alert of late for fear of being embarrassed by a knowledgeable recruit. The classroom quieted abruptly.

Sergeant Harris strode to the front of the class, spread his notes on the lectern and lit the first of the several cigarettes he would smoke during his lecture. He had a face like porous concrete, but Roy thought he wore his uniform well. The tailored blue wool seemed particularly attractive on tall slim men, and Roy wondered how he would look when he had the blue uniform and black Sam Browne.

"We're going to continue with search and seizure of evidence," said Harris, scratching the bald spot at the crown of his rust-colored hair.

"By the way, Fehler," said Sergeant Harris, "you were right yesterday about the uncorroborated testimony of an accomplice being sufficient to prove the corpus delicti. But it isn't enough to convict."

"No, of course not," said Roy, nodding his thanks to Harris for the acknowledgment. He wasn't sure whether Harris appreciated the significance of a few well-placed brain-teasing questions. It was the student who brought a class to life. He had learned this from Professor Raymond who had encouraged him to specialize in criminology when he was drifting aimlessly in the social sciences unable to find a specialty which really interested him. And it was Professor Raymond who begged him not to drop out of college, because he had added so much to the three classes he had taken from the kindly round little man with the burning brown eyes. But he was tired of college; even the independent study with Professor Raymond had begun to bore him. It had come to him suddenly one sleepless night when the presence of Dorothy and her pregnancy was oppressing him that he ought to leave college and join the police department for a year, two years, until he learned something of crime and criminals that might not be available to the criminologist.

The next day he applied at City Hall wondering if he should phone his father or wait until he was actually sworn in, as he would be in about three months, if he passed all the tests and survived the character investigation which he knew would pose no problem. His father was terribly disappointed and his older brother Carl had reminded him that his education had already cost the family business in excess of nine thousand dollars, especially since he could not wait until he finished college to marry, and that in any event, a criminologist would be of little use to a restaurant supply business. Roy had told Carl that he would pay back every cent, and he certainly intended to, but it was difficult living on the policeman's beginning salary which was not the advertised four hundred and eighty-nine dollars a month—not when they deducted for your pension, Police Relief, the Police Protective League, the Police Credit Union which loaned the money for the uniforms, income tax, and the medical plan. But he vowed he'd pay Carl and his father every cent. And he'd finish college and be a criminologist eventually, never making the money his brother Carl would make, but being infinitely happier.

"Yesterday we talked about the famous cases like Cahan, Rochin, and others," said Sergeant Harris. "And we talked about Mapp versus Ohio which any rookie would know was illegal search and seizure, and I mentioned how it sometimes seems to policemen that the court is lying in wait for bad cases like Mapp versus Ohio so they can restrict police power a little more. Now that you're policemen, or almost policemen, you're going to become very interested in the decisions handed down by the courts in the area of search and seizure. You're going to be upset, confused, and generally pissed off most of the time, and you're going to hear locker room bitching about the fact that most landmark decisions are five to four, and how can a working cop be expected to make a sudden decision in the heat of combat and then be second-guessed by the Vestal Virgins of the Potomac, and all that other crap. But in my opinion, that kind of talk is self-defeating. We're only concerned with the U.S. and California supreme courts and a couple of appellate courts. So don't worry about some of these freakish decisions that an individual judge hands down. Even if it's your case and it's one you wanted to win. Chances are the defendant will be busted again before long and we'll get another crack at him. And the judge's decision ends right there on the bench. It's not going to have a goddamn thing to do with the next case you try.

"Now I know I got you guys pretty confused yesterday with the problems of search incident to a lawful arrest. We know we can search when?" Sergeant Harris waved a burning cigarette vaguely toward the rear of the room.

Roy didn't bother to turn toward the voice which answered, "When you have a search warrant, or when you have consent, or incident to a lawful arrest." The voice Roy knew belonged to Samuel Isenberg, the only other cadet whom Roy felt might challenge him scholastically.

"Right," said Sergeant Harris, blowing a cloud of smoke through his nose. "Half you people will never get a search warrant in your entire careers. Most of the two hundred thousand arrests we make in a year are made on the basis of reasonable cause to believe a felony has been committed, or because a crime has been committed in the officer's presence. You're going to stumble onto crimes and criminals and bang! You've got to move, not take six hours to get a search warrant. It's for that reason that we're not going to talk about this kind of search. I've saved the other kind of search until today because to me it's the most challenging—that's search incident to a lawful arrest. If the court ever takes this kind of search away from us we'll be nearly out of business."

Isenberg raised his hand, and Sergeant Harris nodded while taking an incredible puff on the cigarette. What was a fairly good-sized butt was now scorching his fingers. He snuffed it out as Isenberg said, "Would you repeat, sir, about the search of the premises ninety-five feet from the defendant's house?"

"I was afraid of that." Harris smiled, shrugged, and lit another cigarette. "I shouldn't bring up those cases. I did what I criticize other officers for doing, bitching about controversial cases and prophesying doom. Okay, I just said that it hasn't yet been defined what *under the defendant's control* means in terms of search of the premises incident to the arrest. The court has deemed in its infinite wisdom that an arrest ninety-five feet away from the house did not give officers the right to go into the house and search under the theory of the defendant having control of the premises. Also, I mentioned that in another case a person sixty feet away was deemed to have control of a car in question. And then I mentioned a third case in which officers arrested some bookmakers in their car a half block away and the court held the search of the car and premises was reasonable.

"But don't worry about that kind of crap. I shouldn't have mentioned it anyway because I'm basically an optimist. I always see the glass half full not half empty. Some policemen predict that the courts will eventually strip us of all our right to search incident to arrest, but that would cripple us. I don't think it will happen. I feel that one of these days the Chief Sorcerer in Washington and his eight little apprentices will get themselves together and all this will be straightened out."

The class tittered and Roy felt himself becoming irked. Harris just couldn't resist criticizing the Supreme Court, thought Roy. He hadn't heard any instructor discuss the law without taking a few shots at the Court. Harris seemed reasonable but he probably felt obligated to do it too. So far, all of the cases Roy had read, that were so bitterly opposed by the instructors, seemed to him just and intelligent. They were based on libertarian principles and it seemed to him unfair to say such thoughtful decisions were unrealistic.

"Okay you guys, quit leading me off on tangents. We're supposed to be talking about searches incident to a lawful arrest. How about this one: Two officers observe a cab double-parked in front of a hotel. The fare, a man, gets out of the front seat. A woman comes out of the hotel and gets in the rear seat. Another man not with the woman walks up and gets in the back seat with the woman. Two policemen observe the action and decide to investigate. They approach and order the occupants out of the cab. They observe the man remove his hand from the juncture of the seat and back cushion. The officers remove the rear cushion and find three marijuana cigarettes. The man was convicted. Was the decision affirmed or denied by the appellate court? Anyone want to make a guess?"

"Denied," said Guminski, a thin, wiry-haired man of about thirty, whom Roy guessed to be the oldest cadet in the class.

"See. You guys are already thinking like cops," Harris chuckled. "You're ready to believe the courts are screwing us every time. Well you're wrong. The conviction was affirmed. But there was something I failed to mention that contributed to the decision. What do you think it might be?"

Roy raised his hand and when Harris nodded, Roy asked, "What time of day was it?"

"Good," said Sergeant Harris. "You might've guessed, it was an unusual hour. About 3:00 A.M. Now on what grounds could they search the cab?"

"Incident to a lawful arrest," said Roy, without raising his hand or waiting for Harris to nod.

"Who were they arresting?" asked Harris.

Roy was sorry he had responded so quickly. He realized he was being trapped. "Not the defendant or the woman," he said slowly, while his mind worked furiously. "The cabdriver!"

The class burst out laughing but was silenced by a wave of Harris' nicotine-stained left hand. Harris bared his large brownish teeth in a grin and said, "Go ahead, Fehler, what's your reasoning?"

"They could arrest the cabbie for double-parking," said Roy. "That's a violation, and then search incident to the lawful arrest."

"Not bad," said Harris. "I like to see you people thinking even when you're wrong."

Hugh Franklin, the broad-shouldered recruit who sat next to Roy at the alphabetically arranged tables, chuckled louder than Roy felt was necessary. Franklin did not like him, Roy was certain. Franklin was an all-American jock strapper. A high school letterman according to the conversations they had the first few days in the academy. Then three years in the navy, where he played baseball and toured the Orient, thoroughly enjoying himself, and now to the police department, when he couldn't make it in Class D professional baseball.

"Why is Fehler wrong?" Harris asked the class, and Roy became annoyed that the entire class should be asked to attack his answer. Why didn't Harris just give the reason instead of asking everyone to comment? Could it be that Harris was trying to embarrass him? Perhaps he didn't like having a recruit in the class who took the trouble to do independent study in criminal law and not just blindly accept the legal interpretations which evolve from the police point of view.

"Yes, Isenberg," said Harris, and this time Roy turned around so that he would not miss Isenberg's annoying manner of answering questions.

"I doubt that the search of the cab could be justified incident to the arrest of the driver for double-parking," said Isenberg carefully, his dark-lidded black eyes moving from Harris to Roy and back to the instructor. "It's true the driver committed a traffic violation and could be cited, and a traffic ticket is technically an arrest, but how could you search the cab for contraband? That has nothing to do with a traffic violation, does it?"

"Are you asking me?" said Harris.

"No sir, that's my answer." Isenberg smiled shyly, and Roy felt disgust for Isenberg's pretense at humility. He felt the same toward Plebesly and the diffidence he showed when someone expressed admiration for his athletic prowess. He believed them both to be conceited men. Isenberg was another one, he knew, who was just discharged from the army. He wondered how many men joined the Department because they were simply looking for a job and how many like himself had more serious motives.

"Was the search incident to the arrest of anyone?" asked Harris.

"No, I don't think so," said Isenberg, clearing his throat nervously. "I don't think anyone was under arrest at the time the officer found the contraband. The officer could detain and interrogate people under unusual circumstances at night according to Giske versus Sanders, and I don't think there was anything unreasonable in ordering them out of the cab. The officers had a justifiable suspicion that something unusual was going on. When the defendant reached behind the seat I think that might be construed as a furtive action." Isenberg's voice trailed off and several recruits including Roy raised their hands.

Harris looked at no one but Roy. "Go ahead, Fehler," he said.

"I don't think the officers had the right to order them out of the cab. And when were they arrested, after they found the narcotics? What if they would have got out of the cab and just walked away? Would the officers have the right to stop them?"

"How about that, Isenberg?" asked Harris, lighting a fresh cigarette with a battered silver lighter. "Could the officers stop them from walking away, before the contraband was found?"

"Uh, yes, I think so," said Isenberg looking at Roy, who interrupted him.

"Were they under arrest then?" asked Roy. "They must have been under arrest if the officers could stop them from walking away. And if they were under arrest what was their crime? The marijuana wasn't found for several seconds after they had them already under arrest."

Roy smiled indulgently to show Isenberg and Harris there were no hard feelings at having proved Isenberg wrong.

"The point is, they were not under arrest, Fehler," said Isenberg, addressing Roy directly for the first time. "We have the right to stop and interrogate. The person is obliged to identify himself and explain what's going on.

And we can resort to any means to make him submit. Yet we haven't arrested him for any crime. If he explains what's going on and it's reasonable, we release him. I think that's what Giske versus Sanders meant. So in this case, the officers stopped, interrogated, and recovered the marijuana during their investigation. Then and only then were the suspects placed under arrest."

Roy knew from Harris' pleased expression that Isenberg was correct.

"How could you prove someone else hadn't dumped the marijuana behind the seat?" asked Roy, unable to dull the sharp edge on his voice.

"I should've mentioned that the cabbie testified to cleaning out the back of the cab earlier in the evening because of a sick passenger who threw up back there," said Harris. "And no one had been in the back seat until the woman and the defendant got in."

"That certainly makes a difference," said Roy, appealing to Harris for some concession to his interpretation.

"Well, that wasn't the issue I was concerned with," said Harris. "It was the question of searching prior to an actual arrest that I wanted someone to bring out of this case, and Isenberg did it beautifully. You all understand, don't you?"

"Yes sir," said Roy, "but the case would certainly have been reversed if the cabbie hadn't testified to cleaning out the back that same evening. That was certainly an important point, sir."

"Yes, Fehler," Sergeant Harris sighed. "You were partly right. I should've mentioned that, Fehler."

AUGUST 1960

4. Huero

Serge gave his shoes a quick buff, threw the shoe brush in his locker, and slammed the metal door. He was late for roll call. It was two minutes after four o'clock. Damn the traffic, he thought. How can I put up with this traffic and smog for twenty years? He paused before the full-length mirror, alone in the locker room. His brass buttons and Sam Browne needed polish. His blue woolen uniform was so lint covered it looked hairy. He cursed as he realized there might be an inspection tonight.

Serge picked up his notebook, the packet of traffic citations and a map book of city streets. He shoved his shiny new five-cell flashlight into the deep pocket of his uniform pants, grabbed his baton, and put his hat on, since his hands were too full to carry it. The other night watch officers were talking noisily as he entered the roll call room. The watch commander's desk was unoccupied. Serge was relieved to see that he too was late and by the time he arrived five minutes later, Serge had dabbed most of the lint from his uniform with a piece of two-inch-wide masking tape which he carried in his notebook for such emergencies.

"After those new uniforms are cleaned a few times you won't have so much trouble with lint," said Perkins, the desk officer, a nineteen-year policeman now on light duty while recovering from a serious heart attack.

"Oh, yeah," Serge nodded, self-conscious of his brand-new, never cleaned blue uniform, announcing that he was one of the rookies just graduated last week from the academy. He and two members of his class had been assigned to Hollenbeck. It wasn't hard to see how they had been selected, he thought. The other officers were Chacon and Medina. He had heard in the academy that most officers with Spanish surnames ended up in Hollenbeck Division but he had hoped he might be an exception. Not everyone recognized Duran as a Spanish name. He had been mistaken for German and even

Irish, especially by people who couldn't believe a Mexican could be fair, freckled, and speak without a trace of a Spanish accent. The Negro officers were not all assigned to the Negro areas; he was irked that the Chicanos were all stuck here in Hollenbeck. He could see the need for Spanish-speaking officers here, but nobody had even bothered to see if he could speak Spanish. It was just "Duran to Hollenbeck," another victim of a system.

"Ramirez," said Lieutenant Jethro, settling his long sagging body in the desk chair and opening the time book.

"Here."

"Anderson."

"Here."

"You're working Four-A-Five."

"Bradbury."

"Here."

"Gonsalvez."

"Here."

"Four-A-Eleven."

Serge answered when his name was called along with his partner for the night, Galloway, whom he had not worked with since arriving in the division. He was scheduled off tomorrow, Sunday, after working six days, and wished he weren't. Every night was a new adventure and he smiled as he realized he would probably be glad for days off soon enough. He tired of everything quickly. Still, this was a more interesting job than most. He couldn't honestly think of one he'd like better. Of course, when he finished college, he might find something better. And then he had to smile again at himself. He had enrolled in two night classes at East Los Angeles Junior College. Six units. Only a hundred and eighteen to go, and here I sit dreaming about finishing college, he thought.

"Okay, here's the crimes," said the lieutenant, after calling the roll. Perkins took the lineup board downstairs to the teletype machine to be forwarded to Communications, so that Communications downtown would know which cars were working in Hollenbeck. The policemen opened their notebooks to a fresh page, and got ready to write.

Lieutenant Jethro was a loose-skinned, sallow man

with a hard mouth and very cold eyes. Serge had learned however that he was the division's best-liked supervisor. The men considered him fair.

"Had a robbery at twenty-nine twenty-two Brooklyn Avenue," he read mechanically. "At Big G restaurant. Today, 9:30 A.M. Suspect: male, Mexican, twenty-three to twenty-five years, five-five to five-six, hundred sixty to hundred seventy pounds, black hair, brown eyes, medium complexion, wearing a dark shirt and dark pants, carried a hand gun, got eighty-five dollars from the cash register and took victim's wallet and I.D. . . . Goddamn it, that's a shitty description!" said Lieutenant Jethro suddenly. "This is what we were talking about last night at roll call training. What the hell good does a description like that do you?"

"Maybe that's all they could get out of the guy, Lieutenant," said Milton, the burly baiter of supervisors who always took the last seat of the last table in the roll call room, and whose four service stripes, indicating twenty years service, entitled him to a constant barrage of sarcasm directed at the sergeants. He was usually pretty quiet around the lieutenant though, Serge thought.

"Bullshit, Milt," said Jethro. "This poor bastard Hector Lopez has been hit a half dozen times this year. I'm always seeing his name on robbery, burglary, or till tap reports. He's become a professional victim, and he usually gives an outstanding description of the suspect. It's just that some officer—in this case, it was a day watch officer—was in a big hurry and didn't try to get a decent description. This is a good example of a worthless piece of paper that can't be any use to the detectives. That description could fit twenty percent of the guys on the street right now."

"It only takes a few minutes extra to get a decent description the dicks can work with," Jethro continued. "How did the guy comb his hair? Did he have a moustache? Glasses? Tattoos? A distinctive walk? How about his teeth? His clothes? There's dozens of little things about clothes that might be important. How did he talk? Did he have a gravel voice? Did he have a Spanish accent? How about that gun? This report says handgun. What the hell does that tell you? I know goddamn well Lopez knows the difference between an automatic and a revolver. And was it chrome plated or blue steel?"

Jethro dropped the papers disgustedly into the folder. "We had lots of crimes last night, but none of the suspect descriptions are worth a shit so I'm not going to read them." He closed the folders and sat back in his chair on the ten-inch platform, looking down at the policemen of the night watch. "Anything you guys want to talk about before we have an inspection?" he asked.

A groan went up at the mention of the word inspection, and Serge rubbed the toes of each shoe on the back of his calves, irritated once more at the Los Angeles traffic which prevented him from arriving at the station early enough to shine them.

Jethro's colorless eyes glinted merrily around the room for a moment. "If no one can think of something to say, we might as well get started with the inspection. We'll have more time to look a little harder."

"Wait a minute, Lieutenant," said Milton, a wet stump of cigar between his little teeth. "Give me a second, I'll think of something."

"Yeah, Milt, I don't blame you for wanting to stall me," said Jethro. "It looks like you shined those shoes with a Hershey bar."

The men chuckled and Milton beamed and puffed from the end seat at the last row of tables in the rear of the squad room. On his first night in Hollenbeck, Milton had informed Serge that the last row of tables belonged to *los veteranos* and that rookies generally sat toward the front of the room. Serge hadn't worked with Milton yet, and was looking forward to it. He was loud and overbearing but the men told him he could learn a lot from Milton if Milton felt like teaching him.

"One thing before inspection," said Jethro. "Who's working Forty-three tonight? You, Galloway?"

Serge's partner nodded.

"Who's working with you, one of the new men? Duran, right? You two check those pin maps before you go out. They're killing us on Brooklyn Avenue about midnight. We've had three window smashes this week and two last week. All about the same time, and they're grabbing quite a bit of loot."

Serge looked at the walls which were lined with identical street maps of Hollenbeck Division. Each map bore different colored pins, some to indicate burglaries, the multicolored pins indicating whether they occurred on morning, day, or night watch. Other maps showed where robberies were occurring. Still others showed locations of car thefts and thefts from vehicles.

"Let's fall in for inspection," said Lieutenant Jethro. This was Serge's first inspection since leaving the academy. He wondered where fourteen men could line up in the crowded room. He saw quickly that they formed one rank along the side wall in front of the pin maps. The tall men fell in toward the front of the room so Serge headed for the front, standing next to Bressler, who was the only officer taller than himself.

"Okay, you're supposed to be at attention," said the lieutenant quietly to a policeman in the center of the rank who was muttering about something.

"At close interval, dress right, dress!"

The policemen, hands on right hips, elbows touching the man to the right, dressed the rank perfunctorily and Jethro didn't bother to check the line.

"Ready, front!"

When Jethro inspected him, Serge stared at the top of the lieutenant's head as he had been taught in boot camp six years ago when he was eighteen, just graduated from high school, broken-hearted that the Korean War ended before he could get in it and win several pounds of medals which he could pin to the beautiful Marine Corps dress blue uniform which they didn't issue you and he never got around to buying because he grew up quickly under the stunning realities of Marine Corps boot camp.

Jethro paused a few extra seconds in front of Ruben Gonsalvez, a jovial dark-skinned Mexican who, Serge guessed, was a veteran of at least ten years with the Department.

"You're getting rounder every day, Ruben," said Jethro in his toneless unsmiling voice.

"Yes, Lieutenant," answered Gonsalvez and Serge did not yet dare to look down the line.

"You been eating at Manuel's again, I see," said Jethro, and with peripheral vision Serge could see the lieutenant touching Gonsalvez's necktie.

"Yes, sir," said Gonsalvez. "The top stains above the tie bar are *chile verde*. The other ones are *menudo*."

This time Serge turned a fraction of an inch and detected no expression on Jethro or Gonsalvez.

"How about you, Milt? When you changing the oil on your necktie?" said Jethro, moving down the line to the white-haired veteran who stood so straight he looked like a tall man but standing next to him Serge guessed he wasn't five feet ten.

"Right after inspection, Lieutenant," said Milton, and Serge sneaked a glance at Jethro, who shook his head sadly and moved to the end of the rank.

"Night watch. One pace forward . . . No, as you were," said Jethro, shuffling to the front of the roll call room. "I'm afraid to inspect you from the rear. Some of you'll probably have bananas or girlie magazines hanging out of your back pockets. Dis-missed!"

So this is how it is, thought Serge, gathering up his equipment, looking for Galloway to whom he had never been introduced. He was afraid the division would be GI and he wasn't sure how long he could take military discipline. This was okay. He could tolerate this much discipline indefinitely, he thought.

Galloway walked up and offered his hand. "Duran?"

"Yeah," said Serge, shaking hands with the freckled young man.

"What do your friends call you?" asked Galloway and Serge smiled as he recognized the hackneyed opening line that policemen use on suspects to determine street names which were usually much more valuable to know than true names.

"Serge. How about you?"

"Pete."

"Okay, Pete, what do you want to do tonight?" asked Serge, hoping that Galloway would let him drive. This was his sixth night and he hadn't driven yet.

"You're just out of the last class, aren't you?" asked Galloway.

"Yeah," said Serge, disappointed.

"You familiar with the city?"

"No, I lived in Chino before coming on the job."

"Guess you better keep books then. I'll drive, okay?"

"You're the boss," Serge said cheerfully.

"No, we're equals," said Galloway. "Partners."

It was satisfying to be able to get settled in the radio car without asking a dozen inane questions or fumbling around with your equipment. Serge felt he could handle the passenger officer's routine duties as well as possible by now. Serge put his flashlight and hat in the back seat along with his baton which was thrust under the back cushion for easy access. He was surprised to see Galloway slide the baton under the back cushion in the front seat, lancelike, right next to him.

"I like my stick closer to me," said Galloway. "It's my blue blanket."

"Four-A-Forty-three, night watch, clear," said Serge into the hand mike as Galloway started the engine of the Plymouth, and backed out of the parking space and onto First Street, the setting sun forcing Serge to put on his sunglasses as he wrote their names on the daily log.

"What did you do before coming on the job?" asked Galloway.

"Marine Corps for four years," said Serge, writing his serial number on the log.

"How do you like police work so far?" asked Galloway.

"Fine," Serge answered, writing carefully as the car bounced over a rut in the street.

"It's a good job," said Galloway. "I'm starting my fourth year next month. Can't complain so far."

The sandy hair and freckles made Galloway look like a high school kid, Serge thought. With four years on the job he has to be at least twenty-five.

"This your first Saturday night?"

"Yeah."

"Quite a difference on weekends. Maybe we'll see a little action."

"Hope so."

"Done anything exciting yet?"

"Nothing," said Serge. "Took some burglary reports. Wrote a few tickets. Booked a couple drunks and a few traffic warrants. Haven't even made a felony arrest yet."

"We'll try to get you a felony tonight." Galloway offered Serge a cigarette and he accepted.

"Thanks. I was going to ask you to stop so I could get some," said Serge, lighting Galloway's with his Zippo that used to have a brass globe and anchor affixed to it. There was now just a naked metallic ring on the lighter where he had pried the Marine Corps emblem off in Okinawa after a salty pfc with a year and a half in the corps had kidded him about only gung-ho recruits carrying P.X. Zippos with big fat emblems on them.

Serge smiled as he remembered how badly the young marines wanted to be salts. How they had scrubbed and bleached their new dungarees and put sea dips in the caps. He hadn't completely gotten over it, he thought, remembering how his new blue uniform made him uneasy tonight when Perkins mentioned the lint.

The incessant chattering on the police radio was still giving Serge trouble. He knew it would be some time before he was able to pick his car number, Four-A-Forty-three, from the jumble of voices that crowded the police frequencies. He was starting to recognize some of the voices of the Communications operators. One sounded like an old maid schoolmarm, another like a youngish Marilyn Monroe, and a third had a trace of a Southern accent.

"We got a call," said Galloway.

"What?"

"Tell her to repeat," said Galloway.

"Four-A-Forty-three, repeat, please," said Serge, his pencil poised over the pad which was affixed to a metal shelf in front of the hot sheet.

"Four-A-Forty-three," said the schoolmarm, "one-two-seven South Chicago, see the woman, four-five-nine report."

"Four-A-Forty-three, roger," said Serge. And to Galloway, "Sorry. I can't pick our calls out of all that noise, yet."

"Takes a little time," said Galloway, turning around in a gas station parking lot, heading east toward Chicago Street.

"Where you living?" asked Galloway, as Serge took a deep puff on the cigarette to finish it before they arrived.

"Alhambra. I got an apartment over there."

"Guess Chino's too far to drive, huh?"

"Yeah."

"Married?"

"No," said Serge.

"Got parents in Chino?"

"No, they're both dead. Got an older brother there. And a sister in Pomona."

"Oh," said Galloway, looking at him like he was a war orphan.

"I have a nice little apartment, and the apartment

house is crawling with broads," said Serge, so his baby-
faced partner would stop being embarrassed at prying.

"Really?" Galloway grinned. "Must be nice being a
bachelor. I got hooked at nineteen, so I wouldn't know."

After turning north on Chicago Street, Galloway gave
Serge a puzzled look as Serge craned his neck to catch
the house numbers on the east side of the street.

"One twenty-seven will be on the west," said Galloway.
"Even numbers are always on the east and south."

"All over the city?"

"All over," Galloway laughed. "Hasn't anybody told
you that yet?"

"Not yet. I've been checking both sides of the street
on every call. Pretty dumb."

"Sometimes the senior officer forgets to mention the
obvious. As long as you're willing to admit you know
nothing, you'll learn fast enough. Some guys hate to
show they don't know anything."

Serge was out of the car while Galloway was still
applying the emergency brake. He removed his stick
from the back seat and slid it in through the baton
holder on the left side of his Sam Browne. He noticed
that Galloway left his baton in the car, but he guessed
he should adhere to the rules very closely for a while,
and the rule was carry your batons.

The house was a one-story faded pink frame. Most of
the houses in East Los Angeles seemed faded. This was
an old part of the city. The streets were narrow and
Serge noticed many aged people.

"Come in, come in, gentlemen," said the snuffling
puckered old woman in an olive-drab dress and band-
aged legs, as they stepped on the tiny porch one at a
time, shouldering their way through a forest of potted
ferns and flowers.

"Step right in, right in," she smiled and Serge was
surprised to see a mouthful of what he was sure were
real teeth. She should have been toothless. A fleshy
goiter dropped from her neck.

"It's not so often we see the policemen these days,"
she smiled. "We used to know all the police at the Boyle
Heights station. I used to know some officers' names,
but already they're retired I guess."

Serge smiled at the Molly Goldberg accent, but he
noticed Galloway was nodding soberly at the old woman

as he sat in the ancient creaking rocker in front of a brightly painted unused fireplace. Serge smelled fish and flowers, mustiness and perfume, and bread in the oven. He removed his cap and sat on the lumpy napless sofa with a cheap oriental tapestry thrown over the back to dull the thrust of the broken springs he felt against his back.

"I'm Mrs. Waxman," said the old woman. "I been right here in this house for thirty-eight years."

"Is that a fact?" said Galloway.

"Would you like something? A cup of coffee, maybe. Or a cupcake?"

"No thank you," said Galloway. Serge shook his head and smiled.

"I used to walk down the police station some summer evenings and chat with the desk officer. There was a Jewish boy worked there named Sergeant Muellstein. You ever know him?"

"No," said Galloway.

"Brooklyn Avenue was really something then. You should have seen Boyle Heights. Some of the finest families in Los Angeles was living here. Then the Mexicans started moving in and all the people ran out and went to the west side. Just the old Jews like me are left with the Mexicans now. What do you think of the church down the street?"

"Which church?" asked Galloway.

"Hah! You don't have to say. I understand you got a job to do." The old woman smiled knowingly at Galloway and winked at Serge.

"They dare to call the place a synagogue," she croaked. "Could you imagine it?"

Serge glanced through the window at the light-studded Star of David atop the First Hebrew Christian Synagogue at the residential corner of Chicago Street and Michigan Avenue.

"You see what's right across the street?" said the old woman.

"What?" asked Serge.

"The United Mexican Baptist Church," said the old woman, with a triumphant nod of her chalk-white head. "I knew it was going to happen. I told them in the forties when they all started moving."

"Told who?" asked Serge, listening intently.

"We could have lived with the Mexicans. An Orthodox Jew is like a Catholic Mexican. We could have lived. Now look what we got. Reform Jews was bad enough. Now, Christian Jews? Don't make me laugh. And Mexican Baptisters? You see, everything is out of whack now. Now there's just a few of us old ones left. I don't even go out of my yard, no more."

"I guess you called us because of Mrs. Horwitz," said Galloway, adding to Serge's confusion.

"Yes, it's the same old story. There ain't nobody can get along with the woman," said Mrs. Waxman. "She tells everybody her husband has a better shop than my Morris. Hah! My Morris is a watchmaker. Do you understand? A real watchmaker! A craftsman, not some junk repairman!" The old woman stood up, gesturing angrily at the center of the room as a trickle of saliva ran uncontrolled from the corner of her wrinkled mouth.

"Now, now, Mrs. Waxman," said Galloway, helping her back to the chair. "I'm going right over to Mrs. Horwitz and tell her to stop spreading those stories. If she doesn't, why I'll threaten to put her in jail."

"Would you? Would you do that?" asked the old woman. "But don't arrest her, mind you. Just give her a pretty good scare."

"We're going over there right now," said Galloway, putting on his cap and standing up.

"Serves her right, serves her right," said Mrs. Waxman, beaming at the two young men.

"Good-bye, Mrs. Waxman," said Galloway.

"Bye," Serge mumbled, hoping that Galloway had not noticed how long it took him to catch on to the old woman's senility.

"She's a regular," Galloway explained, starting the car and lighting a cigarette. "I guess I been there a dozen times. The old Jews always say 'Boyle Heights,' never Hollenbeck or East L.A. This *was* the Jewish community before the Chicanos moved in."

"Doesn't she have a family?" asked Serge, marking the call in the log.

"No. Another abandoned old lady," said Galloway. "I'd rather some asshole shoot me in the street tonight than end up old and alone like her."

"Where's Mrs. Horwitz live?"

"Who knows? West side probably, where all the Jews with money went. Or maybe she's dead."

Serge borrowed another of Galloway's cigarettes and relaxed as Galloway patrolled slowly in the late summer dusk. He stopped in front of a liquor store and asked Serge what brand he smoked and entered the store without asking for money. Serge knew that this meant the liquor store was Galloway's cigarette stop, or rather it belonged to the car, Four-A-Forty-three. He had accepted the minor gratuity when each partner he had worked with offered it. Only one, a serious, alert young policeman named Kilton, had stopped at a place where Serge had to pay for cigarettes.

Galloway came back after repaying the liquor store proprietor with a few minutes of small talk and flipped the cigarettes into Serge's lap.

"How about some coffee?" asked Galloway.

"Sounds good."

Galloway made a U-turn and drove to a small sidewalk restaurant on Fourth Street. He parked in the empty parking lot, turned up the police radio and got out leaving the door to the car open so they could hear the radio.

"Hi, baby face," said the bleached blonde working the counter, who spoiled her eyes by drawing her eyebrows at a ridiculous angle.

If there was one thing most Mexicans had it was good heads of hair, thought Serge. Why had this one destroyed hers with chemicals?

"Afternoon, Sylvia," said Galloway. "Meet my partner, Serge Duran."

"*Qué tal, huero?*" said Sylvia, pouring two steaming cups of coffee which Galloway did not offer to pay for.

"Hi," said Serge, sipping the burning coffee and hoping the remark would pass.

"*Huero?*" said Galloway. "You a Chicano, Serge?"

"What do you think, *pendejo?*" Sylvia laughed raucously, showing a gold-capped eyetooth. "With a name like Duran?"

"I'll be damned," said Galloway. "You sure look like a paddy."

"He's a real *huero,* baby," said Sylvia with a flirtatious smile at Serge. "He's almost as fair as you."

"Can't we talk about something else?" asked Serge, irritated more at himself for being embarrassed than at these two grinning fools. He told himself he was not ashamed of being Mexican, it was simply less complicated to be an Anglo. And an Anglo he had been for the past five years. He had only returned to Chino a few times after his mother died and one of those times was for a fourteen-day leave with his brother when they buried her. He had tired of the dreary little town in five days and returned to the base, selling his unused leave to the Marine Corps when he was discharged.

"Well, it's good to have a partner who can speak Spanish," said Galloway. "We can use you around here."

"What makes you think I can speak Spanish?" asked Serge, very careful to maintain the narrow cordiality in his voice.

Sylvia looked at Serge strangely, stopped smiling, and returned to the sink where she began washing a small pile of cups and glasses.

"You one of those Chicanos who can't speak Spanish?" Galloway laughed. "We got another one like that, Montez. They transfer him to Hollenbeck and he can't speak Spanish any better than me."

"I don't need it. I get along well enough in English," said Serge.

"Better than me, I hope," smiled Galloway. "If you can't *spell* better than me we'll be in lots of trouble when we make our reports."

Serge gulped down the coffee and waited anxiously as Galloway tried in vain to get Sylvia talking again. She smiled at his jokes but remained at the sink and looked coldly at Serge. "Bye-bye, baby face," she said, as they thanked her for the free coffee and left.

"It's too bad you don't speak Spanish real good," said Galloway as the sun dropped through the smoggy glow in the west. "With a paddy-looking guy like you we could overhear lots of good information. Our arrestees would never guess you could understand them and we could learn all kind of things."

"How often you pick up a sitting duck?" asked Serge, to change the subject, checking a license plate against the numbers on the hot sheet.

"Ducks? Oh, I get one a week maybe. There's plenty of hot cars sitting around Hollenbeck."

"How about rollers?" asked Serge. "How many hot cars do you get rolling?"

"Hot rollers? Oh, maybe one a month, I average. They're just teen-age joyriders usually. Are you just half Mexican?"

Bullshit, thought Serge, taking a large puff on the cigarette, deciding that Galloway would not be denied.

"No, I'm all Mexican. But we just didn't talk Spanish at home."

"Your parents didn't talk it?"

"My father died when I was young. My mother talked half English and half Spanish. We always answered in English. I left home when I got out of high school and went in the Marine Corps for four years. I just got out eight months ago. I've been away from the language and I've forgotten it. I never knew very much Spanish to begin with."

"Too bad," Galloway murmured and seemed satisfied.

Serge slumped in the seat staring blankly at the old houses of Boyle Heights and fought a mild wave of depression. Only two of the other policemen he had worked with had forced him to explain his Spanish name. Damn curious people, he thought. He asked nothing of people, nothing, not even of his brother, Angel, who had tried in every way possible to get him to settle in Chino after leaving the corps, and to go into his gas station with him. Serge told him he didn't plan to work very hard at anything and his brother had to put in thirteen hours every day in the grimy gas station in Chino. He could have done that. Maybe marry some fertile Mexican girl and have nine kids and learn to live on tortillas and beans because that's all you could afford when things were lean in the *barrio*. Well here he was working in another Chicano *barrio* he thought with a crooked smile. But he'd be out of here as soon as he finished his year's probationary period. Hollywood Division appealed to him, or perhaps West Los Angeles. He could rent an apartment near the ocean. The rent would be high, but maybe he could share the cost with another policeman or two. He had heard stories of the aspiring actresses who languish all over the westside streets.

"You ever worked the west side?" he asked Galloway suddenly.

"No, I just worked Newton Street and here at Hollenbeck," Galloway answered.

"I hear there're lots of girls in Hollywood and West L.A.," said Serge.

"I guess so," said Galloway and the leer looked ridiculous with the freckles.

"You hear a lot of pussy stories from policemen. I've been wondering how true they are."

"A lot of them are true," said Galloway. "It seems to me that policemen do pretty well because for one thing girls trust you right off. I mean a girl isn't going to be afraid to meet a guy after work when she sees him sitting in a black and white police car in a big blue uniform. She knows you're not a rapist or a nut or something. At least she can be pretty sure. That means something in this town. And she can also be pretty sure you're a fairly clean-cut individual. And then some girls are attracted by the job itself. It's more than the uniform, it's the authority or something. We got a half dozen cop chasers in every division. You'll get to know some of them. All the policemen know them. They try their damnedest to lay every guy at the station. Some are actually pretty good-looking. You met Lupe, yet?"

"Who's she?" asked Serge.

"She's one of Hollenbeck's cop chasers. Drives a Lincoln convertible. You'll run into her before long. Good lay, I heard." Galloway leered again through the freckles and Serge had to laugh aloud.

"I'm looking forward to meeting her," said Serge.

"There's probably lots of stuff in Hollywood. I never worked those fancy silk stocking divisions so I wouldn't know. But I'd be willing to bet there's more here on the east side than anywhere."

"Let's drive around the division, do you mind?" asked Serge.

"No, where do you want to go?"

"Let's tour the streets, all around Boyle Heights."

"One fifty-cent tour of Hollenbeck Division coming up," said Galloway.

Serge stopped looking for a traffic violator and he didn't check the hot sheet even once for the sitting duck he craved. He smoked and watched people and houses. All the houses were old, most of the people were Mexican. Most of the streets were too narrow, and Serge guessed they were designed decades before anyone dreamed that Los Angeles would be a city on wheels. And when they did realize it, the east side was too old and too poor and the streets stayed too narrow, and the houses got older. Serge felt his stomach tighten and his face grew unaccountably warm as he saw the second-hand stores. *Ropa usada,* the signs said. And the *panadería* filled with sweet breads, cookies and cakes, usually a bit too oily for him. And the scores of restaurants with painted windows announcing that *menudo* was served on Saturdays and Sundays and Serge wondered how anyone could eat the tripe and hominy and thin red broth. Especially he wondered how he had been able to eat it as a child, but he guessed it was because they had been hungry. He thought of his brother Angel and his sister Aurora and how they would squeeze half a lemon in the *menudo,* sprinkle in oregano and slosh corn tortillas in the broth faster than his mother could make them. His father had been a tubercular whom he barely remembered as a smiling man with bony wrists, lying in bed all the time, coughing and smelling bad from the sickness. He only produced three children and little else in this world and Serge couldn't at the moment think of another family on his street with only three children except the Kulaskis and they were Anglos, at least to the Chicanos they were Anglos, but now he thought how humorous it was to have considered these Polacks as Anglo. He also wondered if it was true that the large quantity of corn the Mexicans consumed by eating tortillas three times a day produced the fine teeth. It was Mexican folklore that this was the case and it was certainly true that he and most of his boyhood friends had teeth like alligators. Serge had been to a dentist for the first time while in the Marine Corps where he had two molars filled.

Night was falling faster now that summer had almost gone and as he watched and listened a strange but oddly familiar feeling swept over him. First it was a tremor in the stomach and then up around the chest and his face felt warm; he was filled with anxious longing, or was it, could it be, nostalgia? It was all he could do to keep from laughing aloud as he thought it must be nostalgia, for this was Chino on a grand scale. He was watching the same people who were doing the same things they had done in Chino, and he thought how strange that part of a man could yearn for the place of his youth even when he despised it, and what produced it, and what it produced. But at least it was the only innocent years he had ever known and there had been his mother. He guessed it was really her that he yearned for and the safety she represented. We all must long for that, he thought.

Serge watched the garish lighted madness on the San Bernardino Freeway as Galloway drove south on Soto back to Boyle Heights. There was a minor accident on the freeway below and a flare pattern had traffic backed up as far as he could see. A man held what looked like a bloody handkerchief to his face and talked to a traffic officer in a white hat who held a flashlight under his arm as he wrote in his notebook. No one really wants to grow up and go out in all this, he thought, looking down at the thousands of crawling headlights and the squatty white tow truck which was removing the debris. That must be what you long for—childhood—not for the people or the place. Those poor stupid Chicanos, he thought. Pitiful bastards.

"Getting hungry, partner?" asked Galloway.

"Anytime," said Serge, deciding to leave Chino five years in the past where it belonged.

"We don't have many eating spots in Hollenbeck," said Galloway. "And the few we do have aren't fit to eat in."

Serge had already been a policeman long enough to learn that "eating spot" meant more than restaurant, it meant restaurant that served free food to policemen. He still felt uncomfortable about accepting the free meals especially since they had been warned about gratuities in the police academy. It seemed however that the sergeants looked the other way when it came to free cigarettes, food, newspapers and coffee.

"I don't mind paying for dinner," said Serge.

"You don't have anything against paying half price, do you? We have a place in our area that pops for half."

"I don't mind at all," Serge smiled.

"We actually do have a place that bounces for everything. It's called El Soberano, that means the sovereign.

We call it El Sobaco. You know what that means, don't you?"

"No," Serge lied.

"That means the armpit. It's a real scuzzy joint. A beer joint that serves food. Real ptomaine tavern."

"Serves greasy tacos, I bet." Serge smiled wryly, knowing what the place would look like. "Everybody drinking and dancing I bet, and every night some guy gets jealous of his girl friend and you get a call there to break up a fight."

"You described it perfect," said Galloway. "I don't know about the food though. For all I know, they might drive a sick bull out on the floor at dinner time and everybody slices a steak with their blades."

"Let's hit the half-price joint," said Serge.

"Tell her to repeat!" Galloway commanded.

"What?"

"The radio. We just got another call."

"Son of a bitch. Sorry, partner, I've got to start listening to that jumble of noise." He pressed the red mike button. "Four-A-Forty-three, repeat."

"Four-A-Forty-three, Four-A-Forty-three," said the shrill voice, who had replaced the schoolmarm, "Three-three-seven South Mott, see the woman, four-five-nine suspect there now. Code two."

"Four-A-Forty-three, roger," said Serge.

Galloway stepped down unexpectedly on the accelerator and Serge bounced off the back cushion. "Sorry," Galloway grinned. "Sometimes I'm a leadfoot. I can't help stomping down on a four-five-nine call. Love to catch those burglars."

Serge was glad to see his partner's blue eyes shining happily. He hoped the thrills of the job would not wear off too soon on himself. They obviously hadn't on Galloway. It was reassuring. Everything in the world seemed to grow so dull so quickly.

Galloway slowed at a red light, looked both ways carelessly and roared across First Street as a westbound station wagon squealed and blasted its horn.

"Jesus," Serge whispered aloud.

"Sorry," said Galloway sheepishly, slowing down but only a little. Two blocks farther, he streaked through a partially blind intersection with a posted stop sign and Serge closed his eyes but heard no squealing tires.

"I don't have to tell you you shouldn't drive like this, do I?" said Galloway. "At least not while you're on probation. You can't afford to catch any heat from the sergeants while you're on probation." Galloway made a grinding right turn and another left at the next block.

"If I obeyed all the goddamn rules of the road like they tell us to, we'd never get there quick enough to catch anyone. And I figure it's my ass if we get in an accident, so what the hell."

How about my ass, you dumb ass, Serge thought, one hand braced on the dashboard, the other gripping the top of the back cushion. He had never envisioned hurtling down busy streets at these speeds. Galloway was a fearless and stupidly lucky driver.

Serge realized that he could not afford to get a quick reputation of troublemaker. New rookies should be all ears and short on mouth, but this was too much. He was going to demand that Galloway slow down. He made the decision just as his sweaty left hand lost its grip on the cushion.

"This is the street," said Galloway. "It's about mid-block." He turned off his headlights and glided noiselessly to the curb, several houses from where the address should have been. "Don't close your door," said Galloway, slipping out of the car and padding along the curb while Serge was still unfastening his seat belt.

Serge got out and followed Galloway, who wore ripple-soled shoes and his key ring tucked in his back pocket. Serge now saw the reason as his own new leather-soled shoes skidded and crunched noisily on the pavement. He tucked the jingling key ring in the back pocket and walked as softly as he could.

It was a dark residential street and he lost Galloway in the gloom, cursing as he forgot the address they were sent to. He broke into a slow run when Galloway, standing in the darkness of a driveway, startled him.

"It's okay, he's long gone," said Galloway.

"Got a description?" asked Serge, noticing the side door of the leaning stucco house was standing open and seeing the tiny dark woman in a straight cotton dress standing near Galloway.

"He's been gone ten minutes," said Galloway. "She doesn't have a phone and couldn't find a neighbor at home. She made the call at the drugstore."

"She saw him?"

"Came home and found the pad ransacked. She must've surprised the burglar, because she heard someone run through the back bedroom and go out the window. A car took off down the alley a second later. She didn't see the suspect, the car or anything."

Two more radio cars suddenly glided down the street, one from each direction.

"Go broadcast a code four," said Galloway. "Just say the four-five-nine occurred ten minutes ago and the suspect left in a vehicle and was not seen. When you're finished come in the house and we'll take a report."

Serge held up four fingers to the policemen in the other cars indicating a code four, that no assistance was needed. As he returned to the house from making the broadcast, he decided that this payday he would invest in a pair of ripple soles or get these leather soles replaced with rubber.

He heard the sobbing as he approached the open side door and Galloway's voice coming from the front of the small house.

Serge did not go into the living room for a moment. He stood and looked around the kitchen, smelling the cilantro and onion, and seeing jalapeño chili peppers on the tile drainboard. He remembered as he saw the package of corn tortillas that his mother would never have any but homemade tortillas in her house. There was an eight-inch-high madonna on the refrigerator and school pictures of five smiling children, and he knew without examining her closely that the madonna would be Our Lady of Guadalupe in pink gown and blue veil. He wondered where the other favorite saint of the Mexicans was hiding. But Martin de Porres was not in the kitchen, and Serge entered the living room, which was small and scantily furnished with outdated blond furniture.

"We bought that TV set so recently," said the woman, who had stopped weeping and was staring at the dazzling white wall where the freshly cut two-foot antenna wire lay coiled on the floor.

"Anything else missing?" asked Galloway.

"I'll look," she sighed. "We only made six payments on it. I guess we got to pay for it even though it's gone."

"I wouldn't," said Galloway. "Call the store. Tell them it's stolen."

"We bought it at Frank's Appliance Store. He's not a rich man. He can't afford to take our loss."

"Do you have theft insurance?" asked Galloway.

"Just fire. We was going to get theft. We was just talking about it because of so many burglaries around here."

They followed her into the bedroom and Serge saw him—Blessed Martin de Porres, the black holy man in his white robe and black cloak and black hands which said to the Chicano, "Look at my face, not brown but black and yet even for me Nuestro Señor delivers miracles." Serge wondered if they still made Mexican movies about Martin de Porres and Pancho Villa and other folk heroes. Mexicans are great believers he thought. Lousy Catholics, really. Not devout churchgoers like Italians and Irish. The Aztec blood diluted the orthodox Spanish Catholicism. He thought of the various signals he had seen Mexicans make to their particular version of the Christian deity as they genuflected on both knees in the crumbling stucco church in Chino. Some made the sign of the Cross in the conventional Mexican fashion, completing the sign with a kiss on the thumbnail. Others made the sign three times with three kisses, others six times or more. Some made a small cross with the thumb on the forehead, then touched the breast and both shoulders, then returned to the lips for another cross, breast and shoulders again, and another small cross on the lips followed by ten signs on the head, breast and shoulders. He loved to watch them then, particularly during the Forty Hours when the Blessed Sacrament was exposed, and he being an altar boy was obliged to sit or kneel at the foot of the altar for four hours until relieved by Mando Rentería, an emaciated altar boy two years younger than he who was never on time for Mass or anything else. Serge used to watch them and he recalled that no matter what sign they made to whatever strange idol they worshiped who was certainly not the traditional Christ, they touched their knees to the floor when they genuflected and did not fake a genuflection as he had seen so many Anglos do in much finer churches in the short time he still bothered to attend Mass after his mother died. And they had looked at the mute stone figures on the altar with consummate veneration. And whether or not they attended Mass every Sunday, you knew that they were communicating with a spirit when they prayed.

He remembered Father McCarthy, the pastor of the parish, when he had overheard him say to Sister Mary Immaculate, the principal of the school, "They are not good Catholics, but they are so respectful and they believe so well." Serge, then a novice altar boy, was in the sacristy to get his white surplice which he had forgotten to bring home. His mother had sent him back to get it because she insisted on washing and starching the surplice every time he served a Mass even though it was completely unnecessary and this would wear it out much too soon and then she would have to make him another one. Serge knew who Father McCarthy meant when he said "they" to the tall craggy-faced Irish nun who cracked Serge's hands unmercifully with a ruler during the first five years of grammar school when he would talk in class or daydream. Then she had changed abruptly the last three years when he was a gangling altar boy tripping over his cassock that was one of Father McCarthy's cut-down cassocks because he was so tall for a Mexican boy, and she doted over him because he learned his Latin so quickly and pronounced it "so wondrously well." But it was easy, because in those days he still spoke a little Spanish and the Latin did not seem really so strange, not nearly so strange as English seemed those first years of grammar school. And now that he had all but forgotten Spanish it was hard to believe that he once spoke no English.

"Ayeeee," she wailed suddenly, opening the closet in the ransacked bedroom. "The money, it's gone."

"You had money?" said Galloway to the angular, dark little woman, who stared in disbelief at Galloway and then at the closet.

"It was more than sixty dollars," she cried. *"Dios mío!* I put it in there. It was sitting right there." Suddenly she began rummaging through the already ransacked bedroom. "Maybe the thief dropped it," she said, and Serge knew that she might destroy any fingerprints on the chest of drawers and the other smooth-surfaced objects in the bedroom, but he had also learned enough by now to know there were probably no prints anyway as most competent burglars used socks on their hands, or gloves, or wiped their prints. He knew that Galloway knew she might destroy evidence, but Galloway motioned him into the living room.

"Let her blow off steam," Galloway whispered. "The only good place for prints is the window ledge anyway. She's not going to touch that."

Serge nodded, took off his hat and sat down. After a few moments, the furious rustling sounds in the bedroom subsided and the utter silence that followed made Serge wish very much that she would hurry and tell them what was missing so they could make their report and leave.

"You're going to find out before too long that we're the only ones that see the victims," said Galloway. "The judges and probation officers and social workers and everybody else think mainly about the suspect and how they can help him stop whatever he specializes in doing to his victims, but you and me are the only ones who see what he does to his victims—right after it's done. And this is only a little burglary."

She should pray to Our Lady of Guadalupe or Blessed Martin, thought Serge. Or maybe to Pancho Villa. That would be just as useful. Oh, they're great believers, these Chicanos, he thought.

5. The Centurions

"Here comes Lafitte," said the tall policeman. "Three minutes till roll call but he'll be on time. Watch him."

Gus watched Lafitte grin at the tall policeman, and open his locker with one hand, while the other unbuttoned the yellow sport shirt. When Gus looked up again after giving his shoes a last touch with the shine rag, Lafitte was fully dressed in his uniform and was fastening the Sam Browne.

"I'll bet it takes you longer to get into your jammies at night than it does to throw on that blue suit, eh Lafitte?" said the tall policeman.

"Your pay doesn't start till 3:00 P.M.," Lafitte answered. "No sense giving the Department any extra minutes. It all adds up in a year."

Gus stole a glance at Lafitte's brass buttons on his shirt pocket flaps and epaulets and saw the tiny holes in the center of the star on the buttons. This proved the buttons had seen a good deal of polishing, he thought. A hole was worn in the middle. He looked at his own brass buttons and saw they were not a lustrous gold like Lafitte's. If he had been in the service he would have learned a good deal about such things, he thought. On the opposite side of the metal lockers was the roll call room, lockers, rows of benches, tables, and the watch commander's desk at the front, all crammed into one thirty by fifty foot room. Gus was told that the old station would be replaced in a few years by a new station, but it thrilled him just as it was. This was his first night in University Division. He was not a cadet now; the academy was finished and he could not believe it was Gus Plebesly inside this tailored blue woolen shirt which bore the glistening oval shield. He took a place at the second row of tables from the rear of the room. This seemed safe enough. The rear table was almost filled with older officers, and no one sat at the front one. The second row from the rear should be safe enough, he thought.

There were twenty-two policemen at this early night watch roll call and he felt reassured when he saw Griggs and Patzloff, two of his academy classmates, who had also been sent to University Division from the academy.

Griggs and Patzloff were talking quietly and Gus debated about moving across the room to their table but he decided it might attract too much attention, and anyway, it was one minute to roll call. The doors at the rear of the room swung open and a man in civilian clothes entered, and a burly, bald policeman at the rear table shouted, "Salone, why ain't you suited up?"

"Light duty," said Salone. "I'm working the desk tonight. No roll call."

"Son of a bitch," said the burly policeman, "too sick to ride around with me in a radio car? What the hell's wrong with you?"

"Gum infection."

"You don't sit on your gums, Salone," said the burly policeman. "Son of a bitch. Now I guess I'll get stuck with one of these slick-sleeved little RE-cruits."

Everyone laughed and Gus's face turned hot and he pretended he didn't hear the remark. Then he realized why the burly policeman had said "slick-sleeved." He glanced over his shoulder and saw the rows of white service stripes on the lower sleeves of the policemen at the rear table, one stripe for each five years' service, and he understood the epithet. The doors swung open and two sergeants entered carrying manila folders and a large square board from which the car plan would be read.

"Three-A-Five, Hill and Matthews," said the pipe-smoking sergeant with the receding hairline.

"Here."

"Here."

"Three-A-Nine, Carson and Lafitte."

"Here."

"Here," said Lafitte, and Gus recognized the voice.

"Three-A-Eleven, Ball and Gladstone."

"Here," said one of the two Negro policemen in the room.

"Here," said the other Negro.

Gus was afraid he would be put with the burly policeman and was glad to hear him answer "Here" when he was assigned with someone else.

Finally the sergeant said, "Three-A-Ninety-nine, Kilvinsky and Plebesly."

"Here," said Kilvinsky and Gus turned, smiling nervously at the tall silver-haired policeman in the back row who smiled back at him.

"Here, sir," said Gus, and then cursed himself for saying "sir." He was out of the academy now. "Sirs" were reserved for lieutenants and higher.

"We have three new officers with us," said the pipe-smoking sergeant. "Glad to have you men. I'm Sergeant Bridget and this ruddy Irishman on my right is Sergeant O'Toole. Looks just like the big Irish cop you see in all the old B movies, doesn't he?"

Sergeant O'Toole grinned broadly and nodded to the new officers.

"Before we read the crimes, I want to talk about the supervisor's meeting today," said Sergeant Bridget as he thumbed through one of the manila folders.

Gus gazed around the room at the several maps of University Division which were covered with multi-colored pins that he thought must signify certain crimes or arrests. Soon he would know all the little things and he would be one of them. Or would he be one of them? His forehead and armpits began to perspire and he thought, I will not think that. It's self-defeating and neurotic to think like that. I'm just as good as any of them. I was tops in my class in physical training. What right do I have to degrade myself. I promised myself I'd stop doing that.

"One thing the captain talked about at the supervisor's meeting was the time and mileage check," said Bridget. "He wanted us to remind you guys to broadcast your time and mileage *every* time you transport a female in a police car—for any reason. Some bitch in Newton Division beefed a policeman last week. Says he took her in a park and tried to lay her. It was easy to prove she lied because the policeman gave his mileage to Communications at ten minutes past eleven when he left her pad and he gave his mileage again at eleven twenty-three when he arrived at the Main Jail. His mileage and the time check proved he couldn't have driven her up in Elysian Park like she claimed."

"Hey Sarge," said a lean swarthy policeman near the front. "If the Newton Street policeman who she accused is Harry Ferndale, she's probably telling the truth. He's so horny he'd plow a dead alligator or even a live one if somebody'd hold the tail."

"Damn it, Leoni," grinned Sergeant Bridget as the others chuckled, "we got some new men here tonight. You roll call pop-offs ought to be trying to set some kind of example, at least on their first night. This is serious shit I'm reading. The next thing the captain wanted us to bring up is that some Seventy-seventh Street officer in traffic court was asked by the defendant's lawyer what drew his attention to the defendant's vehicle to cite it for an illegal turn, and the officer said because the defendant was driving with his arm around a well-known Negro prostitute."

The roll call room burst into laughter and Bridget held up a hand to quiet them. "I know that's funny and all that, but number one, you can prejudice a case by implying that you were trying to suppress prostitution, not enforce traffic laws. And number two, this little remark got back to the guy's old lady and he's beefing the policeman. An investigation started already."

"Is it true?" asked Matthews.

"Yeah, he was with a whore I guess."

"Then let the asshole beef," said Matthews, and Gus realized that they used "asshole" as much here in the divisions as the instructors did in the academy and he guessed it was the favorite epithet of policemen, at least Los Angeles policemen.

"Anyway, the captain says no more of it," Bridget continued, "and another thing the old man says is that you guys are not at *any* time to push cars with your police vehicle. Snider on the day watch was giving a poor stranded motorist a push and he jumped the bumper and busted the guy's taillights and dented his deck lid and the prick is threatening to sue the city if his car isn't fixed. So no more pushing."

"How about on the freeway, or when a stalled car has a street bottled up?" asked Leoni.

"Okay, you and I know there are exceptions to everything in this business, but in almost all cases no pushing, okay?"

"Has the captain ever done police work out in the street?" asked Matthews. "I bet he had some cushy office job since he's been on the Department."

"Let's not get personal, Mike," smiled Bridget. "The next thing is these preliminary investigations in burglary and robbery cases. Now, you guys aren't detectives, but you aren't mere report writers either. You're supposed to conduct a preliminary investigation out there, not just fill in a bunch of blanks on a crime report." Bridget paused and lit the long-stemmed pipe he had been toying with. "We all know that we seldom get good latent prints from a gun because of the broken surface, but Jesus Christ, a couple weeks ago an officer of this division didn't bother worrying about prints on a gun a suspect dropped at the scene of a liquor store robbery! And the dicks had a damned good suspect in custody the next day but the dumb ass liquor store owner was some idiot who claimed he was new in the business in this part of town and he couldn't tell Negroes apart. There wouldn't have been any case at all because the officer handled the suspect's gun and ruined any prints there might have been, except for one thing—it was an automatic. Lucky for the officer, because he might've got a couple days suspension for screwing up the case like that."

"Were the prints on the clip?" asked Lafitte.

"No, the officer screwed those up when he took the clip out, but there were prints on the cartridges. They got part of the friction ridges on the center portion of the suspect's right thumb on several of the shells where he'd pushed them in the clip. The officer claimed the liquor store owner had handled the gun first so the officer decided all possibility of getting prints was destroyed. I'd like to know how the hell he knew that. It doesn't matter who handles the gun, you should still treat it like it's printable and notify the latent prints specialists."

"Tell them about the rags," said Sergeant O'Toole without looking up.

"Oh yeah. In another job recently, an officer had to be reminded by a sergeant at the scene to book the rags the suspect used to bind the victim. And the suspect had brought the rags with him! Christ, they could have laundry marks or they could be matched up with other rags that the dicks might later find in the suspect's pad or on some other job. I know you guys know most of this shit, but some of you are getting awful careless.

Okay, that's all the bitching I have for you, I guess. Any questions on the supervisor's meeting?"

"Yeah, you ever talk about the good things we do?" asked Matthews.

"Glad you asked that, Mike," said Sergeant Bridget, his teeth clenched on the black pipe stem. "As a matter of fact the lieutenant wrote you a little commendation for the hot roller you got the other night. Come on up and sign it."

"In eighteen years I guess I got a hundred of these things," grumbled Matthews, striding heavy-footed to the front of the room, "but I still get the same goddamn skinny paycheck every two weeks."

"You're getting almost six bills a month, Mike. Quit your kicking," said Bridget, then turning to the others said, "Mike went in pursuit and brought down a hot car driven by a damn good burglar and he likes a little 'at-a-boy' once in a while just like the rest of us, despite his bitching. You new men are going to find out that if you have a yen for lots of thanks and praise, you picked the wrong profession. Want to read the crimes, William, me boy?" he said to Sergeant O'Toole.

"Lots of crimes in the division last night, but not too many good descriptions," said O'Toole with a trace of a New York accent. "Got one happy moment on the crime sheet though. Cornelius Arps, the Western Avenue pimp, got cut by one of his whores and he EX-pired at 3:00 A.M. in General Hospital."

A loud cheer went up in the room. It startled Gus.

"Which whore did it?" shouted Leoni.

"One calls herself Tammy Randolph. Anybody know her?"

"She worked usually around Twenty-first and Western," said Kilvinsky, and Gus turned for another appraisal of his partner who looked more like a doctor than what he imagined a policeman should look like. The older ones, he noticed, looked hard around the mouth and their eyes seemed to watch things not just look at things, but to watch as though they were waiting for something, but that might be his imagination, he thought.

"How'd she do him?" asked Lafitte.

"You'll never believe this," said O'Toole, "but the old canoe maker at the autopsy today claimed that she punctured the aorta with a three and a half inch blade! She hit him so hard in the side with this little pocket knife that it severed a rib and punctured the aorta. Now how could a broad do that?"

"You never saw Tammy Randolph," said Kilvinsky quietly. "A hundred and ninety pounds of fighting whore. She's the one that beat hell out of the vice officer last summer, remember?"

"Oh, is that the same bitch?" asked Bridget. "Well, she atoned for it by juking Cornelius Arps."

"Why didn't you get the lieutenant to write her an at-a-boy like he did me?" asked Matthews as the men laughed.

"Here's a suspect wanted for attempted murder and two-eleven," said O'Toole. "Name is Calvin Tubbs, male, Negro, born 6-12-35, five ten, one eighty-five, black hair, brown eyes, medium complexion, wears his hair marcelled, full moustache, drives a 1959 Ford convertible, white over maroon, license John Victor David one seven three. Hangs out here in University at Normandie and Adams, and at Western and Adams. Robbed a bread truck driver and shot him for the hell of it. They made him on six other jobs—all bread trucks. He's bought and paid for, you can render that asshole."

"Really raping those bread trucks and buses, ain't they?" said Matthews.

"You know it," said O'Toole, glancing over the bifocals. "For the benefit of you new men, we should tell you it's not safe to ride a bus in this part of town. Armed bandits rob a bus almost every day and sometimes rob the passengers too. So if you have a flat tire on your way to work, call a cab. And the bread truck drivers or anybody else that's a street vendor gets hit regular, too. I know one bread truck driver that was held up twenty-one times in one year."

"That guy's a professional victim," said Leoni.

"He can probably run a show-up better than the robbery dicks," said Matthews.

Gus glanced over at the two Negro officers who sat together near the front, but they laughed when the others did and showed no sign of discomfort. Gus knew that all the "down heres" referred to the Negro divisions and he wondered if all the cracks about the crimes affected them personally. He decided they must be used to it.

"Had kind of an interesting homicide the other night," O'Toole continued in his monotone. "Family beef. Some dude told his old lady she was a bum lay and she shot him twice and he fell off the porch and broke his leg and she ran inside, got a kitchen knife and came back and started cutting where the jagged bone stuck out. Almost got the leg all the way off by the time the first radio car got there. They tell me they couldn't even take a regular blood test. There was no blood left in the guy's veins. Had to take it from the spleen."

"Wonder if she *was* a bum lay," said Leoni.

"By the way," said Sergeant Bridget, "any of you guys know an old lady named Alice Hockington? Lives on Twenty-eighth near Hoover?"

No one answered and Sergeant Bridget said, "She called last night and said a car came by on a prowler call last week. Who was it?"

"Why do you want to know?" asked a bass voice from the last table.

"Goddamn suspicious cops," Bridget said, shaking his head. "Well screw you guys then. I was just going to tell you the old girl died and left ten thousand dollars to the nice policemen who chased a prowler away. Now, who wants to cop out?"

"That was me, Sarge," said Leoni.

"Bullshit," said Matthews, "that was me and Cavanaugh."

The others laughed and Bridget said, "Anyway, the old girl called last night. She didn't really die, but she's thinking about it. She said she wanted that handsome tall young policeman with the black moustache (that sounds like you, Lafitte) to come by every afternoon and check for the evening newspaper. If it's still on her porch at five o'clock it means she's dead and she wants you to bust the door in if that happens. Because of her dog, she said."

"She afraid he'll starve or she afraid he won't starve?" asked Lafitte.

"The sympathy of these guys really is touching," said Bridget.

"Can I go on with the crimes or am I boring you guys," said O'Toole. "Attempt rape, last night, 11:10 P.M., three-six-nine West Thirty-seventh Place. Suspect awoke victim by placing hand over her mouth, said,

'Don't move. I love you and I want to prove it.' Fondled victim's private parts while he held a two-inch blue steel revolver in the air for her to see. Suspect wore a blue suit . . ."

"Bluesuit?" asked Lafitte. "Sounds like a policeman."

"Suspect wore blue suit and light-colored shirt," O'Toole continued. "Was male, Negro, twenty-eight to thirty, six foot two, hundred ninety, black, brown, medium complexion."

"Sounds exactly like Gladstone. I think we can solve this one," Lafitte said.

"Victim screamed and suspect jumped out window and was seen getting into a late model yellow vehicle parked on Hoover."

"What kind of car you got, Gladstone?" asked Lafitte and the big Negro policeman turned and grinned, "She wouldn't have screamed if it'd been me."

"The hell she wouldn't," said Matthews. "I seen Glad in the academy showers one time. That would be assault with a deadly weapon."

"Assault with a friendly weapon," said Gladstone.

"Let's go to work," said Sergeant Bridget, and Gus was glad there was no inspection because he didn't think his buttons would pass and he wondered how often they had inspections here in the divisions. Not very often, he guessed, from the uniforms he saw around him, which were certainly not up to academy standards. He guessed things would be relaxed out here. Soon, he would be relaxed too. He would be part of it.

Gus stood with his notebook a few steps from Kilvinsky and smiled when Kilvinsky turned around.

"Gus Plebesly," said Gus, shaking Kilvinsky's wide, smooth hand.

"Andy's the first name," said Kilvinsky looking down at Gus with an easy grin. Gus guessed he might be six feet four.

"Guess you're stuck with me tonight," said Gus.

"All month. And I don't mind."

"Whatever you say is okay with me."

"That goes without saying."

"Oh, yes sir."

"You don't have to sir me," Kilvinsky laughed. "My gray hair only means that I've been around a long time. We're partners. You have a notebook?"

"Yes."

"Okay, you keep books for the first week or so. After you learn to take a report and get to know the streets a little bit, I'll let you drive. All new policemen love to drive."

"Anything. Anything is okay with me."

"Guess I'm ready, Gus. Let's go downstairs," said Kilvinsky, and they walked side by side through the double doors and down the turning stairway of old University station.

"See those pictures, partner?" said Kilvinsky pointing to the glass-covered portraits of University policemen who had been killed on duty. "Those guys aren't heroes. Those guys just screwed up and they're dead. Pretty soon you'll get comfortable and relaxed out there, just like the rest of us. But don't get too comfortable. Remember the guys in the pictures."

"I don't feel like I'll ever get comfortable," Gus said.

"You will, partner. You will," said Kilvinsky. "Let's find our black and white and go to work."

The inadequate parking lot was teeming with blue uniforms as the night watch relieved the day watch at 3:45 P.M. The sun was still very hot and ties could remain off until later in the evening. Gus wondered at the heavy long-sleeved blue uniforms. His arms were sweating and the wool was harsh.

"I'm not used to wearing such heavy clothes in the heat," he smiled to Kilvinsky, as he wiped his forehead with a handkerchief.

"You'll get used to it," said Kilvinsky, sitting carefully on the sun-heated vinyl seat and releasing the seat lock to slide back and make room for his long legs.

Gus placed the new hot sheet in the holder and wrote 3-A-99 on the notebook pad so that he would not forget who they were. That seemed odd, he thought. He was now 3-A-99. He felt his heart race and he knew he was more excited than he should be. He hoped it was just that—excitement. There was nothing yet to fear.

"The passenger officer handles the radio, Gus."

"Okay."

"You won't hear our calls at first. That radio will just be an incoherent mess of conversation for a while. In a week or so you'll start to hear our calls."

"Okay."

"Ready for a night of romance, intrigue and adventure on the streets of the asphalt jungle?" asked Kilvinsky dramatically.

"Sure," Gus smiled.

"Okay, kid," Kilvinsky laughed. "You a little thrilled?"

"Yes."

"Good. That's the way you should be."

As Kilvinsky drove from the station parking lot he turned west on Jefferson and Gus flipped down the visor and squinted into the sun. The radio car smelled faintly of vomit.

"Want a tour of the division?" asked Kilvinsky.

"Sure."

"Almost all the citizens here are Negroes. Some whites. Some Mexicans. Mostly Negroes. Lots of crime when you have lots of Negroes. We work Ninety-nine. Our area is *all* black. Close to Newton. Ours are eastside Negroes. When they got some money they move west of Figueroa and Vermont and maybe west of Western. Then they call themselves westside Negroes and expect to be treated differently. I treat everyone the same, white or black. I'm civil to all people, courteous to none. I think courtesy implies servility. Policemen don't have to be servile or apologize to anyone for doing their job. This is a philosophy lesson I throw in free to every rookie I break in. Old-timers like me love to hear themselves talk. You'll get used to radio car philosophers."

"How much time do you have on the Department?" asked Gus, looking at the three service stripes on Kilvinsky's sleeve which meant at least fifteen years. But he had a youthful face if it weren't for the silver hair and the glasses. Gus guessed he was in good condition. He had a powerful-looking body.

"Twenty years this December," said Kilvinsky.

"You retiring?"

"Haven't decided."

They rode silently for several minutes and Gus looked at the city and realized he knew nothing about Negroes. He enjoyed the names on the churches. On a corner he saw a one-story, white-washed frame building with a handmade sign which said, "Lion of Judah and Kingdom of Christ Church," and on the same block was the "Sacred Defender Baptist Church" and in a moment he saw the "Hearty Welcome Missionary Baptist Church" and on and on he read the signs on the scores of churches and hoped he could remember them to tell Vickie when he got home tonight. He thought the churches were wonderful.

"Sure is hot," said Gus, wiping his forehead with the back of his hand.

"You don't have to wear your lid in the car, you know," said Kilvinsky. "Only when you get out."

"Oh," said Gus, taking off the hat quickly. "I forgot I had it on."

Kilvinsky smiled and hummed softly as he patrolled the streets, letting Gus sightsee and Gus watched how slowly he drove and how deliberately. He would remember that. Kilvinsky patrolled at fifteen miles an hour.

"Guess I'll get used to the heavy uniform," said Gus, pulling the sleeve from his sticky arms.

"Chief Parker doesn't go for short sleeves," said Kilvinsky.

"Why not?"

"Doesn't like hairy arms and tattoos. Long sleeves are more dignified."

"He spoke to our graduating class," said Gus, remembering the eloquence of the chief and the perfect English which had deeply impressed Vickie who sat proudly in the audience that day.

"He's one of a vanishing kind," said Kilvinsky.

"I've heard he's strict."

"He's a Calvinist. Know what that is?"

"A puritan?"

"He professes to be Roman Catholic, but I say he's a Calvinist. He won't compromise on matters of principle. He's despised by lots of people."

"He is?" said Gus, reading the signs on the store windows.

"He knows evil when he sees it. He recognizes the weakness of people. He has a passion for order and the rule of law. He can be relentless," said Kilvinsky.

"You sound as if you kind of admire him."

"I love him. When he's gone, nothing will be the same."

What a strange man Kilvinsky is, Gus thought. He talked absently and if it weren't for the boyish grin, Gus would have been uncomfortable with him. Then Gus watched a young Negro strutting across Jefferson

Boulevard and he studied the swaying, limber shoulder movement, bent-elbowed free swinging arms, and the rubber-kneed big stepping bounce and as Kilvinsky remarked, "He's walkin' smart," Gus realized how profoundly ignorant he was about Negroes and he was anxious to learn about them, and about all people. If he could just learn and grow he would know something about people after a few years in this job. He thought of the squirming muscle in the long brown arms of the young man who was now blocks behind him. He wondered how he would fare if the two of them were face to face in a police-suspect confrontation when he had no partner and he could not use his sidearm and the young Negro was not impressed with his glittering golden shield and suit of blue. He cursed himself again for the insidious fear and he vowed he would master it but he always made this vow and still the fear came or rather the promise of fear, the nervous growling stomach, the clammy hands, the leathery mouth, but enough, enough to make him suspect that when the time came he would not behave like a policeman.

What if a man the size of Kilvinsky resisted arrest? Gus thought. How could I possibly handle him? There were things he wanted to ask, but was ashamed to ask Kilvinsky. Things he might ask a smaller man, after he got to know him, if he ever did get to really know him. He had never had many friends and at this moment he doubted that he could find any among these uniformed men who made him feel like a small boy. Maybe it had all been a mistake, he thought. Maybe he could never be one of them. They seemed so forceful and confident. They had seen things. But maybe it was just bravado. Maybe it was that.

But what would happen if someone's life, maybe Kilvinsky's life, depended on his conquest of fear which he had never been able to conquer? Those four years of marriage while he worked in a bank had not prepared him to cope with that. And why hadn't he the courage to talk to Vickie about things like this, and then he thought of the times he had lain beside her in the darkness, particularly after lovemaking, and he had thought of these things and prayed to have the courage to talk to Vickie about it, but he hadn't, and no one knew that *he* knew that he was a coward. But what would it ever

have mattered that he was a coward if he had stayed in
the bank where he belonged? Why could he do well in
wrestling and physical training, but turn sick and impo-
tent when the other man was not playing a game? Once
in P.T. when he was wrestling with Walmsley he had applied the wristlock too firmly as Officer Randolph had
shown them. Walmsley became angry and when Gus
saw his eyes, the fear came, his strength deserted him
and Walmsley easily took him down. He did it viciously
and Gus did not resist even though he knew he was
stronger and twice as agile as Walmsley. But that was
all part of being a coward, that inability to control your
body. Is the hate the thing I fear? Is' that it? A face full
of hate?

"Come on granny, let the clutch out," Kilvinsky said
as a female driver in front of them crept toward the
signal causing them to stop instead of making the yellow
light.

"One-seven-three west Fifty-fourth Street," said Kilvinsky, tapping on the writing pad between them.

"What?" asked Gus.

"We got a call. One-seven-three west Fifty-fourth
Street. Write it down."

"Oh. Sorry, I can't make any sense out of the radio
yet."

"Roger the call," said Kilvinsky.

"Three-A-Ninety-nine, roger," said Gus into the hand
mike.

"You'll start picking our calls out of all that chatter
pretty soon," said Kilvinsky. "Takes a while. You'll get
it."

"What kind of call was it?"

"Unknown trouble call. That means the person who
called isn't sure what the problem is, or it means he
wasn't coherent or the operator couldn't understand him,
or it could mean anything. I don't like those calls. You
don't know what the hell you have until you get there."

Gus nervously looked at the storefronts. He saw two
Negroes with high shiny pompadours and colorful one-
piece jump suits park a red Cadillac convertible in front
of a window which said, "Big Red's Process Parlor," and
below it in yellow letters Gus read, "Process, do-it-
yourself process, Quo Vadis, and other styles."

"What do you call the hairdos on those two men?" asked Gus.

"Those two pimps? That style is just called a process, some call it a marcel. Old-time policemen might refer to it as gassed hair, but for police reports most of us just use the word 'process.' Costs them a lot of money to keep a nice process like that, but then, pimps have lots of money. And a process is as important to them as a Cadillac. No self-respecting pimp would be caught without both of them."

Gus wished the sun would drop, then it might cool off. He loved summer nights when the days were hot and paper-dry like this one. He noticed the crescent and star over the white two-story stucco building on the corner. Two men in close-cropped hair and black suits with maroon neckties stood in front of the wide doors with their hands behind their backs and glared at the police car as they continued south.

"That a church?" asked Gus to Kilvinsky, who never looked toward the building or the men.

"That's the Muslim temple. Do you know about Muslims?"

"I've read a little in the papers, that's all."

"They're a fanatical sect that's sprung up recently all over the country. A lot of them are ex-cons. They're all cop haters."

"They look so clean-cut," said Gus, glancing over his shoulder at the two men whose faces were turned in the direction of the police car.

"They're just part of what's happening in the country," said Kilvinsky. "Nobody knows what's happening yet, except a few people like the chief. It may take ten years to figure it all out."

"What *is* happening?" asked Gus.

"It's a long story," Kilvinsky said. "And I'm not sure myself. And besides, here's the pad."

Gus turned and saw the one-seven-three over the mailbox of the green stucco house with a trash-littered front yard.

Gus almost didn't see the trembling old Negro in khaki work clothes huddled on an ancient wicker chair on the dilapidated porch of the house.

"Glad yo'all could come officahs," he said, standing,

quivering, with sporadic looks toward the door standing ajar.

"What's the problem?" asked Kilvinsky, climbing the three stairs to the porch, his cap placed precisely straight on the silver mane.

"Ah jist came home and ah saw a man in the house. Ah don' know him. He jist was sittin' there starin' at me and ah got scairt and run out heah and ovah nex' do' and ah use mah neighbah's phone and while I was waitin' ah look back inside an' theah he sits jist rockin', an' Lord, ah think he's a crazy man. He don' say nothin' jist sits an' rocks."

Gus reached involuntarily for the baton and fingered the grooved handle, waiting for Kilvinsky to decide their first move and he was embarrassed by his relief when he understood, when Kilvinsky winked and said, "Wait here, partner, in case he tries to go out the back door. There's a fence back there so he'd have to come back through the front."

Gus waited with the old man and in a few minutes he heard Kilvinsky shout, "Alright you son of a bitch, get out of here and don't come back!" And he heard the back door slam. Then Kilvinsky opened the screen and said, "Okay, Mister, come on in. He's gone."

Gus followed the gnarled old man, who removed the crumpled hat when he crossed the threshold.

"He sho' is gone, officahs," said the old man, but the trembling had not stopped.

"I told him not to come back," said Kilvinsky. "I don't think you'll be seeing him again around this neighborhood."

"God bless yo'all," said the old man, shuffling toward the back door and locking it.

"How long's it been since you had a drink?" asked Kilvinsky.

"Oh, couple days now," said the old man, smiling a black-toothed smile. "Check's due in the mail any day now."

"Well, just fix yourself a cup of tea and try to get some sleep. You'll feel lots better tomorrow."

"Ah thanks yo'all," said the old man as they walked down the cracked concrete sidewalk to the car. Kilvinsky didn't say anything as he drove off and Gus said finally,

"Those d.t.'s must be hell, huh?"

"Must be hell," Kilvinsky nodded.

"We got a coffee spot down the street," said Kilvinsky. "It's so bad you could pour it in your battery when she dies, but it's free and so are the doughnuts."

"Sounds good to me," said Gus.

Kilvinsky parked in the littered coffee shop parking lot and Gus went inside to get the coffee. He left his cap in the car and felt like a veteran, hatless, striding into the coffee shop where he watched a wizened, alcoholic-looking man who was listlessly pouring coffee for three Negro counter customers.

"Coffee?" he said to Gus, coming toward him with two paper cups in his hand.

"Please."

"Cream?"

"Only in one," said Gus, as the counterman drew the coffee from the urns and placed the cups on the counter as Gus self-consciously tried to decide the most diplomatic way to order doughnuts which were free. You didn't wish to be presumptuous even though you wanted a doughnut. It would be so much simpler if they just paid for the coffee and doughnuts, he thought, but then that would counter the tradition and if you did something like that the word might be passed that you were a troublemaker. The man solved his dilemma by saying, "Doughnuts?"

"Please," said Gus, relieved.

"Chocolate or plain? I'm out of glazed."

"Two plain," said Gus, realizing that Kilvinsky had not stated his preference.

"Tops for the cups?"

"No, I can manage," said Gus and a moment later discovered that this chain of coffee shops made the hottest coffee in Los Angeles.

"It's sure hot," he smiled weakly, in case Kilvinsky had seen him spill coffee on himself. His forehead perspired from the sudden flash of pain.

"Wait till you're on the morning watch," said Kilvinsky. "Some chilly winter night about 1:00 A.M. this coffee will light a fire in you and see you through the night."

The sun was dropping on the horizon but it was still hot and Gus thought a Coke would have been better than a cup of coffee but he had already noticed that policemen were coffee drinkers and he guessed he may as well get used to it because he was going to be one of them, come what may.

Gus sipped the steaming coffee a full three minutes after it sat on the roof of the police car and found that he still could not stand the temperature; he waited and watched Kilvinsky out of the corner of his eye and saw him taking great gulps as he smoked a cigarette and adjusted the radio until it was barely audible, still much too low for Gus, but then, Gus knew he could not pick their calls out of that chaotic garble of voices anyway, so if Kilvinsky could hear it, it was enough.

Gus saw a stooped ragpicker in filthy denim trousers and a torn, grimy, checkered shirt several sizes too large, and a GI helmet liner with a hole on the side through which a snarled handful of the ragpicker's gray hair protruded. He pushed a shopping cart stolidly down the sidewalk, ignoring six or seven Negro children who taunted him, and until he was very close Gus could not guess what his race was but guessed he was white because of the long gray hair. Then he saw that he was indeed a white man, but covered with crusty layers of filth. The ragpicker stopped near crevices and crannies between and behind the rows of one-story business buildings. He probed in trash cans and behind clumps of weeds in vacant lots until he discovered his prizes and the shopping cart was already filled with empty bottles which the children grabbed at. They shrieked in delight when the ragpicker made ineffectual swipes at their darting hands with his hairy paws too broad and massive for the emaciated body.

"Maybe he was wearing that helmet on some Pacific island when it got that hole blown in it," said Gus.

"It'd be nice to think so," said Kilvinsky. "Adds a little glamour to the old ragpicker. You should keep an eye on those guys, though. They steal plenty. We watched one pushing his little cart along Vermont on Christmas Eve clouting presents out of cars that were parked at the curb. Had a pile of bottles and other trash on top and a cartload of stolen Christmas presents beneath."

Kilvinsky started the car and resumed his slow patrol and Gus felt much more at ease after the coffee and doughnut which domesticized the strange feeling he had here in the city. He was so provincial, he thought, even though he grew up in Azusa, and made frequent trips to Los Angeles.

Kilvinsky drove slowly enough for Gus to read the signs in the windows of the drugstores and neighborhood markets, which advertised hair straighteners, skin brighteners, scalp conditioner, pressing oil, waxes and pomades. Kilvinsky pointed to a large crudely lettered whitewashed warning on a board fence which said, "Bab bog," and Gus noticed the professional lettering on the pool hall window which said, "Billard Parler." Kilvinsky parked in front of the pool hall, telling Gus he had something to show him.

The pool hall, which Gus supposed would be empty at the dinner hour, was teeming with men and a few women, all Negro except for two of the three women who slouched at a table near the small room at the rear of the building. Gus noticed one of the women, a middle-aged woman with hair like flames, scurried into the back room as soon as she spotted them. The pool players ignored them and continued the nine ball contests.

"Probably a little dice game going in the back," said Kilvinsky as Gus eagerly studied everything about the place, the floor caked with grime, six threadbare pool tables, two dozen men sitting or standing against the walls, the blaring record player being overseen by a pudgy cigar chewer in a blue silk undershirt, the smell of stale sweat and beer, for which there was no license, cigarette smoke, and through it all a good barbecue smell. Gus knew by the smell that whatever else they were doing in the back room, somebody was cooking, and that seemed very strange somehow. The three women were all fiftyish and very alcoholic-looking, the Negro being the slimmest and cleanest-looking of the three although she too was foul enough, Gus thought.

"A shine parlor or pool hall down here is the last stop for a white whore," said Kilvinsky following Gus's eyes. "There's what I brought you in here to see." Kilvinsky pointed at a sign high on the wall over the door which led to the back room. The sign read, "No liquor or narcotics allowed."

Gus was relieved to get back in the air, and he inhaled deeply. Kilvinsky resumed patrol and Gus was already starting to know the voices of the female Communications operators, particularly the one with the deep young voice on frequency thirteen, who would occasionally whisper "Hi" into the mike or "roger" in coy response to the policemen's voices he could not hear. It had been a surprise to him that the radios were two-way radios and not three-way, but it was just as well, he thought, because the jumble of women's voices was hard enough to understand without more voices from all the radio cars being thrown in.

"I'll wait till dark to show you Western Avenue," said Kilvinsky and now Gus could definitely feel the refreshing coolness of approaching night although it was far from dark.

"What's on Western Avenue?"

"Whores. Of course there're whores all over this part of town, but Western is the whore center of the city. They're all over the street."

"Don't we arrest them?"

"*We* don't. What would we arrest them for? Walking the street? Just *being* whores? No crime in that. Vice officers arrest them when they tail them to their trick pad, or when they operate the girl undercover and get an offer of prostitution."

"I wonder what working vice would be like?" Gus mused aloud.

"You might get a chance to find out someday," Kilvinsky said. "You're kind of small and . . . oh, a little more docile than the average pushy cop. I think you'd be a good undercover operator. You don't look like a policeman."

Gus thought of being here in the streets in plainclothes, perhaps without a partner, and he was glad such assignments were voluntary. He watched a very dark-skinned homosexual mincing across Vernon Avenue when the light turned green.

"Hope we don't lose our masquerading laws," said Kilvinsky.

"What's that?"

"City ordinance against a man dressing up like a woman or vice versa. Keeps the fruits from going around full drag and causing all sorts of police problems. I got a feeling though that that's another law on the way out. Better write that address down."

"What address?"

"We just got a call."

"We did? Where?" asked Gus, turning the radio louder and readying his pencil.

"Three-A-Ninety-nine, repeat," said Kilvinsky.

"Three-A-Ninety-nine, Three-A-Ninety-nine, a forgery suspect there now, at Forty-one-thirty-two south Broadway, see the man at that location, code two."

"Three-A-Ninety-nine, roger," said Gus, rubbing his palms on his thighs impatiently, and wondering why Kilvinsky didn't drive a bit faster. After all, it was a code two call.

They were only three blocks from the call but when they arrived another car was already parked in the front of the market and Kilvinsky double-parked until Leoni walked out of the store and over to their car.

"Suspect's a female wino," said Leoni, leaning in the window on Gus's side. "Guy offered her ten bucks to try and pass a hundred and thirty dollar payroll check. Probably a phony, but it looks pretty good. Check writer was used. The bitch said the guy was middle-aged, red shirt, average size. She just met him in a gin mill."

"Negro?" asked Kilvinsky.

"What else?"

"We'll take a look around," Kilvinsky said.

Kilvinsky circled the block once, studying people and cars. Gus wondered what they were supposed to be looking for because there were less than ten men in the immediate area who were middle-sized and none of them had on a red shirt, but on his second pass around the block, Kilvinsky turned sharply into a drugstore parking lot and zoomed across the alley toward a man who was walking toward the sidewalk. Kilvinsky jammed on the brakes and was on his feet before Gus was certain he was stopping.

"Just a minute," said Kilvinsky to the man who continued walking. "Hold it, there."

The man turned and looked quizzically at the two policemen. He wore a brown checkered shirt and a black felt stingy brim with a fat yellow feather. He was neither middle-aged nor of average size, but rather he was in his early thirties, Gus guessed, and was tall and portly.

"What you want?" asked the man and Gus noticed the deep scar which followed the cheek line and was at first not apparent.

"Your identification, please," said Kilvinsky.

"What for?"

"I'll explain in a minute, but let me see your I.D. first. Something just happened."

"Oh," sneered the man, "and I'm suspicious, huh? I'm black so that makes me suspicious, huh? Black man is just ol' Joe Lunchmeat to you, huh?"

"Look around you," Kilvinsky said, taking a giant stride forward, "you see anybody that ain't black except my partner and me? Now I picked you cause I got a motherfuckin' good reason. Break out that I.D. cause we ain't got time for shuckin'."

"Okay, Officer," said the man, "I ain't got nothin' to hide, it just that the PO-lice is always fuckin' over me ever' time I goes outside and I'm a workin' man. I works ever' day."

Kilvinsky examined the social security card and Gus thought how Kilvinsky had talked to the man. His rage was profound and with his size it had cowed the Negro, and Kilvinsky had talked like a Negro, exactly like a Negro, Gus thought.

"This I.D. ain't shit, man," said Kilvinsky. "Got something with your thumb print or a picture on it? Got a driver's license maybe?"

"What I need a drivin' license fo'? I ain't drivin'."

"What you been busted for?"

"Gamblin', traffic tickets, suspicious, a time or two."

"Forgery?"

"No, man."

"Flim flam?"

"No, man. I gambles a little bit, I ain't no criminal, no jive."

"Yeah, you jivin'," said Kilvinsky. "Your mouth is dry; you're lickin' your lips."

"Sheee-it, man, when the bluesuits stops me, I always gets nervous."

"Your heart is hammerin'," said Kilvinsky, placing a hand on the man's chest. "What's your real name?"

"Gandy. Woodrow Gandy. Just like it say on that card," said the man who now was obviously nervous. He shuffled his feet and could not control the darting pink tongue which moistened brown lips every few seconds.

"Hop in the car, Gandy," said Kilvinsky. "There's

an old drunk across the street. I want her to take a look at you."

"Ohooo man, this is a roust!" said Gandy as Kilvinsky patted him down. "This is a humbug and a roust!"

Gus noticed that Gandy knew which side of the police car to sit in, and Gus sat behind Kilvinsky and reached across locking the door on Gandy's side.

They drove back to the bank and found Leoni sitting in his radio car with a frazzled bleary-eyed Negro woman about forty who peeked out the window of Leoni's car toward Gandy when Kilvinsky pulled alongside.

"That's him. That the nigger that got me in all this trouble!" she shrieked, and then to Gandy she said, "Yeah, you, you bastard, standin' there finger poppin' and talkin' so smart to ever'one and tell me how easy I could earn ten dollars and how smart you was and all, you black son of a bitch. That's the one, Officer, I done told you I would be yo' witness and I means it, no jive. I tol' you he had a big flappy mouf like Cheetah. He the one all right. If I'm lyin', I'm flyin'."

Gandy turned away from the drunken woman and Gus was embarrassed by her words, but Gandy seemed completely unconcerned and Gus was astonished at how they degraded one another. He guessed they learned from the white man.

It was after nine o'clock when they finally got Gandy in the booking office of University jail. It was an antiquated jail and looked like a dungeon. Gus wondered what the cells were like. He wondered why they didn't take Gandy's shoelaces like they do in movies, but he remembered hearing a policeman in the academy saying that you can't stop a man from committing suicide who really wants to and then he described the death of the prisoner who tied strips of a pillowcase around his neck and then to the barred door. The man did a backflip, breaking his neck, and the officer quipped that deaths in jail caused tons of paper work and were very inconsiderate on the part of the deceased. Of course everybody laughed as policemen always did at grim humor and attempts at humor.

Over the booking officer's desk was a sign which read, "Support your local police. Be a snitch," and a toy spear perhaps three feet long decorated with African symbols and colorful feathers. It had a rubber blade and a sign over it said, "Search your prisoners thoroughly." Gus wondered if the Negro policemen were offended by this and for the first time in his life he was becoming acutely aware of Negroes in general, and he guessed he would become even more so because he would now spend most of his waking hours here among them. He wasn't sorry, he was interested, but he was also afraid of them. But then, he would probably be almost as fearful of any people no matter where he was stationed, and then he thought, what if Gandy had resisted arrest and what if Kilvinsky were not with him. Could he have handled a man like Gandy?

As the booking officer typed, Gus thought of Gus, Jr., three years old, and how chesty he was. Gus knew he would be a big husky boy. Already he could throw a man-sized basketball halfway across the living room and this was their favorite toy even though they broke one of Vickie's new decanters with it. Gus clearly remembered his own father's rough and tumble play although he never saw him again after the divorce, and how they had played. He remembered the moustache with wisps of gray among the brown and the big dry hard hands which tossed him confidently and surely into the air until he could hardly breathe for the laughter. He described this to his mother once when he was twelve, and old enough to see how miserably sad it made her. He never mentioned his father again and tried to be more helpful to his mother than ever because he was four years older than John and was his mother's little man she said. Gus guessed he was fiercely proud of the fact that he had worked since he was a small boy to help support the three of them. Now the pride was gone and it was a genuine hardship to set aside fifty dollars a month for her and John, now that he and Vickie were married and he had his own family.

"Ready to go, pard?" asked Kilvinsky.

"Oh, sure."

"Daydreaming?"

"Yeah."

"Let's go eat now, and do the arrest report later."

"Okay," said Gus, brightening at the thought. "You aren't too mad to eat, are you?"

"Mad?"

"For a minute I thought you were going to eat that suspect alive."

"I wasn't mad," said Kilvinsky, looking at Gus in surprise as they walked to the car. "That was just my act. Change the words once in a while, but I use the same tune. Don't they teach you about interrogation in the academy anymore?"

"I thought you were blowing your top."

"Hell, no. I just figured he was the type who only respected naked strength, not civility. You can't use that technique on everybody. In fact, if you try it on some guys you might find yourself on your back looking up. But I figured he'd quiet down if I talked his language, so I did. You have to size up each suspect fast and make up your mind how you're going to talk to him."

"Oh," said Gus. "But how did you know he was the suspect? He didn't look like her description. His shirt wasn't even red."

"How did I know," Kilvinsky murmured. "Let's see. You haven't been to court yet, have you?"

"No."

"Well, you'll have to start answering the question, 'How did you know?' I don't honestly know how I knew. But I knew. At least I was pretty sure. The shirt wasn't red, but it wasn't green either. It was a color that could be called red by a fuzzy-eyed drunk. It was a rusty brown. And Gandy was standing a little too casually there in the parking lot. He was too cool and he gave me too much of an 'I got nothing to hide' look when I was driving by and eyeballing everybody that could possibly be the guy. And when I came back around he had moved to the other side of the lot. He was still moving when I turned the corner but when he sees us he stops to show us he's not walking away. He's got nothing to hide. I know this means nothing by itself, but these are some of the little things. I just *knew*, I tell you."

"Instinct?"

"I think so. But I wouldn't say that in court."

"Will you have trouble in court with this case?"

"Oh no. This isn't a search and seizure case. If we had a search and seizure case going, that feeling and those little things he did wouldn't be enough. We'd lose. Unless we stretched the truth."

"Do you stretch the truth sometimes?"

"I don't. I don't care enough about people in general to get emotionally involved. I don't give a shit if I busted Jack the Ripper and lost him on an unreasonable search. As long as the asshole stays off *my* property, I don't worry about it. Some policemen become avenging angels. They have a real animal who's hurt a lot of people and they decide they have to convict him even if it means lying in court, but I say it's not worth it. The public isn't worth your risking a perjury rap. And he'll be back on the street before long anyway. Stay frosty. Relax. That's the way to do this job. You can beat it then. You take your forty percent after twenty years, and your family, if you still have one, and you make it. Go to Oregon or Montana."

"Do you have a family?"

"I'm single now. This job isn't conducive to stable family relationships, the marriage counselors say. I think we're near the top in suicide rate."

"I hope I can do this job," Gus blurted, surprised at the desperate tone in his own voice.

"Police work is seventy percent common sense. That's about what makes a policeman, common sense, and the ability to make a quick decision. You've got to cultivate those abilities or get out. You'll learn to appreciate this in your fellow policemen. Pretty soon, you won't be able to feel the same way about your friends in the lodge or church or in your neighborhood because they won't measure up to policemen in these ways. You'll be able to come up with a quick solution for *any* kind of strange situation because you have to do it every day, and you'll get mad as hell at your old friends if they can't."

Gus noticed that now that night had come, the streets were filling with people, black people, and the building fronts shone forth. It seemed that every block had at least one bar or liquor store and all the liquor store proprietors were white men. It seemed to Gus that now you didn't notice the churches, only the bars and liquor stores and places where crowds of people were standing around. He saw boisterous crowds around hamburger stands, liquor stores, certain porches of certain apartment houses, parking lots, shine stands, record stores, and a suspicious place whose windows advertised that this was a "Social Club." Gus noticed the peephole in the door and he wished that he could be inside there unnoticed, and his curiosity was stronger than his fear.

"How about some soul food, brother?" asked Kilvinsky with a Negro accent as he parked in front of the neat lunch counter on Normandie.

"I'll try anything," Gus smiled.

"Fat Jack makes the best gumbo in town. Lots of shrimp and crab meat and chicken and okra, easy on the rice and lots of down home flavor. Real Looos-iana gumbo."

"You from the South?"

"No, I just appreciate the cooking," Kilvinsky said, and held the door as they entered the restaurant. Soon they were served the huge bowl of gumbo and Gus liked the way Fat Jack said, "They was full of shrimps tonight." He poured some hot sauce on the gumbo as Kilvinsky did even though it was tangy enough, but it was delicious, even the chopped-up chicken necks and the crab claws which had to be picked and sucked clean. Kilvinsky poured more ladles of hot sauce over the spicy gruel and ate half a pan of corn bread. But it was spoiled a little because they each left a quarter tip for the waitress and that was all, and Gus felt guilty to accept a gratuity and he wondered how he would explain it to a sergeant. He wondered if Fat Jack and the waitresses called them freeloaders behind their backs.

At 11:00 P.M. while cruising the dark residential streets north of Slauson Avenue, Kilvinsky said, "You ready to go work the whore wagon?"

"The what?"

"I asked the sergeant if we could take the wagon out tonight to roust the whores and he said it'd be okay if the air was quiet and I haven't heard a radio call in University Division for a half hour, so let's go in and get the wagon. I think you might find it educational."

"There don't seem to be too many whores around," said Gus. "There were those two at Vernon and Broadway you pointed out and one on Fifty-eighth, but . . ."

"Wait till you see Western Avenue."

After arriving at the station Kilvinsky pointed to the blue panel truck in the station parking lot with the white "Los Angeles Police Department" on the side. The back end was windowless and two benches were attached to each wall of the truck. A heavy steel screen separated the passengers from the front of the cab.

"Let's go tell the boss we're going out in the wagon," said Kilvinsky, and after another fifteen-minute delay while Kilvinsky joked with Candy the policewoman at the desk, they were in the wagon which rumbled down Jefferson Boulevard like a blue rhino. Gus thought he would hate to be sitting on the wooden bench in the back of this hard-riding wagon.

Kilvinsky turned north on Western Avenue and they had not driven two blocks on Western until he found himself counting the sauntering, wriggling, garishly dressed women who strolled down the sidewalks mostly *with* the traffic so that the cars would pull conveniently to the curb. The bars and restaurants on and near Western were bulging with people and there was a formidable fleet of Cadillac convertibles parked in the lot of "Blue Dot McAfee's Casbah."

"Pimping is profitable," said Kilvinsky, pointing to the Cadillacs. "There's too much money in pussy. I suspect that's why it's not legalized in many countries. Too much profit and no overhead. The pimps would control the economy in no time."

"Christ, it looks like it's legal *here!*" said Gus, taking in the colorful figures on both sides of Western who were leaning in the windows of parked cars, standing in groups or sitting on the low walls in front of the residences. Gus noticed that the prostitutes looked with concern at the blue wagon as it rumbled north toward Adams Boulevard.

"I believe in giving them one pass down Western to show the wagon's out. If they stay on the street we pick them up. Sure a lot of money in wigs out there, huh?"

"God, yes," said Gus, looking at an incredibly buxom prostitute standing alone on the corner of Twenty-seventh. He was astounded at how attractive some of them were and he noticed that they all carried purses.

"They've got purses," Gus said.

"Oh, yeah," Kilvinsky smiled. "Just for show. High skinny heels and purses, short skirts or tight pants. Uniform of the day. But don't worry, they don't carry any bread in those purses. All women in these parts carry their money in their bras."

When they got to Washington Boulevard, Kilvinsky turned around.

"There were twenty-eight whores on the Avenue," said

Gus. "And I think I missed counting some right at first!"

"The people around here have got to stop it," said Kilvinsky, lighting a cigarette and inserting it in a plastic cigarette holder. "Soon as they bitch loud enough the judges will give the girls some time and they'll go underground again. I know a whore with seventy-three prior arrests. Most time she ever did was six months on two separate occasions. This whore wagon is completely illegal by the way."

"What do we do with them? Where do we take them? I was wondering about that."

"For a ride, that's all. We pick them up and ride them around for an hour or so and take them to the station and run a make to see if they have any traffic warrants and let them go from the station. It's illegal as hell. We'll be stopped from doing it one of these days, but right now it works. The girls hate to be picked up in the wagon. Stopgap measure. Let's take those two."

Gus saw no one at first and then saw a movement in the shadows near the phone booth at the corner of Twenty-first Street and two girls in blue dresses walked west on Twenty-first. They ignored Kilvinsky's, "Evening ladies," until both policemen were out of the cab and Kilvinsky was holding the back door of the wagon open.

"Shit, fuck, Kilvinsky, you always picks on me," said the younger of the two, a yellow girl in an auburn wig who, Gus supposed, was even younger than himself.

"Who's the baby?" asked the other, pointing at Gus and appearing resigned to climbing the high step into the back of the panel. She hiked the flesh-tight blue satin dress up to her hips to make the step. "Give me a lift, baby," she said to Gus but didn't hold out her hand. "Grab a handful of mah big ass and push."

Kilvinsky chewed on the cigarette holder and eyed Gus with frank amusement, and Gus saw her firm pantiless buttocks like a dark melon with a sliver removed. He held her around the waist and boosted her up as she shrieked with laughter and Kilvinsky chuckled softly as he locked the double doors and they climbed back in the cab.

The next girl they picked up at Adams, and there were not so many now that everyone knew the wagon was out, but they picked up three more at Twenty-seventh, one of whom cursed Kilvinsky viciously because someone had made her ride in the wagon only last night and it wasn't her turn again, she said.

Once the prostitutes were in the wagon, they chattered and laughed pleasantly enough. It seemed to Gus that a few of them might be enjoying the respite from the street and Kilvinsky assured him that there was truth in this when Gus asked him, because their work was very dangerous and demanding, what with robbers and sadists prowling for prostitutes. The pimps provided little protection except from other pimps who were constantly trying to enlarge their own stables.

The tall policeman who had talked to Lafitte in the locker room was standing with his partner at Twenty-eighth beside the open door of the radio car talking to two prostitutes. The tall one motioned them to the curb.

"Got two for you, Andy," said the tall policeman.

"Yeah, you should make sergeant for this, you blue-eyed devil," said the umber-colored girl, with a natural hairdo, and a severe short-skirted black dress.

"She doesn't like you, Bethel," said Kilvinsky to the tall policeman.

"He don't know how to talk to a woman," said the girl. "Nobody likes this funky devil."

"I don't see any women," said Bethel, "just two whores."

"Yo' wife's a whore, bastard," spat the girl, leaning forward at the waist. "She fucks fo' peanuts. I gets two hundred dollars every day fo' fuckin' you pitiful paddy motherfuckers. Yo' wife's the real whore."

"Get in the wagon, bitch," said Bethel, shoving the girl across the sidewalk and Gus grabbed her to keep her from falling.

"We goin' to fix you whiteys, one day," said the girl, sobbing. "You devil! I never feel you blue-eyed devils, do you hear? I feel nothin'! You paddy motherfuckers never make me feel nothin' with yo' needle dicks. You ain't gonna git away wif pushin' me aroun', hear me?"

"Okay, Alice, hop in, will you," said Kilvinsky, holding the girl's arm as she yielded and climbed into the wagon.

"That there suckah don't evah talk right to nobody," said a voice inside the blackness of the wagon. "He think people is dogs or somethin'. We is motherfuckin' ladies."

"I haven't met you yet," said Bethel, offering his hand to Gus who shook it, looking up at the large brown eyes of Bethel.

"This is quite an experience," said Gus haltingly.

"It's a garbage truck," said Bethel. "But this ain't too bad, really. You ought to work Newton Division . . ."

"We've got to get going, Bethel," said Kilvinsky.

"One thing, Plebesly," said Bethel, "at least working around here you never run into nobody smarter than you."

"Do I have to get in the wagon, too?" asked the second girl and for the first time Gus noticed she was white. She had a high-styled black wig and her eyes were dark. She had a fine sun tan but she was definitely a white woman and Gus thought she was exceptionally pretty.

"Your old man is Eddie Simms, ain't that right, nigger?" Bethel whispered to the girl, whom he held by the upper arm. "You give all your money to a nigger, don't you? You'd do just anything for that slick-haired boy, wouldn't you? That makes you a nigger too, don't it, nigger?"

"Get in the wagon, Rose," said Kilvinsky taking her arm, but Bethel gave her a push and she dropped her purse and fell heavily into Kilvinsky, who cursed and lifted her into the wagon with one large hand while Gus picked up the purse.

"When you get more time on the job you'll learn not to manhandle another officer's prisoner," said Kilvinsky to Bethel as they got back in the wagon.

Bethel faced Kilvinsky for a moment, but said nothing, turned, got back in his car, and was roaring halfway up Western before Kilvinsky ever started the motor.

"Got lots of problems, that kid," said Kilvinsky. "Only two years on the Department and already he's got lots of problems."

"Hey," said a voice from the back of the wagon as they bounced and jogged across Jefferson and began an aimless ride to harass the prostitutes. "Yo'all need some pillas back here. This is terrible bumpy."

"Your pillow is built in, baby," said Kilvinsky and several girls laughed.

"Hey silver hair. How 'bout lettin' us out ovah on Vermont or somewhere," said another voice. "I jist got to make me some coin tonight."

"Kilvinsky got soul," said another voice. "He git us some scotch if we ask him pretty. You got soul, don't you, Mr. Kilvinsky?"

"Baby, Ah gots more soul than Ah kin control," said Kilvinsky and the girls burst into laughter.

"He sho' kin talk that trash," said a throaty voice that sounded like the girl who had cursed Bethel.

Kilvinsky parked in front of a liquor store and shouted over his shoulder, "Get your money ready and tell me what you want." Then to Gus, "Stay in the wagon. I'll be back."

Kilvinsky went around to the back and opened the door.

"Dollar each," said one of the girls and Gus heard the rustle of clothing and paper and the clink of coins.

"Two quarts of milk and a fifth of scotch. That okay?" asked one of the girls and several voices muttered, "Uh huh."

"Give me enough for paper cups," said Kilvinsky, "I'm not going to use my own money."

"Baby, if you'd turn in that bluesuit, you wouldn't have to worry 'bout money," said the one called Alice. "I'd keep you forever, you beautiful blue-eyed devil."

The girls laughed loudly as Kilvinsky closed the wagon and entered the liquor store, returning with a shopping bag in a few minutes.

He handed the bag in the door and was back in the cab and moving when Gus heard the liquor being poured.

"Change is in the bag," said Kilvinsky.

"Gud-dam," muttered one of the prostitutes. "Scotch and milk is the best motherfuckin' drink in the world. Want a drink, Kilvinsky?"

"You know we can't drink on duty."

"I know somethin' we can do on duty," said another one. "And yo' sergeant won't smell it on yo' breath. Less'n you want to get down on yo' knees and French me."

The girls screamed in laughter and Kilvinsky said, "I'm too damn old for you young girls."

"You ever change yo' mind, let me know," said Alice, "a foxy little whore like me could make you young again."

Kilvinsky drove aimlessly for more than a half hour while Gus listened as the prostitutes laughed and talked shop, each girl trying to top the last one with her account of the "weird tricks" she had encountered.

"Hell," said one prostitute, "I had one pick me up right here on Twenty-eighth and Western one night and take me clear to Beverly Heels for a hundred bucks and that bastard had me cut the head of a live chicken right there in some plushy apartment and then squish the chicken aroun' in the sink while the water was runnin' and he stood there and comed like a dog."

"Lord! Why did you do it, girl?" asked another.

"Shee-it, I didn't know what the suckah wanted till he got me in that place and handed me the butcher knife. Then I was so scared I jist did it so he wouldn' git mad. Ol' funky bastard, he was. Didn' think he could even git a stiff one."

"How 'bout that freak that lives up there in Van Nuys that likes to French inside a coffin. He sho' is a crazy motherfucker," said a shrill voice.

"That milk bath guy picked Wilma up one night, didn't he Wilma?" said another.

"Yeah, but he ain't nothin' too weird. Ah don' mind him, 'cept he lives too far away, way up in North Hollywood in one of them pads on a mountain. He jist gives you a bath in a tub full of milk. He pays damn good."

"He don' do nothin' else?"

"Oh, he Frenches you a little, but not too much."

"Shit, they almost all Frenches you anymore. People is gettin' so goddamn weird all they evah wants to do is eat pussy."

"That right, girl. I was sayin' that the other day (pour me a little scotch, honey) people jist French or git Frenched anymore. I can't remember when a trick wanted to fuck me for his ten dollars."

"Yeah, but these is all white tricks. Black men still likes to fuck."

"Shee-it, I wouldn' know 'bout that. You take black tricks, baby?"

"Sometimes, don't you?"

"Nevah. Nevah. My ol' man tol' me any who' dum 'nuff to take black tricks deserves it if she gits her ass robbed or cut. Ah never fucked a niggah in my life fo' money. An' ah never fucked a white man fo' free."

"Amen. Give me another shot of that scotch, baby, ah wants to tell you 'bout this here rich bitch from Hollywood that picked me up one night an' she wanted to give me a hunderd an' fifty dollars to go home an' let her eat mah pussy an' her husband is sittin' right there in the car with her an' she tells me he jist likes to watch."

Gus listened to tale after tale, each more bizarre than the last and when the voices were slurring, Kilvinsky said, "Let's head for the station and let them go a few blocks away. They're too drunk to take them in the station. The sergeant would want us to book them for being drunk and then they might tell him where they got the booze."

As the wagon bounced toward the station, the night drawing to a close, Gus found himself more relaxed than he had been for days. As for a physical confrontation, why, it might never happen and if it did, he would probably do well enough. He was feeling a lot better now. He hoped Vickie would be awake. He had so much to tell her.

"You're going to learn things down here, Gus," said Kilvinsky. "Every day down here is like ten days in a white division. It's the intensity down here, not just the high crime rate. You'll be a veteran after a year. It's the thousands of little things. Like the fact that you shouldn't use a pay phone. The coin chutes of all the public phones around here are stuffed so you can't get any coins back. Then once every few days the thief comes along and pulls the stuffing out with a piece of wire and gets the three dollars worth of coins that've collected there. And other things. Kid's bikes. They're all stolen, or they all have stolen parts on them, so don't ask questions to any kid about his bike or you'll be tied up all night with bike reports. Little things, see, like New Year's Eve down here sounds like the battle of Midway. All these people seem to have guns. New Year's Eve will terrify you when you realize how many of them have guns and what's going to happen someday if this Civil Rights push ever breaks into armed rebellion. But the time passes fast down here, because these people keep us eternally busy and that's important to me. I only have a short time to go for my pension and I'm interested in time."

"I'm not sorry I'm here," said Gus.

"It's all happening here, partner. Big things. This Civil Rights business and the Black Muslims and all are just the start of it. Authority is being challenged and the Negroes are at the front, but they're just a small part of it. You're going to have an impossible job in the next five years or I miss my guess."

Kilvinsky steered around an automobile wheel which was lying in the center of the residential street, but he rolled over another which lay on the other side of the street, unobserved, until they were on it. The exhausted blue van bounced painfully on its axle and a chorus of laughter was interrupted by an explosion of curses.

"Goddamn! Take it easy, Kilvinsky! You ain't drivin' no fuckin' cattle truck," said Alice.

"It's the great myth," said Kilvinsky to Gus, ignoring the voices behind them, "the myth whatever it happens to be that breaks civil authority. I wonder if a couple of centurions might've sat around like you and me one hot dry evening talking about the myth of Christianity that was defeating them. They would've been afraid, I bet, but the new myth was loaded with 'don'ts,' so one kind of authority was just being substituted for another. Civilization was never in jeopardy. But today the 'don'ts' are dying or being murdered in the name of freedom and we policemen can't save them. Once the people become accustomed to the death of a 'don't,' well then, the other 'don'ts' die much easier. Usually all the vice laws die first because people are generally vice-ridden anyway. Then the ordinary misdemeanors and some felonies become unenforceable until freedom prevails. Then later the freed people have to organize an army of their own to find order because they learn that freedom is horrifying and ugly and only small doses of it can be tolerated." Kilvinsky laughed self-consciously, a laugh that ended when he put the battered cigarette holder in his mouth and chewed on it quietly for several seconds. "I warned you us old coppers are big bullshitters, didn't I, Gus?"

6. The Swamper

"How about driving to a gamewell phone? I got to call the desk about something," said Whitey Duncan, and Roy sighed, turning the radio car right on Adams toward Hooper where he thought there was a call box.

"Go to Twenty-third and Hooper," said Duncan. "That's one of the few call boxes that works in this lousy division. Nothing works. The people don't work, the call boxes don't work, nothing works."

Some of the policemen don't work, thought Roy, and wondered how they could have possibly assigned him with Duncan five nights in a row. Granted, August was a time when the car plan was short due to vacations, but Roy thought that was a feeble reason and inexcusable supervisory technique to give a rookie officer to a partner like Duncan. After his second night with Whitey he had even subtly suggested to Sergeant Coffin that he would like to work with an aggressive younger officer, but Coffin had cut him off abruptly as though a new officer had no right to ask for a specific car or partner. Roy felt that he was being penalized for speaking up by being inflicted with Duncan for five days.

"I'll be right back, kid," said Whitey, leaving his hat in the radio car as he strolled to the call box, unsnapped the gamewell key from the ring hanging on his Sam Browne, and opened the box which was attached to the far side of a telephone pole out of Roy's line of sight. Roy could only see some white hair, a round blue stomach and shiny black shoe protruding from the vertical line of the pole.

Roy was told that Whitey had been a foot policeman in Central Division for almost twenty years and that he could never get used to working in a radio car. That was probably why he insisted on calling the station a half dozen times a night to talk to his friend, Sam Tucker, the desk officer.

After a few moments, Whitey swaggered back to the car and settled back, lighting his third cigar of the evening.

"You sure like to use that call box," said Roy with a forced smile, trying to conceal the anger brought about by the boredom of working with a useless partner like Whitey when he was brand-new and eager to learn.

"Got to ring in. Let the desk know where you're at."

"Your radio tells them that, Whitey. Policemen have radios in their cars nowadays."

"I'm not used to it," said Whitey. "Like to ring in on the call box. Besides, I like to talk to my old buddy, Sam Tucker. Good man, old Sammy."

"How come you always call in on the same box?"

"Habit, boy. When you get to be old Whitey's age, you start doing everything the same."

It was true, Roy thought. Unless an urgent call intervened, they would eat at precisely ten o'clock every night at one of three greasy spoon restaurants that served Whitey free meals. Then, fifteen minutes would be spent at the station for Whitey's bowel movement. Then back out for the remainder of the watch, which would be broken by two or three stops at certain liquor stores for free cigars and of course the recurrent messages to Sam Tucker from the call box at Twenty-third and Hooper.

"How about driving through the produce market?" said Whitey. "I never took you in there yet, did I?"

"Whatever you say," Roy sighed.

Whitey directed Roy through bustling narrow streets blocked by a maze of trucks and milling swampers who were just coming to work. "Over there," said Whitey. "That's old Foo Foo's place. He has the best bananas in the market. Park right there, kid. Then we'll get some avocados. They're a quarter apiece, right now. You like avocados? Then maybe a lug of peaches. I know a guy on the other side of the market, he has the best peaches. Never a bruise." Whitey lumbered out of the car, and put on his hat at a jaunty beat officer's angle, grabbed his baton, probably from force of habit, and began twirling it expertly in his left hand as he approached the gaunt Chinese who was sweating in a pair of khaki shorts and an undershirt as he threw huge bunches of bananas onto a produce truck. The Chinese bared his gold and silver bridgework when Whitey approached and Roy lit a cigarette and watched in revulsion as Whitey put his baton in the ring on his belt and helped Foo Foo toss bananas onto the truck.

Professional policeman, Roy thought viciously, as he remembered the suave, silver-haired captain who had lectured them in the academy about the new professionalism. But it seemed the fat cop stealing apples died hard. Look at the old bastard, thought Roy, throwing bananas in full uniform while all the other swampers are laughing their heads off. Why doesn't he retire from the Department, and then he could swamp bananas full time. I hope a tarantula bites him on his fat ass, Roy thought.

How they could have sent him to Newton Street Station, Roy could not understand. What was the sense of giving them three choices of divisions if they were then ignored and sent arbitrarily from the academy to a station twenty miles from home. He lived almost in the valley. They could have sent him to one of the valley divisions or Highland Park or even Central which was his third choice, but Newton Street he had not counted on. It was the poorest of the Negro divisions and the drabness of the area was depressing. This was the "east side" and he already had learned that as soon as the newly emigrated Negroes could afford it, they moved to the "west side," somewhere west of Figueroa Street. But the fact that the majority of the people here were Negro was the one thing that appealed to Roy. When he left the Department to be a criminologist he intended to have a thorough understanding of the ghetto. He hoped to learn all that was necessary in a year or so, and then transfer north, perhaps to Van Nuys or North Hollywood.

When they finally left the produce market, the back seat of the radio car was filled with bananas, avocados and peaches, as well as a basket of tomatoes which Whitey had scrounged as an afterthought.

"You know you got a right to half of these," said Whitey as they loaded the produce into his private car in the station parking lot.

"I told you I didn't want any."

"Partners got to share and share alike. You got a right to half of it. How about the avocados? Why don't you take the avocados?"

"Son of a bitch," Roy blurted, "I don't want it! Look here, I'm just out of the academy. I've got eight months more to do on my probationary period. They can fire me on a whim anytime between now and then. No civil service protection for a probationer, you know. I can't be taking gratuities. At least not things like this. Free meals—cigarettes—coffee—that stuff seems to be traditional, but what if the sergeant saw us in the produce market tonight? I could lose my job!"

"Sorry, kid," said Whitey with a hurt expression. "I didn't know you felt that way. I'd take all the heat if we'd got caught, you should know that."

"Yeah? What would I use as an excuse? That you put a gun to my head and forced me to go with you on that shopping tour?"

Whitey completed the transfer of fruit without further comment and didn't speak again until they were back patrolling their district, then he said, "Hey, partner, drive to a call box, I got to ring in again."

"What the hell for?" said Roy, not caring what Whitey thought anymore. "What's going on? You got a bunch of broads leaving messages at the desk for you or something?"

"I just talk to old Sam Tucker," said Whitey with a deep sigh. "The old bastard gets lonesome there at the desk. We was academy classmates, you know. Twenty-six years this October. It's tough on him being colored and working a nigger division like this. Some nights he feels pretty low when they bring in some black bastard that killed an old lady or some other shitty thing like that, and these policemen shoot off their mouth in the coffee room about niggers and such. Sam hears it and it bothers him, so he gets feeling low. Course, he's too old to be a cop anyway. He was thirty-one when he came on the job. He ought to pull the pin and leave this crappy place."

"How old were you when you came on, Whitey?"

"Twenty-nine. Hey, drive to the call box on Twenty-third. You know that's my favorite box."

"I ought to know by now," said Roy.

Roy parked at the curb and waited hopelessly while Whitey went to the call box and talked to Sam Tucker for ten minutes.

Police professionalism would come only after the old breed was gone, Roy thought. That didn't really trouble him though, because he had no intention of making a career of police work. That reminded him he had better get busy and register for the coming semester if he hoped to keep on schedule and complete his degree as planned. He wondered how anyone could want to do this kind of work for a career. Now that the training phase was over, he was part of a system he would master, learn from, and leave behind.

He glanced in the car mirror. The sun had given him a fine color. Dorothy said she'd never seen him so tan, and whether it was the uniform or his fitness she obviously found him more desirable and wanted him to make love to her often. But it may have been only because she was pregnant with their first baby and she knew that soon there would be none of it for a while. And he did it, though the enormous mound of life almost revolted him and he pretended to enjoy it as much as he did when she was lithe with a satin stomach that would probably bear stretch scars forever now that she was pregnant. That was her fault. They had decided not to have children for five years, but she had made a mistake. The news had staggered him. All his plans had to be changed. She could no longer work as a senior steno at Rhem Electronics, and she had been making an excellent wage. He would have to stay with the Department an extra year or so to save money. He would not ask his father or Carl for assistance, not even for a loan now that they all knew he would never enter the family firm.

Trying to please them was the reason he changed his major three times until he took abnormal psychology with Professor Raymond, and learned from the flabby little scholar who he was. The kindly man, who had been like a father, had almost wept when Roy told him he was leaving college to join the Los Angeles Police Department for a year or two. They had sat in Professor Raymond's office until midnight while the little man coaxed and urged and swore at Roy's stubbornness and at last gave in when Roy convinced him he was tired and probably would fail every class next semester if he remained, that a year or two away from the books but in close touch with life would give him the impetus to return and take his bachelor's and master's degrees. And who knows, if he were the scholar that Professor Raymond believed he could be, he might even keep right on while he had the momentum and get his Ph.D.

"We might be colleagues someday, Roy," said the professor, fervently shaking Roy's dry hand in both his moist soft ones. "Keep in touch with me, Roy."

And he had meant to. He wanted to talk with someone as sensitive as the professor about the things he had learned so far. He talked with Dorothy, of course. But she was so involved in the mysteries of childbirth that he doubted that she listened when he brought home the tales of the bizarre situations he encountered as a policeman and what they meant to a behaviorist.

While waiting for Whitey, Roy tilted the car mirror down and examined his badge and brass buttons. He was tall and slim but his shoulders were broad enough to make the tailored blue shirt becoming. His Sam Browne glistened and his shoes were as good as he could get them without the fanatical spit shine that some of the others employed. He kept the badge lustrous with a treated cloth and some jeweler's rouge. He decided that when his hair grew out he would never cut it short again. He had heard that a butch haircut sometimes grows out wavier than before.

"You're absolutely beautiful," said Whitey, jerking open the door and flopping into the seat with a fatuous grin at Roy.

"I dropped some cigarette ash on my shirt," said Roy, tilting the mirror to its former position. "I was just brushing it off."

"Let's go do some police work," said Whitey, rubbing his hands together.

"Why bother? We only have three more hours until end of watch," said Roy. "What the hell did Tucker tell you to make you so happy?"

"Nothing. I just feel good. It's a nice summer night. I just feel like working. Let's catch a burglar. Anybody show you yet how to patrol for burglars?"

"Thirteen-A-Forty-three, Thirteen-A-Forty-three," said the operator and Whitey turned up the volume, "see the woman, landlord-tenant dispute, forty-nine, thirty-nine south Avalon."

"Thirteen-A-Forty-three, roger," said Whitey into the hand mike. Then to Roy, "Well, instead of catching crooks, let's go pacify the natives."

Roy parked in front of the house on Avalon which was easy to find because of the porch light and the fragile white-haired Negro woman standing on the porch watching the street. She was perhaps sixty and smiled timidly when Roy and Whitey climbed the ten steps.

"This is it, Mr. PO-lice," she said, opening the battered screen door. "Won't you please come in?"

Roy removed his hat upon entering and became annoyed when Whitey failed to remove his also. It seemed that everything Whitey did irritated him.

"Won't you sit down?" she smiled, and Roy admired the tidy house she kept which looked old and clean and orderly like her.

"No, thanks, ma'am," said Whitey. "What can we do for you?"

"I got these here people that lives in the back. I don't know what to do. I hopes you can help me. They don't pay the rent on time never. And now they's two months behind and I needs the money terrible bad. I only lives on a little social security, you see, and I just got to have the rent."

"I appreciate your problem, ma'am, I sure do," said Whitey. "I once owned a duplex myself. I had some tenants that wouldn't pay and I had a heck of a time. Mine had five kids that like to've torn the place down. Yours have any kids?"

"They does. Six. And they tears up my property terrible."

"It's rough," said Whitey, shaking his head.

"What can I do, sir? Can you help me? I begged them to pay me."

"Sure wish we could," said Whitey, "but you see this is a civil matter and we only deal in criminal matters. You'd have to get the county marshal to serve them with a notice to quit and then you'd have to sue them for unlawful detainer. That's what they call it and that would take time and you'd have to pay a lawyer."

"I don't have no money for a lawyer, Mr. PO-lice," said the old woman, her thin hand touching Whitey beseechingly on the arm.

"I appreciate that, ma'am," said Whitey, "I sure do. By the way, is that corn bread I smell?"

"It sho' is, sir. Would you like some?"

"Would I?" said Whitey, removing his hat and leading the old woman to the kitchen. "I'm a country-raised boy. I grew up in Arkansas on corn bread."

"Would you like some?" she smiled to Roy.

"No, thank you," he said.

"Some coffee? It's fresh."

"No ma'am, thank you."

"I don't know when I had such good corn bread," said Whitey. "Soon's I finish, I'm going back and talk to your tenants for you. They in the little cottage in the rear?"

"Yes, sir. That's where they is. I sure would appreciate that and I'm going to tell our councilman what a fine PO-lice force we have. You always so good to me no matter what I calls for. You from Newton Street Station, ain't you?"

"Yes, ma'am, you just tell the councilman that you liked the service of old Whitey from Newton Street. You can even call the station and tell my sergeant if you want to."

"Why I'll do that, I surely will, Mr. Whitey. Can I get you some more corn bread?"

"No, no thank you," said Whitey, wiping his entire face with the linen napkin the old woman got for him. "We'll have a little talk with them and I bet they get your rent to you real quick."

"Thank you very much," the old woman called, as Roy followed Whitey and his flashlight beam down the narrow walkway to the rear of the property. Roy's frustration had subsided in his pity for the plight of the old woman and his admiration of her neat little house. There weren't enough like her in the ghetto, he thought.

"It's too damned bad that people would take advantage of a nice old woman like that," said Roy as they approached the rear cottage.

"How do you know they did?" asked Whitey.

"What do you mean? You heard her."

"I heard one side of a landlord-tenant dispute," said Whitey. "Now I got to hear the other side. You're the judge in all these dispute calls we get. Never make a decision till both sides present their cases."

This time Roy bit his lip to enforce his silence. The absurdity of this man was beyond belief. A child could see the old woman had a just grievance and he knew before the door opened that the cottage would be a filthy hovel where miserable children lived in squalor with deadbeat parents.

A coffee-colored woman in her late twenties opened the door when Whitey tapped.

"Mrs. Carson said she was going to call the PO-lice," said the woman with a tired smile. "Come in, Officers."

Roy followed Whitey into the little house which had a bedroom in the back, a small kitchen, and a living room filled by the six children who were gathered around an ancient television with a dying picture tube.

"Honey," she called, and a man padded into the room from the back, wearing frayed khaki trousers and a faded blue short-sleeved shirt which revealed oversized arms and battered hard-working hands.

"I just didn't think she'd really call the law," he said with an embarrassed smile at the officers, as Roy wondered how the cottage could be kept this clean with so many small children.

"We're two weeks behind in our rent," he drawled. "We never been behind befo' 'cept oncet and that was fo' three days. That ol' lady is mighty hard."

"She says you're over two months behind," said Roy.

"Looky here," said the man, going to the kitchen cupboard and returning with several slips of paper. "Here's last month's receipt and the month befo' and the one befo' that, clear back to January when we fust came here from Arkansas."

"You from Arkansas?" said Whitey. "Whereabouts? I'm from Arkansas too."

"Wait a minute, Whitey," said Roy, then turned back to the man. "Why would Mrs. Carson say you were behind in your rent? She said you never pay her on time and she's told you how she needs the money and that your kids have destroyed her property. Why would she say that?"

"Officer," said the man, "Mrs. Carson is a very hard lady. She owns most of this side of Avalon from Fo'ty-ninth Street on down to the co'ner."

"Have your children ever destroyed her property?" asked Roy weakly.

"Look at my house, Officer," said the woman. "Do it look like we the kind of folks that would let a chil' tear up a house? Once James there broke her basement window chucking a rock at a tin can. But she added that on our rent payment and we paid fo' it."

"How do you like California?" asked Whitey.

"Oh, we likes it fine," smiled the man. "Soon's we can save a little we wants to maybe buy a small house and get away from Mrs. Carson."

"Well, we got to be going now," said Whitey. "Sure sorry you're having troubles with your landlady. I want to wish you good luck here in California, and listen, if you ever happen to make any down-home Arkansas meals and have some left over you just call Newton Street Station and let me know, will you?"

"Why, we'll do that, sir," said the woman. "Who'll we ask fo'?"

"Just say old Whitey. And you might tell the sergeant old Whitey gave you good service. We need a pat on the back once in a while."

"Thank you, Officer," said the man. "It's surely a comfort to meet such fine po-licemen here."

"So long, kids," shouted Whitey to the six beaming brown faces which by now were gazing reverently at the policemen. They all waved good-byes as Roy followed the fat blue swaggering figure back down the narrow walkway to the car.

While Whitey was lighting a cigar Roy asked, "How did you know the old lady was lying? You probably answered calls there before, right?"

"Never did," said Whitey. "Goddamn cigars. Wonder if good cigars draw better than cheap ones?"

"Well how did you know then? You must've suspected she was lying."

"I never said she was lying. I don't say it now. There's two sides to every beef. Experience'll teach you that. You got to listen to the first guy like he's giving you the gospel and then go to the second guy and do the same thing. You just got to be patient, use horse sense and this job is easy."

Handling a rent dispute doesn't make you a policeman, Roy thought. There's more to police work than that.

"You ready to teach me how to catch a burglar now?" asked Roy, knowing the satirical edge on his voice was apparent.

"Okay, but first I got to make sure you can handle a simple landlord-tenant beef. First thing you already learned, don't take no sides. Next thing, a landlord-tenant beef or anything else could involve a psycho, or a crook with something in the pad he don't want you to see, or somebody that's so pissed off at his landlord or tenant that he's ready to climb the ass of anybody that comes through the door."

"So?"

"So be careful. Walk into any pad like a policeman not an insurance man. Stick your flashlight in your back pocket if there's light on in the pad, and keep your lid on your head. Then you got two hands ready to use. You start strolling in these pads with a light in one hand and a hat in the other you might find you need a third hand quick some night and you'll be a real courteous corpse with your hat in your hand."

"I didn't think the old lady was very dangerous."

"I had a senile old lady stick a pair of scissors right through the web of my hand one time," said Whitey. "You do what you want, I just give the tips for what they're worth. Hey, kid, how about letting me call in. Head for my call box, will you?"

Roy watched Whitey at the call box and fumed. Patronizing stupid bastard, he thought. Roy realized he had a lot to learn, but he wanted to learn it from a real policeman, not from an overweight old windbag who was a caricature of a police officer. The incessant chatter of the police radio subsided for a moment and Roy heard a dull clink of glass.

Then the realization struck him and he smiled. How foolish not to have guessed it before! He couldn't help grinning when Whitey returned to the car.

"Let's go to work, kid," said Whitey, as he got back in.

"Sure thing, partner," said Roy. "But first, I think I'll call in. I want to leave a message with the desk."

"Wait a minute!" said Whitey. "Let's drive to the station. You can tell him personally."

"No, it'll just take a minute, I can use this call box," said Roy.

"No! Wait a minute! The box is screwed up. Just before I hung up, it started buzzing. Almost busted my eardrum. It ain't working right!"

"Well, I'll just try it," said Roy, and moved as though to get out of the car.

"Wait, please!" said Whitey, grabbing Roy's elbow.

"Let's go in right now. I got to take a shit terrible bad. Take me to the station right now and you can give your message to Sam."

"Why, Whitey," Roy grinned triumphantly, and with Whitey's perspiring face this close, the fresh whiskey odor was overpowering, "you always crap fifteen minutes after we eat dinner. You told me your guts start rumbling right after your evening meal. What's the matter?"

"It's my age," said Whitey, staring sadly at the floorboard as Roy gunned the engine and drove into the traffic lane, "when you get my age you can't depend on nothing, not even your guts, especially not your guts."

AUGUST 1961

7. Guerra!

They were told by the Gang Squad detective that the war had actually started six weeks ago when the Junior Falcons jumped a seventeen-year-old member of *Los Gavilanes* named Felix Orozco who had made the consummate and final mistake of running out of gas in Falcon territory in a striped nineteen forty-eight Chevrolet that the Falcons knew belonged to a *Gavilán*. Felix was beaten to death with his own tire iron which he had used to break the wrist of the first Falcon who had come at him with a sharpened screwdriver. The girl friend of Felix Orozco, thirteen-year-old Connie Madrid, was not killed by the Junior Falcons but her face was badly ripped by a whistling slash of the car antenna that was broken off the car by El Pablo of the Junior Falcons who, it was believed by the detectives, was the one responsible for flogging Felix Orozco with the limber piece of steel as he lay, already dead probably, from countless kicks to the head and face.

Connie had been a less than cooperative witness and now after two hearing postponements in juvenile court, it was believed by the homicide team that she would probably deny in court that she saw anything.

Since the death of Felix, there had been seven cases of gang reprisals involving *Los Gavilanes* and the Junior Falcons, but on one occasion a member of the Easystreeters, named Ramon Garcia, was mistaken for a Junior Falcon and the Easystreeters announced against *Los Gavilanes*. Then, *Los Rojos*, who had no love for the Junior Falcons but who hated the Easystreeters, saw the opportunity once and for all to join a powerful ally and destroy the hated Easystreeters. Hollenbeck Division was plunged into a war that produced at least one gang incident every night, and made Serge more than ever want to transfer to Hollywood Division.

He had been getting used to Hollenbeck. It was a small division, and after a year, he was getting to know people. It helped being familiar with the regulars and when you saw someone like Marcial Tapia—who had been a burglar for over twenty years—when you saw him driving a pickup truck in the Flats (when he lived his entire life in Lincoln Heights) and the Flats was an area of commercial buildings, factories, and businesses, which were closed on weekends and it was five o'clock Sunday afternoon and all the businesses were closed—well then, you had better stop Marcial Tapia and check the contents of the truck bed which was covered with three barrels of trash and refuse. Serge had done this just three weeks before and found seven new portable television sets, an adding machine, and two typewriters beneath the pile of rubble. He had received a commendation for the arrest of Tapia, his second commendation since becoming a policeman. He had made an excellent arrest report detailing the probable cause for the arrest and search, telling how Tapia had committed a traffic violation which had caused him to stop the truck, and how he had observed the rabbit ear antenna protruding from the pile of trash. He also told how Tapia had appeared exceptionally nervous and evasive when questioned about the telltale antenna, and how when it was all added up he, being a reasonable and prudent man, with a year's experience as a police officer, believed there was something being concealed in the truck and this was how he told it in court, and it was, of course, all bullshit. He had stopped Tapia only because he recognized him and knew his background and suspected what he was doing in the commercial area of the Flats on a Sunday afternoon.

It infuriated him that he had to lie, at least it used to infuriate him, but it soon came easy enough to him when he saw that if he stuck strictly to the truth he would probably lose more than half of his arrests which involved probable cause to stop and search, because the courts were not reasonable and prudent in their assessment of what was reasonable and prudent. So Serge had decided irrevocably several months ago that he would never lose another case that hinged on a word, innuendo, or interpretation of an action by a black-robed idealist who had never done police work. It wasn't that he was trying to protect the victims, he believed that if you did not enjoy taking an asshole off the street, even if it's only for a little while, then you are in the wrong business.

"Why so quiet?" asked Milton, as he propped his elbow on the seat cushion and puffed his foul cigar, looking utterly content because they had just finished an enormous plate of chile verde, rice, and frijoles at a Mexican restaurant where Milton had been eating for eighteen years. He could eat his chile as hot as any Mexican after working Hollenbeck so long, and Raul Muñoz, the owner, challenged Milton by serving them his special chile "not for gringo tastes." Milton had consumed the chile with a bland expression saying it was tasty but not hot enough. Serge however had drunk three strawberry sodas with his meal and had his water refilled twice. That had not quenched the fire and he had ordered a large glass of milk finally. His stomach was just now becoming normal.

"What the hell. You never ate real Mexican food before?" asked Milton as Serge drove slowly through the dark summer night, enjoying the cool breeze which made the long-sleeved blue woolen uniform shirt bearable.

"I never ate that kind of green chile," said Serge, "you think it's safe to light a cigarette?"

"I think if I ever get married again, I'll marry a *Mexicana* who can make that kind of chile verde that bites back," Milton sighed, blowing cigar smoke out the window.

Serge was Milton's regular partner this month and so far he could tolerate the overweight blustering old policeman. He thought that Milton liked him, even though he always called him a "damn rookie" and sometimes treated him as though he had been on the Department fifteen days rather than fifteen months. But then, he once heard Milton call Simon a damn rookie and Simon had eight years on the Department.

"Four-A-Eleven," said the Communications operator, "at eighteen-thirteen Brooklyn, see the woman, A.D.W. report."

Serge waited for Milton to roger the call, which of course was his job as passenger officer, but the old glutton was too comfortable, with one fat leg crossed over the other, a hand on his belly and a pleading look at Serge.

"Four-A-Eleven, roger," said Serge and Milton nodded his gratitude at not having to move just yet.

"I think I'll trade you in for a police dog," said Serge, seeing by his watch that it was 9:45. Only three hours to go. It had been a quick evening, though uneventful for a Saturday night.

"At least you can catch a number for me," said Serge to Milton, who had closed his eyes and leaned his head against the door post.

"Okay, Sergio, my boy, if you're going to nag me," said Milton, pronouncing it Ser-jee-oh instead of with a soft throaty g in two syllables as it was meant to be pronounced.

Milton shined the spotlight at the housefronts trying to read a number. Serge did not like to be called Sergio no matter how it was said. It was a name from his childhood and childhood was so far in the past that he could hardly remember. He had not seen his brother Angel nor his sister Aurora since Aurora's birthday dinner at Angel's house when he had brought presents to Aurora and all his nephews and nieces. He had been scolded by Aurora and Angel's wife Yolanda for coming by so seldom. But since his mother was gone he had little reason to return to Chino and he realized that when the memory of his mother would begin to fade, his visits would probably be no more than twice a year. But so far, his memories of her were still very vivid and it was difficult to understand because he had never thought of her so frequently when she lived. In fact, when he left her at eighteen to join the Marine Corps, he had intended never to live at home again, but to leave the bleak little neighborhood and go perhaps to Los Angeles. He had not at that time considered being a policeman. Then he thought of how she, like all Mexican mothers, called her sons *mi hijo* and said it like one word which made it more intimate than "my son" in English.

"Must be the gray house," said Milton. "That one. The one with the balcony. Jesus Christ, those timbers are rotten. I wouldn't walk on that balcony."

"With your weight I wouldn't walk on the First Street bridge," said Serge.

"Goddamn rookies, no respect for senior partners anymore," said Milton as Serge parked the radio car.

The house sat on the edge of an alley and north of the

alley was a commercial building, windowless on the south wall. The builder of the edifice had made the error of plastering the building with a coat of soft irresistible yellow paint. Serge guessed that the wall had not remained inviolate for two days after it was completed. This was a gang neighborhood, a Mexican gang neighborhood, and Mexican gang members were obsessed with a compulsion to make their mark on the world. Serge stopped for a moment, taking the last puff on his cigarette while Milton got his notebook and flashlight. Serge read the writing on the wall in black and red paint from spray cans which all gang members carried in their cars in case they would spot a windfall like this creamy yellow irresistible blank wall. There was a heart in red, three feet in diameter, which bore the names of "Ruben and Isabel" followed by *"mi vida"* and there was the huge declaration of an Easystreeter which said *"El Wimpy de los Easystreeters,"* and another one which said "Ruben *de los Easystreeters,"* but Ruben would not be outdone by Wimpy and the legend below his name said *"de los Easystreeters y del mundo,"* and Serge smiled wryly as he thought of Ruben who claimed the world as his domain because Serge had yet to meet a gang member who had ever been outside Los Angeles County. There were other names of Junior Easystreeters and Peewee Easystreeters, dozens of them, and declarations of love and ferocity and the claims that this was the land of the Easystreeters. Of course at the bottom of the wall was the inevitable *"CON SAFOS,"* the crucial gang incantation not to be found in any Spanish dictionary, which declared that none of the writing on this wall can ever be altered or despoiled by anything later written by the enemy.

As Serge read, the disgust welled in him but it was interrupted by a blast of horns and a caravan of cars moving down State Street decorated with strings of pink and white paper carnations announcing a Mexican wedding. The men in the cars wore white dinner jackets and the girls chiffon dresses of blue. The bride of course wore white and a white veil which she wore pulled back as she kissed her new husband who Serge guessed could not be more than eighteen. The car directly behind the bride and groom's blasted the horn louder than the rest to sound approval at the prolonged kiss.

"In a few months we'll be called in to handle their family disputes," said Serge, grinding the cigarette out on the sidewalk.

"Think it'll take that long before he starts kicking the hell out of her?" asked Milton.

"No, probably not," said Serge as they walked to the house.

"That's why I told the lieutenant if he had to stick me with a rookie, to give me that half-breed Mexican Sergio Duran," said Milton slapping Serge on the shoulder. "You may be short on experience, Sergio my boy, but you're as cynical as any twenty-year cop on the Department."

Serge did not correct Milton who had referred to him on another occasion as his half-caste partner. He had never claimed to be only half-Mexican, but the idea had spread somehow and Serge merely acquiesced by his silence when some overly inquisitive partner asked him if it were true his mother had been an Anglo which would certainly explain why he didn't speak Spanish and why he was such a big man and so fair. At first it had bothered him for someone to think his mother was other than what she had been, but damn it, it was better this way he told himself. Otherwise, he would have been constantly plagued like Ruben Gonsalvez and the other Chicano cops with hundreds of duties involving translation. And it was true, it was utterly true that he no longer spoke the language. Certainly he understood things that were said, but he had to concentrate fully to understand a conversation and it was not worth the effort to him. And he forgot the words. He could not answer even if he did understand a little. So it was better this way. Even with a name like Sergio Duran you could not be expected to speak Spanish if your mother was not Mexican.

"Hope this goddamn balcony doesn't cave in while we're in the pad," said Milton, flipping the remains of his wet cigar in the alley as they knocked on the screen door.

Two little boys came to the door and held it open silently.

"Is Mama home?" asked Milton, tapping the shorter one under the chin.

"Our father is a policeman too," said the taller one, who was very thin and dirty. His eyes were as black as his hair and he was obviously excited at having the policemen in his house.

"He is?" said Serge, wondering if it were true. "You mean he's a guard of some kind?"

"He's a policeman," said the boy, nodding for emphasis. "He's a *capitán de policía*. I swear it."

"Where?" asked Serge. "Not here in Los Angeles?"

"In Juárez, Mexico," answered the boy. "Where we come from."

Milton chuckled, and when Serge turned he reddened as he saw Milton was laughing at him, not at the boy.

That was something he hadn't yet mastered completely, the capacity to mentally challenge anything, *anything* that people told you because it was usually erroneous, exaggerated, rationalized or downright deceptive.

"Go get Mama," said Milton, and the shorter child obeyed immediately. The taller one stood staring at Serge in wonder.

The boy reminded Serge of someone, he couldn't remember who. The same hollow eyes of opaque blackness, bony arms, and a buttonless shirt that had never been completely clean. A boy in the old life perhaps, or one of the Korean children who shined their shoes and swept the barracks. No, it was one from the old life, a childhood friend had eyes like that, but he couldn't remember which one. Why should he try? The memory failure was further proof the cord was irreparably severed, the operation a success.

The child stared at the shiny black Sam Browne belt, the key ring with the huge brass key which unlocked police call boxes, and the chrome-plated whistle which Serge had bought to replace the plastic one the Department supplied. While Serge glanced up the stairs toward the woman who was answering the child they had sent, he felt a light touch on the key ring. When he looked down the child was still staring, but his hands were at his sides.

"Here kid," said Milton, removing the whistle from his key ring. "Take it outside and blow your brains out. But I want it back when I leave, hear me?"

The boy smiled and took the whistle from Milton. Before he stepped from the house, the shrill screams of the whistle pierced the summer night.

"Christ, he'll have the whole neighborhood complaining," said Serge, moving toward the door to call the boy.

"Let him," said Milton, grabbing Serge's arm.

"You gave it to him," Serge shrugged. "It's your whistle."

"Yep," said Milton.

"He'll probably steal the goddamn thing," said Serge, disgustedly.

"You're probably right. That's what I like about you, kid, you're a realist."

It was an old two-story house and Serge guessed it housed a family on each floor. They were standing in a living room which had two twin beds shoved into a far corner. The kitchen was in the rear of the house and another room which he could not see into. It was probably another bedroom. It was a very large old house, very large for one family. At least it was very large for one family on welfare, as he guessed this one was, for there were no man signs around the house, only children's and women's things.

"Up here, please," said the woman, who stood at the top of the staircase in the darkness. She was pregnant and carried a baby in her arms who was not more than a year old.

"The light over the steps is out. I'm sorry," she said, as they used their flashlights to light the creaking, precarious steps.

"In here, please," she said entering the room to the left of the landing.

It looked very much like the room downstairs, a combination living room and bedroom where at least two children slept. There was a half-dead portable television on a low end table and three girls and the boy they had sent upstairs were sitting in front of it watching a grotesque cowboy whose elongated head sat atop an enormous avocado body.

"That TV needs repair," said Milton.

"Oh yes," she smiled. "I'm going to get it fixed soon."

"You know Jesse's TV Shop on First Street?" asked Milton.

"I think so," she nodded, "near the bank?"

"Yeah. Take it to him. He's honest. He's been around here at least twenty years that I know of."

"I will, thank you," she said, giving the fat baby to the oldest girl, a child of about ten, who was sitting on the end of the blanket-covered couch.

"What's the problem?" asked Serge.

"My oldest boy got beat up today," said the woman. "He's in the bedroom. When I told him I called the cops, he went in there and won't come out. His head is bleeding and he won't let me take him to General Hospital or nothing. Could you please talk to him or something?"

"We can't talk if he won't open the door," said Serge.

"He'll open it," said the woman. Her huge stomach was tearing the shapeless black dress at the seams. She shuffled barefoot to the closed door at the rear of a cluttered hallway.

"Nacho," she called. "Nacho! Open the door! He's stubborn," she said turning to the two policemen. "Ignacio, you open it!"

Serge wondered when was the last time Nacho had been kicked in the ass by his mother. Never, probably. If there had ever been a real father living in the pad, he probably didn't care enough to do the job. He would never have dared to defy his own mother like this, Serge thought. And she had raised them without a father. And the house was always spotless, not like this filth. And she had worked and he was glad because if they had given away welfare in those days like they did today, they probably would have accepted it because who could refuse money.

"Come on, Nacho, open the door and let's stop playing around," said Milton. "And hurry up! We're not going to stand around all night."

The lock turned and a chunky shirtless boy of about sixteen opened the door, turned his back, and walked across the room to a wicker chair where he had apparently been sitting. He held a grimy washcloth to his head, the webs of his fingers crusty with blood and car grease.

"What happened to you?" asked Milton, entering the room and turning up a table lamp to examine the boy's head.

"I fell," he said, with a surly look at Milton and another at Serge. The look he gave his mother infuriated Serge who shook a cigarette from his pack and lit it.

"Look, we don't care whether your head gets infected or not," said Milton. "And we don't care if you want to be stupid and get in gang beefs and die like a stupid *vato* in the street. That's your business. But you think about it, because we're only going to give you about two minutes to decide whether you want to let us take you to the hospital and get your head sewed up and tell us what happened, or whether you want to go to bed like that and wake up with gangrene of the superego which usually only takes three hours to kill you. I can see that wound is already getting green flakes all over it. That's a sure sign."

The boy looked at Milton's expressionless beefy face for a moment. "All right, you might as well take me to the hospital," he said, snatching a soiled T-shirt from the bedpost.

"What happened? *Los Rojos* get you?" asked Milton, turning sideways to get down the narrow creaking stairway with Nacho.

"Will you bring him home?" asked the woman.

"We'll take him to Lincoln Heights Receiving Hospital," said Serge. "You'll have to bring him home."

"I don't got a car," said the woman. "And I got the kids here. Maybe I can get Ralph next door to take me. Can you wait a minute?"

"We'll bring him home after he's fixed up," said Milton.

It was that kind of thing that made Serge damn mad at Milton at least once every working night. It was not their responsibility to bring people home from the hospital, or jail, or anywhere else they took them. Police cars made one-way trips. It was Saturday night and there were lots more interesting things to do than nursemaid this kid. It would never have occurred to Milton to ask him what *he* wanted to do, thought Serge. Serge would need ten more years as a cop before he rated simple consideration from Milton. Besides, that was the trouble with people like these, someone was always doing for them what they should do for themselves.

"We'll have him back in less than an hour," said Milton to the panting woman who rested her big belly against the precarious banister and apparently decided not to descend the entire stairway.

When Serge turned to go he noticed that above the doorway in the living room of the downstairs family were two eight-by-four-inch holy cards. One was Our Lady of Guadalupe and the other Blessed Martin de Porres. In the center was another card, a bit larger, which contained a green and gold horseshoe covered with glitter and a border of four-leaf clovers.

Nacho had mastered the stride of the Mexican gang member and Serge was looking at him as they crossed the front yard. He didn't see the car cruising slowly down the street, lights out, until it was close. At first he thought it was another radio car on early prowler patrol and then he saw it was a green metal-flaked Chevrolet. Four or five heads barely showed above the window ledges which told Serge automatically that the seats were dropped and that it was probably a gang car.

"Who are those low riders?" Serge asked, turning to Nacho, who was gaping in terror at the car. The car stopped near Nacho's alley and for the first time the low riders seemed to notice the radio car which was partially hidden from view behind a junk-laden van parked in front.

Nacho bolted for the house at the same moment that Serge realized these were *Los Rojos* who had attacked the boy and were probably returning to be more thorough.

Nacho's little brother gave a happy blast on the police whistle.

"*La jura!*" said a voice from the car, apparently seeing the policemen step from the shadows into the light from the open doorway. The driver turned on the lights and the car lurched forward and stalled as Serge ran toward it, ignoring Milton who shouted, "Duran, get your ass back here!"

Serge had a half-formed thought of jerking the cursing driver out of the car as he ground the starter desperately, but when Serge was ten feet from the car he heard a pop, and an orange fiery blossom flashed from the interior of the car. Serge froze as he instinctively knew what it was before his mind fully comprehended, and the Chevy started, faltered, and roared east on Brooklyn Avenue.

"The keys!" Milton roared, standing beside the open driver's door of the radio car. "Throw the keys!"

Serge obeyed immediately although still stunned by the realization that they had fired at him point-blank. He barely jumped in the passenger seat when Milton squealed from the curb and the flashing red light and siren brought Serge back to reality.

"Four-A-Eleven in pursuit!" Serge yelled into the open microphone, and began shouting the streets they were passing as the Communications operator cleared the frequency of conversation so that all units could be informed that Four-A-Eleven was pursuing a 1948 Chevrolet eastbound on Marengo.

"Four-A-Eleven, your location!" shouted the Communications operator.

Serge turned the radio as loud as it would go and rolled up the window but could still hardly hear Milton and the operator over the din of the siren and the roaring engine as Milton gained on the careening low riders who narrowly missed a head-on collision with a left turner.

"Four-A-Eleven approaching Soto Street, still eastbound on Marengo," Serge shouted, and then realized his seat belt was not fastened.

"Four-A-Eleven your location! Come in Four-A-Eleven!" shouted the Communications operator as Serge fumbled with the seat belt, cursed, and dropped the mike.

"They're bailing out!" Milton shouted and Serge looked up to see the Chevrolet skidding to a stop in the middle of Soto Street as all four doors were flung open.

"The one in the right rear fired the shot. Get him!" Milton yelled as Serge was running in the street before the radio car finished the jolting sliding stop.

Several passing cars slammed on brakes as Serge chased the *Rojo* in the brown hat and yellow Pendleton shirt down Soto and east on Wabash. Serge was utterly unaware that he had run two blocks at top speed when suddenly the air scorched his lungs and his legs turned weak, but they were still running through the darkness. He had lost his baton and his hat, and the flashlight fluttering in his swinging left hand lighted nothing but empty sidewalk in front of him. Then his man was gone. Serge stopped and scanned the street frantically. The street was quiet and badly lit. He heard nothing but his outraged thudding heart and the sawing breaths that frightened him. He heard a barking dog close to his left, and another, and a crash in the rear yard of a run-down yellow frame house behind him. He turned off the flashlight, picked a yard farther west and crept between two houses. When he reached the rear of the house he stopped, listened, and crouched down. The first dog, two doors away, had stopped barking, but the other in the next yard was snarling and yelping as though he was bumping against a taut chain. The lights were going on and Serge waited. He jerked his gun out as the figure appeared from the yard gracefully with a light leap over the wooden fence. He was there in the driveway silhouetted against the whitewashed background of the two-car garage like the paper man on the pistol range, and Serge was struck with the thought that he was no doubt a juvenile and should not be shot under any circumstances but defense of your life. Yet he decided quite calmly that this *Rojo* was not getting another shot at Serge Duran, and he cocked the gun which did not startle the dark figure who was twelve feet away, but the flashlight did, and there he'was in the intense beam of the five cell. Serge had already taken up the slack of the fleshy padding of the right index finger and this *Rojo* would never know that only a microscopic layer of human flesh over unyielding finger bone kept the hammer from falling as Serge exerted perhaps a pound of pull on the trigger of the cocked revolver which was pointed at the stomach of the boy.

"Freeze," Serge breathed, watching the hands of the boy and deciding that if they moved, if they moved at all . . .

"Don't! Don't," said the boy, who stared at the beam, but stood motionless, one foot turned to the side, as in a clumsy stop-action camera shot. "Oh, don't," he said and Serge realized he was creeping forward in a duck walk, the gun extended in front of him. He also realized how much pressure he was exerting on the trigger and he always wondered why the hammer had not fallen.

"Just move," Serge whispered, as he circled the quivering boy and moved in behind him, the flashlight under his arm as he patted the *Rojo* down for the gun that had made the orange flash.

"I don't got a weapon," said the boy.

"Shut your mouth," said Serge, teeth clenched, and as he found no gun his stomach began to loosen a bit and the breathing evened.

Serge handcuffed the boy carefully behind his back, tightening the iron until the boy winced. He uncocked and holstered the gun and his hand shook so badly that for a second he almost considered holstering the gun still cocked because he was afraid the hammer might slip while he uncocked it.

"Let's go," he said, finally, shoving the boy ahead of him.

When they got to the front street, Serge saw several people on the porches, and two police cars were driving slowly from opposite directions, spotlights flashing, undoubtedly looking for him.

Serge shoved the boy into the street and when the beam of the first spotlight hit them the radio car accelerated and jerked to a stop in front of them.

Ruben Gonsalvez was the passenger officer, and he ran around the car throwing open the door on the near side.

"This the one who fired at you?" he asked.

"You prove it, *puto*," the boy said, grinning now in the presence of the other officers and the three or four onlookers who were standing on porches, as dogs for three blocks howled and barked at the siren of the help car which had raced code three to their aid.

Serge grasped the boy by the neck, bent his head and shoved him in the back seat, crawling in beside him and forcing him to the right side of the car.

"Tough now that you got your friends, ain't you, *pinchi jura*," said the boy and Serge tightened the iron again until the boy sobbed, "You dirty motherfucking cop."

"Shut your mouth," said Serge.

"*Chinga tu madre!*" said the boy.

"I should have killed you."

"*Tu madre!*"

And then Serge realized he was squeezing the hard rubber grips of the Smith & Wesson. He was pressing the trigger guard and he remembered the way he felt when he had the boy in his sights, the black shadow who had almost ended him at age twenty-four when his entire life was ahead, for reasons not he nor this little *vato* could understand. He had not known he was capable of this kind of terrifying rage. But to be almost murdered. It was utterly absurd.

"*Tu madre*," the boy repeated, and the fury crept over Serge again. It wasn't the same in Spanish, he thought. It was so much filthier, almost unbearable, that this gutter animal would dare to mention her like that . . .

"You don't like that, do you, gringo?" said the boy, baring his white teeth in the darkness. "You understand some Spanish, huh? You don't like me talking about your moth . . ."

And Serge was choking him, down, down, to the floor he took him, screaming silently, staring into the exposed whites of swollen horrified eyes, and Serge through the irresistible shroud of smothering fury probed for the little bones in front of the throat, which if broken . . . and then Gonsalvez was holding Serge across the forehead and bending him backward in a bow. Then he was lying flat on his back in the street and Gonsalvez was kneeling beside him, panting and babbling incoherently in Spanish and English, patting him on the shoulder but keeping a firm grip on one arm.

"Easy, easy easy," said Gonsalvez. "*Hombre*, Jesus Christ! Sergio, *no es nada*, man. You're okay, now. Relax, *hombre. Hijo la* . . ."

Serge turned his back to the radio car and supported himself against it. He had never wept, he thought, never in his life, not when she died, not ever. And he did not weep now, as he shakily accepted the cigarette which Gonsalvez had lit for him.

"Nobody saw nothing, Sergio," said Gonsalvez, as Serge sucked dully on the cigarette, filled with a hopeless sickness which he did not want to analyze now, hoping he could maintain control of himself because he was more afraid than he had ever been in his life, and he knew vaguely it was things in himself he feared.

"Good thing those people on the porch went in the pad," Gonsalvez whispered. "Nobody saw nothing."

"I'm going to sue you, motherfucker," said the raspy sobbing voice inside the car. "I'm going to get you."

Gonsalvez tightened his grip on Serge's arm. "Don't listen to that *cabrone*. I think he's going to have bruises on his neck. If he does, he got them when you arrested him in the backyard. He fought with you and you grabbed him by the neck during the fight, got it?"

Serge nodded, not caring about anything but the slight pleasure the cigarette was giving him as he breathed only smoke, exhaling a cloud through his nose as he sucked in another fiery puff.

When Serge sat in the detective squad room at two o'clock that morning, he appreciated Milton as he never had before. He came now to understand how little he had known about the blustering, red-faced old policeman who, after a whispered conversation with Gonsalvez, took charge of the young prisoner, reported verbally to the sergeant and the detectives, and generally left Serge to sit in the detective squad room, smoke, and go through the motions of participating in the writing of reports. The night watch detectives and juvenile officers were all kept overtime interrogating suspects and witnesses. Four radio cars were assigned to search the streets, yards, sidewalks and sewers in the route of the pursuit from the point of inception to the dark driveway where Serge made his arrest. But as of two o'clock the boy's gun had not been found.

"Want some more coffee?" asked Milton, placing a mug of black coffee on the table where Serge sat listlessly penciling out a statement on the shooting that would be retyped on the arrest report.

"They find the gun yet?" asked Serge.

Milton shook his head, taking a sip from his own cup. "The way I figure it, the kid you chased had the gun with him and dumped it when he was in those yards. You realize the thousands of places a gun could be concealed in one junky little yard? And he was probably in several yards jumping fences. He could've thrown it on the roof of one of the houses. He could've pulled up a little grass and buried it. He could've thrown it as far as he could over to the next street. He could've got rid of it during the pursuit, too. The guys couldn't possibly check every inch of every yard, every ivy patch, every roof of every building, and every parked car along the route where he could've thrown it."

"Sounds like you think they won't find it?"

"You should be ready for the possibility," Milton shrugged. "Without the gun, we've got no case. These con wise little mothers are sticking together pretty damn good on their stories. There was no gun, they say."

"You saw the muzzle flash," said Serge.

"Sure, I did. But we got to prove it was a gun."

"How about that kid Ignacio? He saw it."

"He saw nothing. At least he says he saw nothing. He claims he was running for the house when he heard the loud crack. Sounded like a backfire, he says."

"How about his mother. She was on the porch."

"Says she saw nothing. She don't want to get involved with these gang wars. You can understand her position."

"I can only understand that little killer has to be taken off the street."

"I know how you feel, kid," said Milton, putting his hand on Serge's shoulder and pulling a chair close. "And listen, that kid didn't mention anything that happened later, you know what I mean. At least not yet, he didn't. I noticed some marks on his neck, but he's pretty dark-complected. They don't show up."

Serge looked into the blackness of the cup and swallowed a gulp of the bitter burning coffee.

"Once a guy swung a blade at me," said Milton quietly. "It wasn't too many years ago. Almost opened up this big pile of guts." Milton patted the bulging belly. "He had a honed, eight-inch blade and he really tried to hit me. Something made me move. I never saw it coming. I was just making a pinch on this guy for holding a little weed, that's all. Something made me move. Maybe I heard it, I don't know. When he missed me, I jumped back, fell on my ass and pulled my gun just as he was getting ready to try again. He dropped the knife and kind of smiled, you know, like, 'This time you win, copper.' I put the gun away, took out the baton and broke two of his ribs and they had to put thirteen stitches in his head. I know I'd have killed him if my partner didn't stop me. I never done that before or since. I mean I never let go before. But I was having personal problems at the time, a divorce and all, and this bastard had tried to render me, and I just let go, that's all. I never had no regrets at what I did to him, understand? I was sick at what I did to myself. I mean, he dragged me down to the jungle floor and made me an animal too, that's what I hated. But I thought about it for a few days and I decided that I had just acted like a regular man and not like a cop. A policeman isn't supposed to be afraid or shocked or mad when some bastard tries to make a canoe out of him with a switchblade. So I just did what any guy might've. But that don't mean I couldn't handle it a little better if it ever happened again. And I'll tell you one thing, he only got a hundred and twenty days for almost murdering me, and that didn't bother him, but I'll bet he learned something from what I did to him and he might think twice before trying to knife another cop. This is a brutal business you're in, kid. So don't stew over things. And if you learn something about yourself that you'd be better off not knowing, well, just slide along, it'll work out."

Serge nodded at Milton to acknowledge what his partner was trying to do. He drained the coffee cup and lit another cigarette as one of the detectives came in the squad room carrying a flashlight and a yellow legal tablet. The detective took off his coat and crossed the room to Milton and Serge.

"We're going to sack up these four dudes now," said the detective, a youthful curly-haired sergeant, whose name Serge couldn't remember. "Three of them are seventeen and they're going to Georgia Street, but I'll tell you for sure they'll be out Monday. We got no case."

"How old is the one that shot at my partner?" asked Milton.

"Primitivo Chavez? He's an adult. Eighteen years old. He'll go to Central jail, but we'll have to kick him out in forty-eight hours unless we can turn up that gun."

"How about the bullet?" asked Serge.

"From where you were standing and from where those guys were sitting in that low rider Chevy, I'm guessing that the trajectory of the bullet would be at least forty-five degrees out the window of the car. It would've hit you in the face if it'd been aimed right, but since it didn't I'm thinking it went approximately between the houses you guys were in and the next one west. That's separated by the other one by about a half acre of vacant lot. In other words, I think the goddamn bullet didn't hit a thing and probably right now is sitting on the freeway out near General Hospital. Sorry, guys, you don't want to nail these four assholes any more than I do. We figure the one cat, Jesus Martinez, is involved in an unsolved gang killing in Highland Park where a kid got blown up. We can't prove that one either."

"How about the paraffin test, Sam," said Milton. "Can't that show if a guy's fired a gun?"

"Not worth a shit, Milton," said the detective. "Only in the movie whodunits. A guy can have nitrates on his hands from a thousand other ways. The paraffin test is no good."

"Maybe a witness or maybe the gun will turn up tomorrow," said Milton.

"Maybe it will," said the detective doubtfully. "I'm glad I'm not a juvenile officer. They only call us in when these assholes start shooting each other. I'd hate to handle them every day for all their ordinary burglaries and robberies and stuff. I'll stick to adult investigation. At least they get a *little* time when I convict them."

"What kind of records they got?" asked Milton.

"About what you'd expect: lots of burglaries, A.D.W.'s, joy riding galore, robberies, narco and a scattered rape here and there. The Chavez kid's been sent to Youth Authority camp once. The others never have been sent to camp. This is Chavez' first bust as an adult. He only turned eighteen last month. At least he'll get a taste of the men's jail for a few days."

"That'll just give him something to talk about when he goes back to the neighborhood," said Milton.

"I guess so," sighed the detective. "He'll already have all the status in the world for getting away with shooting at Duran. I've been trying to learn something from all these little gang hoods you guys bring in. Want to hear something? Follow me." The detective led the way to a locked door which when opened revealed a small closet filled with sound and recording equipment. The detective turned on the switch .to the recorder and Serge recognized the insolent thin voice of Primitivo Chavez.

"I never shot nobody, man. Why should I?"

"Why not?" said the detective's voice.

"That's a better question," said the boy.

"It would be smart to tell the truth, Primo. The truth always makes you feel better and clears the way for a new start."

"New start? I like my old start. How about a smoke?"

The tape spun silently for a moment and Serge heard

the flicker and spurt of a match and then the detective's steady voice again.

"We'll find the gun, Primo, it's only a matter of time."

The boy laughed a thin snuffling laugh and Serge felt his heart thump as he remembered how he felt when he had the skinny throat.

"You ain't never going to find no gun," said the boy. "I ain't worried about that."

"You hid it pretty good, I bet," said the detective. "You got some brains, I imagine."

"I didn't say I had a gun. I just said you ain't never going to find no gun."

"Read that," the detective suddenly commanded.

"What's that?" asked the boy, suspiciously.

"Just a news magazine. Just something I found laying around. Read it for me, *ése*."

"What for, man? What kind of games you playing?"

"Just my own little experiment. Something I do with all gang members."

"You trying to prove something?"

"Maybe."

"Well prove it with somebody else."

"How far you go in school, Primo?"

"Twelfth grade. I quit in twelfth grade."

"Yeah? Well you can read pretty good, then. Just open the magazine and read anything."

Serge heard the rustle of pages and then a moment of silence followed by, "Look man, I don't got time for kid games. *Véte a la chingada.*"

"You can't read can you, Primo? And they passed you clear through to the twelfth grade hoping that being in the twelfth grade would make you a twelfth grader and then they made it tough when they realized they couldn't give an illiterate a diploma. These do-gooders really fucked you up, didn't they Primo."

"What're you talking about, man? I'd rather talk about this shooting you say I did than all this other shit."

"How far you been in your life, Primo?"

"How far?"

"Yeah, how far. You live in the housing projects down by the animal shelter, right?"

"Dogtown, man. You can call it Dogtown, we ain't ashamed of that."

"Okay, Dogtown. What's the farthest you ever been from Dogtown? Ever been to Lincoln Heights?"

"Lincoln Heights? Sure, I been there."

"How many times? Three?"

"Three, four, I don't know. Hey, I had enough of this kind of talk. I don't know what the hell you want, *Ya estuvo.*"

"Have another cigarette," said the detective. "And take a few for later."

"Okay, for cigarettes I can put up with this bullshit."

"Lincoln Heights is maybe two miles from Dogtown. You ever been farther?"

The tape was silent once again and then the boy said, "I been to El Serreno. How far is that?"

"About a mile farther."

"So I seen enough."

"Ever see the ocean?"

"No."

"How about a lake or river?"

"I seen a river, the goddamn L.A. River runs right by Dogtown, don't it?"

"Yeah, sometimes there's eight inches of water in the channel."

"Who cares about that shit anyway. I got everything I want in Dogtown. I don't want to go nowhere."

The tape was silent once more and the boy said, "Wait a minute. I been somewhere far. A hundred miles, maybe."

"Where was that?"

"In camp. The last time I got busted for burglary they sent me away to camp for four months. I was fucking glad to get back to Dogtown."

The detective smiled and turned off the recorder. "Primitivo Chavez is a typical teen-age gang member, I'd say."

"What're you trying to prove, Sam?" asked Milton. "You going to rehabilitate him?"

"Not me," the detective smiled. "Nobody could do it now. You could give Primo two million bucks and he'd never leave Dogtown and the gang and the fun of cutting down one of the Easystreeters—or a cop, maybe. Primo is too old. He's molded. He's lost."

"He deserves to be," said Milton bitterly. "That little son of a bitch'll die by the sword."

8. Classrooms

"I've already explained to you twice that your signature on this traffic citation is merely a promise to appear. You are not admitting guilt. Understand?" said Rantlee, with a glance at the group of onlookers that suddenly formed.

"Well, I still ain't signin' nothin'," said the tow truck driver, slouched back against his white truck, brown muscular arms folded across his chest. He raised his face to the setting sun at the conclusion of a sentence and cast triumphant looks at the bystanders who now numbered about twenty, and Gus wondered if now were the time to saunter to the radio car and put in a call for assistance.

Why wait until it started? They could be killed quickly by a mob. But should he wait a few more minutes? Would it seem cowardly to put in a call for backup units at this moment, because the truck driver was merely arguing, putting up a bluff for the onlookers? He would probably sign the ticket in a moment or so.

"If you refuse to sign, we have no choice but to arrest you," said Rantlee. "If you sign, it's like putting up a bond. Your word is the bond and we can let you go. You have the right to a trial, a jury trial if you want one."

"That's what I'm going to ask for, too. A jury trial."

"Fine. Now, please sign the ticket."

"I'm goin' to make you spend all day in court on your day off."

"Fine!"

"You jist like to drive around givin' tickets to Negroes, don't you?"

"Look around, Mister," said Rantlee, his face crimson now. "There ain't nobody on the streets around here, *but* Negroes. Now why do you suppose I picked on you and not somebody else?"

"Any nigger would do, wouldn't it? I jist happened to be the one you picked."

"You just happened to be the one that ran the red light. Now, are you going to sign this ticket?"

"You specially likes to pick on wildcat tow truckers, don't you? Always chasin' us away from accident scenes so the truckers that contract with the PO-lice Department can git the tow."

"Lock up your truck if you're not going to sign. Let's get going to the station."

"You don't even got my real name on that ticket. My name ain't Wilfred Sentley."

"That's what your license says."

"My real name is Wilfred 3X, whitey. Gave to me by the prophet himself."

"That's fine. But for our purposes, you can sign your slave name to this ticket. Just sign Wilfred Sentley."

"You jist love workin' down here, don't you? You jist soil your shorts I bet, when you think about comin' here every day and fuckin' all the black people you can."

"Yeah, get it up in there real tight, whitey," said a voice at the rear of the crowd of teen-agers, "so it feels real good when you come."

This brought peals of laughter from the high school crowd who had run across from the hot dog stand on the opposite corner.

"Yes, I just love working down here," said Rantlee in a toneless voice, but his red face betrayed him and he stopped. "Lock your truck," he said finally.

"See how they treats black people, brothers and sisters," the man shouted, turning to the crowd on the sidewalk which had doubled in the last minute and now blocked access to the police car, and Gus's jaw was trembling so that he clamped his teeth shut tight. It's gone too far, thought Gus.

"See how they is?" shouted the man, and several children in the front of the crowd joined a tall belligerent drunk in his early twenties who lurched into the street from the Easy Time Shine Parlor and announced that he could kill any motherfuckin' white cop that ever lived with his two black hands, which brought a whoop and cheer from the younger children who urged him on.

Rantlee pushed through the crowd suddenly and Gus knew he was going to the radio, and for an agonizing moment Gus was alone in the center of the ring of faces, some of which he told himself, would surely help him. If anything happened someone would help him. He told himself it was not hate he saw in every face because his imagination was rampant now and the fear subsided only slightly when Rantlee pushed his way back through the crowd.

"Okay, there're five cars on the way," Rantlee said to Gus and turned to the truck driver. "Now, you sign or if you want to start something, we got enough help that'll be here in two minutes to take care of you and anybody else that decides to be froggy and leap."

"You got your quota to write, don't you?" the man sneered.

"No, we used to have a quota, now I can write every goddamn ticket I want to," Rantlee said, and held the pencil up to the driver's face. "And this is your last chance to sign, 'cause when the first police car gets here, you go to jail, whether you sign or not."

The man took a step forward and stared in the young policeman's gray eyes for a long moment. Gus saw that he was as tall as Rantlee and just as well built. Then Gus looked at the three young men in black Russian peasant hats and white tunics who whispered together on the curb, watching Gus. He knew it would be them that he would have to contend with if anything happened.

"Your day is comin'," said the driver, ripping the pencil from Rantlee's hand and scrawling his name across the face of the citation. "You ain't goin' to be top dog much longer."

While Rantlee tore the white violator's copy from the ticket book, the driver let Rantlee's pencil fall to the ground and Rantlee pretended not to notice. He gave the ticket to the driver who snatched it from the policeman's hand and was still talking to the dispersing crowd when Gus and Rantlee were back in the car, pulling slowly from the curb while several young Negroes grudgingly stepped from their path. They both ignored a loud thump and knew that one of the ones in the peasant caps had kicked their fender, to the delight of the children.

They stopped for a few seconds and Gus locked his door while a boy in a yellow shirt in a last show of bravado sauntered out of the path of the bumper. Gus recoiled when he turned to the right and saw a brown face only a few inches from his, but it was only a boy of about nine years and he studied Gus while Rantlee impatiently revved the engine. Gus saw only childlike curiosity in the face and all but the three in the peasant caps were now walking away. Gus smiled at the little face and the black eyes which never left his.

"Hello, young man," said Gus, but his voice was weak.

"Why do you like to shoot black people?" asked the boy.

"Who told you that? That's not . . ." The lurching police car threw him back in his seat and Rantlee was roaring south on Broadway and west on Fifty-fourth Street back to their area. Gus turned and saw the little boy still standing in the street looking after the speeding radio car.

"They never used to gather like that," said Rantlee lighting a cigarette. "Three years ago when I first came on the job, I used to like working down here because Negroes understood our job almost as well as we did and crowds never used to gather like that. Not nowadays. They gather for any excuse. They're getting ready for something. I shouldn't let them bait me. I shouldn't argue at all. But the pressure is starting to get to me. Were you very scared?"

"Yeah," said Gus, wondering how obvious it was that he was paralyzed out there, like he had been on only a few other occasions in the past year. One of these days, he was going to have to take direct forceful action when he was paralyzed like that. Then he'd know about himself. So far, something always intervened. He had escaped his fate, but one of these days, he'd know.

"I wasn't a bit scared," said Rantlee.

"You weren't?"

"No, but somebody shit on my seat," he grinned, smoking the cigarette and they both laughed the hearty laugh of tension relieved.

"Crowd like that could do you in two minutes," said Rantlee, blowing a plume of smoke out the window, and Gus thought that he hadn't shown the slightest fear to the onlookers. Rantlee was only twenty-four years old and looked younger with his auburn hair and rosy complexion.

"Think we ought to cancel the assistance you called for?" asked Gus. "We don't need them now."

"Sure, go ahead," said Rantlee and eyed Gus curiously

as Gus said, "Three-A-Ninety-one, cancel the assistance
to Fifty-first and south Broadway, crowd has dispersed."
Gus received no reply and Rantlee grinned wider and Gus
for the first time noticed that the radio was dead. Then
he saw the mike cord dangling impotently and he realized that someone had jerked the wire out while they
had been surrounded.

"You were bluffing them when you told him help was
coming."

"Was I ever!" said Rantlee, and Gus was very glad
to be driving toward the radio shop and after that to the
Crenshaw area which was the "silk stocking" part of
University Division, where large numbers of whites still
resided. The Negroes there were "westside Negroes" and
the sixty-thousand-dollar homes in Baldwin Hills over-
looked the large department stores, where you would not
be surrounded by a hostile ring of black faces.

On the side of a stucco apartment building facing the
Harbor Freeway, Gus saw sprayed in letters four feet
high "Oncle Remus is an Oncle Tom," and then Rantlee
was on the freeway speeding north. In a few moments
the tall palms which line the freeway in south central
Los Angeles were replaced by the civic center buildings
and they were downtown driving leisurely toward the
police building radio shop to have the mike replaced.

Gus admired the beautiful women who always seemed
to be plentiful on the downtown streets and he felt a
faint rumble of heat and hoped Vickie would still be
awake tonight. Despite the precautions, Vickie was not
the same lover she had been, but he guessed it was only
natural. Then he felt the creeping guilt which he had
been experiencing periodically since Billy was born and
he knew it was ridiculous to blame himself, but yet any
intelligent man would have seen to it that a twenty-
three-year-old girl did not give birth to three children in
less than five years of marriage, especially when the girl
was not really mature, depending on her man for all but
the most basic decisions, when she believed her man was
a strong man, and oh, what a laugh that was.

Since he had admitted to himself that marriage had
been a mistake, it had somehow become easier. Once you
face something you can live with it, he thought. How
could he have known at age eighteen what things were
all about? He still didn't know but at least he now knew

life was more than a ceaseless yearning for sex and romantic love. Vickie had been a pretty girl with a fine
body and he had had to settle for plain girls all his life,
even in his senior year in high school when he could not
find a date for the Christmas formal, ending up with
Mildred Greer, his next door neighbor, who was only
sixteen and built like a shot-putter. She had embarrassed
him by wearing a pink chiffon that would have been old-
fashioned ten years before. So it was not his fault entirely that he had married Vickie when they were much
too young and knew nothing except each other's bodies.
What else mattered at age eighteen?

"You see that guy with the mop of blond hair?" asked
Rantlee.

"Which guy?"

"The one in the green T-shirt. You see him make us
and run through the parking lot?"

"No."

"Funny, how many people get black and white fever
and start moving fast in the opposite direction. You can't
go after them all. You think about them though. They
make you hinky. What's their secret? You always wonder."

"I know what you mean," said Gus and then wondered how a pretty girl like Vickie could be so dependent
and weak. He had always thought that attractive people
should naturally have a certain amount of confidence.
He always thought that if he had been a big man that
he would not have been so afraid of people, so unable
to converse freely with anyone but intimate friends. The
intimate friends were few in number, and at this moment
other than his boyhood friend, Bill Halleran, he could
think of no one he really wanted to be with. Except
Kilvinsky. But Kilvinsky was so much older and he had
no family now that his ex-wife was remarried. Every time
Kilvinsky came to his house for dinner he played with
Gus's children and then became morose, so that even
Vickie noticed it. As much as he liked Kilvinsky, whom
he felt was a teacher and more than a friend, he didn't
really see him much after Kilvinsky had decided to
transfer to Communications Division which he said was
out to pasture for old cops. Last month he had retired
suddenly and was gone to Oregon where Gus pictured
him in an extra-large khaki shirt and khaki trousers, his

silver hair matted down from the baseball cap he always wore when he fished.

The fishing trip to the Colorado River that he had taken with Kilvinsky and three other policemen had been a wonderful trip and now he could think of Kilvinsky like he had been at the river, chewing on the battered cigarette holder while he all but ignored the burning cigarette it held, casting and reeling in the line with ease, showing that the wide hard hands were nimble and quick, not merely strong. Once when Kilvinsky had been to their house for dinner, right after they bought the three-bedroom house and were still short on furniture, Kilvinsky had taken little John into the almost bare living room and tossed him in the air with his big sure hands until John and even Gus who watched were laughing so hard they could hardly breathe. And, inevitably, Kilvinsky became gloomy after the children went to bed. Once when Gus asked him about his family he said they were now living in New Jersey and Gus realized he must not question him further. All of the other policeman friends were "on duty" friends. Why couldn't he like anyone else the way he liked Kilvinsky, he wondered.

"I gotta transfer out of University," said Rantlee.

"Why?"

"Niggers are driving me crazy. Sometimes I think I'll kill one someday when he does what that bastard in the tow truck did. If someone would've made the first move those savages would've cut off our heads and shrunk them. Before I came on this job I wouldn't even use the word nigger. It embarrassed me. Now it's the most used word in my vocabulary. It says everything I feel. I've never used it in front of one yet but I probably will sooner or later and he'll beef me and I'll get suspended."

"Remember Kilvinsky?" asked Gus. "He always used to say that the black people were only the spearhead of a bigger attack on authority and law that was surely coming in the next ten years. He always said not to make the mistake of thinking your enemy was the Negro. It wasn't that simple, he said."

"It's strange as hell what happens to you," said Rantlee. "I'm finding myself agreeing with every right wing son of a bitch I ever read about. I wasn't brought up that way. My father's a flaming liberal and we're getting so we hate to see each other anymore because a big argument starts. I'm even getting to become sympathetic with some of these rabid anticommunist causes. Yet at the same time I admire the Reds for their efficiency. They can keep order, for chrissake. They know just how far you can let people go before you pull the chain. It's all mixed up, Plebesly. I haven't figured things out yet." Rantlee ran his hand through his wavy hair and tapped on the window ledge as he talked and then turned right on First Street. Gus thought he wouldn't mind working Central Division because downtown Los Angeles seemed exciting with the lights and the rush of people, but it was also sordid if you looked closely at the people who inhabit the downtown streets. At least most of them were white and you didn't have the feeling of being in an enemy camp.

"Maybe I'm wrong in blaming it all on the Negroes," said Rantlee. "Maybe it's a combination of causes, but by God the Negroes are a big part of it."

Gus hadn't yet finished his coffee when their radio was repaired and he hurried to the radio shop bathroom and on the way out noticed in the mirror that his always thin straw-colored hair was now falling out badly. He guessed he'd be bald at thirty, but what did it matter anyway he thought wryly. He noticed also that his uniform was becoming shiny which was the mark of a veteran but it was also fraying at the collar and the cuffs. He dreaded the thought of buying another because they were outrageously expensive. The uniform dealers kept the price up all over Los Angeles and you had to pay it.

Rantlee seemed in better spirits as they drove back down the Harbor Freeway to their beat.

"Hear about the shooting in Newton Street?"

"No," said Gus.

"They got a policeman on the fire for shooting a guy that works in a liquor store on Olympic. Officer rolls up to the store answering a silent alarm, and just as he's getting ready to peek in the window to see if it's for real or phony, the proprietor comes running out and starts screaming and pointing toward the alley across the street. One officer runs in the alley and the other circles the block and picks a spot where he thinks anybody back there would come out, and in a few minutes he hears running footsteps and hides behind the corner of an apartment house with his gun out and ready, and in a few seconds a guy comes busting around the corner with a Mauser in his hand and the officer yells freeze and the guy whirls around and the officer naturally lets go and puts five right in the ten ring." Rantlee placed his clenched fist against his chest to indicate the tight pattern of the bullets.

"So what's wrong with the shooting?" asked Gus.

"The guy was an employee in the store who was chasing the suspect with his boss's gun."

"The officer couldn't have known. I don't see any real problem. It's unfortunate, but . . ."

"The guy was black and some of the black newspapers are playing it up, you know, how innocent people are killed every day by the storm troops in occupied south central Los Angeles. And how the Jew proprietor in the ghetto sends his black lackeys to do the jobs he hasn't got the guts to do. Odd how the Jews can support the blacks who hate them so much."

"I guess they haven't forgotten how they suffered themselves," said Gus.

"That's a kind thought," said Rantlee. "But I think it's because they make so goddamn much money off these poor ignorant black people from their stores and rents. They sure as hell don't live among them. Jesus Christ, now I'm a Jew hater. I tell you, Plebesly, I'm transferring to the valley or West L.A. or somewhere. These niggers are driving me crazy."

They were barely back to their area when Gus logged the family dispute call on Main Street.

"Oh, no," Rantlee groaned. "Back on the goddamn east side." And Gus noticed that Rantlee, who was not a particularly slow driver, headed for the call at a snail's pace. In a few minutes they were parked in front of an ancient two-story house which was tall and narrow and gray. It seemed to be used by four families and they knew which door to knock on by the shouts which could be heard from the street. Rantlee kicked three times against the base of the door to be heard over the din of voices inside.

A sagging square-shouldered woman of about forty opened the door. She held a plump brown baby in one arm and in the other she held a bowl of gray baby food and a spoon. The baby food was all over the infant's face and his diaper was as gray as the siding of the house.

"Come in, Officers," she nodded. "I'm the one who called."

"Yeah, that's right, you punk ass bitch, call the law," said the watery-eyed man in a dirty undershirt. "But while they're here, tell them how you drinks away the welfare check and how I has to support these here kids and three of them ain't even mine. Tell them."

"Okay, okay," said Rantlee, holding up his hands for silence and Gus noticed that the four children sprawled on the sagging couch watched the TV set with little or no interest in the fight or the officers' arrival.

"You some husban'," she spat. "You know, when he drunk, Officer, he jist climbs on me and starts ruttin'. Don't make no diff'ence if the chirrun is here or not. That the kind of man he is."

"That is a gud-dam lie," said the man, and Gus saw they were both half drunk. The man must have been fifty but his shoulders were blocklike and his biceps heavily veined. "I'm goin' tell you like it is," he said to Rantlee. "You a man and I'm a man and I works ever' day."

Rantlee turned to Gus and winked and Gus wondered how many black men he had heard preface a remark to him with, "You a man and I'm a man," fearful that the white law did not truly believe it. They knew how policemen could be impressed by the fact that they worked and did not draw welfare. He wondered how many black men he had heard saying, "I works ever' day," to the white law, and well they might, Gus thought, because he had seen how it *did* work, how a policeman could be talked out of issuing a traffic ticket to a black man with a workman's helmet, or a lunch bucket, or a floor polisher, or some other proof of toil. Gus realized that policemen expected so little of Negroes that a job alone and clean children were unalterable proof that this was a decent man as opposed to the ones with dirty children, who were probably the enemy.

"We didn't come to referee a brawl," said Rantlee. "Why don't we quiet down and talk. You come in here, sir, and talk to me. You talk to my partner, ma'am," Rantlee walked the man into the kitchen to separate them which was of course what Gus knew he would do.

Gus listened to the woman, hardly hearing her, because he had heard similar stories so many times and after they had told the officers their problems, the problems would diminish. Then they could probably talk the man into taking a walk for a while and coming home when things had cooled off and that was the whole secret of handling disputes.

"That man is a righteous dog, Officer," said the woman, shoving a spoonful of food into the pink little mouth of the greedy baby who would only be silenced by the spoon. "That man is terrible jealous and he drink all the time and he don't really work. He live on my county check and he jist lay up here and don't never give nothin' to me 'cept chirrun. I jist wants you to take him out of here."

"You legally married?" asked Gus.

"No, we's common law."

"How long you been together?"

"Ten years and that is too long. Last week, when I cashed my check and bought some groc'ries and came home, why that man snatched the change right outten my hand and went out and laid up wif some woman fo' two days and come back here wif not a cent and I takes him back and then tonight that nigger hits me wif his fist 'cause I ain't got no mo' money fo' him to drink up. An' that's as true as this baby here."

"Well, we'll try to talk him into leaving for a while."

"I wants him outten this house fo' good!"

"We'll talk to him."

"I'm tryin' to raise my chirruns right 'cause I sees all these chirruns nowadays jist jumpin' rope and smokin' dope."

A loud burst of staccato raps startled Gus and the woman stepped to the door and opened it for a furious, very dark, middle-aged man in a tattered flannel bathrobe.

"H'lo Harvey," she said.

"I'm gittin gud-dam sick of the noise in this apartment," said the man.

"He hit me agin, Harvey."

"You goin' to have to git out if you can't git along. I got other tenants in this house."

"What do you want?" shouted the woman's husband who crossed the living room in three angry strides. "We got our rent paid up. You got no right in here."

"This is my house. I get all the right I need," said the man in the bathrobe.

"You git yo' raggedy ass outa my apartment before I throws you out," said the man in the undershirt and Gus saw that the landlord was not as fierce as he seemed and he took a step backward even though Rantlee stepped between them.

"That's enough," said Rantlee.

"Why don't you take him out, Officers," said the landlord, wilting before the glare of the smaller man in the undershirt.

"Yeah, so you kin come sniffin' roun' here after my woman. That would tickle you wouldn' it?"

"Why don't you go back to your apartment, sir," said Rantlee to the landlord, "until we get things settled."

"Don't worry, Officers," said the man in the undershirt, drilling the landlord with his watery black eyes, the blue black lips forming a deliberate sneer, "I wouldn't hurt that. That's pussy."

Nobody can manage an insult like them, Gus thought. And he looked with awe at the rough black face, and how the nostrils had flared, and the eyes and mouth and nostrils had joined to create the quintessence of contempt. "I wouldn' even touch that wif a angry hand. That ain't no man. That's jist pussy!"

They can teach me, thought Gus. There is no other people like them. There was fear, but he could learn things here. And where could he go where there would not be fear?

9. Spade Bit

It was Wednesday and Roy Fehler hurried to the station because he was sure he would be on the transfer list. Most of his academy classmates had their transfers by now and he had been requesting North Hollywood or Highland Park for five months. When he did not find his name on the transfer he was bitterly disappointed and now he knew he must intensify his efforts in college to complete his degree so he could quit this thankless job. And it was thankless, they all knew it. They all talked about it often enough. If you want gratitude for your work, be a fireman they always said.

He had done his best for the past year. He had brought compassion to all his dealings with the Negro. He had learned from them, and hoped he had taught them something. It was time to move on now. He had wanted to work on the other side of town. There was still so much to learn about people yet they left him here at Newton Street. They had forgotten him. He'd increase his unit load next semester, and to hell with concentrating his efforts on being a good police officer. What had it gotten him? He had earned only six units in the past two semesters and had gotten only C's because he read law and police science textbooks when he should have been working on course assignments. At this rate it would take years to finish his degree. Even Professor Raymond seldom wrote anymore. Everyone had forgotten him.

Roy examined his lean body in the full-length mirror and thought the uniform still fit as well as the day he left the academy. He hadn't been exercising but he watched what he ate and thought he still wore the blue suit well.

He was a few minutes late for roll call and muttered "Here" when Lieutenant Bilkins called his name, but he didn't hear Bilkins read the daily crimes and wanted suspects even though he mechanically wrote the information in his notebook just as all the others did. Sam Tucker came straggling in ten minutes after roll call, still adjusting his tie clip with his heavily veined blue-black hands as he sat down at the bench in front of the first row of tables.

"If we could get old Sam to quit counting his money, we could get him here on time," said Bilkins, glancing down at the grizzled Negro officer with his blank narrow eyes.

"Today's rent day, Lieutenant," said Tucker. "Got to stop by my tenants' and collect my share of their welfare checks before they blow it on booze."

"Just like you Jew landlords," sniffed Bilkins, "bleed the ghetto black man, keep him down in the east side."

"You don't think I'd let them live in West L.A. with me, do you?" said Tucker with a perfectly sober expression which brought a burst of laughter from the already sleepy morning watch officers.

"For you guys who don't know, Sam owns half of Newton Division," said Bilkins. "Police work is a hobby with him. That's why Sam's always late the first Wednesday of every month. If we could stop him from counting his money we could get him here on time. And if we could break all the mirrors in the joint, we could get Fehler here on time."

Roy cursed himself for flushing deeply as the roll call boomed with the chuckles of his fellow officers. That was unfair as hell, he thought. And it wasn't that funny. He knew he was a bit vain, but so was everyone.

"By the way, Fehler, you and Light keep an eyeball out for the hot prowl suspect in your district. The prick hit again last night and I think it's only a matter of time till he hurts somebody."

"Did he leave his calling card again?" asked Light, Roy's partner this month, a round-shouldered, two-year Negro policeman, slightly taller than Roy and a difficult man for Roy to understand. He couldn't seem to develop rapport with Light even though he went out of his way as he always did with Negroes.

"He dropped his calling card right on the fucking kitchen table this time," said Bilkins dryly, running a big hand over his bald head and puffing on a badly scarred pipe. "For you new guys that don't know what we're talking about, this cat burglar has hit about fifteen times in the past two months in Ninety-nine's district. He never woke nobody in any of his jobs except once when he woke a guy who had just got home and wasn't sleeping too sound yet. He slugged the guy in the chops with a metal ashtray and bailed out the window, glass and all. His calling card is a pile of shit, his shit, which he dumps in some conspicuous place."

"Why would he do that?" asked Blanden, a curly-haired young policeman with large round eyes, who was new and aggressive, too aggressive for a rookie, Roy thought. And then Roy thought the act of defecation was clearly what Konrad Lorenz called "a triumph reaction," the swelling and flapping of the geese. It was utterly explainable, thought Roy, simply a biological response. He could tell them about it.

"Who knows?" Bilkins shrugged. "Lots of burglars do it. It's a fairly common M.O. Probably to show their contempt for the squares and the law and everything, I guess. Anyway, he's a shitter and wouldn't it be nice if somebody would wake up some night and grab a shot-gun and catch the bastard squatting on their kitchen table just squeezing out a big one, and baloooey, he'd be shitting out a new hole."

"Is there any description on this guy yet?" asked Roy, still smarting from Bilkins' gratuitous remark about the mirror, but man enough he thought, to overlook immaturity in a superior.

"Nothing new. Male, Negro, thirty to thirty-five, me-dium-sized, processed hair, that's it."

"He sounds like a real sweetheart," said Tucker.

"His mother should've washed him out with a douche bag," said Bilkins. "Okay, I been inspecting you for the last three minutes and you all look good except Whitey Duncan who's got dried barbecue sauce all over his tie."

"Do I?" said Whitey, looking toward the tie which was ridiculously short hanging over a belly which Roy thought had swelled three inches in the past year. Thank heavens he didn't have to work with Whitey anymore.

"I saw Whitey this afternoon down at Sister Maybelle's Barbeque Junction on Central Avenue," said Sam Tucker, grinning at Whitey affectionately. "He comes to work two hours early on payday and runs down to Sister May-belle's for an early supper."

"Why the hell would Whitey need money to eat?" shouted a voice in the back of the room and the men chuckled.

"Who said that?" said Bilkins. "We don't accept gratuities or free meals. Who the hell said that?" Then to
Tucker, "What do you think Whitey's up to, Sam? Think
he's got the hots for Maybelle?"

"I think he's trying to pass, Lieutenant," Tucker answered. "He was sitting there amongst ten or fifteen
black faces and he had barbecue sauce from his eyebrows to his chin. Shit, you couldn't even see that pudgy
pink face. I think he's trying to pass. Everybody wants
to be black, nowadays."

Bilkins puffed and blew gray clouds and the fathomless
eyes roved the roll call room. He seemed satisfied that
they were all in good spirits and Roy knew he would
never send them out in the morning watch until they
were laughing or otherwise cheerful. He had overheard
Bilkins telling a young sergeant that no man who did
police work from midnight to 9:00 A.M. should be subject to any kind of GI discipline. Roy wondered if Bilkins wasn't too soft on the men because Bilkins' watch
was never the high producer in arrests or traffic citations or anything else, except perhaps in good cheer
which was a commodity of doubtful value in police work.
Police work is serious business, Roy thought. Clowns
should join a circus.

"Want to drive or keep score?" asked Light after roll
call and Roy realized Light must want to drive because
he had driven last night and knew it was Roy's turn to
drive tonight. He asked, therefore he must be hoping for
another night at the wheel. Roy knew that Light was
self-conscious because Roy was such an excellent report
writer and that when working with Roy, Light hated to
keep the log and make the reports as the passenger officer must do.

"I'll keep books if you want to drive," said Roy.

"Suit yourself," said Light, holding a cigarette between
his teeth and Roy often thought he was one of the
darkest Negroes he had ever seen. It was hard to see
where his hairline began, he was so dark.

"You want to drive, don't you?"

"Up to you."

"You want to or don't you?"

"Okay I'll drive," said Light and Roy was starting the
night out annoyed. If a man had a deficiency why in the
hell didn't he admit the deficiency instead of running

away from it? He hoped he had helped Light recognize some of his defense mechanisms with his blunt frankness. Light would be a much happier young man if he could come to know himself just a little better, thought Roy. He always thought of Light as his junior even though he was twenty-five, two years older than Roy. It was probably his college training, he thought, which brought him of age sooner than most.

As Roy was crossing the parking lot to the radio car, he saw a new Buick stop in the green parking zone in front of the station. A large-busted young woman jumped from the car and hurried into the station. Probably a policeman's girl friend he thought. She was not particularly attractive, but down here any white girl attracted attention, and several other policemen turned to watch. Roy felt a sudden longing for his freedom, for the carefree liberty of his early college days before he met Dorothy. How could he ever have thought they could be compatible? Dorothy, a receptionist in an insurance office, barely a high school graduate, having got her diploma only after a math class was waived by an understanding principal. He had known her too long. Childhood sweethearts are the stuff of movie mags. Romantic nonsense, he thought bitterly, and it had never been anything but bickering and misery since Dorothy became pregnant with Becky. But, God, how he loved Becky. She had flaxen hair and pale blue eyes like his side of the family, and she was incredibly intelligent. Even their pediatrician had admitted she was an extraordinary child. It was ironic, he thought, that her conception had shown him irrevocably the mistake he had made in marrying Dorothy, in marrying anyone so young, when he still had the promise of a splendid life to come. Yet, almost from the moment of birth Becky had shown him still another life, and he felt something utterly unique which he recognized as love. For the first time in his life he loved without question or reason, and when he held his daughter in his arms and saw himself in her violet irises, he wondered if he could ever leave Dorothy because he worshiped this soft creature. He was drawn to the tranquility she could produce in him instantly, at almost any moment, when he pressed the tiny white cheek to his own.

"Want some coffee?" asked Light as they cleared from

the station, but at that moment the Communications operator gave them a call to Seventh Street and Central. Roy heard the call and heard Light and wrote the address of the call as well as the time the call was received. He did all this mechanically now and never for a moment stopped thinking of Becky. It was becoming too easy, this job, he thought. He could make the necessary moves while only ten percent of his mind was functioning as a policeman.

"There he is," said Light as he made a U-turn in the intersection at Seventh Street. "Looks like a ragpicker."

"He is," said Roy in disgust as he shined his spotlight on the supine figure, sleeping on the sidewalk. The front of his trousers was soaked with urine and a sinuous trickle flowed down the sidewalk. Roy could smell the vomit and the excrement while still twenty feet away. The drunk had lost one torn and dismal shoe in his travels and a ragged felt hat, three sizes too big, lay crushed beneath his face. His hands clawed at the concrete and his bare foot dug in when Light struck him on the sole of the other foot with his baton, but then he became absolutely still as though he had grabbed for the softness and security of his bed, and having found it, relaxed and returned to the slumber of the consummate alcoholic.

"Goddamn Winos," said Light, striking the man more sharply on the sole of the shoe. "He's got piss, puke, and lord knows what, all over him. I ain't about to carry him."

"Neither am I," said Roy.

"Come on, wino. Goddamn," said Light, stooping down and placing the knuckles of his thick brown index fingers into the hollow behind the ears of the wino. Roy knew how strong Light was, and cringed when his partner applied the painful pressure to the mastoids. The wino screamed and grabbed Light's wrists and came up vertically from the ground clinging to the powerful forearms of the policeman. Roy was surprised to see the man was a light-skinned Negro. The race of the ragpicker was almost indistinguishable.

"Don't hurt me," said the wino. "Don't, don't, don't, don't."

"We don't want to hurt you, man," said Light, "but we ain't carrying your smelly ass. Let's walk." Light released the man who collapsed softly to the sidewalk and then tumbled back lightly on a fragile elbow and Roy thought when they're this far gone with malnutrition, when they bear the wounds of rats and even alley cats that have nibbled at the pungent flesh as they lay for hours in ghastly places, when they're like this, it's impossible to estimate how close to death they are.

"You got gloves on?" asked Light, bending down and touching the wino's hand. Roy shined the flashlight beam in the lap of the man and Light recoiled in horror.

"His hand. Damn, I touched it."

"What is it?"

"Look at that hand!"

Roy thought at first that the wino was wearing a glove which had been turned inside out and was hanging inside out by the fingertips. Then he saw it was the flesh of the right hand which was hanging from all five fingers. The pink muscle and tendon of the hand were exposed and Roy thought for a minute that some terrible accident had torn his flesh off, but he saw the other hand was beginning to shed the flesh so he concluded the man was deteriorating like a corpse. He was long dead and didn't know it. Roy walked to the radio car and opened the door.

"I hate like hell to go to all the trouble of absentee booking a drunk at the General Hospital prison ward," said Roy, "but I'm afraid this guy's about dead."

"No choice," Light shrugged. "I imagine the police been keeping him alive for twenty years now, though. Think we're doing him a favor each time? It would've been over long ago if some policeman would just've let him lay."

"Yeah, but we got a radio call," said Roy. "Somebody reported him lying here. We couldn't ride off and leave him."

"I know. We got to protect our own asses."

"You wouldn't leave him anyway, would you?"

"They'll dry him out and give him ninety days and he'll be right back here, come Thanksgiving. Eventually he'll die right here in the street. Does it matter when?"

"You wouldn't leave him," Roy smiled uneasily. "You're not that cold, Light. He's a human being. He's not a dog."

"That right?" said Light to the wino who stared

dumbly at Roy, his blue-lidded eyes crusty yellow at the corners.

"You really a man?" asked Light, tapping the wino gently on the sole of his shoe with the baton. "You sure you ain't a dog?"

"Yeah, I'm a dog," croaked the wino and the policemen looked at each other in amazement that he could speak. "I'm a dog. I'm a dog. Bow wow, you motherfuckers."

"I'll be damned," grinned Light, "maybe you're worth saving after all."

Roy found the absentee booking of a prisoner at General Hospital to be a complicated procedure which necessitated a stop at Central Receiving Hospital and then a trip to Lincoln Heights Jail with the prisoner's property which in this case was the handful of rags that would be burned, and the presentation of the jail clinic with the treatment slips and finally the completion of paper work at the prison ward of the General Hospital. He was exhausted at three-thirty when Light was driving back to their division and they stopped at the doughnut shop at Slauson and Broadway for some bad but very hot coffee and free doughnuts. The Communications operator gave them a family dispute call. Light cursed and threw his empty paper cup in the trash can at the rear of the doughnut shop.

"A family dispute at four in the morning. Son of a bitch."

"I felt like taking it easy for a while too," Roy nodded. "I'm getting hungry, and not for these goddamn doughnuts. I feel like some real food."

"We usually wait till seven o'clock," said Light, starting the car while Roy gulped down the last of his coffee.

"I know we do," said Roy. "That's the trouble with this goddamn morning watch. I eat breakfast at seven o'clock in the morning. Then I go home and go to bed and when I get up in the late afternoon, I can't stand anything heavy so I eat breakfast again, and then maybe around eleven just before I come to work I grab a couple eggs. Jesus, I'm eating breakfast three times a day!"

Light settled the family dispute the easiest way by taking the husband's identification and calling into R and I where he found there were two traffic warrants out for his arrest. As they were taking him out of the house, his wife, who had called them to complain of his beating her, begged them not to arrest her man. When they put him in the radio car she cursed the policemen and said, "I'll get bail money somehow. I'll get you out, baby."

It was almost five o'clock when they got their prisoner booked and drove back to their beat.

"Want some coffee?" asked Light.

"I've got indigestion."

"Me too. I get it every morning about this time. Too damned late to go to the hole."

Roy was glad. He hated "going to the hole" which meant hiding your car in some bleak alley or concealed parking lot, sleeping the fitful frantic half-awake sleep of the morning watch policeman, more nerve-racking than restful. He never objected when Light did it though. He just sat there awake, dozing, mostly awake, and thought about his future and his daughter Becky who was inextricably tied to any dream of the future.

It was 8:30 A.M. and Roy was sleepy. The morning sun was scorching his raw eyeballs when they got the silent robbery alarm call to the telephone company just as they were heading for the station to go home.

"Thirteen-A-Forty-one, roger," said Roy and rolled up his window so that the siren would not drown out the radio broadcasting, but they were close and Light did not turn on the siren.

"Think it's a false alarm?" asked Roy nervously as Light made a sweeping right turn through a narrow gap in the busy early morning commuter traffic. Suddenly Roy was wide awake.

"Probably is," Light muttered. "Some new cashier probably set off the silent alarm and didn't know she did it. But that place has been knocked over two or three times and it's usually early in the morning. Last time the bandit fired a shot at a clerk."

"Can't get too much money early in the morning," said Roy. "Not many people come in this early to pay bills."

"Hoods around here will burn you down for ten bucks," said Light, and he turned sharply toward the curb and Roy saw that they had arrived. Light parked fifty feet from the entrance to the building where the lobby was already filling with people paying their utility bills. All of the customers were Negro as were many of the employees.

Roy saw the two men at the cashier's counter turn and look toward him as he came through the front door. Light had gone to cover the side door and now Roy took a step toward the men. They turned before he got very far into the lobby and were almost to the door when he realized they were the only two in the place who could possibly be robbery suspects. The other customers were either women or couples, some with children.

He thought of the embarrassment it would cause them if it was a false alarm, how there was so much talk these days that black men could not proceed about their business in the ghetto without being molested by white policemen, and he had seen what he considered overly aggressive police tactics. Yet he knew he must challenge them and for his own protection should be ready because they had after all received a silent robbery alarm call. He decided to let them reach the sidewalk and then to talk to them. Nobody behind the cashier's windows had signaled him. It was undoubtedly a false alarm, but he must talk to them.

"Freeze!" said Light, who had approached from behind him noiselessly and was standing with his gun leveled at the middle of the back of the man in the black leather jacket and green stingy brim who was preparing to shove the swinging door. "Don't touch that door, brother," said Light.

"What is this?" said the man closest to Roy, who started to place his left hand in his trouser pocket.

"You freeze, man, or your ass is gone," Light whispered and the man raised the mobile hand sharply.

"What the fuck is this?" the man in the brown sweater said and Roy thought he was almost as dark as Light but not nearly as hard looking. At the present moment Light looked deadly.

Roy heard four car doors slam and three uniformed officers responding to the hot shot call came running toward the front door while another came in the side door Light had entered.

"Search them," said Light as the men were pushed outside, and Light walked across the floor to the cashier's cage with Roy.

"Who pushed the button?" Light called to the gathering circle of employees, most of whom were unaware that something unusual was happening until the policemen rushed through the door.

"I did," said a tiny blond woman who stood three windows away from where the two men had been doing business.

"Were they trying to rob the place or not?" asked Light impatiently.

"Well, no," said the woman. "But I recognized the one in the hat. He's the one who robbed us with a gun last June. He robbed my window. I'd know him anywhere. When I saw him this morning, I just pushed the button to get you here quick. Maybe I just should have phoned."

"No, I guess it's okay to use the silent button in cases like that," Light grinned. "Just don't push the button when you want us here to arrest a drunk out front."

"Oh no, Officer. I know that button is for emergencies."

"What were they doing?" asked Light to the pretty Mexican girl who worked the counter where the men were standing.

"Just paying a bill," said the girl. "Nothing else."

"You sure about that guy?" Light asked the timorous blond.

"I'm positive, sir," said the woman.

"Good work, then," said Light. "What's your name? The robbery detectives will probably be calling you in a little while."

"Phyllis Trent."

"Thanks, ma'am," said Light and he walked long-legged across the lobby while Roy followed.

"Want us to take them?" asked the day watch officer who had the two men handcuffed and standing next to his radio car.

"Damn right," said Light. "We're morning watch. Man, we want to go home. That guy have anything in that left front pocket? He sure wanted to get in there."

"Yeah, a couple joints, wrapped in a rubber band, and a little loose pot in his shirt pocket in a sandwich bag."

"Yeah? How about that. I thought it was a gun. If that asshole had decided to go for it quick, I'd have figured it was a gun for sure. He'd be crossing the river Jordan about now."

"The river Styx," smiled the day watch officer, opening the door for the man in the black leather jacket, handcuffed now.

As they were driving to the station, Roy thought several times he should let the whole incident pass, but he sensed Light was unhappy with the way he had handled the situation in the lobby. Finally Roy said, "How did you tumble to them being suspects, Light? Did one of the employees give you a sign?"

"No," said Light, chewing on the filter of a cigarette, as they sped north on Central Avenue. "They were the only likely-looking pair in the place, didn't you think?"

"Yes, but for all we knew it was a false alarm."

"Why didn't you stop them before I came up, Fehler? They were almost out the door. And why didn't you have your gun ready?"

"We didn't know for sure they were suspects," Roy repeated, feeling the anger well up.

"Fehler, they were, in fact, suspects, and if old stingy brim had brought his iron with him this trip, you'd be laying back there on that floor, you know that?"

"Goddamn it, I'm not a rookie, Light. I didn't think the situation warranted me drawing a gun, so I didn't."

"Let's clear the air, Fehler, we got a whole month to work together. Tell me something truthfully, if they'd been white would you've been quicker to take positive action?"

"What do you mean?"

"I mean that you're so goddamn careful not to offend black people in any way that I think you risk your goddamn life and *mine* so's not to look like a big blond storm trooper standing there frisking a black man in a public place in front of all those black people. What do you think of that?"

"You know what's wrong with you, Light? You're ashamed of your people," blurted Roy, and it was out before he could retract it.

"What the hell do you mean?" asked Light and Roy cursed himself but it was too late now and the words he was repressing had to be released.

"Alright Light, I know your problem and I'm going to tell you what it is. You're too damned tough on your people. You don't have to be cruel to them. Don't you see, Light? You feel guilty because you're trying so hard to pull yourself from that kind of degrading ghetto environment. You feel shame and guilt for them."

"I'll be damned," said Light, looking at Roy as if for the first time. "I always knew you were a little strange, Fehler, but I didn't know you were a social worker."

"I'm your friend, Light," said Roy. "That's why I'm telling you."

"Yeah, well listen, friend, I don't look at a lot of these people as black or white or even as people. They're assholes. And when some of these kids grow up they'll probably be assholes too, even though I feel sorry as hell for them right now."

"Yes, I understand," said Roy, nodding tolerantly, "there's a tendency of the oppressed to embrace the ideals of the oppressor. Don't you see that's what happened to you?"

"I'm not oppressed, Fehler. Why do white liberals have to look at every Negro as an oppressed black man?"

"I don't consider myself a liberal."

"People like you are worse than the Klan. Your paternalism makes you worse than the other kind. Quit looking at these people as Negroes or problems. I worked a silk stocking division out on the west side when I first came out of the academy and I never thought of a Caucasian asshole in terms of race. An asshole is an asshole, they're just a little darker here. But not to you. He's a Negro and needs a special kind of protective handling."

"Wait a minute," said Roy. "You don't understand."

"The hell I don't," snapped Light, who had now pulled to the curb at Washington and Central and turned in the seat to face Roy squarely. "You been here over a year now, haven't you? You know the amount of crime in the Negro divisions. Yet the D.A. won't hardly file a felony assault if it's a Negro victim and suspect involved. You know what the detectives say, 'Forty stitches or a gunshot is a felony. Anything less is a misdemeanor.' Negroes are expected to act that way. White liberals have said, 'That's alright, Mister Black man,' and they're always careful to say Mister. 'That's alright, you have been oppressed and therefore you are not entirely responsible for your actions. We guilty whites are responsible,' and what does the black man do then? Why, he takes full advantage of his tolerant white brother's misplaced kindness, just like the white would do if the positions were reversed because people in general are just plain assholes unless they got a spade bit in their mouths. Remember, Fehler, people need spades, not spurs."

Roy felt the blood rush to his face and he cursed his stammer as he struggled to master the situation. Light's outburst had been so unwarranted, so sudden . . . "Light, don't get excited, we're not communicating. We're not . . ."

"I'm not excited," said Light, deliberately now. "It's just that sometimes I've been close to busting since I started working with you. Remember the kid at Jefferson High School last week? The robbery report, remember?"

"Yes, what about it?"

"I wanted to tell you this then. I was choking on my frustration the way you patronized that little bastard. I went to high school right here in southeast L.A. I saw that same kind of shakedown every day. The blacks were the majority and the white kids were terrorized. 'Gimme a dime, motherfucker. Gimme a dime or I'll cut yo' ass.' Then we gave whitey a punch in the mouth whether or not we got the dime. And these were *poor* white kids. Poor as us, sometimes from mixed marriages and shack jobs. You didn't want to book that kid. You wanted to apply your double standard because he was a downtrodden black boy and the victim was white."

"You don't understand," said Roy bleakly. "Negroes hate the whites because they know they're faceless non-human creatures in the eyes of the whites."

"Yeah, yeah, I know that's what intellectuals say. You know, Fehler, you're not the only cop that's read a book or two."

"I never said I was, goddamn it," said Roy.

"I tell you Fehler, those white boys in my school were without faces to *us*. What do you think of that? And we terrorized those poor bastards. The few I ever got to know didn't hate us, they were afraid of us, because of our numerical superiority. Get off your knees when you're talking to Negroes, Fehler. We're just like whites. Assholes, most of us. Just like whites. Make the Negro answer to the law for his crimes just like a white man.

Don't take away his manhood by coddling him. Don't make him a domestic animal. All men are the same. Just keep him on a mean spade bit with a long shank. When he gets too spirited, jerk those reins, man!"

AUGUST 1962

10. The Lotus Eaters

Serge listened to the dreary monotone of Sergeant Burke who was conducting roll call training. He looked around the roll call room at Milton and Gonsalvez and the new faces, all of whom he knew by now since his return to Hollenbeck. He remembered how Burke's roll call training used to bore him and still did. But he was no longer annoyed by it.

The five months from January to June which he had spent in Hollywood Division was by now a grotesque candy-striped memory which seemed to have never happened. Though he had to admit it had been educational. Everyone in Hollywood is a phony, a fruit, or a flim-flam man, a partner had warned him. At first the glamour and hilarity fascinated him and he slept with some of the most beautiful girls he would ever see, satin blondes, silky redheads, dark ones he avoided, for those were all he had in Hollenbeck Division. They were not all aspiring actresses, these lovely girls who are drawn to Hollywood from everywhere, but they all yearned for something. He never bothered to find out what. As long as they yearned for him for a few hours, or pretended to, that was all he asked of them.

And then it all began to depress him, especially the intense look of the revelers when he got to know them. He shared an apartment with two other policemen and he could never go to bed before three o'clock because the blue light would be burning, indicating that one of them had been lucky and please give them some more time. They were very lucky, his roommates, who were equally handsome, wholesome-looking, and accomplished handlers of women. He had learned from them, and by being a roommate had been satisfied with the chaff when the chaff was a pale trembling creature who was all lips and breasts and eyes. It didn't even matter if she ate bennies frantically and babbled of the prospective modeling job which would thrust her into the centerfold of *Playboy*. And there was another who, in the middle of the heated preliminaries of lovemaking said, "Serge, baby, I realize you're a cop and all, but I know you're no square and you wouldn't mind if I smoked a little pot first, would you? It makes it all so much better. You should try it. We'll be so much better lovers." He thought about letting her do it, but the bennies were only a misdemeanor and marijuana was a felony, and he was afraid to be here while she did it, and besides, she had annihilated his ego and desire with her need for euphoria. When she disappeared into the bedroom for the marijuana, he put on his shoes and coat and crept out the door, an ache in his loins.

There were lots of other girls, waitresses and office girls, some of whom were ordinary, but then there was Esther, who was the most beautiful girl he had ever met. Esther who had called the police to complain about the peepers who were a constant annoyance to her, but her apartment was on the ground floor and she dressed with her drapes open because she "just loved the cooling breezes." She seemed genuinely surprised when Serge suggested she draw her drapes at night or move to an upstairs apartment. It had started out passionately between them but she was totally unique, with her moist lips and face and hands. Her eyes too were moist as was most of her torso, particularly the ample breasts. A fine layer of not unpleasant perspiration covered her during the lovemaking so that sleeping with Esther was like a steam and rub, except it was not as therapeutic—because even though a night-long bout with Esther left him exhausted, he did not feel cleansed from the inside out as he did when he left the steam room at the police academy. Perhaps Esther could not open his pores. Her heat was not purgative.

Her style of love had begun strangely enough, but then a few of her more bizarre improvisations began to repel him slightly. One bawdy Saturday, he had become drunk in her apartment, and she had become drunk too except she drank only a fourth as much as he. She made frequent trips to the bedroom which he did not question. Then that evening when he was preparing to take her and she was more than ready, they had tumbled and clawed their way to the bed and suddenly the things she was whispering through the drunken mist became coherent. It wasn't her usual string of obscenities and he listened stunned to what she suggested. Then it was not passion but frenzy he saw in the moist eyes and she stepped half naked to the closet and dragged out various accouterments, some of which he understood and others he did not. She told him that the young couple next door, Phil and Nora, whom he had decided were a pleasant pair, were ready for a "fabulously exciting evening." If he would only say the word they would be there in a minute and it could begin.

When he left Esther's apartment a moment later she was uttering a stream of grotesque curses that made him shiver with nausea.

A few nights later Serge was asked by his partner, Harry Edmonds, why he was so quiet and although he answered that there was nothing wrong, he was deeply aware that he was unhappy in Hollywood where life was ethereal and complicated. The most routine call became impossible in this place. Burglary reports would often turn into therapy sessions with unhappy neurotics who had to be subjected to a crude psychoanalysis to determine the true deflated value of a wristwatch or fur coat stolen by a Hollywood burglar who often as not turned out to be as neurotic as his victim.

At ten minutes past nine, that night, Serge and Edmonds received a call to an apartment on Wilcox not far from Hollywood station.

"This is a pretty swinging apartment house," said Edmonds, a young policeman with sideburns a bit too long and a moustache that Serge thought ridiculous on him.

"You got calls here before?" asked Serge.

"Yeah, the manager's a woman. A dyke, I think. She only rents to broads far as I can see. There's always some beef here. Usually between the manager and some boyfriend of one of the female tenants. If the girls want to have girl parties, she never bitches."

Serge carried his eight by eleven notebook under his arm and tapped on the manager's door with his flashlight.

"You call?" he asked the lean, sweater-clad woman who held a bloody towel in one hand and a cigarette in the other.

"Come in," she said. "The girl you want to talk to is in here."

Serge and Edmonds followed the woman through a

colorful green-gold and blue living room into the kitchen. Serge thought the black sweater and close-fitting pants very becoming. Although her hair was short it was silver-tipped and styled attractively. He guessed her age at thirty-five and wondered if Edmonds was right that she was a lesbian. Nothing in Hollywood could surprise him anymore, he thought.

The quivering brunette was seated at the kitchen table holding a second towel, ice-filled, to the left side of her face. Her right eye was swollen shut and her lower lip was turning blue but was not badly cut. Serge guessed the blood must have been from her nose which was not bleeding now and didn't look broken. It wasn't a particularly good-looking nose at best, he thought, and he looked at her crossed legs which were nicely shaped, but both knees were scraped. The torn hose hung from her left leg and had fallen down around the shoe, but she seemed too miserable to care.

"Her boyfriend did it," said the manager, who waved them to the wrought iron leather-padded chairs which surrounded the oval table.

Serge opened his notebook, leafing past the burglary and robbery reports and removed a miscellaneous crime report.

"Lover's quarrel?" he asked.

The brunette swallowed and the tear-filled eyes overflowed into the blood-stained towel.

Serge lit a cigarette, leaned back and waited for her to stop, realizing vaguely that this might not be *complete* melodrama since the injuries were real and probably quite painful.

"What's your name?" he asked, finally, as he realized it was ten o'clock and their favorite restaurant preferred that they eat before ten-thirty when the paying customers needed most of the counter space.

"Lola St. John," she sobbed.

"This is the second time that bastard beat you, isn't it, honey?" asked the manager. "Give the officers the same name you were using when you made the last report."

"Rachel Sebastian," she said, dabbing at the tender lip and examining the towel.

Serge erased the Lola St. John and wrote the other name across the top.

"You prosecute him last time he beat you?" Serge asked. "Or did you drop the charges?"

"I had him arrested."

"Then you dropped the charges and refused to prosecute?"

"I love him," she muttered, touching the lip with a pink tongue tip. An exquisite jewel formed at the corner of each eye, gumming with mascara.

"Before we go to a lot of trouble, are you going to go through with the prosecution this time?"

"This time I had it. I will. I swear by all that's holy."

Serge glanced at Edmonds and began filling in the boxes on the crime report. "How old are you?"

"Twenty-eight."

That was the third lie. Or was it the fourth? Sometime he meant to count the lies at the completion of a report.

"Occupation?"

"Actress."

"What else you do? When you're between acting jobs, I mean."

"I'm sometimes night manager and hostess at Frederick's Restaurant in Culver City."

Serge knew the place. He wrote "carhop" in the space for victim's occupation.

The manager uncoiled and crossed the kitchen to the refrigerator. She refilled a clean towel with ice cubes and returned to the battered woman.

"That son of a bitch is no good. I won't have him back here, honey. I want you for a tenant and all, but that man cannot come in this building."

"Don't worry, Terry, he won't," she said, accepting the towel, which was pressed to her jaw.

"Has he beat you on only one prior occasion?" asked Serge, beginning the narrative of the report, wishing he had sharpened the pencil at the station.

"Well, actually, I had him arrested another time," she said. "I'm just a sucker for a big good-looking guy, I guess." She smiled and fluttered the unclosed eye at Serge and he guessed she was signaling that he was big enough to suit her.

"What name were you using that time?" asked Serge, thinking she was probably blousy at best, but the legs were good and the stomach was still pretty flat.

"That time I was using Constance Deville, I believe. I was under contract to Universal under that name. Wait a minute, that was in sixty-one. I don't think . . . Christ, it's hard to think. That man of mine knocked something loose. Let's see."

"Were you drinking tonight?" asked Edmonds.

"It started in a bar," she nodded. "I think I was using my real name, then," she added thoughtfully.

"What's your real name?" asked Serge.

"God my head hurts," she moaned. "Felicia Randall."

"You want to see your own doctor?" asked Serge, not mentioning that free emergency care was available to crime victims because he did not want to take this woman to the hospital and bring her back.

"I don't think I need a doct . . . Wait a minute, did I say Felicia Randall? Christ almighty! That's not my *real* name. I was born and raised Dolores Miller. Until I was sixteen, I was Dolores Miller. Christ almighty! I almost forgot my real name! I almost forgot who I was," she said, looking at each of them in wonder.

Later that month, while patrolling Hollywood Boulevard at about 3:00 A.M. with a sleepy-eyed partner named Reeves, Serge had taken a good look at the people who walk the streets of the glamour capital at this hour. Mostly homosexuals of course, and he was getting to recognize some of them after seeing them night after night as they preyed on the servicemen. There were lots of other hustlers who in turn preyed on the homosexuals, not for lust but for money which they got one way or the other. This accounted for a good number of beatings, robberies and killings and until the hour of sunrise when his watch ended, Serge was forced to arbitrate the affairs of these wretched men and he was still revolted with all of it a week later when he returned to Alhambra and rented his old apartment. He talked with Captain Sanders of Hollenbeck Division who agreed to arrange a transfer back to Hollenbeck because he said he remembered Serge as an excellent young officer.

Burke was winding up the roll call training which nobody ever listened to and Serge did not at this moment even know the subject of the lesson. He decided he would drive tonight. He didn't feel like making reports so he'd do the driving. Milton always let him do exactly as he wished. He liked working with Milton and he even liked Burke's slow deliberate ways. There were worse supervisors. It was good to be back in the old station.

Serge was even beginning to lose his dislike for the area. It was not Hollywood, rather it was the opposite of glamorous. It was dull and old and poor with tall narrow houses like gravestones and the smell of the Vernon slaughterhouses remained. It was the place where the immigrants came upon their arrival from Mexico. It was the place where the second and third generation remained, who could not afford to improve their lot. He knew now of the many Russian Molokan families, the men with beards and tunics and the women with covered heads, who lived between Lorena and Indiana Streets after Russian flats had been changed to a low-priced housing project. There was a sizable number of Chinese here in Boyle Heights and Chinese restaurants had Spanish menus. There were many Japanese, and the older women still carried sun parasols. There were the old Jews of course, few now, and sometimes nine old Jews had to scour Brooklyn Avenue and finally hire a drunken Mexican for a minyan of ten to start prayers in temple. These old ones would soon all be dead, the synagogues closed, and Boyle Heights would be changed without them. There were Arab street hawkers selling clothing and rugs. There were even gypsies who lived near North Broadway where many Italians still lived, and there was the Indian church on Hancock Street, the congregation being mostly Pima and Navajo. There were many Negroes in the housing projects of Ramona Gardens and Aliso Village whom the Mexicans only tolerated, and there were the Mexican Americans themselves who made up eighty percent of the population of Hollenbeck Division. There were few white Anglo-Protestant families here unless they were very poor.

There were few phonies in the Hollenbeck area, Serge thought as he slowed on Brooklyn Avenue to park in front of Milton's favorite restaurant. Almost everyone is exactly as he seems. It was very comforting to work in a place where almost everyone is exactly as he seems.

11. The Veteran

"Two years ago tonight I came to University," said Gus. "Fresh out of the academy. It doesn't seem possible. Time has passed."

"You're about due for a transfer, aren't you?" asked Craig.

"Overdue. I'm expecting to be on the next transfer."

"Where you want to go?"

"I don't care."

"Another black division?"

"No, I'd like a change. Little further north, maybe."

"I'm glad I came here. I can learn fast down here," said Craig.

"Be careful you don't learn too fast," said Gus and dropped the Plymouth into low as he slowed for the red light because he was getting tired driving. It had been a very quiet evening and policemen toyed with the cars out of boredom after several hours of slow monotonous patrol. It was only nine-thirty. They shouldn't have eaten so early, Gus thought. The rest of the night would drag.

"Have you ever been in a shooting?" asked Craig.

"No."

"How about a real knockdown fight?"

"I haven't," said Gus. "Not a real fight. A few belligerent bastards, but not a real fight."

"You've been lucky."

"I have," said Gus, and for a second it started coming over him again, but he had learned how to subdue it. He was seldom afraid for no reason anymore. The times when he was afraid he had good reason to be. He had worked with an old-time policeman one night who had told him that in twenty-three years he had never had a real fight or fired his gun in the line of duty, or even been close to death except in a few traffic chases and he didn't think a policeman had to become involved in such things unless he went out of his way to become involved. The thought was comforting except that this policeman had spent his career in West Valley and Van Nuys Division which was the next thing to being retired, and he had only been in University for a few months, a disciplinary transfer. Still, Gus thought, after two years he had escaped the confrontation he feared. But did he really fear so much now, he wondered? The blue suit and badge, and the endless decisions and arbitration of other people's problems (when he didn't really know the answers but on the street at midnight there was no one else to find an answer except him and therefore he had made the choices for others and on a few occasions lives had depended on his decisions), yes, these decisions, and the blue suit and the badge had given him confidence he never dreamed he might possess. Though there were still agonizing self-doubts, his life had been deeply touched by this and he was as happy as he ever expected to be.

If he could transfer to a quiet white division, he would probably be happier if he were not troubled by guilt at being there. But if he could be satisfied that he had the necessary courage and had nothing further to prove to himself, why then he could transfer to Highland Park, and be closer to home and finally content. But that of course was bullshit because if police work had taught him anything it had taught him that happiness is for fools and children to dream of. Reasonable contentment was a more likely goal.

He began thinking of Vickie's widening hips and how twenty pounds even on a pretty girl like Vickie could make such a difference so that sometimes he was unsure whether their infrequent lovemaking was because she was so terribly frightened of another pregnancy, for which he couldn't blame her, or was it because she was growing less and less attractive. It wasn't just the bulkiness which had transformed a sleek body that was made for a bed, it wasn't just that, it was the breakdown of personality which he could only blame on a youthful hasty marriage and three children which were too much for a weak-willed girl of less than average intelligence who had always depended upon others, who now leaned so heavily on him.

He guessed he would be up all night with the baby if her cold weren't any better, and he felt a tiny surge of purgative anger but he knew he had no right to be angry with Vickie who was the prettiest girl who had ever shown an interest in him. After all, he was certainly not a trophy to cherish. He glanced in the rearview mirror and saw that his sandy hair was very thin now and he had been forced to reassess his guess; he knew he would be bald long before he was thirty and he already had tiny wrinkles at the corners of his eyes. He laughed at himself for his disappointment in Vickie for getting fat. But that wasn't it, he thought. That wasn't it at all. It was her.

"Gus, do you think policemen are in a better position to understand criminality than, say, penologists or parole officers or other behavioral scientists?"

"My God," Gus laughed. "What kind of question is that? Is that a test question?"

"As a matter of fact it is," said Craig. "I'm taking psych at Long Beach State and my professor has quite a background in criminology. He thinks policemen are arrogant and clannish and distrust other experts, and believe they're the only ones who really understand crime."

"That's a fair assessment," said Gus. He reminded himself that this would be the last semester he could afford to rest because he would get out of the habit of going to school. If he ever wanted the degree he would have to get back in classes next semester without fail.

"Do you agree with that?" asked Craig.

"I think so."

"Well I've only been out of the academy a few months but I don't think policemen are clannish. I've still got all my old friends."

"I still have mine," said Gus. "But you'll see after a year or so that you feel a little different about them. They don't know, you see. And criminologists don't know. Police see a hundred percent of criminality. We see noncriminals and real criminals who're involved in crime. We see witnesses to crimes and victims of crimes and we see them during and immediately after crimes occur. We see the perpetrators during and right after and we see victims sometimes before the crimes occur and we know they're going to be victims, and we see perpetrators before and we know they're going to be perpetrators. We can't do a damned thing about it even though we know through our experience. We *know*. Tell that to your professor and he'll think *you* need a psychologist. Your professor sees them in a test tube and in an institution and he thinks these are criminals, these unfortunate unloved losers he's studying, but what he doesn't realize is that so many thousands of the winners out here are involved in crime just as deeply as his unloved losers. If he really knew how much crime occurs he wouldn't be so damned smug. Policemen are snobs, but we're not smug because this kind of knowledge doesn't make you self-satisfied, it just scares you."

"I never heard you talk so much, Gus," said Craig, looking at Gus with new interest, and Gus felt an urge to talk about these things because he never talked about them very much except to Kilvinsky when he was here. He had learned all these things from Kilvinsky anyway, and then his experience had shown Kilvinsky was right.

"You can't exaggerate the closeness of our dealings with people," said Gus. "We see them when nobody else sees them, when they're being born and dying and fornicating and drunk." Now Gus knew it was Kilvinsky talking and he was using Kilvinsky's very words; it made him feel a little like Kilvinsky was still here when he used the big man's words and that was a good feeling. "We see people when they're taking anything of value from other people and when they're without shame or very much ashamed and we learn secrets that their husbands and wives don't even know, secrets that they even try to keep from themselves, and what the hell, when you learn these things about people who aren't institutionalized, people who're out here where you can see them function every day, well then, you really *know*. Of course you get clannish and associate with others who know. It's only natural."

"I like to hear you talk, Gus," said Craig. "You're usually so quiet I thought maybe you didn't like me. You know, us rookies worry about everything."

"I know," said Gus, moved by Craig's frank boyishness.

"It's valuable to hear an experienced officer talk about things," said Craig, and it was very hard for Gus to control a smile when he thought of Craig thinking of him as a veteran.

"While I'm philosophizing, you want a definition of police brutality?" asked Gus.

"Okay."

"Police brutality means to act as an ordinary prudent person, without a policeman's self-discipline, would surely act under the stresses of police work."

"Is that one of the Chief's quotes?"

"No, Kilvinsky said that."

"Is he the guy who wrote the book on police supervision?"

"No, Kilvinsky was a great philosopher."

"Never heard of him."

"On punishment Kilvinsky said, 'We don't want to punish offenders by putting them in institutions, we only want to separate ourselves from them when their pattern of deviation becomes immutably written in pain and blood.' Kilvinsky was drinking a little when he said that. He was usually much more earthy."

"You knew him?"

"I studied under him. He also said, 'I don't care if you supply the asshole with dames and dope for the rest of his life as long as we keep him in the joint.' In fact, Kilvinsky would have out-liberaled the most ardent liberal when it came to prison reforms. He thought they should be very agreeable places. He thought it was stupid and useless and cruel to try to punish *or* to try to rehabilitate most people with 'the pattern' as he called it. He had it pretty well doped out to where his penal institutions would save society untold money and grief."

"Three-A-Thirteen, Three-A-Thirteen," said the operator. "See the man, family dispute, twenty-six, thirty-five south Hobart."

"Well, it's fun to talk on a quiet night," said Gus, "but duty calls."

Craig rogered the call as Gus turned the car north and then east toward Hobart.

"I wish I had had this Kilvinsky for a professor," said Craig. "I think I'd have liked him."

"You'd have loved him," said Gus.

When Gus stepped out of the radio car he realized how unusually quiet a night it had been for a Thursday. He listened for a moment but the street lined on both sides with one-story private residences was absolutely still. Thursday, in preparation for weekend activity, was usually a fairly busy night and then he realized that welfare checks would arrive in the next few days. With no money the people were quiet this Thursday.

"I think it's the house in the rear," said Craig, shining his flashlight to the right of the darkened pink stucco front house. Gus saw the lighted porch and followed Craig down the walk to the rear house where a shirtless Negro stepped out of the shadows with a baseball bat in his hand and Gus had his revolver unsnapped, in his hand, crouching instinctively before he realized why. The man threw the ball bat to the ground.

"Don't shoot. I called you. I'm the one that called. Don't shoot."

"Jesus Christ," said Gus, seeing the Negro lurch drunkenly to his left, waving his big hands to the officers as he held them high overhead.

"You could get killed like that, jumping out with a club," said Craig, snapping his holster.

Gus could not find the pocket in the holster and had to use both shaking hands to put the gun away, and could not speak, did not dare to speak because Craig would see, anyone would see how unreasonably frightened he had been. He was humiliated to see that Craig was merely startled and was already asking questions of the drunken Negro while his own heart was hammering blood into his ears so that he couldn't make out the conversation until the Negro said, "I hit the motherfucker with the bat. He layin' back there. I think I done killed him and I wants to pay the price."

"Show us," Craig commanded, and Gus followed the two of them to the rear of the cottage which was pink like the front house, but a frame building not stucco, and Gus sucked deeply at the air to still his beating heart. In the rear yard they found the lanky Negro with a head like a bloody bullet lying on his face and beating the ground with a bony fist as he moaned softly.

"Guess I didn' kill him," said the drunken Negro. "Sho' thought he was dead."

"Can you get up?" asked Craig, already obviously accustomed to bloody scenes, knowing that most people can shed a great deal of blood and unless wounds are of certain types, people can usually function quite well with them.

"Hurts," said the man on the ground and rolled over on one elbow. Gus saw that he too was drunk and he grinned foolishly at the officers and said, "Take me to the hospital and git me sewed up will you, Officer?"

"Shall I call an ambulance?" asked Craig.

"Doesn't really need one," said Gus, his voice steady now, "but you may as well. He'd get blood all over the radio car."

"Don't want to press no cha'ges Officer," said the bloody man. "Jist want sewed up."

What if I'd shot him, thought Gus while Craig's voice echoed through the narrow walkway and was followed by a static explosion. A female voice blared out and Craig adjusted the volume and repeated his request for an ambulance. Someday I'll become scared like that and I *will* kill someone and I'll cover it up neatly just as I could have covered up this one because a man leaped out of the darkness with an upraised club. But Craig was only startled; he didn't even clear the holster and there I was crouched with three pounds of pressure on the trigger and thank God, I didn't cock the gun unconsciously or I'd have killed him sure. As it was, the hammer was moving back double action, moving, and God, what if Craig hadn't been in front of me, I know I'd have killed him. His body had reacted independent of his mind. He'd have to think about that later. This could be the thing that might save him if *real* danger came. If it ever comes I hope it comes suddenly, he thought, without warning like a man leaping out of darkness. Then my body might save me, he thought.

As his heart pounded more slowly, Gus remembered that he had put off his running program for a week and he must not do that, because if you lose momentum you'll stop. He decided to go to the academy and run tonight after he got off duty. It would be a beautiful night and of course there would be no one else on the track except possibly Seymour, the leathery old motor officer who was a hulking man with a huge stomach, wide hips, and a face like eroded clay from riding the motorcycle more than twenty years. Sometimes Gus would find Seymour out there lumbering around the police academy track at 3:00 A.M. blowing and steaming. After his shower, when he was dressed in the blue uniform, riding breeches, black boots and white helmet, why then Seymour looked formidable again and not nearly as fat. He rode the motor lightly and could do wonders with the heavy machine. He had been a friend of Kilvinsky and how Gus had enjoyed the nocturnal runs when Kilvinsky was with him, and how they would rest on the turf. He had loved listening to Kilvinsky and Seymour discussing the old times on the police department when things were simple, when good and evil were definitive. He remembered how he would pretend to be as tired as Kilvinsky when they had covered their fifteen laps, gone to the steam room and then the showers, but actually he could have run fifteen more without exhausting himself. It was a beautiful night tonight. It would be good to get on the cool grass and run and run. He would try to run five miles tonight, five hard fast miles, and then he would not need a steam bath. He would shower, go home, and sleep into the afternoon tomorrow if it were not too hot to sleep, if the children would let him sleep, and if Vickie would not need him to help her replace a light bulb that was simply too high to reach after she became dizzy standing on a chair. Or to help her shop because it was impossible to shop nowadays alone even if you could leave the children with your neighbor because the markets were horribly confusing and you couldn't find anything, and sometimes you just wanted to scream, especially when you thought of returning to a house with three children and oh, God, Gus, what if I'm pregnant again? I'm five days overdue. Yes I'm sure, I'm sure.

"Ambulance on the way," said Craig, clicking back down the walkway and Gus made a mental note to suggest to Craig that he get rubber-soled shoes or at least to remove the cleat from his heels because even working uniformed patrol, it paid to walk quietly a good part of the time. It was hard enough to do with a jingling key ring and creaking Sam Browne and jostling baton.

"Why did you hit him?" asked Craig, and by now the bloody man was sitting up and wailing as the pain was apparently penetrating the drunken euphoria.

"Ah tol' him I was goin' to do it nex' time he messed wif Tillie. Las' time I came home early I catched them in bed sleepin' an' drunk on mah whiskey an' there they was comf'table wif Tillie's bare ass right up there nex' to him and that thing still there inside her an' I reached ovah an' pulled it out and I woke him up an' tol' him if he evah did that again why I would whop him up side the head and I came home early tonight and I catched them agin an' I did it."

"I had it comin', Charlie," said the bloody man. "You right. You right."

Gus heard the wail of the ambulance siren in the distance and looked at his watch. By the time they finished the arrest report it would be end-of-watch and he could go to the academy and run and run.

"Don' you worry, Charlie, I won't have you arrested," said the bloody man. "You the bes' friend I evah had."

"I'm afraid Charlie has to go to jail, friend," said Craig, helping the bloody man to his feet.

"I won' sign no complaint," warned the bloody man and then winced as he stood erect and touched his head tenderly.

"Doesn't matter if you do or not," said Gus. "This is a felony and we're going to put him in jail just in case you up and die on us in the next few days."

"Don' you worry, Charlie," said the bloody man. "I ain't goin' to die on you."

"You can talk to the detectives tomorrow about refusing to prosecute," said Gus as they all walked to the front. "But tonight, your friend is going to jail."

The winking piercing red siren light announced the arrival of the ambulance even though the driver had killed the siren. Gus flashed his light to show the driver the house and the ambulance slid in at the curb and the attendant jumped out. He took the arm of the bloody man as the driver opened the door.

"Don' you worry now, Charlie, I won' persecute you," said the bloody man. "An' Ah'll take good care of Tillie too while you in jail. Don' you worry none 'bout her neither. Hear?"

12. Enema

Roy's heart thumped as the telephone rang in the receiver which he held pressed to his ear. The door to the vice squad office was locked and he knew the rest of the night watch teams would not be straggling into the office for at least a half hour. He decided to call Dorothy from a police department phone to save the long distance charge. It was hard enough trying to make rent payments in two places and support himself after he sent his monthly payment to Dorothy. Then there was his car payment and it was becoming apparent he would soon have to sell the Thunderbird and settle for a lower priced car when this was one of the few luxuries he had left.

He was almost glad she wasn't home and was about to hang up when he heard the unmistakable pitch of Dorothy's unmistakable voice which so often made a simple greeting sound like a question.

"Hello?"

"Hello, Dorothy, hope I didn't disturb you."

"Roy? I was in the shower."

"Oh, I'm sorry, I'll call back."

"No, it's alright. I'm in my bathrobe. What is it?"

"Is it the gold robe I got you for your last birthday?"

"We were already separated on my last birthday, Roy. It was the year before you got me a gold robe and this isn't it."

"Oh. How's Becky?"

"You just saw her last week, Roy. She's still the same."

"Goddamnit, Dorothy, can't you even spare me an occasional kind word."

"Yes, Roy, but please don't let's get started again on the same old thing. The divorce will be final in just eighty-nine days and that's it. We're not coming back to you."

Roy swallowed hard and the tears rushed to his eyes.

He didn't speak for several seconds until he was sure he had control.

"Roy?"

"Yes, Dorothy."

"Roy, this is useless."

"God, I'll do anything you say, Dorothy. Please come home. Don't go through with it."

"We've been over this again and again."

"I'm terribly lonely."

"A handsome man like you? A golden-haired, blue-eyed Apollo like Roy Fehler? You didn't have any trouble finding companionship while we were together."

"Christ, Dorothy, it only happened once or twice. I've told you all about it."

"I know, Roy. It wasn't that. You weren't particularly unfaithful as far as men go. But I just stopped caring. I just don't care for you anymore, can't you understand that?"

"Please give her to me, Dorothy," Roy sobbed brokenly, and then the dam burst and he began crying in the mouthpiece, turning toward the door fearful that one of the other vice officers would come in early, and humiliated that he was doing this and letting Dorothy hear it.

"Roy, Roy, don't do that. I know how you're suffering without Becky."

"Give her to me, Dorothy," Roy sniffed, wiping his face on the sleeve of his orange checkered sport shirt which he wore hanging out of his belt to cover the gun and handcuffs.

"Roy, I'm her mother."

"I'll pay you anything, Dorothy. My father has some money set aside for me in his will. Carl once hinted to me that if I ever changed my mind about going in the family store, I could maybe get my hands on it. I'll get it. I'll give it to you. Anything, Dorothy."

"I'm not selling my baby, Roy! When the hell are you going to grow up?"

"I'll move back with Mom and Dad. Mom could take care of Becky while I work. I've already talked to Mom. Please, Dorothy, you don't know how I love her. I love her so much more than you do."

The line was dead for a moment and Roy was coldly afraid she had hung up, then she said, "Maybe you do,

Roy. Maybe in your own way you do. But I don't think
you love her for herself. It's something else you see in
her. But it doesn't matter who loves her more. The point
is that a child, especially a little girl, needs a mother."

"There's *my* mother . . ."

"Goddamnit Roy, will you shut up and stop thinking
about yourself for just once in your life? I'm trying to
tell you Becky needs a mother, a real mother, and I
happen to be that mother. Now my lawyer's told you
and I've told you that you can have more than adequate
visitation rights. You can have whatever is reasonable.
I'll be very liberal in that regard. I don't think I've
been unfair in my child support demands. And surely,
the dollar a year alimony isn't too difficult to manage."

Roy heaved three deep breaths and the sting of his
humiliation swept over him. He was thankful he had
finally decided to make his final plea by telephone because he feared this might happen. He had been so dis-
traught through the divorce that he could hardly control
simple emotions anymore.

"You're very generous, Dorothy," he said, finally.

"I wish you everything good, so help me God I do."

"Thank you."

"Can I give you some advice, Roy? I think I know you
better than anyone."

"Why not? I'm vulnerable to anything right now. Tell
me to drop dead, I'll probably do it."

"No you won't Roy. You'll be all right. Listen, get on
course and go somewhere. You studied criminology after
switching your major two or three times. You said you'd
only be a policeman for a year or so and it's already
more than two years and you're nowhere near your degree. But that's okay if being a policeman is what you
want. But I don't think it is. You've never really liked
it."

"It's better than working for a living."

"Please don't joke now, Roy. This is the last free advice I'll ever be giving you. Get on course. Even if it's
going back to your dad's store. You could do a lot
worse. I don't think you'll be a successful policeman.
You always seemed unhappy with some aspect of the
job or other."

"Maybe I'd be miserable at anything."

"Maybe so, Roy. Maybe so. Anyway, do what you

think is best, and I'm sure I'll be seeing you often when
you come to get Becky."

"You can bet on that."

"Good-bye, Roy."

Roy sat at the cluttered table in the vice office and
smoked, even though he had a severe case of indigestion
and suspected an incipient ulcer. He finished the first
cigarette and used the smoldering coal to light another.
He knew the fire in his stomach would worsen and that
was alright too. He thought for an instant about the
new untested Smith & Wesson two-inch which rested
lightly on his hip and had made him so acutely aware
that for the first time in his police career he was working a plainclothes assignment. For the first time he
realized how badly he wanted that assignment, and how,
when the watch commander had asked him if he would
care for a loan to the vice squad for thirty days, he had
jumped at it. He began feeling a little better and decided
it was foolish and melodramatic to think of the Smith
& Wesson as he had for that moment. Things were not
that bad yet. He still had hope.

The lock turned and the door swung open in one motion and Roy did not recognize the balding loudly
dressed man who came in with a gun belt slung over his
shoulder and a paper sack in his hand.

"Hello," said Roy, standing up and hoping the evidence
of tears was no longer in his face.

"Hi," said the man, extending his hand. "You must
be a new man."

"I'm Roy Fehler. I'm on loan to vice for the month.
This is only my third night here."

"Oh? I'm Frank Gant. I been on days off since Monday. I heard we were borrowing someone from patrol."
He had a massive hand and shook hands violently. "I
didn't think anyone was here. Usually the first night
watch guy that arrives unlocks the door."

"Sorry," said Roy. "I'll unlock the door next time."

"Oh that's okay. You met the rest of the crew?"

"Yeah. You were the only one I didn't meet."

"Saved the best till last," Gant smiled, putting the
paper sack on top of a metal file cabinet.

"My lunch," he said, pointing to the sack. "You brown
bagging it?"

"No, I've bought my lunch the last two nights."

"Might as well brown bag it," said Gant. "You'll find there are lots of disadvantages to working vice. When you take off that blue suit you lose your eating spots. We have to pay for our meals or else brown bag it. I brown bag it. Working vice is expensive enough."

"Guess I'll do the same. I can't stand to spend too much money these days."

"You'll be expected to spend some," said Gant, sitting down at the table and opening the log to make the entry for August third. "They give us a few bucks a week to operate on, and we usually blow that the first night. From then on, you use your own dough if you want to operate. Me, I try not to spend too much. I got five kids."

"I'm with you," said Roy.

"They give you any money yet?"

"We operated a bar last night for liquor law violations," said Roy. "I chitted for two dollars, but really I spent five. I lost three on the deal."

"That's the way vice is," Gant sighed. "It's a damn good job and if you like to work you'll love it here, but the bastards won't give us enough money to work on."

"I'd like to work vice as a regular assignment. Maybe this is a good chance to show what I can do."

"It is," said Gant, opening a bulging manila folder and removing some forms which Roy had already come to recognize as vice complaints. "How long you been in Central, Roy? I don't believe I ever saw you before."

"Just a few months. I came from Newton."

"Down in the jungle, huh? Bet you're glad to get away from there."

"I wanted a change."

"Any change is for the better when you get away from there. I used to work Newton, but that was before the Civil Rights push. Now that they been promised nigger heaven it's not the same working down there. I'll never go back."

"It's a very complicated problem," said Roy, lighting another cigarette as he rubbed his burning stomach and blew a gray plume of smoke through his nose.

"We got some splibs in Central too, but not too many. Just over on the east side and in the projects mostly, and a few others scattered around. Too much business and industry in the downtown area for them to swarm in."

"I'd like to help you with the paper work," said Roy, becoming irritated and uncomfortable as he always did when anyone talked about Negroes like this.

"No, that's okay. These are old vice complaints that there's a follow-up due on. You wouldn't know what to write. Why don't you look through the whore book. It's good to get to know the regulars. Or read over some of the arrest reports to see how vice pinches are made. You made a whore pinch yet?"

"No, we tailed a couple last night but we lost them. We've been mostly operating the bars. We got a bartender for serving a drunk, but that's the only pinch we made in two nights."

"Well Gant's back so we'll go to work now."

"You're not a sergeant are you?" asked Roy, realizing that he still wasn't sure who all were working vice officers and who were supervisors. The whole atmosphere was very informal and different from patrol.

"Hell no," Gant laughed. "I should be, but I can't pass the damned exam. Been failing that son of a bitch for fourteen years. I'm just a policeman like you."

"Not too sure of the chain of command around here," Roy smiled.

"How much time you got on?"

"Almost three years," said Roy and then was afraid Gant would pin him down to months because two years and three months was certainly not "almost three years."

"Different on vice, isn't it? Calling your sergeant by his first name and all that. Far cry from patrol, huh? This is a close group. Vice work has to be. It's intimate work. You'll be in close and up tight with all kinds of people. You'll see every kind of depravity you ever imagined and some you can't even imagine when you see it. They only let a guy work eighteen months of this shit. Too goddamned sordid, that and the kind of life you lead. Hanging around in bars all night, boozing and playing around with broads. You married?"

"No," said Roy, and was struck with a spasm of indigestion that made him rub his stomach again.

"The whores don't tempt nobody, at least they shouldn't after you been around them awhile and get to know them. But there's a lot of pretty sexy toadies that hang around in some of these bars, lonely broads on the make, you know, just amateurs, freebies, and we're always hanging around too. It gets kind of tempting. Only thing Sergeant Jacovitch demands of us troops is that we don't play around on company time. If we meet something nice, we should make a date for our night off. Jake says if he catches us fooling around in some gin mill with a babe, she better be a professional whore or he'll bounce us off the squad."

"I'm going through a divorce right now. I'm not really thinking too much about women." Roy said it, and hoped Gant would ask him when the divorce was final or make some other comment about Roy's problem because he had a sudden urge to talk to someone, anyone, about it, and perhaps Gant had also been through it. So many policemen had.

"You know the division pretty well, Roy?" asked Gant, disappointing him.

"Pretty well."

"Well, you can study that pin map on the wall," said Gant, waving aimlessly at the wall as he made an entry on a work sheet which Roy knew would later be typed onto the vice complaint.

"What will we work tonight, whores?"

"Whores, yeah. We got to get some pinches. Haven't been doing too much lately. Maybe some fruits. We work fruits when we need some bookings. They're the easiest."

Roy heard voices and Phillips, a swarthy young man with unruly hair and a bristling moustache, walked through the door.

"Hello everybody," he announced, throwing a binocular case on the table, and carrying a set of walkie-talkies under his arm.

"What're the CC units for?" asked Gant. "Some kind of big deal tonight?"

"Maybe," said Phillips nodding to Roy. "Just before we went home last night we got a call from Ziggy's bull dagger informant that The Cave was going to have some lewd movies going tonight. We might try to operate the place."

"Hell, Mickey the bartender knows every goddamn one of us. How we going to operate it? I made so damn many pinches in there, they'd know me if I came in a gorilla suit."

"A gorilla suit would be normal dress in that ding-a-ling joint," said Phillips.

"You know The Cave?" asked Gant to Roy.

"That fruit joint on Main?" asked Roy, remembering a fight call he had received there on his first night in Central Division.

"Yeah, but it's not just fruits. There's lesbians, sadists, masochists, hypes, whores, flim flammers, paddy hustlers, hugger muggers, ex-cons of all descriptions, and anybody else with a kink of some kind or other. Who in the hell's going to operate for us, Phillips?"

"Guess?" said Phillips, grinning at Roy.

"Oh yeah," said Gant. "Nobody around the streets knows you yet."

"I was there in uniform once," said Roy, not relishing the idea of going alone into The Cave.

"In uniform you're just a faceless blue man," said Gant. "Nobody will recognize you now that you're in plainclothes. You know, Phillips, I think old Roy here will do alright in there."

"Yeah, those fruits'll go for that blond hair," said Phillips with a chuckle.

The other night watch team came in. Simeone and Ranatti were neighbors as well as partners and drove to work together. Sergeant Jacovitch came in last and Roy, still an outsider not accustomed to the vice squad routine, read arrest reports while the others sat around the long table in the cluttered office doing their paper work. They were all young men, not much older than himself except for Gant and Sergeant Jacovitch, who were approaching middle age. They all dressed nearly alike with bright-colored cotton shirts hanging outside their pants, and comfortable cotton trousers which it didn't matter if they soiled or tore while climbing a tree or crawling along a darkened hedge as Roy had done the night before when they had followed a whore and a trick to the trick pad, but had lost them when they entered the dingy apartment house because they were spotted by a tall Negro with processed hair who was undoubtedly a lookout. Roy noticed they all wore soft-soled shoes, crepe or ripple soles, so they could creep and peek and pry and Roy was not completely certain that he would like to receive an eighteen-month assignment to vice because he respected the privacy of others. He believed that this

undercover surveillance smacked of fascism and he believed that people, damn it, were trustworthy and there
were very few bad ones despite what cynical policemen
said. Then he remembered Dorothy's admonition that
he had never really liked this job, but what the hell,
he thought, vice work should be fascinating. At least for
a month.

"Bring your arrest reports in here, Roy," called Jacovitch, who slid his chair to the side. "Might as well sit
in here and listen to all the bullshit while you're reading
the lies on those arrest reports."

"What lies?" asked Ranatti, a handsome, liquid-eyed
young man who wore an upside-down shoulder holster
over a T-shirt. His outer shirt, a long-sleeved navy blue
cotton was hung carefully over the back of his chair
and he checked it often to make sure the tail was not
dragging the floor.

"The Sarge thinks we exaggerate sometimes on our
arrest reports," said Simeone to Roy. He was younger
looking than Ranatti, rosy cheeked, and had slightly
protruding ears.

"I wouldn't say that," said Jacovitch. "But I've tried
a dozen operators on Ruby Shannon and you guys are
the only ones ever did any good."

"What're you beefing about Jake, we got a case on her
didn't we?" Ranatti beamed.

"Yeah," said Jacovitch, with a wary glance first at
Ranatti, then at Simeone. "But she told me you zoomed
her. You know the lieutenant doesn't want any hummer pinches."

"Aw, it was no hummer, Jake," said Simeone, "she just
went for old Rosso here." He jerked a finger toward
the grinning Ranatti.

"Sure seems funny," said Jacovitch. "She can usually
smell a cop a block away, and Ranatti fooled her.
Shit, he looks like he's fresh off the beat."

"No, look, Jake," said Ranatti. "We really hooked her
legal, honest we did. I operated her in my own inimi-
table style. You know, played a slick young pool room
dago, and she went for it. Never dreamt I was the heat."

"Another thing, it's unusual for Ruby to go on a six-
forty-seven A," said Jacovitch. "She groped you, huh,
Rosso?"

"Honest to God, she honked my horn," said Ranatti,

raising a rather stubby right hand heavenward. "Gave it two toots with a thumb and forefinger before I laid the iron on her wrists."

"I don't trust either of you bastards," said Jacovitch to the grinning young men. "Lieutenant Francis and me were cruising the whore spots last week and we stopped and talked to Ruby at Fifth and Stanford. She mentioned the cute little Eye-talian cop that booked her on a hummer. She claims she laid a hand on your knee and you pinched her for lewd conduct right then."

"Look, boss, I'm lewd from the knee on up. Don't you believe those Latin lover stories?"

They all chuckled and Jacovitch turned to Roy. "What I'm trying to tell these guys is to lay off the hummers. We got a lieutenant that's very explicit about nice legal pinches. If the whore doesn't say the right words to you for a violation or if she doesn't grope you lewdly, there's no basis for a legal bust."

"What if she shakes you down for a gun, Jake?" asked Simeone, lighting a fat cigar that looked comical in the puffy young lips. "If she does that, I say she ought to get busted for lewd conduct. You can embellish your report a bit."

"Goddamn, Sim, no embellishment. That's what I'm trying to get through to you. Look, I'm not the whole show, I'm just one of the clowns. The boss says we do police work straight arrow."

"Okay, Jake, but vice is a different kind of police work," said Gant, joining in the conversation for the first time.

"Look," said Jacovitch in exasperation. "Do you really want to roust these whores? If you do, you got to make what amounts to a false arrest report and then perjure yourself to convict her. It's not worth it. There'll always be whores. Why risk your job for a lousy misdemeanor? And while I'm on the subject, the boss is a little hinky about some of these tails you been pulling where you tail the whore to the trick pad and hear her offer the guy a French for ten bucks."

"So?" said Simeone, not smiling now. "We made one like that last week. Something wrong with it?"

"The lieutenant told me he drove by one of the apartment houses where a team made a bust like that. He didn't say it was you, Sim, but he did say that the goddamn place had a windowless concrete wall on the side where the offer was supposed to be heard by the officers."

"Goddamn it," said Gant, standing up suddenly, and striding across the room to his lunch sack, where he removed another cigar. "What does that fucking boy-lieutenant think this is, a college debating class with all the fucking rules laid down. I never bitched about him before, Jake, but do you know one night he asked me if I'd been drinking? Can you beat it? Ask a vice officer if he's been drinking. I said fuck, yes, Lieutenant, what the hell do you think I should do when I'm operating a bar. Then he asked me if we always pay for our booze and whether we accept sandwiches from bar owners who know we're heat. He wants a bunch of goody goody teetotalers with their lunch money pinned to their underwear. I'm quitting the squad if this prick gets any worse."

"Take it easy. Jesus," said Jacovitch, looking fearfully toward the door. "He's our boss. We got to have a little loyalty."

"That guy's blossoming out, Jake," said Simeone. "He's trying to be the youngest captain on the job. You got to watch the blossomers, they'll use their troops for manure."

Jacovitch looked helplessly at Roy and Roy was certain he would be admonished later by Jacovitch to keep silent about the bitching in the vice squad. He was a poor example of a supervisor if he let it die like this, thought Roy. He should never have let it go this far, but now that it had, he should set them straight. The lieutenant was the officer in charge, and if Roy were in charge, by God, he would hope his sergeant did not permit the men to insult him.

"Let's talk about something else, you mutineers," Jacovitch announced nervously, jerking his glasses off and wiping them although they seemed to Roy perfectly clean.

"Did you guys hear how many marines Hollywood vice busted last weekend?" asked Simeone, and Roy thought Jacovitch looked obviously relieved that the conversation had shifted.

"What's happening in Hollywood?" asked Gant.

"What always happens?" said Simeone. "The joint is lousy with faggots. I hear they got twenty marines in fruit pinches last weekend. They're going to notify the general at Camp Pendleton."

"That pisses me off," said Gant. "I was in the corps, but things were different in those days. Even marines are different now."

"Yeah, I hear there're so many fruit marines being busted, the jarheads at Camp Pendleton are afraid to be seen eating a banana," said Ranatti. "They eat it sideways now like an ear of corn."

"Anybody had a chance to work on the vice complaint at the Regent Arms?" asked Jacovitch.

"Maybe we could use our loaner here for that one," said Ranatti, nodding at Roy. "I think operating that joint is the only way. We prowled it. I got a ladder up to the balcony on the second floor and saw the room where those two whores are tricking, but I couldn't get close enough to the window."

"Trouble is, they're damn particular who they take," said Simeone. "I think one or maybe two bellboys are working with them and sending up the tricks. Maybe Roy here could check in and we could set something up."

"Roy's too young," said Gant. "We need an old guy like me, but I been around so long one of those whores would probably recognize me. How about you, Jake? You're old enough and prosperous looking. We'll make you an out of town sport and set something up."

"Might be alright," said Jacovitch, running his fingers through his thinning black hair. "But the boss doesn't like the sergeants to operate too much. I'll see what he thinks."

"The Clarke Apartments is expanding their operations too," said Ranatti. "Apartments six, seven, and eight all have hot beds in them now. Sim and me were staked out there last night for less than an hour and we must've seen these three whores take twelve or thirteen tricks in there one after another. The trick checks in at the desk each time too, so the place is making a fortune."

"One hot bed can make you plenty," Jacovitch nodded.

"These three are really busy. They don't even bother changing sheets," said Ranatti.

"That used to be a square place," said Gant. "I used to take a date there after work whenever I'd get lucky.

Too bad they had to get involved in prostitution. Nice old guy runs the joint."

"Too much money in vice," said Jacovitch looking at each of them. "It can corrupt anybody."

"Hey, you guys hear what Harwell did in the restroom at the Garthwaite Theater?" asked Simeone.

"Harwell's a day watch vice officer," said Jacovitch to Roy. "He's about as psycho as Simeone and Ranatti. We all got our crosses to bear."

"What did he do this time?" asked Gant, completing his scribbled notes on a page of yellow legal-size paper.

"He was working the restroom on the vice complaint from the manager, and he spots a brand-new glory hole between the walls of the toilets, so he plops his big ass down on the last stool without dropping his pants and he just sits there smoking his big cigar and pretty soon some fruit comes in and goes straight to the glory hole and sticks his joint through at old Harwell. Lopez was watching from the trap behind the air conditioning on the east wall and he could see real good since we had the manager take the doors off all the johns to discourage the fruits. He said when the guy's joint came poking through the hole, why old Harwell tapped the ashes off that big cigar and blew on the coal till it was glowing red then ground it right into the head of the guy's dick. Says the fruit was screaming on the floor when they left."

"That bastard's psycho," Jacovitch murmured. "This is his second tour on vice. I had my doubts about him. Bastard's psycho."

"You ever hear about the glory hole in Bloomfield's Department Store in the ladies dressing room?" asked Ranatti. "Where the wienie wagger shoved it through at the old babe changing clothes and she stuck a hatpin clear through it and the son of a bitch was pinned right there when the cops arrived."

"I heard that one for years," said Phillips. "I think some cop dreamed that one up for a good locker room story."

"Well, the one about Harwell is true," said Simeone. "Lopez told me. Said they got the hell out right away. Harwell wanted to book the fruit. Can you imagine, after he damn near burned his dick off, he wants to put him in jail? Lopez told him, 'Let's get the hell out of here and the fruit'll never know it was a cop that did it.'"

"Bastard's going to get fired someday," Jacovitch grumbled.

"Look, you got to keep your sense of humor working this job," Ranatti grinned. "You'd go nuts if you didn't."

"I'd like to've seen that," said Gant. "Was the fruit a white guy?"

"Pretty close," said Simeone. "He was Italian."

"You asshole," said Ranatti.

"You guys remember this is trash night," said Jacovitch.

"What a pain in the ass," said Simeone. "I forgot. Jesus Christ, I wore decent clothes tonight."

"Trash night is the night we help the day watch," said Jacovitch to Roy. "We've agreed to rummage through the garbage cans real late at night on the night before the weekly trash pickup. The day watch gives us the addresses of the places they suspect are bookie joints and we check their trash cans."

"I can tell all my friends I'm a G-man," Ranatti muttered. "G for garbage."

"It worked pretty good so far," said Jacovitch to Roy. "We've found betting markers in garbage cans in three places. That gave day watch something to work on."

"And I go home smelling like a garbage dump," said Ranatti.

"One night we were rummaging in the cans back of Red Cat Sam's restaurant," said Simeone, grinning at Jacovitch, "and we find a big hog's head. Goddamn hog had a head like a lion. Old Red Cat's a splib, specializes in soul food. Anyway, we brought the head back for Jake, here. We stuck it in his wall locker and went home. Next night we come to work early to make sure we see him open it and that's the goddamn night this new lieutenant gets transferred in, unbeknownst to us. And they gave Jake's locker to him. He opened that door and didn't say a goddamn thing. Nothing! Nobody said nothing. We just all pretended like we were doing our paper work or something, and didn't say nothing!"

"He told me later that he thought this was an initiation for the new commander," said Jacovitch, lighting a cigarette and coughing hoarsely. "Maybe that's why he's made it so tough on us."

"Let's not talk about him anymore. I get depressed," said Gant. "You guys ready to go to work?"

"Wait a minute before you go," said Jacovitch. "We got something pretty big cooking tonight. We're going to take The Cave at 1:00 A.M. I know you guys've probably heard rumors because it's impossible to keep a secret in this outfit. Anyway, we got some good scam from a reliable snitch that The Cave is having a lewd movie show tonight. I can't understand it unless Frippo the owner is just plain desperate for business. Anyway, the word is out and the goddamn place is going to be packed tonight. Do you know anything about The Cave, Roy?"

"A little," Roy nodded.

"We been hitting them pretty hard lately," said Jacovitch. "One more good bust and I think we can get his liquor license. Tonight should be it. You guys drop whatever you're doing and meet me here at about midnight. We're borrowing about a dozen uniformed policemen from patrol and two teams from Administrative Vice are going to assist. The movie show is supposed to start about one and we're going to have Roy inside. As soon as the movie starts, Roy, you casually walk to the restroom. We already heard from the snitch that nobody's going to get in or out the front door after it starts. Stick a cigarette out the window and wave it around. We'll be sitting outside where we can see that window. Then we'll use the key and come in the front door."

"You have a key to the place?" asked Roy.

"Yeah," Ranatti grinned. "That's it in the corner." He pointed to a four-foot metal post with a heavy steel plate welded on the end and handles affixed to each side so that four men could swing it.

"It should come off with no problems," Jacovitch said. "I don't think you'll have any trouble, but if you should, like if something screwy should happen—if you're made as a vice officer, if you're in any danger at all—you just pick up a barstool or a beer mug or anything and toss it through the front window. Then we'll be right in. But you won't have any trouble."

"Do I just sit there and have a drink?" asked Roy.

"Yeah. Order beer and drink out of the bottle," said Ranatti. "You don't dare drink out of a glass in the slimy place. Hey, Sim, is Dawn LaVere still hustling out of The Cave?"

"I saw her out front last week," Simeone nodded.

"Watch for that bitch, Roy. She's the smartest whore I ever saw. She can spot a cop quick. If she suspects you're vice she'll start her act. Sit next to you, put a hand around your waist and pat you down for a gun and handcuffs while she's tucking a big tit under your armpit to keep you busy. She'll feel your key ring or get her hands on it if she can to see if you got call box keys or handcuff keys. And she'll feel for two wallets because she knows most policemen carry one wallet with their money and another one for their badge. I'd advise you to leave your badge and gun and everything with Gant before you go in."

"I don't know about that," said Jacovitch. "He'd better be armed. I don't want him getting hurt."

"A gun can screw up the deal, Jake," Ranatti protested. "He might as well get used to taking a few chances. We all got to if we want to work vice."

"I don't know. I'll think about it," said Jacovitch.

"Another thing, don't let old Dawn kiss you," giggled Ranatti. "She loves to snuggle around with guys she's hustling. Real affectionate whore, but she's got VD and TB."

"Runny at both ends," Simeone nodded. "All the time."

"She gobbles about twenty joints a night," said Ranatti. "Dawn once told me she don't even screw anymore. Most guys would rather have head jobs and that's a lot easier for her. She don't even have to undress."

"She a dyke?" asked Gant.

"Oh yeah," said Ranatti. "She lives over on Alvarado with some big fat bull dagger. Told me one time she can't stand to lay a man anymore."

"A vice officer hears all the girls' problems," said Phillips to Roy. "We get to know all these assholes so well."

"Want Roy to work with me?" asked Gant to Jacovitch.

"I want the four of you to work together tonight," said Jacovitch. "I don't want you guys getting hung up on something and not be ready to go on The Cave when it's time. You four go out together. You can take two cars, but decide what you're going to do till midnight and do it together. Phillips'll work with me."

"Let's go down on Sixth and see if Roy can operate a streetwalker," said Gant to Ranatti and Simeone who were already taking their small flashlights out of the drawer of a filing cabinet.

"Trash night and I'm wearing a brand-new shirt," Ranatti grumbled, buttoning the shirt gingerly. Roy noticed it fitted well and the shoulder holster was completely concealed. He wondered if he should invest in a shoulder holster. He decided to wait. He was only working vice this month and it might be a long time before he was given a permanent plainclothes assignment. Surely though, someone would want him soon. Felony car, vice, someone would want him. He was sure it was evident to everyone that he was an exceptionally good policeman but police work was temporary and he knew he should be thinking about what courses he would be taking this semester. He seemed to have lost his drive in that direction. Maybe, he thought, I'll take a vacation this semester.

They took two cars. Gant was driving a two-tone green Chevrolet which the vice officers had done their best to camouflage by putting oversized tires on the back. Someone had hung a fuzzy object from the mirror and Gant told Roy that Simeone was responsible for the college decals plastered all over the rear window. Still, Roy thought, it looked like a stripped down, low priced, plainclothes police car. The Department, according to Gant, was very tight with expenditures of funds for undercover operation.

Gant drove Roy to the parking lot where he had his private car.

"Listen Roy," said Gant. "We'll be in the vacant lot behind the yellow apartment building north of Sixth just off Towne Avenue. You make a pass by there and see where we are. Then you cruise a few blocks down on Sixth and you should see a hustler or two even this early in the evening. If you get her, bring her back to the meeting place."

"Okay," said Roy.

"You sure you learned last night what you need for a whore pinch?" asked Gant.

"Offer of sex for money," said Roy. "Seems simple enough."

"Okay, Roy, go ahead," said Gant. "If you see a whore you suspect is a man dressed up as a woman, don't hit on him. Pass him by and try another one. We don't

operate fruits alone. They're the most dangerous un-
predictable bastards in the world. You just hit on women
—*real* women."

"Okay," Roy said, getting anxious to start. It was a
dark night, and being out here on the city streets in
plainclothes was like being out here for the very first
time. It was eerie and exciting. His heart began thudding.

"Go ahead, kid," said Gant. "Take it easy though."

Roy noticed that his hands became extremely clammy
and the steering wheel slippery as he turned east on
Sixth Street. It wasn't that he was alone, because he was
not really alone with Gant and Ranatti and Simeone
staked out just a few blocks away. But he was for the
first time out in the streets minus the security of the
badge and blue suit, and though he knew this street
fairly well, it seemed altogether strange. A vice officer
loses the comfort of the big brass shield, he thought. He
acquires an identity. Without the blue suit he becomes a
mere man who must function as a street dweller. His
confidence was waning. Was it more than nervousness?
He put a hand on his chest and measured the thuds. Was
it fear?

Roy saw a streetwalker at Fifth and Stanford. She
was an emaciated Negro with straight legs and Roy
guessed she was an addict with her look of yearning. She
smiled as he drove slowly by.

"Hello blondie," she said, walking up to Roy's car on
the passenger side and peering in.

"Hello there," Roy said, forced a smile, and cursed
silently at his quivering voice.

"Haven't I seen you around?" she asked, still smiling
an uninviting bad-toothed smile as she glanced around
the car, probing, and Roy guessed that she suspected immediately.

"I've never been here before," Roy answered. "A
friend told me about this place. Said I could have a good
time."

"What do you do for a living, baby?" she smiled.

"Insurance man."

"That's funny, you look just like a cop to me," she
said, drilling him with her eyes.

"A cop?" he laughed brokenly. "Not me."

"You look exactly like a young cop," she said unblinkingly while he withered.

"Look, you're making me nervous with this cop talk," said Roy. "Can I get a good time around here, or not?"

"Maybe you could," she said. "What do you have in mind?"

Roy remembered last night's admonishment by Jacovitch about entrapment and he knew she was trying to lead him into making the offer himself.

"Don't you know?" he said, trying a coy smile but uncertain how it looked.

"Give me a card, baby, I might want to buy some insurance sometime."

"Card?"

"A business card. Give me a business card."

"Look, I'm a married man. I don't want you to know my name. What're you trying to do, blackmail me?" said Roy, congratulating himself on his quick thinking and making a note to borrow some cards from an insurance office for any future operations.

"Okay," she smiled easily. "Tear your name off the card or scratch it out with that pen in your shirt pocket. Just let me see that you have a card."

"I don't have any with me," said Roy. "Come on, let's get down to business."

"Uh huh," she said, "let's do that. And my business is minding my own business. Any insurance man that ain't got a million cards in his wallet is a mighty poor insurance man."

"So I'm a poor insurance man. What the hell," said Roy hopelessly as she turned to walk away.

"You ain't even a good vice cop," she sneered over her shoulder.

"Bitch," said Roy.

"Paddy, blue-eyed motherfucker," said the prostitute.

Roy turned right on the next street, drove south to Seventh then back up to Sixth where he parked his car a half block away with the lights out and watched the prostitute talking to a tall Negro in a gray felt hat who nodded and walked quickly down the block to a fat prostitute in a green satin dress whom Roy hadn't seen before. She ran inside the building and talked with two women in the doorway who were just coming out. Roy drove to the meeting place where he found Gant sitting in the back seat of Ranatti and Simeone's car.

"Might as well go somewhere else," said Roy. "I'm burned."

"What happened?" asked Gant.

"A skinny whore in a brown dress recognized me from working uniform in this area," Roy lied. "I saw her look at me and run and tell all the whores on the block. It's no use, I'm burned here."

"Let's go over to the park and bust a quick fruit or two," said Ranatti. "We haven't made a fruit pinch for a few days."

After leaving his private car in the station parking lot Roy rejoined Gant in the vice car and they drove toward the park. Roy was disappointed that he had so far been unable to make a vice arrest, but he decided he'd operate successfully in The Cave later tonight and it now occurred to him that he had no idea how to arrest a homosexual.

"What're the elements of a fruit pinch?" asked Roy.

"That's easier than a whore bust," said Gant, driving casually through the early evening traffic. "If he makes a lewd offer in a public place, that's it. Or if he gropes you. But as far as I'm concerned you don't have to let a man grab your joint. If it looks like he's making a move to honk you, just grab his hand and he's busted. We'll say on the arrest report he touched your privates. I don't give a shit what Jacovitch says about legal arrests and embellishing arrest reports, I don't let nobody touch my tool unless she's wearing a dress and I know for sure there's a female body under the dress."

"Seems like you could just settle for the verbal offer," said Roy.

"Yeah, you could. But some faggots are real aggressive. You say hello and bang, they got you by the dork. I don't expect you to submit to that crap. Just operating fruits is bad enough. But maybe we won't have to operate them. Maybe we can catch them in the trap."

"I heard lots of talk about *the trap*. What is it?" asked Roy, feeling a bit uncomfortable about the prospect of working fruits.

"That's what we call a vantage point," said Gant, accelerating up the hill on Sixth Street past Central Receiving Hospital. "There's lots of places where fruits hang out, like public restrooms. Well, some of these places install vents covered with heavy mesh screen or something like that, where we can peek through into the restroom area. Most of the places take the doors off the shithouses for us too. Then we sit in *the trap,* as we call it, and peek through into the restroom. Of course there's legal technicalities like probable cause and exploratory searches involved here, but I'll tell you about that when we make the arrest report—if we catch any. Sometimes we use the CC units and let one guy sit in the trap with a radio and if he sees some fruit action in the john, he whispers to us over the radio and in we come. Let me warn you about fruits. I don't know what you're expecting, but I can tell you that a fruit can look like anything. He can be a big manly guy with a wife and kids and a good job, he can be a professional man, or a priest, or even a cop. We've caught people from every walk of life in these traps. All kinds of people got kinks, and in my opinion, any guy with this particular kind of kink that has to indulge it occasionally will sooner or later look for a public restroom or some other sleazy fruit hangout. It's part of the cruddy thrill I guess. I talked to a million fruits in my time and lots of them cop out to needing a little action in a place like this once in a while even when they can have their kicks in private with a discreet boyfriend. I don't know why, I just know they do it. So the thing is, you might run into a pretty square kind of fruit in here. Like I said, a respectable married guy or something, and when he finds out you're the law, that son of a bitch might come uncorked. Suddenly he pictures a big scandal where Mama and the kiddies and all his friends read on the front page of the *Times* that old Herbie is really a cocksucker. That's what's going on in his sweaty brain. And you be careful, because if you was taking him for murder he wouldn't be near as panicky or dangerous. This prick might literally try to kill you to get away. I say don't get yourself hurt for a lousy misdemeanor pinch that ain't worth a goddamn in court anyway. You know what the average fruit gets? About a fifty-dollar fine and that's it. He'd have to have a bunch of priors to draw any jail time. But these fruits don't know all this and if they don't know it they don't think of it when you're arresting them. All they're thinking about is getting away from you. And they're fucked up in the head anyway or they wouldn't be there in the first place, so you just be careful working fruits."

"I will," said Roy, feeling his heart race again. He hadn't bargained for the dangers of vice work. When he first learned he was going to vice he vaguely pictured girls and drinking. He thought of how he had never actually been in a fight in the two years he had been a policeman. He had to assist a partner wrestle a man to the ground a few times where the handcuffs were applied without too much trouble. But he had never actually struck a man, nor had anyone ever struck him. And a vice officer carried no baton. "Do you carry a sap?" Roy asked.

"You bet," said Gant, lifting his shirt and showing Roy the huge black beaver-tail sap he carried inside his waistband.

"Maybe I ought to buy one," said Roy.

"I think you ought to have one," Gant nodded. "Vice officers get in some good ones and that onesies on twosies wristlock they teach you in the academy never seems to work when you're squirming around on some piss-covered restroom floor with some bloody sweaty fruit, or maybe battling some hugger mugger's pimp in some dark hotel lobby when your partner doesn't know where the hell you are."

"This job doesn't sound too good after all," Roy smiled weakly.

"I'm just telling the worst that can happen," said Gant. "They're the things that happen to young hot dogs like Ranatti and Simeone. But you stick with the old salts like me and nothing's going to happen. We won't make as many pinches as those guys but we'll go home in one piece every night."

Gant parked the vice car a half block from the park and walked to the hedgerow on the south side of the duck pond where they found Ranatti and Simeone sprawled on the grass smoking and throwing pieces of popcorn to a hissing black gander who accepted the tribute but scorned them for their charity.

"Nobody appreciates something for nothing," said Ranatti, pointing his cigarette at the ferocious gander who tired of the popcorn and waddled to the water's edge.

"We going to operate, or work the trap?" asked Gant.

"Whatever you want," Simeone shrugged.

"What do you want to do, Roy?" asked Gant.

"Hell, I'm too new to know," said Roy. "If we operate that means we walk around and pose as fruits?"

"Just be available," said Simeone. "You don't have to swish around or play with your coins in your pants pocket or anything. Just hang around and talk to the fruits that hit on you. Usually one or two of us operate out around the trees and the other two wait somewhere. If you get an offer you bring the fruit to the waiting place. Tell him you got a car nearby or a pad, or tell him anything. Just get him to us, then we all take him. One man never takes a fruit alone."

"I already told him that," said Gant.

"Or, if you're squeamish about playing fruit, and I don't blame you if you are," said Ranatti, " 'cause I never could stand to operate them—well, then we can go to the trap. Then you only watch them in a lewd act. You don't have to actually mingle with them like when you operate."

"Let's do that," said Roy.

"You two want inside or outside?" asked Simeone to Gant.

"Outside. What do you think?"

"What did you ask him for?" said Ranatti.

"He respects his elders," said Gant as they began strolling through the park. It was a warm summer evening, and a slight breeze cooled Roy's face as it came off the pond. Many of the ducks were asleep, and aside from the steady flow of nearby traffic it was quiet and restful here.

"It's a beautiful place," said Roy.

"The park?" said Ranatti. "Oh, yeah. But it's full of faggots and thieves and assholes in general. No decent people dare hang around here after dark."

"Except us vice officers," said Simeone.

"He said decent people," Gant reminded him.

"Once in a while some squares that're new in town might come around here after dark with the family, but they soon see what's happening. They used to lock up the johns at night, but some brainy park administrator decided to leave them open. The open restrooms draw fruits like flies."

"Fruit flies," said Simeone.

"We used to only have a hundred fruits a night around here. Now we got a thousand. Maybe we can get the restrooms closed again."

"That's it over there," said Gant to Roy, pointing at the large stucco outbuilding squatting near a clump of elms that rustled in the wind which had grown stronger.

"Roy, you and me'll wait behind those trees over there," said Gant. "When they come out of the trap we'll see them and run over and help them."

"One time," said Simeone, "there were only two of us here and we caught eight fruits in there. One was gobbling another's joint, and the other six were standing around fondling anything they could find."

"A real circle jerk," said Ranatti. "We snuck out of the trap and didn't know what the hell to do with eight of them. Finally Sim spots a pile of roofing tiles at the corner of the tool shed and he sticks his head in and yells, 'All you fruits are under arrest.' Then he slams the door shut and backs off to the pile of tiles and starts heaving them at the door every time one of them tries to get out. He was really enjoying it, I think. I ran to the call box on the corner and put out a help call and when the black and whites got here we still had all eight fruits trapped in the crapper. But the wall of the building looked like a machine gun squad had strafed it."

"See what I told you before about sticking with me and staying out of trouble," said Gant, walking toward the clump of trees where they would wait. "Why don't you go in with them for a while, Roy? You might as well see what it's all about."

Ranatti removed his key ring from his pocket and unlocked the padlock on a massive tool shed which was attached to the side of the building. Roy entered the shed and was followed by Ranatti who held the door for him and closed it behind them. It was deep and black in the shed except for a patch of light six feet up on the wall near the roof of the shed. Ranatti took Roy's elbow and guided him through the darkness and pointed to a step and a three-foot platform leading up to the patch of light. Roy stepped up and looked through the heavy gauge sheets of wire mesh into the interior of the restroom. The room was about thirty by twenty feet, Roy thought. He envisioned the dimension might be a question by the defense if he ever had to go to court on an arrest he made here. There were four urinals and four stools behind them separated by metal walls. Roy noticed there were no doors on the front of the stalls and several peepholes were drilled in the metal walls which separated the toilets.

They waited silently for several minutes and then Roy heard feet shuffling on the concrete walk leading toward the front door. An old stooped tramp slouched in toting a bundle which he opened when he got inside. The tramp took four wine bottles from the dirty sack and drained the half mouthful of wine which remained in each of them. Then he put the bottles back into the bundle and Roy wondered what value they could have. The old man wobbled over to the last stool where he removed his filthy coat, lunged sideways against the wall, righted himself, and took the floppy hat from his tremendous shaggy head. The tramp dropped his pants and sat down in one motion and a tremendous gaseous explosion echoed through the restroom.

"Oh Christ," Simeone whispered. "Just our luck."

The stench filled the room instantly.

"Jesus Christ," said Ranatti, "this place smells like a shithouse."

"Were you expecting a flowershop?" asked Simeone.

"This is a degrading job," Roy muttered and went to the door for some fresh air.

"Well, the old thief's got enough asswipe stashed to last a week," said Simeone in a loud voice.

Roy looked back into the restroom and saw the tramp still sitting on the toilet, slumped against the side wall snoring loudly. A huge wad of toilet paper protruded from the top of his ragged undershirt.

"Hey!" Simeone called. "Wake up you old ragpicker. Wake up!"

The tramp stirred, blinked twice and closed his eyes again.

"Hey, he's not sleeping real sound yet," said Ranatti. "Hey! Old man! Wake up! Get your ass up and out of here!"

This time the tramp stirred, grunted and opened his eyes with a snap of his head.

"Get the hell out of here, you old crud!" said Simeone.

"Who said that?" asked the tramp, leaning forward on

the toilet, trying to peek around the wall of the toilet stall.

"It's me. God!" said Ranatti. "Get the hell out of here."

"Wise son of a bitch, huh?" said the tramp. "Jus' wait a minute."

As the tramp was struggling back into his pants, Roy heard footsteps and a pale, nervous-looking man with a receding hairline and green-tinted glasses entered the restroom.

"A fruit," Ranatti whispered in Roy's ear.

The man looked in each toilet stall and seeing only the uninteresting tramp in the last stall, walked to the urinal on the far side of the room.

The tramp did not buckle his belt but merely tied the leather around his waist. He slammed the floppy hat back on his head and picked up the bundle. Then he saw the man standing at the last urinal. The tramp put down the bundle.

"Hello God," said the tramp.

"Beg your pardon?" said the man, still standing at the urinal.

"Ain't you God?" asked the tramp. "Didn't you tell me to get the hell out of here? Well I might not look like much, but no son of a bitch tells me to get my ass out of a public shithouse, you son of a bitch." The tramp put down his bundle deliberately while the terrified man re-zipped his trousers. As the man skidded toward the door across the slippery floor of the restroom the tramp threw a wine bottle that crashed on the doorjamb and showered the man with glass fragments. The tramp hobbled to the door and looked after his fleeing enemy, then returned to his bundle and hefted it to his shoulder. With a toothless triumphant grin he staggered from the restroom.

"Sometimes you get a chance to do good things for people in this job," said Simeone lighting a cigarette, making Roy wish he would not smoke in the stifling dark enclosure of the shed.

It was perhaps five minutes when another step was heard. A tall, muscular man of about thirty entered, walked to the sink and ran a comb deliberately through his wavy brown hair without glancing to his left. Then he examined the wide collar of a green sport shirt worn beneath a lightweight well-fitting lime sweater. Then he

walked to each toilet stall and looked inside. He then
walked to the urinal which had been occupied by the
pale man, unzipped his trousers and stood there not
urinating. Ranatti nodded in the darkness to Roy but
Roy did not believe he could be a fruit. The man stood
at the urinal for almost five minutes craning his neck
occasionally toward the door when a sound was heard
outside. Twice Roy thought someone would enter and
he now knew of course what the man was waiting for,
and he shivered in the back of his neck and decided
when another one came in he did not want to watch,
was not curious enough to watch because already he felt
slightly nauseated. He always had the idea that fruits
were all swishes, hence identifiable, and it sickened him
to see this average-looking man in here, and he did not
want to watch. Then an old man entered. Roy didn't see
him until he was through the door and stepping lightly
to the urinal at the opposite end of the line. The old
man was perhaps seventy, dressed nattily in a blue pin-
stripe with natural shoulders and matching vest, and a
blue silk tie over a pale blue shirt. His hair was pearl
white and styled. His hands were lightly veined and
he picked nervously at invisible lint on the impeccable
suit. He looked at the tall man at the other urinal and
smiled and the light glinted off his silver collar pin and
Roy was struck with a wave of revulsion not impercepti-
ble like before, but gut wrenching as the old man, still
holding his hands near his groin out of Roy's line of
sight, hopped along the urinals until he was standing
next to the tall man. He laughed softly and so did the
tall man who said, "You're too old." Roy whispered in-
credulously to Ranatti, "He's an old man! My God, he's
an old man!"

"What the hell," Ranatti whispered dryly, "fruits
grow old too."

The old man left after being repulsed another time.
He stopped in the doorway but finally left in dejection.

"He didn't really do anything lewd," Simeone whispered to Roy. "He just stood next to him at the urinal.
No touching or anything. He didn't even jerk off. No
good for an arrest."

Roy thought the hell with it he had seen enough and
decided to join Gant on the cool clean grass in the in-
vigorating air when he heard voices and feet scraping

and decided to see who or what would enter. He heard a man say something in rapid Spanish and a child answered. The only thing Roy understood was "Sí Papá." Then Roy heard the man walking away from the doorway and he heard other children's voices talking Spanish. A boy of about six skipped in the restroom not looking at the tall man and ran to a toilet where he turned his back to the watchers, dropped his short pants to the floor revealing his plump brown behind, and urinated in the toilet while he hummed a child's song. Roy smiled for a moment, but then he remembered the tall man. He saw the tall man's hand moving frantically in the area of his crotch and then he stepped away from the urinal and masturbated as he faced the boy but hurriedly returned to the urinal when a child's shrill laugh pierced the silence from the outside. The boy adjusted his pants and ran from the restroom still humming, and Roy heard him shout, "Carlos! Carlos!" to a child who answered from a long way across the park. The child never saw the tall man who now grunted while he stood at the old place and his hand moved more frantically than before.

"See? Our job *is* worth doing," Simeone grinned viciously. "Let's take that bastard."

As the three men broke from the shed door, Simeone whistled and Gant came running from the clump of swaying elms. Roy saw a man and three children across the expanse of darkness strolling across the grass carrying shopping bags. They were almost out of the park.

Simeone led the way into the restroom with his badge in his hand. The man looked at the four vice officers and fumbled with the zipper of his trousers.

"You like kids?" Simeone grinned. "I'll bet you got some little bubblegummers of your own. Want to bet, Rosso?" he said and turned to Ranatti.

"What is this?" asked the man, his face white, jaw twitching.

"Answer me!" Simeone commanded. "You got kids? And a wife?"

"I'm getting out of here," said the man, walking toward Simeone who shoved him back against the wall of the restroom.

"No need for that," said Gant, standing on the threshold.

"I'm not getting rough," said Simeone. "I just want to know if he's got a wife and kids. They almost always do. Do you, man?"

"Yes, of course. But why are you arresting me? Lord, I didn't do anything," he said as Simeone handcuffed his hands behind his back.

"Always handcuff fruits," Simeone smiled to Roy. "Always. No exceptions."

As they were leaving the park, Roy walked behind with Gant.

"How do you like working fruits, kid?" asked Gant.

"Not too good," Roy answered.

"Look over there," said Gant, pointing toward the pond where a slender young man in tight coffee-colored pants and a lacy orange shirt was mincing along the edge of the water.

"That's what I thought all fruits looked like," said Roy.

The young man stopped every thirty feet or so, genuflected, crossed himself, and prayed silently. Roy counted six genuflections before he reached the street where he disappeared in the pedestrian traffic.

"Some of them are pretty pitiful. That one's trying to resist," Gant shrugged, offering Roy a cigarette which he accepted. "They're the most promiscuous creatures that ever walked the earth. They're so goddamned unsatisfied they're always seeking. Now you see why we try to work whores, and gambling, and bars as much as possible. And remember, you can get the shit kicked out of you working fruits. On top of all the rest of the crap you got to put up with, it's dangerous as hell."

Roy's mind drifted back then, back to college. He had been reminded of someone. Of course! he thought suddenly, as he remembered the mannerisms of Professor Raymond. It had never occurred to him before! Professor Raymond was a fruit!

"Can we work whores tomorrow night?" asked Roy.

"Sure, kid," Gant laughed.

At midnight, Roy was getting tired of sitting in the vice office watching Gant do his paper work as he talked baseball with Phillips and Sergeant Jacovitch. Ranatti and Simeone had not returned since taking the fruit to jail, but Roy heard Jacovitch mention their names during a phone conversation and he cursed when he hung up and muttered something to Gant while Roy glanced over vice reports in the other room.

Ranatti and Simeone rushed in just after midnight. "Ready to raid The Cave?" Ranatti grinned.

"I got a call, Rosso," said Jacovitch quietly. "Some whore called and asked for the sergeant. Said her name was Rosie Redfield and that you guys tore the wiring out of her car and flattened her tires."

"Us?" said Ranatti.

"She named you," said Jacovitch soberly to the young men who did not seem overly surprised.

"That's the whore that thinks she owns Sixth and Alvarado," said Simeone. "We told you about her, Jake. We busted her three times last month and she got her cases consolidated and got summary probation. We've done everything to try to get her to hustle someplace else. Hell, we got two vice complaints about her hustling on that corner."

"Did you know where she parked her car?" asked Jacovitch.

"Yeah, we know," Ranatti admitted. "Did she say she saw us fucking up her car?"

"No, if she did, I'd have to take a personnel complaint against you. You realize that, don't you? There'd be an investigation. She just suspects it was you."

"This ain't no game we're playing out there," said Simeone. "We've done our best to get rid of that bitch. She's not just a whore, she's a booster and a hugger mugger and everything else. She's a rotten bitch and works for Silver Shapiro and he's a rotten pimp and extortionist and God knows what all."

"I'm not even going to ask you if you did it," said Jacovitch, "but I'm warning you guys for the last time about this kind of stuff. You got to stay strictly within the law and Department regulations."

"You know what, Jake?" asked Ranatti, sitting heavily in a chair, and propping a crepe-soled shoe on a typewriter table. "If we did just that, we wouldn't convict one asshole a week. The goddamn streets wouldn't be safe even for us."

It was five minutes till one when Roy parked his private car at Fourth and Broadway and walked toward Main in the direction of The Cave. It was a warm evening, but he shivered as he stood waiting for a green light. He knew the rest of the squad was ready and already in position and he knew there was no particular danger in this, but he was unarmed and felt terribly alone and vulnerable. He walked timorously through the oval doorway of The Cave and stood for a moment adjusting his eyes to the blackness, bumping his head on a plaster stalactite which hung down next to the second entryway. The spacious interior was jammed with people and he shouldered his way to the bar, already beginning to perspire, and found a space to stand between a leering red-haired homosexual and a Negro prostitute who looked him over and apparently did not find him as interesting as the balding man to her left who nervously rubbed his shoulder against her large loose breasts.

Roy started to order a whiskey and soda, remembered Ranatti, and asked for a bottle of beer instead. He ignored the glass, wiped the mouth of the bottle with his hand and drank from the bottle.

Roy saw several booths and tables occupied by lesbians, the butches fondling the femmes, kissing shoulders and arms. Homosexual male couples filled a good part of the room but when one couple tried to dance, mannish female waitresses ordered them to sit, pointing at the "No Dancing" sign. There were prostitutes of all descriptions some of whom were plainly men masquerading as women, but the Negro next to him was certainly a woman, he thought, as she shook a shoulder strap free so the bald man could see more of the vast brown orbs.

Roy saw a group of leather jackets behind a latticework partition which seemed to be drawing a group of onlookers and he squeezed past several people milling in the aisles and beating the tables with glasses to the strident sounds of an outrageous red jukebox. When he got to the latticework he peered through and saw two young men, long sideburned twins with chain belts, arm wrestling on a swaying table with a burning candle at each side of the table to scorch the back of the loser's hand. Two men watched fascinated from a booth to Roy's right. One was collegiate-looking and blond. The other was equally clean-cut, with thick dark hair. They looked as out of place as Roy felt he must look, but when the curling hair on one wrestler's hand began sizzling in the flame of the candle, the young blond man squeezed the thigh of the other, who responded with an excited gasp, and as the candle burned flesh, he held the ear of his blond friend and twisted it violently. No one but Roy seemed to notice, as the onlookers worshiped the searing flame.

Roy returned to the bar and ordered a second beer and a third. It was almost one-thirty and he thought the information had been false when suddenly the juke-box was unplugged and the crowd became silent.

"Lock the door," shouted the bartender, a hairy giant, who announced to the crowd, "The show starts now. Nobody leaves till it's over."

Roy watched the butch waitress switch on the movie projector which was placed on a table near the lattice-work that divided the two sections of the room. The white wall was the projection screen and the crowd burst into laughter as a silent Woody Woodpecker cartoon flashed on the wall.

Roy was trying to figure it all out when Woody Woodpecker was suddenly replaced by two oiled naked men who were wrestling on a filthy mat in a ramshackle gymnasium. A cheer went up from the leather jackets across the floor, but after a few moments the scene shifted abruptly to two naked women, one young and reasonably attractive, the other puffy and middle-aged. They nibbled and kissed and fondled on an unmade bed for a few moments while the lesbian tables whistled, but the scene shifted another time to a backyard where a woman in a puckered bathing suit orally copulated a fat man in khaki shorts and most of the crowd laughed but no one cheered. Then it was back to the naked male wrestlers which brought some more groans and catcalls from the leather jackets. When the film slipped off the sprocket and the picture jumped out of focus in a crucial scene in the lewd wrestling match, Roy was surprised to see the bald man, who had previously been interested in the Negro prostitute, jerk off his brown loafer and begin banging on the bar shouting, "Fix it! Hurry up, fix the goddamn thing!" After that, he left the prostitute and joined the leather jackets in the other room.

They were still working on the film when Roy sidled along the bar toward the men's restroom. He walked unnoticed through a doorway and found himself in a dimly lit corridor and saw a sign marked "Women?" on the left and "Men?" on the right. He entered the men's restroom, smelled marijuana unmistakably, and found a leather jacket just coming from the toilet by the open window.

Roy pretended to wash his hands while the young man, in Levis, cleated boots, and leather jacket, fumbled drunkenly with the chain around his waist. He had an enormous head with unkempt hair and a ragged light brown moustache.

Roy stalled for a moment and fidgeted with a paper towel but could not get to the window for the signal.

Finally the leather jacket looked at him. "I'm not interested right now, blondie," he leered. "See me later. Give me your phone number."

"Go to hell," Roy said, infuriated, forgetting the window for a moment.

"Oh, you got a little spunk? I like that," said the leather jacket and he put his fists on his hips and looked even thicker through the chest and back. "Maybe you could interest me after all," he grinned lasciviously.

"Stay right there," warned Roy to the advancing barrel-chested sadist, who began uncoiling the chain around his waist.

Roy then, at that moment, for the first time in his life knew real fear, hopeless fear, which debilitated, overwhelmed, flashed and froze him. He was panic-stricken and never clearly knew how he had done it, but he knew later that he kicked the assailant once, just as the chain writhed and slid around his fist. The leather jacket screamed and fell to the floor holding his groin with one hand but grabbed Roy's leg with the other and as Roy pulled frantically the whiskered face pressed on his leg and Roy felt the teeth, but jerked free as the teeth closed on his calf. He heard a tearing noise and saw a patch of his trousers hanging from the whiskered mouth, and then Roy leaped over him into the toilet area and thought wildly that the other leather jackets had heard the scream. Roy hurled a metal wastebasket through the glass and scrambled out the window, dropping five feet to a concrete walk where he was struck by the beam of a flashlight in the hand of a uniformed policeman.

"You the vice officer we're waiting for?" the officer whispered.

"Yeah, let's go," Roy said and ran for the front of The Cave where he saw a dozen blue uniforms already approaching. The vice car zoomed up in the front of the bar and Gant and Ranatti alighted carrying "the key" and they slammed it into the double doors of The Cave as Roy shuffled across the sidewalk and sat on the fender of the vice car and felt like he would vomit.

Roy stepped back away from the entrance and decided he was too sick to go back into that foul steamy place and he watched the door finally fall from the hinges and the wagon pulled up in front. Now there were at least fifteen bluesuits and they formed a sweeping V and Roy was panting from his heart-cracking effort, thinking now he would vomit, and he watched the vast blue wedge of bodies insert itself into the opening of The Cave. Soon the blue line disappeared inside and the others came squirming, running, tumbling out. The drunks were thrown into the wagon expertly by two big policemen wearing black gloves. The others were shoved into various directions, and Roy, holding a handkerchief over his mouth, watched them as they spilled into the street, all gray and brown and faceless now as the lights over the entrance were turned off and the garish colors and frivolity were extinguished. Roy wondered when they would stop coming but after five minutes they still flowed out into the street, noisy and perspiring. Roy thought he could smell them, and they flowed swiftly up and down the street when they hit the sidewalk, those who were not being booked. Soon Roy saw two policemen helping the leather-covered bear out the door and he was still holding his groin. Roy was about to tell them to book that one, but he saw he was being put in the wagon anyway so he remained silent and continued watching in sickened fascination until the street was quiet and the cathartic blue wedge of policemen withdrew from the mouth of The Cave. The wagon drove off as Ranatti and Simeone and Gant had the owner and two barmaids in custody and were nailing the broken front door closed and padlocking it.

"What's the matter, kid?" asked Gant walking up to Roy who still had the handkerchief held to his mouth.

"I had a little scuffle in there."

"You did?" said Gant, putting a hand on each of Roy's shoulders.

"I'm sick," said Roy.

"Did you get hurt?" asked Gant, his eyes wide as he examined Roy's face.

"I'm just sick," said Roy, shaking his head. "I just saw the asshole of the world get a blue enema."

"Yeah? Well get used to it, kid," said Gant. "Everything you seen in there will be legal before long."

"Let's get out of here," Simeone called from behind the wheel of the vice car. He pointed at a crawling yellow street cleaner which was inching down Main Street. Roy and Gant squeezed in the car with the arrestees and Simeone and Ranatti.

Roy leaned out the window as they drove away and saw the street cleaner squirt a stream of water over the street and curb around The Cave. The machine hissed and roared and Roy watched the filth being washed away.

AUGUST 1963

13. The Madonna

Serge wondered if any of his academy classmates had plainclothes assignments yet. Probably Fehler or Isenberg and a few of the others had made it to vice or to a felony squad. But not many of them, he guessed. He had been astonished when Sergeant Farrell asked him if he would like to work felony cars this month and then if he worked out it might be a permanent assignment.

This was his second week in F-Cars. He had never realized how much more comfortable it could be to do police work in a business suit rather than the heavy woolen uniforms and unwieldy Sam Browne belt. He wore a four-inch lightweight Colt which he had just bought last payday after seeing how heavy the six-inch Smith rides on your hip in a plainclothes holster.

He suspected that Milton had recommended him to Sergeant Farrell for the F-Car. Milton and Farrell were friends and Farrell seemed to like and respect the old man. However he got here, it was fine to get out of the black and white car for a while. Not that the street people did not know them, two men in business suits, in a low priced, four-door Plymouth—two men who drove slowly and watched streets and people. But at least they were inconspicuous enough to avoid being troubled by the endless numbers of people who need a policeman to solve an endless number of problems that a policeman is not qualified to solve, but must make an attempt to solve, because he is an easily accessible member of the establishment and traditionally vulnerable to criticism. Serge happily blew three smoke rings which would have been perfect except that the breeze took them, the breeze which was pleasant because it had been a very hot summer and the nights were not as cool as Los Angeles nights usually are.

Serge's partner, Harry Ralston, seemed to sense his contentment.

"Think you're going to like F-Cars?" he grinned, turning toward Serge who was slumped in the seat, admiring an exceptionally voluptuous girl in a clinging white cotton dress.

"I'm going to like it," Serge smiled.

"I know how you feel. It's great to get out of uniform, ain't it?"

"Great."

"I was in uniform eight years," said Ralston. "I was really ready. Got five years in felony cars now, and I still like it. Beats uniform patrol."

"I've got a lot to learn," said Serge.

"You'll learn. It's different from patrol. You're already learning that, I think."

Serge nodded, dropping the cigarette out the window, a luxury he never could have allowed himself in a black and white car where some citizen with an ax to grind might take his car number and report him to his sergeant for the vehicle code violation of dropping the lighted substance from a car.

"Ready for code seven?" asked Ralston, looking at his watch. "It's not nine o'clock yet, but I'm hungry as hell."

"I can eat," said Serge, picking up the mike. "Four-Frank-One requesting code seven at Brooklyn and Mott."

"Four-Frank-One, okay seven," said the Communications operator and Serge checked his watch to be sure and clear over the radio when their forty-five minutes were up. It irritated him that the Department made them work an eight hour and forty-five minute shift. Since the forty-five minutes was his own time, he made sure he used every minute of it.

"Hello, Mr. Rosales," said Ralston, as they took the booth on the far wall nearest the kitchen. It was noisy and hot from the stoves in this particular booth, but Ralston loved to be near the kitchen smells. He was a man who lived to eat, Serge thought, and his incredible appetite belied his lankiness.

"Good evening, señores," smiled the old man, coming from behind the counter where three customers sat. He wiped the table which needed no wiping. He poured two glasses of water for them after swiping at the inside of Ralston's already sparkling glass with a dazzling white towel he carried over a sloping shoulder. The old man wore a full moustache which exactly suited him, Serge thought.

"What will you have, señores?" asked Mr. Rosales, giving them each a hand-printed menu that misspelled the dishes in Spanish on the right side as well as in English on the left side. They can live here all their lives and never learn English, thought Serge. They never learn Spanish either. Just a strange anglicized version of both, which the educated, old country Mexicans scoff at.

"I'll have *huevos rancheros*," said Ralston, with an accent that made Serge wince in spite of himself.

The old man seemed to love it however, when Ralston tried Spanish. "And you, señor?"

"I guess I'll have *chile relleno*," said Serge with a pronunciation that was every bit as anglicized as Ralston's. All of the officers knew by now that he spoke no Spanish and understood only a few words.

"Smell the onions and green chile," said Ralston while Mr. Rosales' pudgy little wife was preparing the food in the back room which had been converted into an inadequately ventilated kitchen.

"How can you tell it's green chile?" asked Serge, feeling jovial tonight. "Maybe it's red chile or maybe it's not chile at all."

"My nose never fails," said Ralston, touching the side of his nostril. "You should quit smoking and your sense of smell would become acute like mine."

Serge thought that a beer would do good with the *chile relleno* and he wondered if Ralston knew Serge better, would he order a beer with his dinner? They were working plainclothes now, and a beer with dinner wouldn't hurt. Vice officers of course drank freely, and detectives were legendary lushes, so why not F-Car officers? he thought. But he realized that he was drinking too much beer lately and was going to have to trim off ten pounds before his next physical or the doctor would surely send his captain "a fat man letter." He hadn't had much beer in Hollywood where martinis were his drink. It had been very easy to get to enjoy martinis. He had been drunk a good deal of his off-duty time. But that was all part of his education, he thought. The body should not be mistreated, at least not badly. He was considering cutting down his smoking to a pack a day and had again begun playing handball at the academy.

There was something about being back in Hollenbeck that restored his health.

He looked more than casually at the girl who brought their dinners, holding the burning dishes with two colorful pot holders, the drops of perspiration shining on her bronze cheekbones and on the too long upper lip. She wore her hair braided, close to the head like an Indian and Serge guessed she was not more than seventeen. Her hands were ghostly white from the flour and they reminded him of his mother's hands. He wondered how long she had been this side of the border.

"Thank you," he said, smiling as she set the plate in front of him. She smiled back, a clean smile, and Serge noticed she wore only a little lipstick. The heavy eyelashes and perfect brows were not man-made.

"*Gracias, señorita,*" said Ralston, leering at the plate of *huevos rancheros* and ignoring the girl who placed it in front of him.

"*De nada, señor,*" she smiled again.

"Cute kid," said Serge, toying with the rice and refried beans which were still too hot to eat.

Ralston nodded with enthusiasm, and dumped another ladle of homemade chile sauce on the eggs, the rice, everything. Then he sloshed his large flour tortilla around through all of it and took an enormous bite.

Mr. Rosales whispered to the girl and she returned to the table just as Serge's food was becoming cool enough to eat and Ralston's was half gone.

"Joo wan'," she said. "Joo weesh . . ." She stopped and turned to Mr. Rosales who nodded his approval.

"Coffee," he urged her. "Coff—ee."

"I don' talk *inglés* good," she laughed to Serge who was thinking how smooth and slim she looked, yet how strong. Her breasts were round and the extra weight womanhood brings could only improve her.

"I'll have some more coffee," Serge smiled.

"*Sí café, por favor,*" said Ralston, a forkful of frijoles poised at his mobile lip.

When the girl disappeared into the kitchen Mr. Rosales came over to the table. "Everything is alright?" he smiled through the great moustache.

"Dee-licious," Ralston murmured.

"Who's the little girl?" asked Serge, sipping at the last of his water which Mr. Rosales hurried to refill.

"She is the daughter of my *compadre*. She just got here from Guadalajara last Monday. I swore to my *compadre* many years ago that if I ever made good in this country I would send for his oldest girl, my godchild, and educate her like an American. He said it would be better to educate a boy and I agreed, but he never had a boy. Not to this day. Eleven girls."

Serge laughed and said, "She looks like she'll do."

"Yes, Mariana is very smart," he nodded enthusiastically. "And she was just eighteen. I am sending her to night school next month to learn English and then we shall see what she wants to do."

"She'll probably find some young guy and get married before you have anything to say about it," said Ralston, punctuating his pronouncement with a repressed belch.

"Maybe so," Mr. Rosales sighed. "You know, it is so much better here than in Mexico that the people do not care to make themselves a great success. Just to be here is so much more than they ever dreamed, that it is enough. They become content to work in a car wash or a sewing factory. But I think that she is a smart girl and will do better."

The girl made three trips to their table during the remainder of the meal, but didn't try English again.

Ralston caught Serge watching her because he said, "She's legal, you know. Eighteen."

"You're kidding. I wouldn't raid a nursery."

"Some baby," said Ralston and Serge hoped he wouldn't light one of his cheap cigars. When they were in the car with the windows open they weren't so bad. "She looks like a young Dolores Del Rio to me," said Ralston, blowing two heavy palls of smoke over the table.

She did not resemble Dolores Del Rio, Serge thought. But she had the thing that made Del Rio the beloved woman of Mexico, an object of veneration by millions of Mexicans who had seldom if ever seen her in a movie—she too had the madonna look.

"What's your last name?" asked Serge, as she made her last trip to the table with a coffee refill. He knew it was customary for policemen who had received a free meal to tip a quarter, but he slipped seventy-five cents under a plate.

"Mande, señor?" she said turning to Mr. Rosales who was busy with a counter customer.

"Your last name," said Ralston carefully. "Mariana *qué?"*

"Ah," she smiled. "Mariana Paloma," and then she turned from Serge's steady gaze and took some of the plates to the kitchen.

"Paloma," said Serge. "A dove. It fits."

"I eat here once a week," said Ralston eyeing Serge curiously. "We don't want to burn the place up with too many free meals."

"Don't worry," said Serge quickly, getting the implication. "This is your eating spot. I'll never come here unless I'm working with you."

"The girl is your business," said Ralston. "You can come off duty if you want, but I'd hate for someone to burn up the eating spot I cultivated for years. He used to charge me half price and now it's free."

"Don't worry," Serge repeated. "And that girl doesn't interest me like that, for God's sake. I've got enough female problems without a kid that can't speak English."

"You single guys," Ralston sighed. "I should have those problems. You got one lined up tonight after work?"

"I got one," Serge answered without enthusiasm.

"She got a friend?"

"Not that I know of," Serge smiled.

"What's she look like?" Ralston leered, now that the hunger drive was apparently slaked.

"A honey blonde. All ass," Serge answered, and that about described Margie who lived in the upstairs rear of his apartment building. The landlady had already warned him about being more discreet when he left Margie's apartment in the morning.

"A real honey blonde, huh?" Ralston murmured.

"What's real?" asked Serge, and then thought, she's real enough in her own way, and it doesn't matter if the glistening honey is the fruit of the hairdresser's art because everything of beauty in the world has been tinted or somehow transformed by a clever artisan. You can always discover how it's done if you look closely enough. But who wants to look? During those times when he needed her, Margie was plenty real, he thought.

"What's a bachelor do besides lay everything in sight?" asked Ralston. "You happy being alone?"

"I don't even want a roommate to share expenses. I like being alone." Serge was the first to get up and turned to look for the girl who was out of sight in the kitchen.

"*Buenas noches,* Señor Rosales," Ralston called.

"*Ándale pues,*" shouted Mr. Rosales, over the din of a too loud mariachi record which someone had played on the jukebox.

"You watch TV a lot?" asked Ralston when they were back in the car. "I'm asking about single life because me and the old lady aren't getting along very good at all right now and who knows what might happen."

"Oh?" said Serge hoping Ralston would not bore him with a long account of his marital problems which so many other partners had done during the long hours on patrol when the night was quiet because it was a week night, when the people were between paydays and welfare checks, and were not drinking. "Well, I read a lot, novels mostly. I play handball at least three or four times a week at the academy. I go to movies and watch a little TV. I got to a lot of Dodger games. There isn't all the carousing you think." And then he remembered Hollywood again. "At least not anymore. That can get old, too."

"Maybe I'll be finding out," said Ralston, driving toward Hollenbeck Park.

Serge took the flashlight from under the seat and placed it on the seat beside him. He turned the volume of the radio up slightly, hoping it would dissuade Ralston from trying to compete with it, but Serge felt certain he was going to hear a domestic tirade.

"Four-Frank-One, clear," said Serge into the mike.

"Maybe you can entice little Dolores Del Rio to your pad if you play your cards right," said Ralston as the Communications operator acknowledged they were clear. Ralston began a slow halfhearted residential burglar patrol in the area east of the park which had been hard hit by a cat burglar the past few weeks. They had already decided that after midnight, they would prowl the streets on foot which seemed to be the only effective way to catch the cat.

"I told you that babies don't interest me," said Serge.

"Maybe she's got a cousin or a fat aunt or something. I'm ready for some action. My old lady shut me off. I could grow a long moustache for her like that actor that plays in all the Mexican movies, what's his name?"

"Pedro Armendariz," said Serge without thinking.

"Yeah, that guy. It seems like he's on every marquee around here, him and Dolores."

"They were even the big stars when I was a kid," said Serge gazing at the cloudless sky which was only slightly smoggy tonight.

"Yeah? You went to Mexican movies? I thought you don't speak Spanish."

"I understood a little when I was a kid," Serge answered, sitting up in the seat. "Anybody could understand those simple pictures. All guns and guitars."

Ralston quieted down and the radio droned on and he relaxed again. He found himself thinking of the little dove and he wondered if she would be as satisfying as Elenita who was the first girl he ever had, the dusky fifteen-year-old daughter of a bracero who was well worn by the time she seduced Serge when he himself was fifteen. He had returned to her every Friday night for a year and sometimes she would have him, but sometimes there would be older boys already there and he would go away to avoid trouble. Elenita was everybody's girl but he liked to pretend she was his girl until one June afternoon when the gossip blazed through the school that Elenita had been taken from school because she was pregnant. Several boys, mostly the members of the football squad, began to talk in frightened whispers. Then came the rumor a few days later that Elenita was also found to have been syphilitic and the frightened whispers became frantic. Serge had terrible fantasies of elephantine pus-filled genitals and he prayed and lit three candles every other day until he felt the danger period had passed even though he never knew for sure if it had, or even whether poor Elenita was really so afflicted. He could ill afford thirty cents for candles in those days when the part-time gas pumping job only netted nine dollars a week which he had to give to his mother.

Then he felt guilty for thinking about the girl Mariana like this because eighteen years, despite what the law said, did not make you an adult. He was twenty-six now and wondered if another ten years would do the job for him. If he could continue to profit from all the lies and cruelty and violence this job had shown him, maybe he could grow up sooner. If he could quit seeing a saint in the tawny face of a perfectly healthy little animal like Mariana he would be so much closer to maturity. Maybe that's the part of being a Chicano I can't shake off, Serge thought, the superstitious longing —brown magic—The Sorceress of Guadelupe—or Guadalajara—a simple bastard yearning for the Madonna in a miserable Mexican restaurant.

14. The Operator

"No wonder Plebesly gets more whore offers than anybody else on the squad. Look at him. Does this boy look
like a cop?" roared Bonelli, stocky, middle-aged and
balding, with dark whiskers which when they were two
days old were dirty gray. They always seemed at least
two days old, and whenever Sergeant Anderson objected, Bonelli just reminded him that this was Wilshire
vice squad and not a goddamned military academy and
he was only trying to look like the rest of the assholes
out on the street so he could fit in better as an undercover operator. He always addressed Anderson by his
first name which was Mike and so did the others because it was customary in a vice squad to be more intimate with your supervisors, but Gus did not like or
trust Anderson and neither did the others. He was on
the lieutenant's list and would probably someday be a
captain at least, but the lanky young man with the blond
sparse moustache was a natural disciplinarian and would
be better, they all concluded, in a patrol function which
was more GI than a vice squad.

"One whore Gus got last week never did believe he
was a cop," laughed Bonelli, throwing his feet up on the
table in the vice office and spilling some cigar ashes on
a report which Sergeant Anderson was writing. Anderson's lips tightened under the pale moustache, but he
said nothing, got up and went to his own desk to work.

"I remember that one, Sal," said Petrie to Bonelli.
"Old Salvatore had to save Gus from that whore. She
thought he was a PO-lice impersonator when he finally
badged her."

They all laughed at Petrie's affected Negro dialect,
even Hunter, the slim Negro officer who was the only
Negro on the night watch. He laughed heartily, but Gus
laughed nervously partly because they were roasting him
but partly because he could never get used to Negro
jokes in front of a Negro even though he had been a
vice officer for three months now and should be accus-

tomed to the merciless chiding which went on ritually every night before they went out to the streets. Each of them subjected the other to cracks which stopped at neither race, religion, or physical defects.

Yet the six policemen and Sergeant Handle, who was one of *them*, went to Bonelli's apartment at least once a week after work and played pool and drank a case of beer at least. Or sometimes they went to Sergeant Handle's house and played poker all night. Once when they had gone to Hunter's apartment which was here in Wilshire Division in the racially mixed neighborhood near Pico and La Brea, Bonelli had made a whispered remark to Hunter that he had been kicked in the shoulder by a whore while making a lewd conduct arrest and that at his age arthritis might set in. Bonelli couldn't pull the sleeve of his outrageous Hawaiian shirt over the hairy shoulder to show Hunter because the shoulder was too large, and finally, Bonelli said, "Anyway, the bruise is the color of your ass." When Hunter's lithe mahogany-colored wife Marie, who had entered the room unnoticed, said, "What, red?" with a perfectly sober expression, Gus began to enjoy the camaraderie which was not affected or strained and did not pretend that being policemen made them brothers or more than brothers.

But they did have a secret which seemed to unite them more closely than normal friendship and that was the knowledge that they *knew* things, basic things about strength and weakness, courage and fear, good and evil, especially good and evil. Even though arguments would rage especially when Bonelli was drunk, they all agreed on very fundamental things and usually did not discuss these things because any policeman who had common sense and had been a policeman long enough would surely learn the truth and it was useless to talk about it. They mostly talked about their work and women, and either fishing, golf, or baseball, depending upon whether Farrell or Schulmann or Hunter was controlling the conversation. But when Petrie was working they talked about movies, since Petrie had an uncle who was a director, and Petrie was starstruck even though he had been a policeman five years.

There were a few more cracks made about Gus's meek appearance and how none of the whores could believe he was a policeman which made him the best whore operator on the watch, but then they began talking about other things because Gus never joked back and it was not as much fun as picking on Bonelli who had a caustic tongue and was quick at repartee.

"Hey Marty," said Farrell to Hunter who was trying to pencil out a follow-up to a vice complaint. He held his forehead in a smooth brown hand while the pencil moved jerkily and stopped often while Hunter laughed at something Bonelli said. It was obvious that Hunter would rather work with Bonelli than any of the others, but Sergeant Anderson figured the deployment carefully so that certain men were working on certain nights because he had fixed opinions on supervision and deployment. He informed them that he was very close to his degree in government and he had twelve units in psychology and only *he* was in a position to know who should work with whom, and Bonelli had whispered gruffly, "How did this cunt get on the vice squad?"

"Hey, Marty," Farrell repeated, until Hunter looked up. "How come you people are always complaining that there aren't enough blacks in this job or that group or something and then when we *do* use enough you still bitch. Listen to this article in the *Times*, 'The NAACP sought a class action on behalf of all the men on death's row because it contends a disproportionate number of them are Negroes.'"

"People are never satisfied," said Hunter.

"By the way Marty, you getting your share of that white liberal pussy that's floating around the *ghetto* these days?" asked Bernbaum.

"Marty's going to pass the sergeant's exam this time, ain't you, Marty," said Bonelli. "He'll get forty points on his own and they'll give him forty more for being black."

"And when we get to be on top, first thing I'm going to do is go after your woman, Sal," said Hunter, glancing up from his report.

"Oh, Christ, Marty, do me a favor, go after Elsie right now, will you? That bitch does nothing but talk about marriage anymore and me with three divorces behind me. I need another wife like . . ."

"Do any of you have any rubbers?" asked Sergeant Anderson, suddenly walking into the working area of the vice office separated from his desk by a row of lockers.

"No, if we think a broad is bad enough for rubbers, we generally get a head job," said Farrell, his close-set blue eyes examining Anderson with humor.

"I was referring to the use of rubbers for evidence containers," said Anderson coldly. "We still use them to pour drinks into, don't we?"

"We got a box in the locker, Mike," said Bonelli, and they became quiet when they saw he disliked Farrell's joke. "Working a bar tonight?"

"We've had a complaint about The Cellar for two weeks now. I thought we'd try to take it."

"They serving after hours?" asked Farrell.

"If you could take time out from your joke writing and look at the vice complaints you'd see that the bartender at The Cellar lives in an apartment upstairs and that after two o'clock he sometimes invites customers up to the pad where he continues to operate a bar. After hours."

"We'll try it for you tonight, Mike," said Bonelli with his conciliatory tone, but Gus thought that the heavily browed brown eyes were not conciliatory. They fixed Anderson with a bland expression.

"I want to work it myself," said Anderson. "I'll meet you and Plebesly at Third and Western at eleven and we'll decide then whether to go together or separate."

"I can't go at all," said Bonelli. "I made too many pinches around there. The bartender knows me."

"Might be a good idea for you to go in with one of us," said Bernbaum, scratching his wiry brush of red hair with a pencil. "We could have a drink and leave. They wouldn't suspect the joint was full of cops. They'd probably be satisfied that everything was cool after us two left."

"I think there's a couple of whores working in there," said Hunter. "Me and Bonelli were in there one night and there was an ugly little brunette and another old bat that sure looked like hookers."

"Alright, we'll all meet at Andre's Restaurant at eleven and talk it over," said Anderson going back to his desk. "And another thing, the streetwalkers are getting pretty thick out there on Sunday and Monday nights, I hear. They must know those are the vice squad's nights off so some of you are going to start working Sundays."

"You guys see those magazines the day watch picked

up at a trick pad?" asked Bernbaum, and the conversation again picked up now that Anderson was finished.

"I seen enough of that garbage to last me a lifetime," said Bonelli.

"No, these weren't regular nudie mags," said Bernbaum. "These were pinup mags, but somebody had taken about a hundred Polaroid pictures of guys' dicks and cut them out and stuck them on the girls in the magazines."

"Psychos. The world is full of psychos," said Farrell.

"By the way, are we working fruits tonight, Marty?" asked Petrie.

"Lord, no. We busted enough last week to last all month."

"Think I'll go on days for a while," said Bernbaum. "I'd like to work books. Get me away from all these slimes you have to bust at night."

"Well I'll guarantee you, bookmakers are assholes," said Bonelli. "They're mostly Jews, ain't they?"

"Oh yeah, the Mafia's all Jews too," said Bernbaum. "I think there's a few Italian bookmakers up on Eighth Street last I heard."

Gus felt Bonelli look at him when Bernbaum said it and he knew Bonelli was thinking about Lou Scalise, the bookmaking agent and collector for the loan sharks whom Bonelli hated with a hatred that now made Gus's palms sweat as he thought of it.

"Incidentally, Petrie," said Marty Hunter, slamming the logbook, "the next time we take a fighter, how about using the sap on *him*, not on *me*. Last night we take Biff's Cocktail Lounge for serving a drunk and when we try to bust the drunk he starts a fight and *I* get sapped by my partner."

"Bullshit, Marty. I just grazed your elbow with the sap."

"Anytime more than one policeman jumps a suspect the policeman ends up getting hurt," said Farrell. "I remember the night we had that fairy lumberjack." They laughed and Farrell looked appealingly to Bonelli. "Yeah the guy was a lumberman from Oregon. And he's a suck*or* not a suck*ee*. Comes to L.A. and wears eye shadow. Anyway, he's swishing around Lafayette Park and gropes Bonelli, remember, Sal?"

"I'll never forget that asshole."

"Anyway, there were five of us in the park that night

and for fifteen minutes we all battle that puke. He threw me in the pond and threw Steve in there twice. We thumped the shit out of each other with saps and it finally ended when Sal held his head underwater for a few minutes. He never did get sapped or even hurt and every one of us policemen had to get patched up."

"Funny thing," said Bernbaum, "when Sal had him about half drowned and he was panicky and all, know what he does? He yells, 'Help, police!' Imagine that, with five policemen all over him, he yells that."

"He know you were policemen?" asked Gus.

"Sure he knew," said Farrell. "He said to Bonelli, 'Ain't no cop in the world can take me.' He didn't figure on five, though."

"I had a guy yell that one time when I was in full uniform," said Bernbaum. "Funny what people say when you're wrestling them off to jail."

"Garbage," said Bonelli. "Garbage."

"You handle these assholes, you got to wash your hands *before* you take a leak," said Hunter.

"Remember the time the swish kissed you, Ben?" said Farrell to Bernbaum, and the ruddy-faced young policeman winced in disgust.

"Walked into a bar where we got a complaint some fruits were dancing," said Hunter, "and this little blond swish flits right up to Ben as we were sitting at the bar and plants a smack right on his kisser and then he dances away into the dark. Ben goes to the head and washes his mouth with hand soap and we leave without even working the joint."

"I heard enough. I'm going to take a crap and then we're going to work," said Bonelli standing up, scratching his stomach and lumbering toward the toilet across the hall.

"You say you're going in there to give birth to a sergeant?" said Farrell, winking at Petrie who shook his head and whispered, "Anderson doesn't appreciate your humor."

When Bonelli returned, he and Gus gathered their binoculars and small flashlights and batons which they would put under the seat of the vice car in case of emergency. After reassuring Anderson they wouldn't forget to meet him they went to their car without deciding what they were going to do.

"Want to work complaints, or whores?" asked Bonelli.

"We got some crappy three eighteens," said Gus. "One about the floating card game in the hotel sounds like fun, but it only goes on Saturdays."

"Yeah, let's work whores," said Bonelli.

"Tail or operate?"

"Feel like operating?"

"I don't mind. I'll get my car," said Gus.

"Got enough gas? That cheap prick Anderson won't break loose with any more operating money till next week. You'd think it was his bread and not the city's."

"I've got gas," said Gus. "I'll take a sweep around Washington and La Brea and meet you in the back of the drive-in in fifteen minutes. Sooner, if I get a whore."

"Get a whore. We need the pinches. This's been a slim month."

Gus drove down West Boulevard to Washington and over Washington toward La Brea, but he hadn't gotten two blocks on Washington until he spotted two prostitutes. He was preparing to swing in toward the curb when he saw one was Margaret Pearl whom he had arrested almost three months ago when he first came to the vice squad and she would surely recognize him so he drove past. Already the pulse beat was advancing.

Gus remembered how it had been when he had first come to vice, or rather, he did not remember clearly. Those first nights and those first few arrests were difficult to envision coherently. There was a red cloud of fear enveloping his memory of those nights and that was something else he could not understand. Why did he see or rather feel a red mist about his memories when he was very much afraid? Why were all such memories red-tinged? Was it blood or fire or what? He had been so thoroughly frightened that the prostitutes had come to his car with their offers without questioning his identity. They hadn't dreamed he was a cop, and he had been a vastly successful vice operator. Now that he had some confidence and was no longer so afraid except of things he should be afraid of, he was having to work much harder to get an offer. He was being turned down occasionally by girls who suspected he might be a policeman. Still, he could get twice the girls that any of the others could, only because he looked less like a policeman than any of them. Bonelli had told him it was not just his size. He was actually as tall and heavy as Marty Hunter. It was his diffidence, and Bonelli said that was a shame because the meek would inherit this miserable earth and Gus was too nice a guy to get stuck with it.

Gus hoped he would spot a white whore tonight. He had only arrested a few white whores and these were in bars on Vermont. He had never gotten a white streetwalker, although there were some of them here in this Negro half of Wilshire Division, but there weren't many. He thought Wilshire Division was a good division to work because of the variety. He could leave this Negro section and drive to the northwest boundaries of the division and be on the Miracle Mile and Restaurant Row. There was great variety in a few square miles. He was glad they had transferred him here, and almost immediately he had been marked as a future vice officer by his watch commander Lieutenant Goskin who had finally recommended him when the opening came. Gus wondered how many of his academy classmates were working plainclothes assignments yet. It was good, and it would be very good when the nauseating fear at last disappeared, the fear of being on the streets alone without the security of the blue uniform and badge. There was not too much else to really fear because if you were careful you would never have to fight anyone alone. If you were careful, you would always have Bonelli with you and Bonelli was as powerful and reassuring as Kilvinsky, but of course he did not have Kilvinsky's intellect.

Gus reminded himself that he had not answered Kilvinsky's last letter and he would do that tomorrow. It had worried him. Kilvinsky did not talk of the fishing and the lake and the peaceful mountains anymore. He talked of his children and his ex-wife and Kilvinsky had never talked of them when he had been here. He told of how his youngest son had written him and how his answer to the boy had been returned unopened and how he and his ex-wife had promised themselves years ago that it would be better if the boy forgot him, but he didn't say why. Gus knew that he had never gone East to visit them at his wife's home, and Gus never knew why, and he thought he would give a great deal to learn Kilvinsky's secrets. The latest letters indicated that

Kilvinsky wanted to tell someone, wanted to tell Gus, and Gus decided to ask the big man to come to Los Angeles for a visit before the summer ended. Lord, it would be good to see his friend, Gus thought.

Then Gus realized he also had to send a check to his mother and John because it was less painful than going to see them and hearing how they could no longer make it on seventy-five a month from him even with the welfare check, because things were so dear today and poor John can't work, what with his slipped disc which Gus knew was an excuse for workman's compensation and a free ride from Gus. He was ashamed of his disgust as he thought of those weaklings and then he thought of Vickie. He wondered why his mother and his brother and his wife were all weaklings and depended so completely on him, and anger made him feel better as always, purged him. He saw a chubby Negro prostitute wiggling down Washington Boulevard toward Cloverdale. He pulled to the curb beside her and feigned the nervous smile which used to come so naturally.

"Hi baby," said the prostitute looking in the window of his car as Gus went through his act of looking around as though fearful of seeing police.

"Hello," said Gus. "Want a ride?"

"I ain't out here to ride, baby," said the prostitute watching him closely. "At least I ain't out here to ride no cars."

"Well I'm ready for anything," said Gus, careful not to use any of the forbidden words of entrapment, even though Sal often argued with him that it is obviously impossible to entrap a whore, and he should only worry about entrapment later while writing the report because following the rules of the game was crazy. But Gus had answered that the rules made it all *civilized*.

"Look, Officer," said the girl suddenly, "why don't you go on up to the academy and play yourself a nice game of handball?"

"What?" said Gus blandly, as she examined his eyes.

"Jist a joke, baby," she said finally. "We got to be careful of vice officers."

"Vice officers? Where?" said Gus gunning his motor. "Maybe we better forget all about this."

"Don't git nervous, honey," she said, getting in the car and moving over to him. "I'll give you such a nice

French that you goin' to be glad you came down here tonight and don't worry none about the vice, I got them all paid off. They never bother me."

"Where should I drive?" asked Gus.

"Down La Brea there. The Notel Motel. They got electric beds that vibrate and mirrors on the walls and ceilings and I got my own room reserved and it ain't goin' to cost you nothin' extra. It's all yours for fifteen dollars."

"That sounds about right," said Gus turning around and bouncing into the drive-in parking lot where Bonelli waited and Sal smiled through the heavy whiskers when he saw the prostitute.

"Hi baby, how's tricks?" said Bonelli opening the door for her.

"Tricks was fine, Mr. Bonelli, till I hit on this one," said the girl looking at Gus in disbelief. "I would a swore he was a trick. He really a cop?"

Gus showed the prostitute his badge and got back in the car.

"He looks too motherfuckin' peaceable to be a cop," said the prostitute in disgust as Gus drove out of the lot for another try before they made the long drive to Lincoln Heights jail.

Gus swept the block twice and then made a wider arc and finally decided to drive north on La Brea toward Venice where he had seen prostitutes the last few nights, and then he saw three Cadillacs parked side by side in the motel parking lot. He recognized a prostitute standing outside the purple Cadillac talking to Eddie Parsons and Big Dog Hanley and another Negro pimp he didn't recognize. Gus remembered the time they had arrested Big Dog when Gus had just arrived in Wilshire Division last year and was still working uniform patrol. They had stopped Big Dog for an unsafe lane change and while Gus was writing the ticket, his partner Drew Watson, an aggressive and inquisitive policeman, had spotted the pearl handle of a .22 revolver protruding from under the seat. He had retrieved it and arrested Big Dog, taking him to the detectives who, since Big Dog was a pimp, and had a five-page rap sheet, decided to book him for robbery, impound his car, and book his roll of flash-money as evidence. When they counted out the bills which came to eight hundred dollars and told Big Dog they were booking the money, he broke down and wept, begging the detective not to book his money because it had been done to him before and it took months to get it back and it was *his* money so please don't book it. This surprised Gus in that Big Dog was at once the most insolent and arrogant of all the pimps and here he was begging for his roll and crying. Then Gus realized that without the roll and the Cadillac, he was nothing, and Big Dog knew it and realized that the other pimps and prostitutes knew it, and he would lose everything. It would be taken away by pimps with a bankroll who commanded respect.

Then Gus saw the white prostitute at Venice and La Brea. He accelerated but she had already reached a red Cadillac hardtop and she was alone and getting in the driver's side when Gus slowed and double-parked next to her. He smiled his carefully rehearsed smile which had seldom failed so far.

"Looking for me, sweetie?" asked the girl, and up close she did not look nearly as good although the tight silver pants and black jersey fit well. Gus could see even in this light that the swirling blond hair was a wig and the makeup was garish.

"I think you're the one I've been looking for," Gus smiled.

"Pull up in front of me and park," said the girl. "Then walk on back here and let's talk."

Gus pulled in at the curb and turned his lights out, slipped the holstered two-inch Smith & Wesson under the seat, got out, and walked back to the Cadillac and up to the driver's side.

"Looking for action, sweetie?" asked the girl with a smile that Gus thought was rehearsed as carefully as his. "Sure am," he shot back with his own version of a smile.

"How much you willing to spend?" she said coyly and reached out the window with a long clawed finger and ran it seductively over his torso while she felt for a gun and he smiled to himself because he had left the gun in the car.

She seemed satisfied not feeling a gun or other evidence that he was a policeman and she apparently saw little use in wasting more time. "How about a nice ten dollar fuck?" she said.

"You don't mince words," said Gus, pulling out the badge he had in his back pocket. "You're under arrest."

"Oh crap," moaned the girl. "Man, I just got out of jail. Oh no," she wailed.

"Let's go," said Gus, opening the door of the Cadillac. "Awright, lemme get my purse," she spat, but turned the key and cramped the wheel hard to the left as the Cadillac lurched forward and Gus, not knowing why, leaped on the side of the car and in only seconds he was clinging to the back of the seat and standing on nothing as the powerful car sped east on Venice. He reached desperately across her for the keys, but she drove her little fist into his face and he slid back and tasted the blood from his nose. His eye caught the speedometer registering sixty and quickly seventy and his lower body was swept backward in a rush of wind and he clung to the seat as the cursing prostitute swerved the Cadillac across three lanes attempting to hurl him to his death and now for the first time he was conscious of exactly what he was doing and he prayed to God the body would not fail him now and it would just cling—that was all—just cling.

There were other cars on Venice. Gus knew this from the blasting horns and squeal of tires but he kept his eyes closed and clung as she beat at his hands with a purse and then with a high-heeled shoe as the Cadillac swerved and skidded on Venice Boulevard. Gus tried to remember a simple prayer from his boyhood because he knew there would be a jarring flaming crash but he couldn't remember the prayer and suddenly there was a giddy sliding turn and he knew this was the end and now he would be hurtled through space like a bullet, but then the car righted itself and was speeding back westbound on Venice the way it had come and Gus thought if he could reach his gun, if he dared release the grip of one hand, he would take her with him to the grave and then he remembered the gun was in his car and he thought if he could crank the wheel now at eighty miles an hour he could flip the Cadillac and that would be as good as the gun. He wanted to, but the body would not obey and would only cling stubbornly to the back cushion of the seat. Then the prostitute began pushing the door open as she cut the wheel back and forth and the force hurtled his feet straight

back and Gus found his voice, but it was a whisper and
she was shrieking curses and the car tape deck had
somehow been turned as loudly as it would go and the
music from the car stereo and roar of the wind and
screams of the prostitute were deafening and he shouted
in her ear, "Please, please, let me go! I won't arrest you
if you'll let me go. Slow down and let me jump!"

She answered by cutting the wheel recklessly to the
right and saying, "Die, you dirty little motherfucker."

Gus saw La Brea coming up and the traffic was
moderate when she slashed through the red light at
ninety miles an hour and Gus heard the unmistakable
screech and crash but still they flew and he knew another car had crashed in the intersection and then all
lanes were blocked east and west just west of La Brea
as a stream of fire trucks lumbered north at the next
intersection. The prostitute slammed on her brakes and
turned left on a dark residential street, but made the
turn much too sharply and the Cadillac slid and righted
and careened to the right and up over a lawn taking out
twenty feet of picket fence which hurtled in clattering
fragments over the hood of the car and cracked the
windshield of the Cadillac which sliced across lawns and
through hedges with the prostitute riding the burning
brakes and the lawns hurtling by were coming slower
and slower and Gus guessed the car was going only
thirty miles an hour when he let go but he hit the grass
with a shock and his body coiled and rolled without
command but he was still rolling when he crashed into
a parked car and sat there for a long moment as the
earth moved up and down. Then he was on his feet as
the lights were being turned on all over the block and
the neighborhood dogs had gone mad and the Cadillac
was now almost out of sight.

Gus then started to run as the people poured from the
houses. He was almost at La Brea when he began to
feel the pain in his hip and his arm and several other
places and he wondered why he was running, but right
now it was the only thing that made sense. So he ran
faster and faster and then he was at his car and driving, but his legs, although they would run, would not be
still enough to maneuver the car, and twice he had to
stop and rub them before reaching the station. He drove
his car to the rear of the station and went in the back

door and down to the bathroom where he examined his gray face which was badly scratched and bruised from the blows. When he washed away the blood it didn't look bad but his left knee was mushy and the sweat dried cold on his chest and back. Then he noticed the terrible smell and his stomach turned as he realized what it was and he hurried to the locker thankful that he kept a sport coat and slacks in case he tore his clothing prowling or in case an assignment demanded a dressier appearance. He crept back down to the restroom and cleansed his legs and buttocks, sobbing breathlessly in shame and fear and relief.

After he was washed, he put on the clean slacks and rolled the trousers and soiled underwear into a ball and threw the stinking bundle outside in the trash can at the rear of the station. He got back in the car and drove to the drive-in where he knew Bonelli would be frantic because he had been gone almost an hour and he was still uncertain if he could carry off the lie when he drove to the rear of the restaurant. He found Bonelli with two radio cars who had begun a search for Gus. He told the lie which he had formulated while the tears choked him as he drove to the restaurant. He had to lie because if they knew they had a policeman who was so stupid he would jump on the side of a car, why they would kick him off the squad, and rightly so, for such an officer certainly would need more seasoning—if not a psychiatrist. So he told them an elaborate lie about a prostitute who had hit him in the face with a shoe and had leaped from his car and how he had chased her through alleys on foot for a half hour and finally lost her. Bonelli had told him it was dangerous to go off alone away from your car but he was so damned glad to see Gus was alright that he dropped it at that not even noticing the clothes change, and they drove to the Main Jail. Several times Gus thought he would break down and weep and in fact he twice stifled a sob. But he did not break down and after an hour or so his legs and hands stopped shaking completely. But he could not eat and when they stopped later for a hamburger he had almost gotten sick at the sight of food.

"You look awful," said Bonelli, after he had eaten and they were cruising down Wilshire Boulevard. Gus was looking out the window at the street and the cars and people, feeling not elated at being still alive but darkly depressed. He wished for a moment that the car had overturned during that bowel-searing moment when she had skidded and he knew they were doing ninety.

"I guess that hassle with the whore was a little too much for me," Gus said.

"How far you say you chased that whore?" asked Bonelli with a look of disbelief.

"Several blocks I guess. Why?"

"I happen to know you run like a cougar. How come you couldn't catch her?"

"Well, the truth is, she kicked me in the balls, Sal. I was ashamed to tell you. I was lying in the alley for twenty minutes."

"Well, why in the hell didn't you say you caught a nut shot for chrissake? No wonder you been looking sick all night. I'm taking you home."

"No. No, I don't want to go home," said Gus and thought he would analyze later why he preferred being at work even now when he was despairing of everything.

"Suit yourself, but I want you to really go through that whore mug book tomorrow night and keep looking till you find that bitch. We're going to get a warrant for battery on a police officer."

"I told you, Sal, she was a new one. I never saw her before."

"We'll find the cunt," said Bonelli and seemed content with Gus's explanation. Gus felt better now and his stomach hardly hurt at all. He sat back and wondered where he would get the money for his mother this pay-day because the furniture payment was due, but he decided not to worry about it because thinking about his mother and John always made his stomach tighten up and he had enough of that tonight.

At eleven o'clock, Sal said, "Guess we better go see the boy leader, huh?"

"Okay," Gus mumbled, unaware that he had been dozing.

"You sure you don't want to go home?"

"I feel fine."

They met Anderson at the restaurant looking sour and impatient as he sipped a cup of creamy coffee and tapped on a table with a teaspoon.

"You're late," he muttered as they sat down.

"Yeah," said Bonelli.

"I took a booth so we wouldn't be overheard," said Anderson, worrying the tip of the sparse moustache with the handle of the teaspoon.

"Yeah, can't be too careful when you're in this business," said Bonelli, and Anderson glanced sharply at the stony brown eyes looking for irony.

"The others aren't coming. Hunter and his partner got a couple whores and the others took a game."

"Dice?"

"Cards," said Anderson and Gus became irritated as he always did when Anderson referred to Hunter and *his partner* or *the others* when there were only eight of them altogether and he should know their names well enough by now.

"The three of us working the bar?" asked Bonelli.

"Not you. They know you so you stay outside. I've got a good place picked out for surveillance across the street in an apartment house parking lot. You be there when we bring out an arrestee, or if we get invited to the apartment for after-hour drinking like I hope, we may just have a drink and leave and call for reinforcements."

"Don't forget to pour the drink in the rubber," said Sal.

"Of course," said Anderson.

"Don't pour too much. Those rubbers break if you pour too much booze in."

"I can manage," said Anderson.

"Especially *that* rubber. Don't pour too much in."

"Why?"

"I used that one on my girl friend Bertha last night. It ain't brand-new anymore."

Anderson looked at Bonelli for a second and then chortled self-consciously.

"He thinks I'm joking," said Bonelli to Gus.

"Great kidders," said Anderson. "Let's get going. I'm anxious to do police work."

Bonelli shrugged to Gus as they followed Anderson to his car and drove behind him to within a block of The Cellar where they decided Anderson and Gus would go in separately at five-minute intervals. They might find an excuse to get together once inside, but they were going to act like strangers.

Once inside, Gus wasn't interested in arrests or police work or anything but the drink in front of him when he sat at the leather-padded bar. He drank two whiskeys with soda and ordered a third, but the peace-giving warmth started before he had finished the second and he wondered if his was the type of personality that was conducive to alcoholism. He guessed it was, and that was one reason he seldom drank, but it was mainly that he hated the taste except for whiskey and soda which he could tolerate. Tonight they were good, and his hand began to beat time to the blaring jukebox and for the first time he looked around the bar. It was a good noisy crowd for a week night. The bar was crowded as were the booths and the tables were almost all occupied. After his third drink he noticed Sergeant Anderson sitting alone at a tiny round table, sipping a cocktail and staring hard at Gus before getting up and going to the jukebox.

Gus followed and fumbled in his pocket for a quarter as he approached the glowing machine which flickered green and blue light across the intense face of Anderson.

"Good crowd," said Gus, pretending to pick out a recording. Gus noticed that his mouth was getting numb and he was lightheaded and the music made his heart beat fast. He finished the drink in his hand.

"Better take it easy on the drinking," whispered Anderson. "You'll have to be sober if we're going to operate this place." Anderson punched a selection and pretended to search for another.

"You operate better if you look like one of the boozers," said Gus, and surprised himself because he never contradicted sergeants, least of all Anderson whom he feared.

"Make your drink last," said Anderson. "But don't overdo it that way either or they'll suspect you're vice."

"Okay," said Gus. "Shall we sit together?"

"Not yet," said Anderson. "There're two women at the table directly in front of me. I think they're hustlers, but I'm not sure. It wouldn't hurt to try for a prostitution offer. If we get it, we could always try to use them to duke us into the upstairs drinking. Then we could bust them when we bust the after-hours place."

"Good plan," said Gus, belching wetly.

"Don't talk so loud for crying out loud."

"Sorry," said Gus, belching again.

"You go back to the bar and watch me. If I'm not doing well with the women you stroll over to their table and hit on them. If you score, I'll invite myself over again."

"Okay," said Gus and Anderson punched the last record on the jukebox and the buzz of voices in the bar threatened to drown out the jukebox until Gus's ears popped and he knew most of the buzz was in his head and he thought of the speeding Cadillac, became frightened, and forced it from his mind.

"Go back to your table now," whispered Anderson. "We've been standing here too long."

"Shouldn't I play a record? That's what I came here for," said Gus, pointing to the glowing machine.

"Oh yes," said Anderson. "Play something first."

"Okay," said Gus, belching again.

"You better take it easy with the booze," said Anderson, as he strode back to his table.

Gus found the blurred record labels too hard to read and just punched the first three buttons on the machine. He liked the hard rock that was now being played and he found his fingers snapping and his shoulders swaying as he returned to the bar and had another whiskey and soda which he drank furtively hoping Anderson would not see. Then he ordered another and picked his way through the crowd to the two women at the table who did indeed look like prostitutes, he thought.

The younger of the two, a slightly bulging silver-tipped brunette in a gold sheath, smiled at Gus immediately as he stood, tapping a foot to the music, in front of their table. He sipped his drink and gave them both a leer which he knew they would respond to, and he glanced at Anderson who glared morosely over his drink and he almost laughed because he hadn't felt so happy in months and he knew he was getting drunk. But his sensibility had become actually more acute, he thought, and he saw things in perspective and God, life was good. He leered from the younger one to the bleached fat one who was fifty-five if she was a day, and the fat one blinked at Gus through alcoholic blue eyes and Gus guessed she was not a true professional hooker, but just a companion for the younger. She would probably join in if the opportunity arose, but who in hell would pay money for the hag?

"All alone?" slurred the older one, as Gus stood before them, growing hilarious now, as he bounced and swayed to the music which was building to a crescendo of drums and electric guitar.

"Nobody's alone as long as there's music and drink and love," said Gus, toasting each of them with the whiskey and soda and then pouring it down as he thought how damned eloquent that was, and if he could only remember it later.

"Well, sit down and tell me more, you cute little thing," said the old blonde pointing to the empty chair.

"May I buy you girls a drink?" asked Gus, leaning both elbows on the table and thinking how the younger one really wasn't too bad except for her bad nose which was bent to the right and her fuzzy eyebrows which began and ended nowhere, but she had enormous breasts and he stared at them frankly and then hurled a lewd smile in her face as he snapped his fingers for the waitress who was giving Anderson another drink.

Both women ordered manhattans and he had whiskey and soda and noticed Anderson looked angrier than usual. Anderson finished two drinks while the fat blonde told a long obscene joke about a little Jew and a blue-eyed camel and Gus roared even though he failed to get the punch line, and when he calmed himself the old blonde said, "We didn't even get introduced. I'm Fluffy Largo. This is Poppy La Farge."

"My name is Lance Jeffrey Savage," said Gus, standing shakily and bowing to both giggling women.

"Ain't he the cutest little shit?" said Fluffy to Poppy.

"Where do you work, Lance?" asked Poppy letting her hand rest against her forearm as she dipped her torso forward revealing a half inch more cleavage.

"I work at a cantaloupe factory," said Gus staring at Poppy's breasts. "I mean a dress factory," he added looking up to see if they caught it.

"Cantaloupes," said Fluffy and burst into a high whooping laugh that ended in a snort.

Damn good, thought Gus. That was damn good. And he wondered how he could so easily think of such spectacularly funny things tonight, and then he looked over at Anderson who was paying for another drink and Gus said to the women, "Hey, see that guy over there?"

"Yeah, the bastard tried to pick us up a minute ago,"

said Fluffy, scratching her vast belly and pulling up a slipping bra strap which had dropped below the shoulder onto the flabby pink bicep.

"I know him," said Gus. "Let's invite him over."

"You know him?" asked Poppy. "He looks like a cop to me."

"Hah, hah, hah," said Gus. "A cop. I knew that sucker for five years. He used to own a string of gas stations. His old lady divorced him though and now he's down to three. Always has plenty of bread on him, though."

"Don't you have any bread, Lance?" asked Fluffy suddenly.

"Just seventy-five bucks," said Gus. "That enough?"

"Well," Fluffy smiled. "We expect to show you a good time after this joint closes and naturally, all good things are expensive."

"What kind of dresses you like, Fluffy?" asked Gus expansively. "I carry samples in my car and I want to see you dolls in some fine goods."

"Really?" said Poppy with a huge grin. "Do you have any size fourteens?"

"I got 'em baby," said Gus.

"You got a twenty-two and a half?" asked Fluffy. "This old green rag is falling apart."

"I got 'em Fluffy," said Gus and now he was annoyed because he had absolutely no feeling in his lower jaw, mouth and tongue.

"Listen, Lance," said Poppy, pulling her chair next to his. "We usually don't sleep with nobody for less than a hundred a night each. But maybe for those dresses, I could let you have it for oh, fifty bucks, and maybe we could talk Fluffy into a twenty-five dollar ride. What do you say, Fluff? He's a damned nice guy."

"He's a cute little shit," said Fluffy. "I'll do it."

"Okay, dolls," said Gus, holding up three fingers to the waitress, even though he sensed Anderson was glaring at him through the smoky darkness.

"Why don't we get started now?" asked Poppy. "It's almost one o'clock."

"Not yet," said Gus. "I hear they swing after hours in this joint. What say we try to get in upstairs after two? After a few drinks and a little fun, we can head for the motel."

"George charges a lot for drinks upstairs," said Poppy. "You only got seventy-five bucks and we need it worse than George."

"Listen," Gus muttered, pitying for a moment a drowning fly who thrashed in a ringed puddle on the cluttered table. "I got a plan. Let's invite that guy I know over here and we'll take him with us upstairs to George's place after the bar closes. And we'll all drink off his money. He's loaded. And then after we drink for a while the three of us'll ditch him and head for the pad. I hate to go to bed yet, I'm having too much fun."

"You don't know what fun is, you cute little shit," said Fluffy, squeezing Gus's thigh with a pudgy pink hand and lurching forward heavily into Gus as she tried to kiss him on the cheek with a mouth that looked like a deflated tire tube.

"Cut that out, Fluff," said Poppy. "Crissake, you get thrown in jail for drunk and what're we going to do?"

"She isn't drunk," said Gus drunkenly, as his elbow slipped off the table from the weight of Fluffy's heavy body.

"We better get out of here and head for the motel right now," said Poppy. "You two are going to fuck up the whole deal if you get busted like a couple common winos."

"Just a minute," said Gus, waving a hand toward where he thought Anderson would be.

"We don't want that guy," said Poppy.

"Shut up, Poppy," said Gus.

"Shut up, Poppy," said Fluffy. "The more, the fuckin' merrier."

"This is the last time I take you with me, Fluffy," said Poppy, taking a big swallow of the cocktail.

"You wanted me?" asked Anderson, and Gus looked up at the red-eyed sergeant standing over him.

"Sure, sure," mumbled Gus. "Sit down . . . Chauncey. Girls, this is Chauncey Dunghill, my old friend. Chauncey, meet Fluffy and Poppy, my new friends." Gus held his whiskey up in a toast to the three of them and swallowed a gulp he could hardly taste.

"Pleased to meet you," said Anderson stiffly and Gus squinted at the sergeant and remembered that Bonelli had told him that Anderson could not operate bars because he got high on two drinks being a teetotaler except when duty called. Gus smiled and leaned over the table seeing the peculiar angle of Anderson's eyes.

"Ol' Chaunce has to catch up with us," said Gus, "if he wants to come with us to George's private bar for a few belts after two."

"Shit," said Poppy.

"Private bar?" said Anderson with a crafty look at Gus, toying with his sparse moustache.

"Sure, these girls are taking us upstairs. They know this guy George and he's got a swinging after-hours joint and you can come as long as you buy all the drinks, right, girls?"

"Tha's right," said Fluffy and kissed Gus on the cheek with a jarring collision and Gus winced in spite of the drink in him and wondered about the diseases prostitutes' mouths must carry. He furtively spilled a little whiskey on his hand and dabbed it on the spot to kill the germs.

"You buying drinks, Chauncey?" asked Fluffy with a challenge in her voice as she looked at Anderson like a boxer eyeing an opponent.

"Four drinks," said Anderson to the waitress.

"Two for you," said Gus.

"What?"

"You got to catch up."

"Well?" said the bored waitress, hesitating.

"You catch up or we don't take you upstairs," said Gus.

"Bring me two daiquiris," said Anderson and glared at Gus who giggled all through the joke about the Jew and the blue-eyed camel which Fluffy repeated for Anderson.

"Chug-a-lug the drink," Gus commanded to Anderson when the daiquiris arrived.

"I'll drink as I please," said Anderson.

"Chug-a-lug, mudder-fug," commanded Fluffy, and the purple pouches under her eyes bulged ominously. Gus cheered as Anderson put the first drink away and smiled weakly at Poppy who was now smoking and nursing her drink.

Gus leered in earnest at her bulging breasts and told Fluffy a joke about a one-titted stripper who couldn't twirl a tassle, but he forgot how it ended and he stopped in the middle. Fluffy whooped and snorted and said it was the funniest joke she ever heard.

When Anderson finished his second drink, he signaled

for five more and now grinned gaily at Poppy, asking her if she had ever been a dancer because she had wonderful legs.

"Chug-a-lug," said Anderson when the drinks arrived.

"Mudder-fug," said Fluffy, and exploded in cackles, bumping heads painfully with Gus.

"This is all right," said Anderson, after his glass was drained, and he picked up his next. "I'm catching up, Poppy."

"Something's goin' to happen," Poppy whined. "You can't get drunk in this business, Fluffy."

"I'm not drunk. Lance's drunk," said Fluffy. "Chauncey's drunk too."

"You're a beautiful girl and I really mean it, Poppy," said Anderson, and Gus roared, "Oooooh, stop it, Chauncey, you're killing me," and then Gus giggled in a prolonged burst of hilarity which threatened to suffocate him. When he recovered he saw that everyone on that side of the bar was laughing at him and that made him laugh harder and he only stopped when Fluffy grabbed him in a bulging embrace, called him a cute little shit, and kissed him on the open mouth. She probably went around the world tonight, he thought, cringing in horror. He took a hurried drink, swishing it around in his mouth and held up his hand for another.

"You had enough to drink," said Anderson with a surly slurred voice.

"Speak for yourself, Chauncey," said Gus trying not to think of how prostitutes used their mouths, as he became nauseous.

"We all had enough to drink," said Poppy. "I know something's going to go wrong."

"You're really a lovely girl, Poppy," said Anderson as he spilled half his drink on her gold purse.

"Bunch of fuckin' drunks," said Poppy.

"I'm sorry, Poppy," said Anderson. "Really I am."

Anderson finished his drink and ordered another round even though Poppy had not touched her last one, and finally Anderson drank his and Poppy's two manhattans when Fluffy dared him to. Gus had a headache and still felt nauseous as he remembered hearing a whore in the wagon saying she once gave twenty-two head jobs in one night, and he looked at Fluffy's mouth which had actually touched the inside of his. He sloshed more of the drink around in his mouth and pushed Fluffy away each time she leaned over and squeezed his thigh and now he found he was becoming angry at everything while only moments ago he was happy. He glared at Anderson's sparse moustache and thought what a miserable son of a bitch he was.

"I'm not feeling too good, Poppy," said Anderson who had been patting her hand and telling her that business was bad and he only made fifty thousand last year as she looked as though she didn't believe him.

"Let's all get out of here," said Poppy. "Can you still walk, Fluffy?"

"I can dance," growled Fluffy, whose head seemed to be sinking lower into the mass of her body.

"I'm getting sick," said Anderson.

"Kiss the son of a bitch," whispered Gus suddenly into Fluffy's ear.

"What?" asked Fluffy, swiping at an indomitable drop of moisture which clung to the ball of her nose.

"Grab that bastard like you did me around the arms and give him a big sloppy kiss and make sure you stick your old tongue right in there."

"But I don't even like the shithead," Fluffy whispered.

"I'll give you an extra five bucks later," whispered Gus.

"Okay," said Fluffy, leaning over the table and knocking an empty glass on the floor as she pinned the arms of the surprised Anderson and ground her mouth against his until he could manage the leverage to plop her back in the chair.

"Why did you do that?" Anderson gasped.

" 'Cause I love you, you shithead," said Fluffy and when the waitress passed with a tray of beers for the adjoining table, Fluffy grabbed a beer from the tray and stuck her chin in the foam and said, "Look at me, I'm a billy goat." Anderson paid for the beer and tipped the angry waitress two dollars.

"Come on, Fluffy," said Poppy after the waitress left, "let's go to the restroom and wash your goddamn face and then we're getting Lance and going to the motel right now. Understand, Lance?"

"Sure, sure, Poppy, whatever you say," said Gus, grinning at the outraged Anderson and feeling happy again.

When they were gone Anderson lurched forward, almost fell to the floor and looked painfully at Gus. "Plebesly, we're too goddamn drunk to do our job. Do you realize that?"

"We're not drunk, Sergeant. You're drunk," said Gus. "I'm getting sick, Plebesly," pleaded Anderson.

"Know what Fluffy told me, Sergeant?" said Gus. "She told me she worked in a whorehouse all day and blew twenty-two guys."

"She did?" said Anderson, holding his hand to his mouth.

"She said she gives around the world or straight French 'cause it's too much trouble to screw and she'll go right up the old poop chute if a guy wants it."

"Don't tell me that, Plebesly," said Anderson. "I'm sick, Plebesly."

"I'm sorry she kissed you, Sergeant," said Gus, "I'm sorry 'cause those spermatozoas are probably swarming down your friggin' throat right this minute and swishing their tails against your friggin' tonsils."

Anderson cursed and stumbled sideways, heading for the exit. His handcuffs fell out and clashed to the floor. Gus stooped carefully, retrieved the handcuffs and weaved his way through the tables after Anderson. Even on the sidewalk outside Gus could hear Poppy's curse when she found the table empty. Then Gus crossed the street, carefully following the wavy white line to the opposite curb. It seemed like a mile to the darkened parking lot where he found Anderson vomiting beside his car and Bonelli looking at Gus with affection.

"What happened in there?" asked Bonelli.

"We drank with two whores."

"Didn't they hit on you? Didn't you get an offer?"

"Yes, but there's too much between us now. I couldn't bear to arrest them."

"You drank Anderson under the table, kid," Bonelli grinned.

"Under the friggin' table. I really did, Sal," Gus squeaked.

"How do you feel?"

"I'm getting sick."

"Come on," said Bonelli, throwing a big hairy arm around Gus's shoulder and patting him on the cheek. "Let's go get you some coffee, son."

15. Conception

The transfer to Seventy-seventh Street station had been a demoralizing blow. Now, after his fourth week in the division Roy could still not believe they would do this to him. He knew that most of his academy class had been transferred to three divisions but he hoped he might escape the third one. After all, he was well liked in Central Division and he had already worked Newton Street and didn't dream they would make him work another black division. But then again, he should have expected it. Everything the Department did was senseless and illogical and none of the command officers cared in the least about intangibles like morale as long as they were efficient, icily efficient, and as long as the public knew and appreciated their efficiency. But Christ, Roy thought, Seventy-seventh Division! Fifty-ninth Place and Avalon, Slauson and Broadway, Ninety-second and Beach, One Hundred and Third, all of Watts for that matter! It was Newton Street magnified ten times, it was violence and crime, and every night he was wading through blood.

The stores, the offices, even the churches looked like fortresses with bars and grates and chains protecting doors and windows and he had even seen private uniformed guards in churches during services. It was impossible.

"Let's go to work," said Lieutenant Feeney to the night watch officers. Feeney was a laconic twenty-year man with a melancholy face who seemed to Roy a decent watch commander, but he had to be because in this hellish division a rigid disciplinarian would drive the men to mutiny.

Roy put on his cap, jammed the flashlight in the sap pocket and picked up his books. He hadn't heard a single thing that was said at roll call. He was getting worse about that lately. Someday he'd miss something important. They must occasionally say something important, he thought.

Roy did not walk down the stairs with Rolfe, his partner. The laughter and voices of the others angered him for no apparent reason. The uniform clung wetly on this hot evening and chafed and hung like an oppressive blue pall. Roy dragged himself to the radio car and was glad it was Rolfe's turn to drive tonight. He hadn't the energy. It would be a sultry night as well as hot.

Roy wrote his name mechanically in the log and wrote Rolfe's name on the line below. He made a few other notations, then slammed the notebook as Rolfe drove out of the station parking lot and Roy turned the wind-wing so that what breeze there was cooled him a little.

"Anything special you want to do tonight?" asked Rolfe, a young, usually smiling ex-sailor who had been a policeman just one year and who still had a bubbling exuberance for police work that Roy found annoying.

"Nothing special," said Roy, closing the windwing when he lit a cigarette which tasted bad.

"Let's drive by Fifty-ninth and Avalon," said Rolfe. "We haven't been giving the pill pushers too much attention lately."

"Okay," Roy sighed, thinking that only one more night and then he was off for three. And then he began thinking of Alice, the buxom nurse who for six months he watched leaving the apartment house across the street from his, but whom he never tried before last week because he was keeping well satisfied by fair and fragile Jenny, the steno who only lived across the hall. Jenny was so available and so convenient and so eager for love at any hour, sometimes too eager. She insisted on lovemaking when he was exhausted from an overtime shift and any sane person should have been long asleep. He would stumble into his apartment and close the door quietly and before he could even get into his pajamas she would be in his bedroom, having heard him enter and having used the key he never should have given her. He would turn around suddenly when he felt her presence in the silent room and she would burst into a fit of giggling because she had scared hell out of him. She would be in her nightgown, not a well-shaped girl, far too thin, but very pretty and insatiable in her lust. He knew there were other men too despite what Jenny said, but he didn't give a damn because she was too much for him anyway, and besides, now that he had met Alice, milky, scrubbed and starched Alice, and had luxuriated in her yielding softness one fortunate night last week, now he was going to have to discourage Jenny.

"Looks like a good crowd this evening," said Rolfe. Roy wished he would be quiet when he was thinking about Alice and her splendid gourd-shaped breasts which in themselves provided him with hours of excitement and wonder. If Jenny was two feverish eyes, Alice was two peace-giving breasts. He wondered if there lived a woman whom he could think of as a whole person. He didn't think of Dorothy at all anymore. But then he realized he never thought of anyone as a whole person anymore. Carl was a mouth, an open mouth that criticized incessantly. His father was a pair of eyes, not devouring him like Jenny's, but entreating him, mournful eyes that wanted him to submit to the suffocation of his and Carl's tyranny.

"If only I could add an S to the Fehler and Son sign," his father had pleaded. "Oh Roy, I'd pay a fortune for that privilege." And then he had come to think of his mother as only a pair of hands, clasped hands, moist hands, talking hands which cajoled, "Roy, Roy, we never see you anymore and when are you leaving that city and coming home where you belong, Roy?"

Then he thought of Becky, and he felt his heart race. He could think of her as a whole person. She was scampering about now and she seemed so happy to see him when he came. He would never let a week pass without seeing her and to hell with Dorothy and her fat-assed henpecked fiancé, because he would never let a weekend pass without seeing Becky. Never. He would bring her presents, spend whatever he wished, and they could go to hell.

The evening dragged even though many radio calls were being given to Seventy-seventh cars. He was afraid to ask for code seven for fear they'd get a call. His stomach was rumbling. He should have eaten lunch today.

"Ask for seven," said Rolfe.

"Twelve-A-Five requesting code seven at the station," said Roy, wishing that he had packed something better than a cheese sandwich in his lunch. It was too close to payday to be buying dinner. He wished there were more eating spots on Seventy-seventh Street. He had long since decided that free food was not unprofessional. Everyone accepted meals and the restaurant proprietors did not seem to mind. They wanted policemen in the place or they wouldn't do it. But he and Rolfe had no eating spot in their district that would even feed them at a discount.

"Twelve-A-Five, continue patrol," said the operator, "and handle this call: See the woman, unknown trouble, eleven-o-four, east Ninety-second Street, code two."

Roy rogered the call and turned to Rolfe, "Shit! I'm starving."

"I hate unknown trouble calls," said Rolfe. "They always make me nervous. I like to know what to expect."

"This goddamned jungle," said Roy, flipping his cigarette out the window. "You don't get off on time, you miss your meals, fifteen radio calls a night. I've got to get a transfer."

"Do you really feel that way?" asked Rolfe, turning to Roy with a surprised look. "I like it here. The time passes fast. We're so busy that it's time to go home when I feel like I just came to work. All this action is pretty exciting to me."

"You'll get over that crap," said Roy. "Turn left here. This is Ninety-second."

There was a woman in a clean white turban standing in the front yard of the house next to eleven-o-four. Rolfe parked and she waved nervously as they got out of the car.

"Evening," said Rolfe as they approached the woman, putting on their caps.

"I'm the one that called Mr. PO-lice," she whispered. "They's a lady in that house that is terrible drunk all the time. She got a new baby, one of them preemeys, jist a tiny bug of a chil', and she always drunk, 'specially when her man at work, and he at work tonight."

"She bothering you?" asked Roy.

"It the baby, Mr. PO-lice," said the woman, her arms folded over the ample stomach, as she glanced several times at the house. "She dropped that chil' on the ground last week. I seed her, but my husband say it ain't none our business, but tonight she was staggerin' around' that front porch wif the chil' again and she almost fell right off the porch and I tol' my husband I was calling the PO-lice and tha's what I done."

"Okay, we'll go have a talk with her," said Roy, walking toward the one-story frame house with a rotting picket fence.

Roy walked carefully up the dangerous porch steps and stood by habit to one side of the doorway as Rolfe stood to the other side and knocked. They heard the shuffling of feet and a crash and then they knocked again. After more than a minute a woman with oily ringlets opened the door and stared at the policemen with watery little eyes.

"What you want?" she asked, weaving from side to side as she held tightly to the doorknob for support.

"We were told you might be having some trouble," said Rolfe with his young easy smile. "Mind if we come in? We're here to help you."

"I know how the PO-lices helps," said the woman, bumping the doorway with her wide shoulder during a sudden lurch sideways.

"Look, lady," said Roy, "We were told your baby might be in some danger. How about showing us that the baby's okay and we'll be on our way."

"Get off my porch," said the woman as she prepared to close the door, and Roy shrugged at Rolfe because they couldn't force their way in with no more cause than her being drunk. Roy decided to stop and buy a hamburger to go with the cheese sandwich that he had begun to crave. Then the baby shrieked. It was not a petulant baby scream of anger or discomfort, but it was a full-blown scream of pain or terror and Rolfe was through the door before the shriek died. Pushing past the drunken woman he bounded across the small living room into the kitchen. Roy was just entering the house when Rolfe emerged from the kitchen carrying the incredibly tiny nightgown-clad baby in his arms.

"She laid the baby on the kitchen table next to her ashtray," said Rolfe, awkwardly rocking the moaning brown-skinned infant. "It got hold of the burning cigarette. Hand's burned, and the stomach too. Look at the hole in the nightgown. Poor thing." Rolfe glared at the angry woman over his shoulder as he cradled the baby in one big arm away from the mother who looked on the verge of drunken decision.

"Give me my chil'," she said stepping toward Rolfe.

"Just a minute, lady," said Roy, grabbing her by a

surprisingly hard bicep. "Partner, I think we've got enough to book her for child endangering. Lady, you're under ar . . ." She drove an elbow into the side of Roy's neck and his head struck the edge of the door with a painful shock and he heard Rolfe shout as she lunged for him and Roy stared transfixed as he saw the fragile, screaming baby being pulled by the woman who had the left arm and Rolfe who had the right leg in one hand while his other hand clawed the air in horror and helplessness.

"Let it go, Rolfe," Roy shouted, as the woman jerked backward viciously and Rolfe followed her, unwilling to surrender the wailing infant completely.

Finally Rolfe released the child, and Roy shuddered as the woman fell heavily back into a chair holding the baby by one leg across her lap.

"Let her keep it, Rolfe!" Roy shouted, still unable to decide what to do because they would surely kill it, but Rolfe had pounced on the woman who was digging and punching at his face, still holding the baby in a death grip, first by the leg, then by the arm when Rolfe pulled a hand free. Roy leaped forward when she grabbed the now silent baby by the throat.

"My God, my God," Roy whispered, as he tore the fingers free one at a time while Rolfe pinned the woman's other arm and she cursed and spat and he had the last finger twisted free and was lifting the trembling little body in one hand when the woman's head snapped forward and her teeth closed first on Roy's hand and he shouted in sudden pain. She released him and bit at the child as Rolfe grabbed the woman's neck, and tried to force the head back, but the large white teeth flashed and snapped again and again at the baby, and then the baby shrieked once more, long and loud. Roy pulled the infant and the nightgown ripped away in the woman's mouth and Roy did not look at the baby, but ran to the bedroom with it and put it on the bed and came back to help Rolfe handcuff her.

It was after midnight when they got the woman booked and the baby admitted to the hospital. It was too late to eat now and Roy could not eat anyway and he told himself for the tenth time to stop thinking about what the baby's body looked like there on the shockingly

white table in the emergency ward. Rolfe had a
unusually silent for the past hour or so.

"Someone else tried to bite me once," Roy sa
denly as he puffed on a cigarette and leaned back in the
car as Rolfe was driving them to the station to complete
the reports. "It wasn't like this at all. It was a man and
he was white, and there was no excuse at all. I was trying to get away from him. It was in a restroom."

Rolfe looked at him curiously and Roy said, "I was
working vice. He was trying to devour me. People are
cannibals I guess. They just eat each other. Sometimes
they don't even have the decency to kill you before they
eat you."

"Hey, there's a waitress I know pretty good down at a
restaurant at a Hundred-fifteenth and Western. I go there
after work for coffee all the time. How about us stopping there for a few minutes before we go to the station? We could at least drink some coffee and unwind.
And who knows, maybe we'll get hungry. I think she'd
bounce for a free meal if the boss isn't there."

"Why not?" said Roy, thinking the coffee sounded
good and it would be a pleasure to drive through the
west side of the division for a change, which was only
part Negro and relatively peaceful. Roy hoped he could
work Ninety-one next month and get as far west and
south as the division went. He had to get away from
black faces. He was starting to change toward them and
he knew it was wrong. But still it was happening.

They were only two blocks from the restaurant and
Roy was already feeling reassured at seeing the pre-
dominantly white faces driving and walking by when
Rolfe said, "Fehler, did you look in that liquor store
we just passed?"

"No, why?" asked Roy.

"There was nobody behind the counter," said Rolfe.

"So he went in the back room," said Roy. "Look, do
you want to play cops and robbers or do we get some
coffee?"

"I'm just going to have a look," said Rolfe, making a
U-turn and driving north again while Roy shook his
head and vowed to ask for an older, more settled partner next month.

Rolfe parked across the street from the store and they

watched the interior for a second. They saw a sandy-haired man in a yellow sport shirt run from the back room to the cash register where he punched several keys, and then they saw him clearly shove the gun inside his belt.

"Officers need help, One one three and Western!" Rolfe whispered into the radio, and then he was out of the car, hatless, flashlight in hand, running low to the north side of the building. He evidently remembered Roy who was just getting around the front of the car because he stooped, turned, and pointed to the rear door indicating that he would take the rear and then he disappeared in the shadows streaking for the darkness of the rear alley.

Roy debated a moment where he should place himself, thought of lying across the hood of a car that was parked directly in front of the store and was probably the suspect's car, but changed his mind and decided to get behind the corner of the building at the southwest corner where he could have a clear line of fire if the man came out the front. He began trembling, wondered for a moment if he could shoot a man, and decided not to think about that.

Then he saw that one of the cars in the bar parking lot next door was occupied by a man and woman who sat in the front seat apparently oblivious to the policemen's presence. Roy saw that they would be directly in the line of fire of the gunman if he would shoot at Roy hiding behind the corner of the building. His conscience nagged and his hand trembled more, and he thought if I leave here to run across the vacant lot and tell them to get the hell out, he might come out the door and I'll be caught out of position. But Jesus Christ, he might kill them and I'd never be able to forget . . . Then he decided, and made a dash to the yellow Plymouth thinking: Stupid bastard, probably sitting there playing with her tits and doesn't even know they might get killed. Roy was beside the car and he saw the girl look at him wide-eyed as he held his revolver at his side. The man opened the door quickly.

"Get that car the hell out of here," said Roy and he never forgot the foolish grin and the look of patent unconcern on the face of the little freckled man who leveled the sawed-off shotgun. Then the yellow and red flame crashed into him and he flew back across the sidewalk. He slid off the curb into the gutter where he lay on his side weeping because he could not get up and he had to get up because he could see the slimy intestines wet in the moonlight flopping out of his lower stomach in a pile. They began touching the street and Roy strained to turn over. He heard footsteps and a man said, "Goddamnit Harry, get in!" and another male voice said, "I didn't even know they was out here!" Then the car started and roared across the sidewalk and off the curb and it sounded like more footsteps farther away. He heard Rolfe shouting, "Stop! Stop!" and heard four or five shots and tires squeal. Then he remembered that the intestines were lying on the street and he was filled with horror because they were lying there in the filthy street getting dirty and he began to cry. He squirmed a little to get on his back and get them bunched up because if he could just shovel them back inside and brush the dirt off them he knew he'd be alright because they were oh so dirty now. But he couldn't lift them. His left arm wouldn't move and it hurt so much to try to reach across the bubbling hole with his right arm so he began to cry again, and thought: Oh, if only it would rain. Oh, why can't it rain in August, and suddenly as he cried, he was deafened by thunder and the lightning flashed and clattered and the rain poured down on him. He thanked God and cried tears of joy because the rain was washing all the dirt off the heap of guts that was hanging out. He watched them shine wet red in the rain, clean and red, as all the filth was flushed away and he was still crying happily when Rolfe leaned over him. There were other policemen there and none of them were wet from the rain. He couldn't understand that.

Roy could not have said how long he had been in the police ward of Central Receiving Hospital. Could not at this moment say if it was days or weeks. It was always the same: blinds drawn, the hum of the air conditioning, the patter of soft-soled footsteps, whispers, needles and tubes which were endlessly inserted and withdrawn, but now he guessed perhaps three weeks had passed. He wouldn't ask Tony who sat there reading a magazine by the inadequate night light with a grin on his effeminate face.

"Tony," said Roy, and the little male nurse put the magazine on the table and walked to the bed.

"Hello Roy," Tony smiled. "Woke up, huh?"

"How long I been sleeping?"

"Not too long, two, three hours, maybe," said Tony. "You were restless tonight. I thought I'd sit in here, I figured you'd wake up."

"It hurts tonight," said Roy, sliding the cover back to look at the hole covered with light gauze. It no longer bubbled and sickened him but it could not be sutured because of its size and had to heal on its own. It had already begun to shrink a little.

"It looks good tonight, Roy," Tony smiled. "Pretty soon no more I.V.'s, you'll be eating real food."

"It hurts like hell."

"Dr. Zelko says you're doing wonderfully, Roy. I'll bet you're out of here in two more months. And back to work in six. Light duty of course. Maybe you can work the desk for a while."

"I need something for the pain tonight."

"I can't. I've had specific orders about that. Dr. Zelko says we were giving you too many injections."

"Screw Dr. Zelko! I need something. Do you know what adhesions are? Your goddamn guts tighten up and come together like they were glued. Do you know what that's like?"

"Now, now," said Tony, wiping Roy's forehead with a towel.

"Look how my leg's swollen. There's a nerve that's damaged. Ask Dr. Zelko. I need something. That nerve keeps me in terrible pain."

"I'm sorry, Roy," said Tony, his smooth little face contorted with concern. "I wish I could do more for you. You're our number one patient . . ."

"Shove it!" said Roy and Tony walked back to his chair, sat down, and continued reading.

Roy stared at the holes in the acoustical ceiling and counted rows but he soon tired of that. When the pain was really bad and they wouldn't give him his medication he sometimes thought of Becky and that helped a little. He thought that Dorothy had been here once with Becky but he couldn't be sure. He was about to ask Tony, but Tony was his night nurse and he wouldn't know if they had visited him. His father and mother had been here several times and Carl had come at least once in the beginning. He remembered that. He had opened his eyes one afternoon and seen Carl and his parents, and the wound started hurting again and his cries of anguish had sent them out and brought the delicious indescribable injection that was all he lived for now. Some policemen had come, but he couldn't say just who. He thought he remembered Rolfe, and Captain James, and he thought he saw Whitey Duncan once through a sheet of fire. Now he was getting frightened because his stomach was clenching like a painful fist as though it didn't belong to him and acted on its own in defiance of the waves of anguish that were punishing it.

"What do I look like?" asked Roy suddenly.

"Pardon, Roy?" said Tony, jumping to his feet.

"Get me a mirror. Hurry up."

"What for, Roy?" Tony smiled, opening the drawer of the table in the corner of the private room.

"Have you ever had a really bad stomachache?" asked Roy. "One that made you sick clear through?"

"Yes," said Tony, bringing the smaller mirror over to Roy's bed.

"Well it was nothing. Nothing, do you understand?"

"I can't give you anything," said Tony, holding the mirror up for Roy.

"Who's that?" said Roy, and the fear swelled and pounded and swelled in him as he looked at the thin gray face with the dark-rimmed eyes and the thousands of greasy globules of sweat that roughened the texture of the face that stared at him in horror.

"You don't look bad at all, now. We thought we were going to lose you for the longest time. Now we know you're going to be alright."

"I've got to have some medication, Tony. I'll give you twenty dollars. Fifty. I'll give you fifty dollars."

"Please, Roy," said Tony returning to his chair.

"If I only had my gun," Roy sobbed.

"Don't talk like that, Roy."

"I'd blow my brains out. But first I'd kill you, you little cocksucker."

"You're a cruel man. And I don't have to stand for your insults. I've done everything I could for you. We all have. We've done everything to save you."

"I'm sorry I called you that. You can't help it if you're

a fruit. I'm sorry. Please get some medication. I'll give you a hundred dollars."

"I'm going out. You ring if you really need me."

"Don't go. I'm afraid to be alone with it. Stay here. I'm sorry. Please."

"Alright. Forget it," Tony grumbled, sitting down.

"Dr. Zelko has terrible eyes," said Roy.

"What do you mean?" Tony sighed, putting down the magazine.

"There's hardly any iris. Just two round black little balls like two slugs of double ought buckshot. I can't bear his eyes."

"Is that the kind of buckshot that hit you, Roy?"

"No. I'd be stinking up a coffin now if it had been double ought buck. It was number seven and a half birdshot. You ever hunt?"

"No."

"He hit me from less than two feet away. Some hit my Sam Browne but I got most of it. He was such a silly-looking man. That's why I didn't bring the gun up. He was so silly-looking I just couldn't believe it. And he was a white man. And that sawed-off shotgun was so silly-looking and monstrous I couldn't believe that either. Maybe if he'd been a regular-looking man and had a regular handgun I could've brought my gun up, but I just held it there at my side and he looked so damned silly when he fired."

"I don't want to hear it. Stop talking about it, Roy."

"You asked me. You asked about the buckshot, didn't you?"

"I'm sorry I did. I'd just better go out for a while and maybe you can sleep."

"Go ahead!" Roy sobbed. "All of you can leave me. Look at what you've done to me though. Look at my body. You made me a freak, all you bastards. I got a huge open hole in my belly and you put another one in me and now I can wake up and find a pile of shit on my chest."

"You had to have a colostomy, Roy."

"Yeah? How would you like to have an asshole in your stomach? How would you like to wake up and look at a bag of shit on your chest?"

"I always clean it up as soon as I see it. Now you try to . . ."

"Yeah," he cried, weeping openly now, "you made me a freak. I got a bloody pussy that won't close and an asshole in front that I can't control and they're both right here on my stomach where I've got to look at them. I'm a goddamn freak." Then Roy wept and the pain worsened but he wept more and the pain made him weep harder and harder until he gasped and tried to stop so that he could control the inexorable pain that he prayed would kill him instantly in one huge crashing red and yellow ball of fire.

Tony wiped his face and was about to speak when Roy's sobbing subsided and he gasped, "I . . . I've got to . . . to turn over. It's killing me like this. Please, help me. Help me get on my stomach for a little while."

"Sure, Roy," said Tony, gently lifting him and then letting the bed down flat and taking the pillow away as Roy rested on the throbbing burning wound and sobbed spasmodically and blew his nose in the tissue Tony gave him.

Roy lay like this for perhaps five minutes and then he could bear it no more and turned, but Tony had stepped out into the corridor. He thought the hell with it he'd turn himself over and maybe the effort would kill him and that would be fine. He raised up on an elbow, feeling the sweat streaming over his rib cage and then moved as quickly as he could and fell on his back again. He felt the sweat flowing freely over his entire body. He felt something else and pulled the Scotch tape loose and glanced at the wound and screamed.

"What is it?" said Tony, running in the room.

"Look at it!" said Roy, staring at the fibrous bloody clump which protruded from the wound.

"What the hell?" said Tony, looking toward the hall and then back at Roy with confusion in his eyes.

Roy gaped at the wound and then at Tony and seeing the worried little face on the nurse began to giggle.

"I'll get a doctor, Roy," said Tony.

"Wait a minute," said Roy, laughing harder now. "I don't need a doctor. Oh Christ, this is too funny." Roy gasped and stopped laughing when another spasm struck him but even the pain could not completely destroy the humor of it. "Do you know what that mess is, Tony? That's the goddamn wadding!"

"The what?"

"The wadding of the shotgun shell! It finally worked itself out. Look close. There's even some shot mixed in there. Two little pieces of shot. Oh Christ, that's funny. Oh, Christ. Go make the announcement to the staff that there was a happy event in the police ward. Tell them that Dr. Zelko's monster strained his new pussy and gave birth to a three-ounce pile of bloody wadding. And it had eyes like Dr. Zelko! Oh Christ, that's funny."

"I'll get a doctor, Roy. We'll clean that up."

"Don't try taking my baby away, you goddamn faggot! I once saw a nigger try to eat her baby when I did that to her. Oh Christ, this is too funny," Roy gasped, wiping the tears away.

AUGUST 1964

16. The Saint

Serge stretched and yawned, then put his feet on the desk in the deserted juvenile office at Hollenbeck station. He smoked and wondered when his partner Stan Blackburn would return. Stan had asked Serge to wait in the office while he did some "personal business" which Serge knew to be a woman whose divorce was not final, who had three children that were old enough to get him into trouble when the romance finally ended. An officer would get at least a suspension for conduct unbecoming, when an adulterous affair was brought to the Department's attention. Serge wondered if he would tomcat around—if—he married.

Serge had accepted the assignment as a juvenile officer only because he was assured he would not be transferred to Georgia Street Station but could remain here in Hollenbeck and work the night watch J-Car. He decided that the juvenile background would look good in his record when he went up for promotion. But first he would have to pass the written exam and it would be extremely doubtful that he would manage that since he couldn't imagine himself knuckling down to a rigid study program. He hadn't been able to make himself study even in his college classes and he smiled as he recalled the brave ambition of a few years ago to work diligently for the degree and advance quickly in his profession. After several false starts, he was now a government major at Cal State and had only accumulated thirty-three units.

But he enjoyed his work here at Hollenbeck and he made more than enough money to support himself. He had a surprisingly sound savings program and he couldn't see any farther than perhaps detective sergeant here at Hollenbeck. That would be enough, he thought. At the end of his twenty years he would be forty-three years old and able to draw forty percent of his salary the rest of his life which would certainly not be lived here in Los Angeles, or anywhere near Los Angeles. He thought of San Diego. It was pleasant down there, but not in the city, some suburb perhaps. There should be a woman and children somewhere in his plans, he knew. It could not be avoided indefinitely. And it was true that he was more and more becoming restless and sentimental. The home and hearth television stories were starting to interest him slightly.

He had been seeing a great deal of Paula. No other girl had ever stirred this much interest in him. She was not a beauty, but she was attractive and her clear gray eyes held your attention unless she was wearing tight-fitting clothes and then she became extremely interesting. He knew she would marry him. She had hinted often enough that she wanted a family. He told her you'd better get started because you're now twenty-two, and she asked him if he'd like to sire her a couple of kids. When he said, "My pleasure," she said they'd have to be legitimate.

Paula had other assets. Her father, Dr. Thomas Adams, was a successful dentist in Alhambra, and would probably bestow a small piece of property on a lucky son-in-law since Paula was his only child and overly indulged. Paula had taken apartment number twelve in his building, formerly occupied by a steno named Maureen Ball, and Serge had hardly noticed the change in women and had begun dating Paula without a break in stride. He knew that some evening, after a good dinner and more than a few martinis, he would probably go through the formality of asking her, and tell her to go ahead and inform the family to prepare the marriage feast because, what the hell, he couldn't go on aimlessly forever.

At eight-thirty the sun had fallen and it was cool enough to take a ride around Hollenbeck. Serge was wishing Stan Blackburn would come back and he was trying to decide whether to resume reading the treatise on the California constitution for the summer school class he wished he hadn't taken, or whether to read a novel which he had brought to work tonight because he knew he would be waiting in the office for several hours.

Blackburn came whistling through the door just as Serge made the decision of the novel over the California constitution. Blackburn had a simpering smile on his face and the evidence of his personal business was easy to see.

"Better wipe the lipstick off your shirt front," said Serge.

"Wonder how it got way down there," said Blackburn with a knowing wink at his mark of conquest.

Serge had seen her once when Blackburn had parked in the alley next to her duplex, and gone inside for a moment. Serge wouldn't have bothered with her even without the dangers of an estranged husband, and children who might report to Daddy.

Blackburn ran a comb through his thinning gray hair, straightened his tie, and dabbed at the lipstick stain on his white shirt.

"Ready to go to work?" asked Serge, swinging his feet off the desk.

"I don't know. I'm kind of tired," Blackburn chuckled.

"Let's go, Casanova," said Serge, shaking his head. "I guess I better drive so you can rest and restore yourself."

Serge decided to drive south on Soto and east toward the new Pomona freeway right-of-way. Sometimes in the late afternoon if it wasn't too hot, he liked to watch the workmen scurrying about to complete another vast Los Angeles complex of steel and concrete, obsolete before it is finished, guaranteed to be strangled by cars one hour after its opening. One thing the freeway had done, it had broken up *Los Gavilanes*. The doctrine of eminent domain had succeeded in gang busting where the police, probation department, and juvenile court had failed— *Los Gavilanes* had dissolved when the state bought the property and the parents of *Los Gavilanes* scattered through East Los Angeles.

Serge decided to drive through the concrete paths at Hollenbeck Park to check for juvenile gang activity. They hadn't made an arrest for a week, mostly because of Blackburn's time-consuming romantic meetings and Serge hoped they might spot something tonight. He liked to do just enough work to keep the sergeant off his back, although nothing had yet been said about their lack of accomplishment this week.

As Serge drove toward the boathouse, a figure disappeared in the bushes and they heard a hollow clunk as a bottle hastily dropped, struck a rock.

"See who that was?" asked Serge as Blackburn lazily ran the spotlight over the bushes.

"Looked like one of the Pee Wees. Bimbo Zaragoza, I think."

"Drinking a little wine, I guess."

"Yeah, that's not like him. He's a glue head."

"Any port in a storm."

"Port. Hah, that's pretty good."

"Think we can drive down below and catch him?"

"No, he's clear across the lake by now." Blackburn leaned back and closed his eyes.

"We better make a pinch tonight," said Serge.

"Nothing to worry about," said Blackburn, eyes still closed as he took the wrappers off two sticks of gum and shoved them in his mouth.

As Serge came out of the park onto Boyle Street he saw two more Pee Wees but Bimbo was not with them. The smaller one he recognized as Mario Vega, the other he couldn't recall.

"Who's the big one?" he asked.

Blackburn opened one eye and shined the light on the two boys who grinned and began walking toward Whittier Boulevard.

"Ape man, they called him. I forget his real name."

As they passed the boys, Serge snorted at the exaggerated cholo walk of ape man: toes turned out, heels digging in, arms swinging freely, this was the trademark of the gang member. This and the curious deliberate ritual chewing on imaginary chewing gum. One wore Levis, the other khakis slit at the bottoms at the seams to "hang tough" over the black polished shoes. Both wore Pendleton shirts buttoned at the cuff to hide the puncture marks which, if they had them, would bring the status of the addict. And both wore navy watch caps as they wear in youth camp, and this showed they were ex-cons whether or not they actually were.

Serge caught a few words of the conversation when they drove slowly past the boys, mostly muffled Spanish obscenities. Then he thought of the books which talked of the formalism of Spanish insults in which acts are only implied. Not so in familiar informal Mexican, he thought. A Mexican insult or vulgarism could surpass in color even the English equivalent. The Chicanos had given life to the Spanish obscenity.

Serge had decided that Blackburn was asleep when at ten past ten the Communications operator said, "All Hollenbeck units, and Four-A-Forty-three, a four-eighty-four suspect just left twenty-three eleven Brooklyn Avenue running eastbound on Brooklyn and south on Soto. Suspect is male, Mexican, thirty-five to forty, five feet eight to ten, a hundred sixty to a hundred and seventy, black hair, wearing a dirty short-sleeved red turtleneck shirt, khaki pants, carrying a plaster statue."

Serge and Blackburn were on Brooklyn approaching St. Louis when the call came out. They passed the scene of the theft and Serge saw the radio car parked in front, the dome light on and an officer sitting inside. The other officer was in the store talking with the proprietor.

Serge double-parked for a moment beside the radio car, and read "Luz del Día Religious Store" on the window.

"What did he get?" he called to the officer who was a new rookie that Serge didn't know.

"A religious statue, sir," said the young officer, probably thinking they were worthy of the "sir" since they were plainclothesmen. Serge was glad to see that his drowsing partner at least opened his eyes when he talked to the rookie. He hated to disillusion the young ones too quickly.

Serge turned south on Soto and began glancing around for the thief. He turned east on First and north on Matthews and spotted the red turtleneck lurching down the street. The witness had given an excellent description he thought, but she didn't say he was drunk.

"Here he comes," said Serge.

"Who?"

"The four-eighty-four suspect from the religious store. This has to be him. Look."

"Yeah, that must be him," said Blackburn, lighting up the weaving drunk with the spotlight. The drunk threw his hands in front of his face.

Serge stopped a few feet in front of the man and they both got out.

"Where's the statue?" asked Blackburn.

"I ain't got nothing, sir," said the man, watery-eyed and bloated. His turtleneck was purple with the stains of a hundred pints of wine.

"I know this guy," said Blackburn. "Let's see, Eddie
. . . Eddie something."

"Eduardo Onofre Esquer," said the man, swaying pre-
cariously. "I 'member you, sir. You bosted me lots of
times for drunk."

"Yeah. Eddie was one of the Brooklyn Avenue winos
for years. Where you been, Eddie?"

"I got a jeer last time, sir. I been in the county for a
jeer."

"A year? For drunk?"

"Not for drunk. Petty theft, sir. I was choplifting a
couple pairs of woman's stocking to sell for a drink."

"And now you're doing the same damn thing," said
Blackburn. "You know petty theft with a prior is a
felony. You're going to go for a felony this time."

"Please sir," sobbed Eddie. "Don' bost me this time."

"Get in, Eddie," said Serge. "Show us where you threw
it."

"Please don' bost me," said Eddie, as Serge started the
car and drove east on Michigan.

"Which way, Eddie?" asked Serge.

"I didn' throw it, sir. I set it down at the church when
I saw what it was."

Blackburn's spotlight lighted up the white robe and
black cowl and black face of Martin de Porres on the
steps in front of the drab gray building on Breed Street.

"When I saw what it was, I put it there on the steps
of the church."

"That ain't no church," said Blackburn. "That's a
synagogue."

"Anyway, I put it there for the priest to find," said
Eddie. "Please don' bost me, sir. I'll go straight home
to my room if you give me a break. I won' steal no
more. I swear on my mother."

"What do you say, partner?" asked Serge, grinning.

"What the hell. We're juvenile officers, ain't we?" said
Blackburn. "Eddie's no juvenile."

"Go home, Eddie," said Serge, reaching over the seat
and unlocking the rear door of the car.

"Thank you, sir," said Eddie. "Thank you. I'm going
home." Eddie stumbled over the curb, righted himself
and staggered down the sidewalk toward home as Serge
retrieved the statue from the steps of the synagogue.

"Thank you, sir," Eddie shouted over his shoulder. "I

didn' know what I was taking. I swear to God I wouldn' steal a saint."

"You about ready to eat?" asked Blackburn, after they left black Martin at the religious store, telling the proprietor they found him undamaged on the sidewalk two blocks away, and that perhaps the thief had a conscience and could not steal Martin de Porres. The proprietor said, *"Quizás, quizás. Quién sabe?* We like to think of a thief with a soul."

Blackburn offered the old man a cigarette and said, "We've got to believe there are good ones, eh señor? Young men like my *compañero* here, they don't need anything, but when they get a little older like you and me they need some faith, eh?"

And the old man nodded, puffed on the cigarette and said, "It is very true, señor."

"Ready to eat?" Serge asked Blackburn.

Blackburn was silent for a minute, then said, "Take me to the station, will you, Serge?"

"What for?"

"I want to make a call. You go eat, and pick me up later."

Now what the hell's going on? Serge thought. This guy had more personal problems than any partner he ever had.

"I'm going to call my wife," said Blackburn.

"You're separated, aren't you?" asked Serge, and was then sorry he said it because innocent remarks like that could leave an opening for a lurid confession of marital problems.

"Yeah, but I'm going to call her and ask her if I can come home. What am I doing living in a bachelor pad? I'm forty-two years old. I'm going to tell her we can make it if we have faith."

That's just swell, Serge thought. Black Martin worked his magic on the horny old bastard.

Serge dropped Blackburn at the station and drove back to Brooklyn deciding he'd have some Mexican food. Some *carnitas* sounded good and there were a couple of places on Brooklyn that gave policemen half price and made *carnitas* Michoacán style.

Then he thought of Mr. Rosales' place. He hadn't been there in a few months and there was always Mariana who looked better and better each time he stopped.

One of these days he might ask her out to a movie. Then he realized he hadn't dated a Mexican girl since high school.

He didn't see Mariana when he first entered the restaurant. He had been coming in once or twice a month, but had missed the last few months—because of a thirty-day vacation and a waitress that Blackburn was trying to seduce at a downtown drive-in who was unaccountably interested in the old boy and was supplying them with hot dogs, hamburgers and occasional pastramis courtesy of the boss who did not know she was doing it.

"Ah, señor Duran," said Mr. Rosales, waving Serge to a booth. "We have not seen you. How are you? Have you been sick?"

"Vacation, Mr. Rosales," said Serge. "Am I too late to eat?"

"No, of course not. Some *carnitas?* I have a new cook from Guanajuato. She can make delicious *barbacoa* and *birria.*"

"Maybe just a couple of tacos, Mr. Rosales. And coffee."

"Tacos. *Con todo?*"

"Yes, lots of chile."

"Right away, señor Duran," said Mr. Rosales, going to the kitchen, and Serge waited but it was not Mariana who returned with the coffee, it was another girl, older, thinner, inexperienced as a waitress, who spilled a little coffee while pouring.

Serge drank the coffee and smoked until she brought him the tacos. He was not as hungry as he thought, even though the new cook made them just as good as the last one. Every bit of fat was trimmed off the tiny chunks of pork and the onions were grated with care, with cilantro sprinkled over the meat. The chile sauce, Serge thought, was the best he ever tasted, but still he was not as hungry as he thought.

Midway through the first taco, he caught Mr. Rosales' eye and the little man hurried to his table. "More café?" he asked.

"No, this is fine. I was just wondering, where's Mariana? New job?"

"No," he laughed. "Business is so good I have two waitresses now. I have sent her to the market. We ran out of milk tonight. She will be back soon."

"How's her English? Improving?"

"You will be surprised. She is a very smart one. She talks much better than I do."

"Your English is beautiful, Mr. Rosales."

"Thank you. And your Spanish, señor? I have never heard you speaking Spanish. I thought you were Anglo until I learned your name. You are half Anglo, perhaps? Or a real Spaniard?"

"Here she comes," said Serge, relieved to have Mariana interrupt the conversation. She was carrying two large bags and closed the door with her foot, not seeing Serge who took a grocery bag from her hand.

"Señor Duran!" she said, her black eyes glowing. "How good it is to see joo."

"How good it is to hear you speak such beautiful English," Serge smiled, and nodded to Mr. Rosales, as he helped her take the milk to the kitchen.

Serge returned to the table and ate heartily while Mariana put on an apron and came to his table with a fresh pot of coffee.

"Two more tacos, Mariana," he said, noting with approval that she had gained a few pounds and was now rounding into womanhood.

"Joo are hungry tonight, señor Duran? We have missed you."

"I'm hungry tonight, Mariana," he said. "I've missed you too."

She smiled and returned to the kitchen and he was surprised that he could have forgotten that clean white smile. Now that he saw it again, he thought it astonishing that he could have forgotten. It was still too thin and delicate a face. The forehead was ample, the upper lip still a bit long, the black eyes heavy-lashed and full of life. It was still the madonna face. He knew the tiny fire of longing still lived in spite of what the world had told him, and that flame was glowing red hot at this moment. He thought he'd let it smolder for a while because it was not unpleasant.

When Mariana brought the second plate of tacos, he brushed against her fingers. "Let me hear you speak English," he said.

"What do joo wish me to say?" she laughed, self-consciously.

"First of all, stop calling me señor. You know my name, don't you?"

"I know it."

"What is it?"

"Sergio."

"Serge."

"I cannot say that word. The end is too harsh and difficult. But Sergio is soft and easy to say. Try it jurself."

"Ser-hee-oh."

"Ay, that sounds berry comic. Can you no' say Sergio?" she laughed. "Sergio. Two sounds. No more. No' three sounds."

"Of course," he smiled. "My mother called me Sergio."

"Joo see," she laughed. "I knew that joo could say it. But why don' joo ever talk Spanish?"

"I've forgotten," he smiled, and thought, you couldn't help smiling at her. She was a delightful little child. "You're a dove," he said.

"What is a dove?"

"Una paloma."

"But that is my name. Mariana Paloma."

"It fits. You're a little dove."

"I am no' so little. It is that joo are a big man."

"Did you ever see a man so big in your country?"

"No' many," she said.

"How old are you, Mariana, nineteen?"

"Jas."

"Say yes."

"Jes."

"Y-y-yes."

"J-j-jes."

They both laughed and Serge said, "Would you like me to teach you to say yes? Yes is easy to say."

"I wish to learn all English words," she answered, and Serge felt ashamed because her eyes were innocent, and she didn't understand. Then he thought, for God's sake, there are plenty of girls even if Paula wasn't enough which she most certainly was. What would it prove to take a simple child like this? Had he lived so long alone that self-gratification had become the only purpose for living?

Still he said, "You don't work Sundays, do you?"

"No."

"Would you like to go somewhere with me? To dinner? Or to a theater? Have you ever seen a real play? With music?"

"Joo want me to go with joo? *De veras?*"

"If Mr. Rosales will let you."

"He will let me go anywhere with joo. He thinks joo are a good man. Joo mean it?"

"I mean it. Where shall we go?"

"To a lake. Can we go to a lake? In the afternoon? I will bring food. I have never seen a lake in this country."

"Okay, a picnic," he laughed. "We call it a picnic when people bring food and go to a lake."

"That is another hard word," she said.

Serge thought several times on Saturday of calling Mr. Rosales' restaurant and calling off the outing. He never was aware of having any particular respect for himself. He realized that he was always one who wanted only to get along, to do things the easiest, least painful way, and if he could have a woman, a book, or a movie, and get drunk at least once a month, he thought that he had mastered life. But now there was the lust for the girl and it was not that he was Don Quixote, he thought, but it was a totally unnecessary bit of cruelty to take a child like her who had seen or done nothing in a short difficult life, and to whom he must seem something special with a one-year-old Corvette and expensive gaudy sports coats which Paula bought for him. He was degenerating, he thought. In three years he'd be thirty. What would he be then?

In order to sleep Saturday night, he made a solemn promise to himself that under no circumstances would he engage in a cheap seduction of a girl who was the ward of a kindly old man who had done him no harm. And besides, he grinned wryly, if Mr. Rosales found out, there would be no more free meals for the Hollenbeck policemen. Free meals were harder to come by than women—even if she were truly the Virgin of Guadalajara.

He picked her up at the restaurant because that Sunday she had to work two hours from ten until noon when the afternoon girl came on. Mr. Rosales seemed very glad to see him and she had a shopping bag full of food which she called her "chopping sack." Mr. Rosales waved to them as they drove away from the restaurant and Serge checked his tank because he intended to drive all the way to Lake Arrowhead. If she wanted a lake, he'd give her the best, he thought, complete with lakeside homes that should open those gleaming black eyes as wide as silver pesos.

"I didn't know if joo would come," she smiled.

"Why do you say that?"

"Joo are always joking with señor Rosales and with the other girl and me. I thought maybe it was a joke."

"You were ready, weren't you?"

"I still thought it was maybe a joke. But I went to a berry early Mass and prepared the food."

"What kind of food? Mexican?"

"*Claro.* I am *Mexicana?* No?"

"You are," he laughed. "You are *muy Mexicana.*"

"And joo are completely an American. I cannot believe that joo could have a name like Sergio Duran."

"Sometimes I can't believe it either, little dove."

"I like that name," she smiled, and Serge thought she's not a wilting flower, this one. She carries her face uplifted and looks right in your eye, even when she's blushing because you've made her terribly self-conscious.

"And I like your red dress. And I like your hair down, long like that."

"A waitress cannot wear her hair like this. Sometimes I think I chould cut the hair like American girls."

"Never do that!" he said. "You're not an American girl. Do you want to be one?"

"Only sometimes," she said, looking at him seriously, and then they were silent for a while but it was not an uncomfortable silence. Occasionally she would ask him about a town they passed or an unusual building. She amazed him by noticing and knowing the names of several species of flowers that were used to decorate portions of the San Bernardino Freeway. And she knew them in English.

She surprised him again when she said, "I love the flowers and plants so much, señor Rosales was telling me I chould perhaps study botany instead of language."

"Study?" he said in amazement. "Where?"

"I am starting college in Se'tember," she smiled. "My teacher at my English class says that my reading of English is good and that I will speak also berry good after I begin to study in college."

"College!" he said. "But little girls from Mexico don't

come here and go to college. It's wonderful! I'm very glad."

"Thank joo," she smiled. "I am happy that joo are pleased with me. My teacher says that I may do well even though I have no' too much ed-joocation because I read and write so good in Spanish. My mother was also a berry good reader and had a good ed-joocation before she married my poor father who had none."

"Is your mother alive?"

"No, not for three years."

"Your father is?"

"Oh jes, he is a big strong man. Always berry alive. But not so much as before Mamá died. I have ten junger sisters. I will earn money and I will send for them one by one unless they marry before I earn money."

"You're an ambitious girl."

"What means this?"

"You have great strength and desire to succeed."

"It is nothing."

"So you'll study botany, eh?"

"I will study English and Spanish," she said. "I can be a teacher in perhaps four jeers or a translator in less time working for the courthouse if I work hard. Botany is just a foolish thought. Could joo see me as an ed-joocated woman?"

"I can't see you as a woman at all," he said, even as he studied her ripe young body. "You're just a little dove to me."

"Ah, Sergio," she laughed, "joo get such things from the books. I used to watch joo, before we became friends, when I would serve the food to joo and jour *compañero,* the other policeman. Joo would carry books in the coat pocket and read while eating. There is not a place in the real life for little doves. Joo must be strong and work berry hard. Still, I like to hear joo say that I am a dove."

"You're only nineteen years old," he said.

"A Mexican girl is a woman long before. I am a woman, Sergio."

They drove again in silence and Serge deeply enjoyed her enjoyment of the passing miles, and vineyards, and towns, which he scarcely noticed.

Mariana was as impressed with the lake as he knew

she would be. He rented a motorboat, and for an hour showed her the lakeside Arrowhead homes. He knew she was speechless at such wealth.

"But there are so many!" she exclaimed. "There must be so many rich ones."

"They're many," he said. "And I'll never be one of them."

"But that is not important," she said, leaning an inch closer to him as he steered the boat out into open water. The bright sunlight reflecting off the water hurt his eyes and he put his sunglasses on. She looked a deeper bronze, and the wind caught her deep brown hair and swept it back at least twelve inches from the nape of her exposed neck. It was four o'clock and the sun was still hot when they finished the lunch on a rocky hill on the far side of the lake which Serge had discovered another time with another girl who liked picnics and making love in open places.

"I thought you were bringing Mexican food," said Serge, finishing his fifth piece of tender chicken and washing it down with strawberry soda which was kept chilled by a plastic bucket of ice in the bottom of the shopping bag.

"I heard that Americans take *pollo frito* on a picnic," she laughed. "I was told that all Americans expected it."

"It's delicious," he sighed, thinking he hadn't had strawberry soda lately. He wondered again why strawberry is by far the favorite flavor of Mexicans, and any Good Humor man in East Los Angeles carries an extra box of strawberry sundaes and Popsicles.

"Señora Rosales wanted me to bring *chicharrones* and beer for joo, but I didn't, because I thought joo would like the other better."

"I loved your lunch, Mariana," he smiled, wondering how long it had been since he tasted the rich crispy pork rinds. Then he realized he had never tasted *chicharrones* with beer because when his mother made them he was too young to drink beer. He found himself suddenly yearning for some *chicharrones* and a cold glass of beer. You always want what you don't have at the moment, he thought.

He watched Mariana as she cleaned up the picnic things, putting the paper plates in an extra shopping bag she brought. In a few minutes he would not have known anyone had eaten there. She was a totally efficient girl, he thought, and she looked dazzling in the red dress and black sandals. She had lovely toes and feet, brown and smooth like the rest of her. He got a sharp pain in the lower part of his chest as he thought about the rest of her and remembered the vow of abstinence he had made to the person he was growing to respect the least in all the world.

When she finished she sat next to him and drew her knees up and put her hands on her knees and her chin on her hands.

"Joo want to know something?" she asked gazing at the water.

"What?"

"I never have seen a lake. Not here. Not in Mexico. Only in movies. This is my first real lake to see."

"Do you like it?" he asked, feeling his palms become a little moist. The pain returned to his chest as his mouth turned dry.

"Joo have given me a fine day, Sergio," she said looking at him with heaviness in her voice.

"So you've enjoyed it?"

"Jas."

"Not jas," he laughed. "Yes."

"Jes," she smiled.

"Like this. Y-y-yes. Here, put your chin forward just a little bit." He held her chin in his fingers and tugged lightly. But her whole face came forward to him.

"Yes," he said, and his fingers trembled. "I told you I'd teach you to say yes."

"Yes," she said.

"You said it."

"Yes, Sergio, oh, yes, yes," she breathed.

"Fly away, little dove," he said not knowing the strange hollow voice. "Please fly away," he said, and yet he held her shoulders fearing she would.

"Yes, Sergio, yes."

"You're making a mistake, little dove," he whispered, but her lip touched his cheek.

"I say yes, Sergio. For you, yes. *Para tí*, yes, yes."

17. Kiddy Cops

Lucy was merely attractive, but her eyes were alert and missed nothing and devoured you when you were talking to her. Yet you were never uncomfortable because of it. Instead, you succumbed to being devoured and you liked it. Yes, you liked it. Gus took his gaze from the road and examined her long legs, crossed at the ankle, hose sheer, pale and subtle. She sat relaxed much like a male partner and smoked and watched the street as Gus cruised, much like a male partner would, but it was nothing like working with a male partner. With some of the other policewomen there was no difference, except you had to be more careful and not get involved in things where there was the slightest element of danger. Not if you could help it, because a policewoman was still a woman, nothing more, and you were responsible for her safety, being the male half of the team. With some policewoman partners it was almost like being with a man, but not with Lucy. Gus wondered why he liked being devoured by those brown eyes which crinkled at the corners. He was normally shriveled by eyes which looked too hard.

"Think you're going to stay with police work, Lucy?" asked Gus, turning on Main Street thinking she would probably enjoy touring the skid row streets. Most new policewomen did.

"I love it, Gus," she said. "It's a fascinating job. Especially here in Juvenile Division. I don't think working the women's jail would've been nearly as good."

"I don't think so either. I can't picture you in there pushing those bull daggers around."

"I can't either," she grimaced, "but I guess sooner or later I'll get assigned there."

"Maybe not," said Gus. "You're a good juvenile officer, you know. For just being a few weeks out of the academy I'd say you're exceptional. They may keep you in Juvenile."

"Oh sure, I'm indispensable," she laughed.

"You're smart and quick and you're the first police-woman I ever enjoyed working with. Most policemen don't like working with women." He pretended to watch the road very closely as he said it because he felt the brown eyes. He hadn't meant to say this. It was only 7:00 P.M., not dark yet, and he didn't want to blush and let her see it. But then, she would probably even see it in the dark with those eyes.

"That's a fine compliment, Gus," said Lucy. "You've been a patient teacher."

"Oh, I don't know it all myself yet," said Gus, working hard at not blushing by thinking of other things as he talked, like where they would eat, and that they should walk through the Main Street bus depot and look for runaway juveniles because Sunday night was a slow night, or maybe they should cruise through Elysian Park and look for the kids who would surely be there on a Sunday drinking beer on the grass. Lieutenant Dilford loved them to make arrests for minors' possession of alcohol and Dilford treated it like patrol watch commanders treated good felony arrests.

"You've been working Juvenile about six months, haven't you?" asked Lucy.

"About five months now. I've still got lots to learn."

"Where did you work before that, Central Vice?"

"Wilshire Vice."

"I can't picture you as a vice officer," she laughed. "When I worked Lincoln Heights Jail on weekend assignments, the vice officers would be in and out all night. I can't picture you as a vice officer."

"I know. I don't look man enough to be a vice officer, do I?"

"Oh, I didn't mean that, Gus," she said, uncrossing her ankles and drilling him with her brown eyes. When they were working they darkened her face which was smooth and milky. "I didn't mean that at all. In fact, I didn't like them because they were loud and talked to policewomen like they talked to their whores. I didn't think all that bravado made them more manly. I think that being quiet and gentle and having some humility is very manly, but I didn't see many vice officers like that."

"Well, they have to construct some kind of defense against all the sordid things they see," said Gus, elated because she as much as admitted that she was fond of him and saw things in him. Then he became disgusted and thought viciously, you simpering little bastard. He thought of Vickie who was recovering from an appendectomy and he hoped she would sleep tonight, and he swore that he would stop this childish flirtation before it went any further because Lucy would soon see it even though she was not a self-conscious person and did not notice such things. But when she did, finally, she would probably say, that's not what I meant, that's not what I meant at all. Simpering little bastard, he thought again, and peeked in the rearview mirror at his sandy receding hair which was hardly noticeable. In a few years he would be completely bald and he wondered if he would still be dreaming of a bright, pale, brown-eyed girl who would smile in pity or perhaps revulsion if she knew the thoughts he had about her.

"What time should we check out the unfit home?" asked Lucy, and Gus was glad she had changed the subject. He couldn't help smiling at the man walking up Hill Street who turned his head to look at Lucy as they passed. He remembered how men used to turn like that to look at Vickie when they were first married, before she got so heavy. He thought of how he and Lucy must look, two young people, he in a suit and tie and white shirt and her in a modest green dress which fit so well. They might be going to dinner, or to the Bowl for a concert, or to the Sports Arena. Of course, all the street people recognized the plain four-door Plymouth as a police car, and knew the man and woman were juvenile officers, but to anyone else they might just be lovers.

"What time, Gus?"

"It's twenty after seven."

"No," she laughed. "What time do we check out the unfit home the lieutenant mentioned?"

"Oh, let's do it now. Sorry, I was dreaming."

"How's your wife recovering from her appendectomy?" asked Lucy. Gus hated to talk about Vickie to her, but she always asked things about his family as partners did, often in the early morning hours when things were quiet and partners talked.

"She's getting along all right."

"How's your little one? He's talking, isn't he?"

"Chattering," Gus smiled, and he never hesitated to

talk about his children to her because she wanted to hear, he was sure of it.

"They look so beautiful in the pictures. I'd love to see them some time."

"I'd like you to," said Gus.

"I hope it's quiet tonight."

"Why? The night passes slow when it's quiet."

"Yes, but I can get you talking then," she laughed. "I learn more about being a cop in the late hours when I get you talking."

"You mean when I tell you all the things Kilvinsky taught me?" he smiled.

"Yes, but I bet you're a better teacher than your friend Kilvinsky was."

"Oh, no. Kilvinsky was the best," said Gus, his face burning again. "That reminds me, I've got to write him. He hasn't been answering my letters lately and I'm worried. Ever since he took the trip East to see his ex-wife and children."

"Are you sure he came back?"

"Yes. I got one letter right after he came back, but it didn't say anything."

"Isn't it strange that he never visited his own children before that?"

"He must've had a reason," said Gus.

"I don't think you could abandon your children like that."

"He didn't abandon them," said Gus quickly. "Kilvinsky wouldn't do that. He's just a mysterious man, that's all. He must've had good reasons."

"If your wife ever left you, you wouldn't abandon your children, Gus, not you. Not for any reason."

"Well, I can't judge him," said Gus, glad darkness was settling on downtown as he stopped for a light.

"He's not the father you are, I bet," said Lucy and she was watching him again.

"Oh, you're wrong," said Gus. "Kilvinsky would be a good father. He'd be as good a father as anyone could want. He could tell you things, and when he talked you knew he was right. Things seemed all in place when he explained them."

"It's getting dark."

"Let's go handle the unfit home," said Gus, growing uneasy at the deprecating talk about Kilvinsky.

"Okay, it was on West Temple, wasn't it?"

"It might be a phony call."

"Anonymous?"

"Yeah, a woman called the watch commander and said a neighbor in apartment twenty-three had a cruddy pad and left a little kid alone all the time."

"I haven't been in a real unfit home yet," said Lucy. "They've all turned out to be false alarms."

"Remember how to tell a real unfit?" smiled Gus.

"Sure. If you stomp your foot and the roaches are so tame they don't run, then you know it's a real unfit."

"Right," Gus grinned. "And if we could bottle the smell we'd win every case in court."

Gus drove through the Second Street tunnel and over the Harbor Freeway and turned north, then west on Temple, the setting sun glowing dirty pink on the horizon. It had been a smoggy day.

"I bet it's the white apartment building," said Lucy pointing toward the three-story stucco with an imitation stone facade.

"Eighteen thirteen. That's it," said Gus parking in front and wondering if he had enough money to buy a decent dinner tonight. With anyone else he ate hamburgers or brown bagged it, but Lucy ate well and liked a hot dinner. He went along with her, pretending this was what he wanted too, even though he had less than five dollars to last until payday, and less than a half tank of gas in his car. Monday night he had an argument with Vickie over the check to his mother which had shrunk to forty-five dollars a month because John was in the army, thank God.

The argument was so violent it made him sick. Lucy had noticed his depression the next evening. And now he thought of how he had blurted it out to Lucy that night, and how kind she had been and how ashamed he had been and still was that he had told her. Yet it had lifted his spirits. And come to think of it, she hadn't asked to eat in a real restaurant since that night, and she had insisted on buying the coffee or Cokes more often than she should.

It was built to wear only for a time, like so many southern California apartment houses. Gus parked in front and they climbed the twenty-four steps to the second floor. Gus noticed that the metal railing, which only vaguely resembled wrought iron, was loose. He drew his hand back and guessed that someday a drunk would stagger from his apartment door and hit the railing and plunge twenty feet to the concrete below, but being drunk, he would probably receive only abrasions. Apartment twenty-three was in the back. The drapes were drawn and the door was closed, and this alone made Gus suspect there was no one home, because in all the other occupied apartments the doors were open. All had outside screen doors and the people were trying to catch the evening breeze because it had been a hot smoggy day.

Gus knocked and rang the tinny chime and knocked again. Finally, Lucy shrugged and they turned to go and Gus was glad because he didn't feel like working; he felt like driving through Elysian Park pretending to look for juvenile drinkers and just look at Lucy and talk to her perhaps on the upper road on the east side near the reservoir which looked like black ice in the moonlight.

"You the cops?" whispered a woman who suddenly appeared inside the dusty screen door of apartment number twenty-one.

"Yes. Did you call?" asked Gus.

"I'm the one," said the woman. "I called but I said I didn't want nobody to know I called. They aren't home now, but the kid's in there."

"What seems to be the problem?" asked Gus.

"Well, come on in. It looks like I'm going to get involved anyway," she muttered holding the screen and licking the absurdly made-up lips which were drawn on halfway to her nose. In fact, all her makeup had a theatrical exaggeration designed for an audience that must be far far away.

"I talked to some Lieutenant Whatzizname and told him that place isn't fit for pigs most of the time and the kid gets left alone and I never see him outside hardly. Last night he was screaming and screaming and I think the old man was beating him 'cause the old lady was screaming too."

"Do you know the people in that apartment?" asked Gus.

"Lord, no. They're trash," said the woman, uncoiling a wiry wisp of blond hair with gray roots. "They only been living here a month and they go out almost every night and sometimes they have a babysitter, a cousin or something, staying with their kid. And sometimes they got nobody staying with him. I learned long time ago to mind my own business but today it was so damn hot they had the door open and I happened to walk by and the place looks like a slit trench and I know what a slit trench is because I like war novels. There was dog crap from this dirty little terrier they got, and food and other crud all over the floor and then when they left the kid today I just said what the hell, I'll call and remain anonymous but now it looks like I can't be anonymous, huh?"

"How old is the child?" asked Gus.

"Three. A little boy. He hardly never comes outside. The old man's a souse. The mother seems okay. Just a dirty little mouse, you know what I mean. A souse and a mouse. I think the old man pushes her around when he's drunk, but it don't matter much to her probably, because she's usually drunk when he is. Fine neighbors. This place had class a few years ago. I'm moving."

"How old are they? The parents?"

"Young people. Not thirty I don't think. Dirty people though."

"You sure the little boy's in there alone? Right now?"

"I saw them leave, Officer. I'm sure. He's in there. He's a quiet little guy. Never hear a peep out of him. He's in there."

"What apartment is the landlady in? We'll need a passkey."

"Martha went to the movies tonight. She told me she was going. I never thought about the key." The woman shook her head and tugged at the frayed waistband of the olive stretch pants that were never meant to be stretched so much.

"We can't just break the door down on this information."

"Why not? The kid's only three and he's in there alone."

"No," said Gus, shaking his head. "He could be in there and maybe they took him when you weren't looking. Maybe a lot of things. We'll just have to come back later when they're home and try to get invited inside to take a look around."

"Goddamn," said the woman. "The one time in my

life I call a cop and try to do a decent thing and look what happens."

"Let me go try the door," said Gus. "Maybe it's open."

"The one time I call the cops," said the woman to Lucy as Gus stepped outside and walked down the walkway to number twenty-three. He opened the screen and turned the knob and the door slid open.

"Lucy," he called, and stepped inside the stifling apartment, looking carefully for the "dirty little terrier" that might suddenly grab him by the ankle. He stepped around a moist stinking brown heap in the center of the floor and decided the dog must be large for a terrier. Then he heard the pat pat on the vinyl tile floor and the gaunt gray dog appeared from the bathroom, looked at Gus, wagged his stumpy tail, yawned, and returned to the bathroom. Gus glanced in the empty bedroom and pointed to the pile in the floor when Lucy entered and she walked around it and followed him into the living room.

"Dirty people," said the woman, who had followed Lucy inside.

"This certainly isn't bad by unfit home standards," explained Gus. "It has to be really dangerous. Broken windows, leaky stove. Clothes hanging over an open flame. Knee-deep in defecation, not just a pile in the floor. And garbage laying around. Clogged toilet. I've seen places where the wall seems to move and then you realize that it's a solid sheet of roaches. This isn't bad. And there's no child in that bedroom."

"He's here I tell you!"

"Look for yourself," said Gus, and stood aside as the woman bounced into the bedroom. Her cheeks shook with every step, she walked so heavily.

It was now quite dark and Lucy switched on the hall light and walked toward the small bathroom.

"He's got to be here," said the woman. "I watched them leave."

"Gus!" said Lucy, and he came to the bathroom door as she switched on the light and he saw the little boy on the floor by the bathtub curled up with the dog on a pile of bath towels. The boy was asleep and even before Lucy turned on the light Gus saw the absurd purple rings around his eyes and the swollen mouth cracked and raw from a recent beating. The boy slobbered and wheezed and Gus guessed the nose was broken. The coagulation had the nostrils blocked and Gus saw the way the hand was bent.

"Dirty people," whispered the woman, and then began crying at once, and Lucy took her out without Gus saying anything. Lucy was back in a moment and neither of them spoke as Lucy lifted him in her arms and took him to the bedroom where he didn't awaken until she had him dressed. Gus marveled at her strength and how she gently managed the broken wrist and never woke him until they were starting out of the apartment.

The boy saw Gus first when he awoke and the swollen eyes stared for a second and then through pain or terror the fearful moaning started which never ceased for the hour they were with the boy.

"We'll be back," said Gus to the woman who stood sobbing in the doorway of her apartment. Gus tried to take the boy when they started down the stairway, but when he touched the boy he recoiled and uttered a shriek. Lucy said, "It's okay, Gus, he's afraid of you. There, there, darling." And she patted him as Gus shined his light on the stairway for her. In a few moments they were driving to Central Receiving Hospital and each time Gus got too near the little boy, the moan became a terrible cry so he let Lucy handle him.

"He doesn't even look three years old," said Gus when they parked in the hospital parking lot. "He's so little."

Gus waited in the hallway while they worked on the boy and when a second doctor was called in to look at the arm, Gus peered through the door and saw the first doctor, a floppy-haired young man, nod to the second doctor and point to the little boy whose battered face, green and blue and purple in the naked light, looked as though it had been painted by a surrealist gone mad. "Dig the crazy clownface," said the first doctor with a bitter smile.

Lucy came out in fifteen minutes and said, "Gus, his rectum was stitched up!"

"His rectum?"

"It had been stitched up! Oh Christ, Gus, I know it's usually the father in these sex things, but Christ, I can't believe it."

"Was it a professional stitching job?"

"Yes. A doctor did it. Why wouldn't the doctor notify the police? Why?"

"There are doctors," said Gus.

"He's afraid of men, Gus. He was just as much afraid of the doctor as he was of you. The nurse and I had to pet him and talk to him so the doctor could get near him." Lucy looked for a moment like she would cry but instead she lit a cigarette and walked with Gus to the phone and waited until he phoned the watch commander.

"He's a bright child," said Lucy, as Gus waited for the lieutenant to come to the phone. "When the nurse asked him who did that to his rectum, he said, 'Daddy did it 'cause I'm a bad boy.' Oh Christ, Gus . . ."

It was eleven o'clock before they completed their reports on the boy who was admitted to General Hospital. The parents hadn't returned home yet and Lieutenant Dilford had another team staked out on the apartment. Gus and Lucy resumed patrol.

"There's no sense thinking about it," said Gus when Lucy was silent for a half hour.

"I know," she said, forcing a smile and Gus thought of her comforting the child and thought how beautiful she had looked then.

"My gosh, it's almost eleven," said Gus. "You hungry?"

"No."

"But can you eat?"

"You eat. I'll have coffee."

"Let's both have coffee," said Gus, driving to a restaurant on Sunset Boulevard where there were booths for two and anyone who noticed them would think they were lovers or perhaps a young married couple. Gus thought of how he was wrinkling at the corners of his mouth much like his mother. He smiled, because on second thought no one would believe he was a *young* lover.

When they were seated in the booth in the bright spacious restaurant Gus noticed the rusty smear on the shoulder of her dress and he thought again of how she had been with the child, of how strong she was in every way and how capable. He wondered what it would be like to live your life with someone whom you did not have to take care of and he wondered what it would be like to have someone take care of you occasionally, or at least pretend to. The anger started to build when he thought of Vickie and his mother and at least the army could take care of his brother for a few years. Gus vowed that if his mother let John freeload off her when he returned from the service that she would do it on her county check because he would refuse to give her another cent. As soon as he thought this he knew it was a lie because he too was basically a weakling, his only strength being that he could earn a living. When it came down to it he would go on giving them money because he was too much of a weakling to do otherwise. How much easier would life be, he wondered, being married to a strong girl like Lucy.

"You've got blood on your dress," said Gus, nodding to the smear on her shoulder and he was immediately sorry he said it because he should be trying to cheer her up.

"I don't care," she said, not bothering to look at it, and something had been building up in him. At that moment he almost blurted something. If those steady eyes had been on him instead of on the table he probably would have blurted it but he didn't, and was glad he didn't, because she probably would have looked at him sadly and said, "But that's not what I meant at all."

Gus noticed the three teen-age girls in the large booth across from them gossiping in shrill voices and smoking compulsively as they tried in vain to handle the two little boys who kept slipping unnoticed to the floor and scampering down the aisle between the booths.

One of the girls with a proud bulging belly smiled often at the children of her adolescent girl friends, who had no doubt long since found the mystery of motherhood to be quite different from what had been anticipated. All three girls had ugly hairdos, high, teased, and bleached, and Gus thought that Vickie had been a mother that young. Then the guilt, which he knew was foolish, began to come again, but he forgot it when one of the young mothers grabbed the red-haired tot and cracked him across the face as she whispered, "Sit down and behave you little son of a bitch."

Their coffee was half drunk when Lucy said, "Have you been thinking about the little boy, Gus?"

"Not at all," said Gus.

"Isn't it hard not to?"

"No it's not. Not after you get the hang of it. And you should learn that as soon as you can, Lucy."

"What should I think about?"

"Your own problems. That's what I've been doing. Worrying about my own petty problems."

"Tell me about *your* problems, Gus," said Lucy. "Give me something else to worry about."

"Well, we haven't made a juvenile arrest for three days. The boss is going to be getting on us. That's something to worry about."

"Do you *really* like juvenile work, Gus? I mean all things considered do you like being a kiddy cop?"

"I do, Lucy. It's not easy to explain, but it's like, well, especially with the little ones, I like the job because *we* protect them. Take the boy tonight. His father will be arrested and maybe the D.A. will be able to show that he did those things to the boy and maybe he won't. The boy will be a very bad witness or I miss my guess. Maybe the mother will tell the truth, but that's doubtful. And by the time the lawyers, headshrinkers, and criminologists have their say, nothing much will happen to him. But at least we got the boy out of there. I'm sure juvenile court won't give him back to them. Maybe we've saved his life. I like to think that we protect the children. To tell you the truth, if the door'd been locked I would've broken it down. I'd just about made up my mind. We're the only ones who can save the little kids from their parents."

"Wouldn't you like to take a man like that and make him confess?" said Lucy, smashing her cigarette butt in the ashtray.

"I used to think I could torture the truth out of people," Gus smiled, "but after I was a policeman for a while and saw and arrested some of the really bad ones, I found that I didn't even want to touch them or be with them. I'd never make the grade in a medieval dungeon."

"I had a very proper and square upbringing," said Lucy, sipping her coffee as Gus stared at a place on her white collarbone where the brown hair touched it and caressed it when she moved her head even slightly. He was disgusted because his heart was racing and his hands were clammy. So he stopped staring at that tender patch of flesh. "My dad teaches high school, like I told you, and Mother would have trouble believing that a parent would even let his child go around without freshly washed drawers. They're good people, you know? How can good people conceive of the existence of really bad people? I was going to be a social worker until I found what L.A.P.D. was paying policewomen. How could I ever be a social worker now that I've caught the scent of evil? People aren't basically good after all, are they?"

"But maybe they're not bad, either."

"But they're not good, damn it. All my professors told me they were good! And people lie. God, how they lie. I can't get over how people lie."

"That was the single most difficult thing for me to learn," Gus said. "I believed people for my first year or so on the job. No matter what anybody said. I wouldn't even listen to Kilvinsky. All my life I believed what people told me was the truth, and I was a lousy policeman until I got over that mistake. Now I know they'll lie when the truth would help. They'll lie when their lives depend on the truth."

"What a rotten way to make a living," said Lucy.

"Not for a man. For a woman, maybe. But you'll find someone and get married. You won't be doing this all your life." Gus avoided her eyes when he said it.

"I'll be sure not to marry a policeman. That would mean I couldn't escape it."

"Cops are terrible husbands anyway," Gus smiled. "Divorce rate is sky high."

"You're a cop and you're not a terrible husband."

"How do you know?" he said, and then was caught and trapped by the brown eyes.

"I know you. Better than I've ever known anyone."

"Well," said Gus, "I don't know . . . well . . ." and then he gave up and succumbed to the unblinking eyes, a happy gray rabbit surrendering to the benevolent lethal embrace of the fox and he decided that wherever the conversation went from here he would go with it willingly. Now his heart hammered joyfully.

"You're a good policeman," she said. "You know how things are and yet you're gentle and compassionate, especially with kids. That's a rare thing you know. How can you know what people are and still treat them like they were good?"

"People are weak. I guess I'm resigned to handling weak people. I guess I know them because I'm so weak myself."

"You're the strongest man I've ever known, and the gentlest."

"Lucy, I want to buy you a drink after work tonight. We'll just have time for one before the bars close. Will you stop at Marty's Lounge with me?"

"I don't think so."

"Oh, I don't mean anything by it," said Gus, cursing himself for saying such a silly thing, because he meant everything by it and of course she knew he meant everything by it.

"This will be our last night together," said Lucy.

"What do you mean?"

"The lieutenant asked me tonight if I'd like to be loaned to Harbor Juvenile starting tomorrow and if it worked out maybe it could be permanent. I told him I'd like to think about it. I've decided."

"But that's too far to drive! You live in Glendale."

"I'm a single girl who lives in an apartment. I can move."

"But you like police work! The Harbor will be too dull. You'll miss the action you get around here."

"Was it terrible growing up without a father, Gus?" she asked suddenly.

"Yes, but . . ."

"Could you ever do that to your children?"

"What?"

"Could you ever make them grow up without a father, or with a weekend father, twice a month?"

He wanted to say "yes" to the eyes that he knew wanted him to say "yes," but he faltered. He often thought later that if he hadn't faltered he might have said "yes," and where would things have gone if he had merely said "yes." But he did not say "yes," he said nothing for several seconds, and her mouth smiled and she said, "Of course you couldn't. And that's the kind of man I want to marry me and give me babies. I should've found you about three kids ago. Now how about taking me to the station? I'm going to ask the lieutenant if I can go home. I have a rotten headache."

There must be something he could say but the more he thought, the less sense all this made. His brain was whirling when he parked in the station lot and while Lucy was putting her things away he decided that now, this moment, he would meet her in the parking lot at her car and he would tell her something. They would work out something because if he didn't do it now, right now, he never would. And his very life, no, his soul was on the line.

"Oh, Plebesly," said Lieutenant Dilford, stepping out of his office and beckoning to Gus.

"Yes, sir?" said Gus, entering the watch commander's office.

"Sit down for a second, Gus. I've got some bad news for you. Your wife called."

"What happened?" asked Gus, leaping to his feet. "The kids? Did something happen?"

"No, no. Your wife and kids are okay. Sit down, Gus."

"My mother?" asked Gus, ashamed at his relief that it was his mother, not his children.

"It's your friend Andy Kilvinsky, Gus. I knew him well when I worked University years ago. Your wife said that she was called tonight by a lawyer up in Oregon. Kilvinsky left you a few thousand dollars. He's dead, Gus. He shot himself."

Gus heard the lieutenant's voice droning monotonously for several seconds before he got up and walked to the front door, and the lieutenant was nodding and saying something as though he approved. But Gus did not know what he was saying as he walked weak-legged down the stairway to his car in the parking lot. He was out of the parking lot and on his way home before he started to cry and he thought of Kilvinsky and cried for him. His head bent in anguish and he thought incoherently of the little boy tonight and of all fatherless children. He could no longer see the road. Then he thought of himself and his grief and shame and anger. The tears came like lava. He pulled to the curb and the tears scalded him and his body was convulsed by shuddering sobs for all the silent misery of life. He no longer knew for whom he wept and he was past caring. He wept alone.

18. The Huckster

"I'm sure glad they sent me to Seventy-seventh Street," said Dugan, the ruddy-faced little rookie who had been Roy's partner for a week. "I've learned a hell of a lot from working a Negro division. And I've had good partners breaking me in."

"Seventy-seventh Street is as good a place to work as any," said Roy, thinking how glad he'd be when the sun dropped below the elevated Harbor freeway. The streets would begin to cool and the uniform would become bearable.

"You been here quite a while now, haven't you, Roy?"

"About fifteen months. You're busy in this division. There's always something happening so you're busy. There's no time to sit and think, and time passes. That's why I like it."

"You ever work in a white division?"

"Central," Roy nodded.

"Is it the same as a black division?"

"It's slower. Not as much crime so it's slower. Time passes slower. But it's the same. People are all murderous bastards, they're just a little darker down here."

"How long have you been back to work, Roy? If you don't mind talking about it. As soon as I transferred in, I heard right away about how you were shot. Not many guys have ever survived a shotgun blast in the stomach, I guess."

"Not many."

"I guess you hate to talk about it."

"I don't hate to but I'm tired talking about it. I talked about it for the past five months when I was working light duty on the desk. I told the story a thousand times to every curious policeman who wanted to see how I screwed up and got myself shot like that. I'm just tired telling it. You don't mind."

"Oh, hell no, Roy. I understand completely. You *are* feeling okay, now, aren't you. I mean I'll be glad to drive *and* keep books any night you want to take it easy."

"I'm okay, Dugan," Roy laughed. "I played three hard games of handball last week. I'm doing fine, physically."

"I figure I'm lucky to have an experienced partner who's been around and done everything. But I ask too many questions sometimes. I have a big Irish mouth that I can't control sometimes."

"Okay, partner," Roy smiled.

"Anytime you want me to shut up just say the word."

"Okay, partner."

"Twelve-A-Nine, Twelve-A-Nine, see the woman, four five nine report, eighty-three twenty-nine south Vermont, apartment B as in boy."

"Twelve-A-Nine, roger," said Dugan, and Roy turned into the orange and purple smog-streaked sunset and drove leisurely to the call.

"I used to think most burglaries happened at night," said Dugan. "When I was a civilian, I mean. I guess the biggest portion happen during the day when people aren't home."

"That's right," said Roy.

"Most burglars wouldn't go in an occupied pad at night, would they?"

"Too dangerous," said Roy, lighting a cigarette, which tasted better than the last, now that it was cooling off.

"I'd sure like to nail a good burglar one of these nights. Maybe we'll get one tonight."

"Maybe," Roy answered, turning south on Vermont Avenue from Florence.

"I'm going to continue my education," said Dugan. "I picked up a few units since getting out of the navy but now I'm going to get serious and go after a degree in police science. You going to school, Roy?"

"No."

"You ever go?"

"I used to."

"Got quite a ways to go for your degree?"

"Twenty units maybe."

"Is that all? That's terrific. You going to sign up this semester?"

"Too late."

"You *are* going to finish?"

"Of course I am," said Roy and his stomach began to

burn from a sudden wave of indigestion and a shudder of nausea followed. Indigestion brought nausea now. His stomach would never be reliable again he supposed, and this bright-eyed rookie was upsetting his stomach with his prying, and his exasperating innocence.

That would change, Roy thought. Not abruptly, but gradually. Life would steal his innocence a bit at a time like an owl steals chicks until the nest is empty and awesome in its loneliness.

"That looks like the pad, partner," said Dugan, putting on his cap and opening the door before Roy stopped the car.

"Wait'll I stop, Dugan," said Roy. "I don't want you breaking a leg. This is only a report call."

"Oh, sorry," Dugan smiled, reddening.

It was an upstairs apartment at the rear. Dugan tapped on the door lightly with the butt of his flashlight as Roy usually did, and as he probably had seen Roy do. Roy also noticed that Dugan had switched to Roy's brand of cigarettes and had bought a new three-cell, big-headed flashlight like Roy's even though his five-cell was only a few weeks old. I always wanted a son, Roy thought, sardonically, as he watched Dugan knock and step carefully to the side of the door as Roy had taught him to do on any call no matter how routine, at any time. And he always had his right hand free, carrying the report notebook and the flashlight in the left. He kept his hat on when they entered a house until they were absolutely sure what they had and only then did they sit down and remove the hats and relax. But Roy never relaxed anymore even when he wanted to relax, even as he concentrated on relaxation, because he must if his stomach would ever heal. He could not afford an ulcer now, could never afford one. He wanted so to relax. But now Dorothy was hounding him to let her new fat middle-aged husband adopt Becky. He had told her he'd see them both dead first and Dorothy had been trying to reach him through his mother whom Dorothy had always found an intercessor. And he was thinking of Becky and how she said "Daddy" and how incredibly beautiful and golden she was. The apartment door was opened by a girl who was not beautiful and golden but Roy thought immediately that she was attractive. She was dark-brown-skinned, too dark he thought, even though her eyes were light brown and flecked with black specks that reminded him of the flecks in his daughter's eyes. Roy guessed she was his age or older and he thought the natural African hairdo was attractive on black women even though he despised it on the men. At least she didn't go in for dangling bone or iron earrings and other pretentious Africana. Just the hairdo. That was alright, he thought. It was natural.

She waved them in and pointed carelessly to the ransacked apartment. Roy saw that the molding had been pried from the door with a quarter-inch screwdriver which was then used to easily shim the door.

"These wafer locks aren't worth anything," said Roy, touching the lock with his flashlight.

"Now you tell me," she smiled and shook her head sadly. "They cleaned me out. They really did."

She was surprisingly tall, he noticed, as she stood next to him, not having to tilt her face very much to look in his eyes. He guessed she was five feet nine. And she was shapely.

"Did you touch anything?" asked Dugan.

"No."

"Let's see if we can find some nice smooth items that prints can be lifted from," said Dugan, putting his notebook down and prowling around the apartment.

"This happened while you were at work?" asked Roy, sitting on a high stool at the kitchen bar.

"Yes."

"Where do you work?"

"I'm a dental technician. I work downtown."

"Live alone?"

"Yes."

"What all is missing?"

"Color TV set. A wristwatch, Polaroid camera. Clothes. Just about everything I own that's worth a damn."

"That's a shame," said Roy, thinking that she was *very* shapely and thinking that he had never tried a black woman and had not tried any woman since recovering from the wound, except for Velma, the overweight beautician whom he had met through his mother's neighbor Mrs. Smedley. Velma hadn't been interesting enough to attract him more than once every two or three weeks and he wondered if the buckshot hadn't done something to diminish his sex drive, and if it did, what the hell, it would be natural for him to lose the full appreciation of one of the few pleasures life seemed to hold for every poor son of a bitch it finally murdered.

"Is there much of a chance of getting the TV back?" she asked.

"Do you know the serial number?"

"Afraid not," she said.

"Not too much chance then."

"Do most burglaries go unsolved?"

"In a way they do. I mean they're not officially cleared. The stolen property is never recovered because burglars sell it real fast to fences or in pawnshops or just to no-questions-asked-people they meet on the street. The burglars usually get caught sooner or later and sometimes the detectives know they're good for lots and lots of jobs, maybe dozens or hundreds, but they usually don't get the property back."

"So the guilty get caught sooner or later, but it doesn't help their victims, is that it?"

"That's about it."

"Bastards," she whispered.

Why doesn't she move, Roy thought. Why doesn't she move farther west to the periphery of the black district. Even if she can't get completely away from it she could move to the salt and pepper periphery where there's less crime. But what the hell, he thought. Some white burglar with a kink would probably strangle her in her bed some night. You can't get away from evil. It leaps all barriers, racial or otherwise.

"It'll take a long time to replace all your losses," said Roy.

"You bet," she said, turning away because there were tears glistening, dampening the heavy fringe of real eyelash. "Want some coffee?"

"Sure," said Roy, glad that Dugan was still rummaging in the bedroom. As he watched her going from the stove to a cupboard he thought: maybe I could go for a little of that. Maybe all of the simple animal pleasures aren't gone for me.

"I'm going to fortify my coffee," she said, handing him a gold-rimmed cup and saucer, cream pitcher, and sugar bowl. She returned to the cupboard, brought out a fifth of unopened Canadian bourbon, cracked the seal, and poured a liberal shot into the coffee.

"I never drink alone," she said, "but tonight I think I'll get loaded. I feel rotten!"

Roy's eyes roved from the girl to the bottle and back and then to the bottle and he told himself that he was not in any danger yet. He only drank because he enjoyed it, because he needed to relax and if the drinking was not good for his stomach, the therapeutic value of a whiskey tranquilizer more than made up for its ill effects. At least he was not interested in drugs. It could have happened in the hospital. It happened to lots of people with long-term painful injuries who were kept on medication. He could get through his shift without a drink, he knew. But he wasn't harming anyone. A few ounces of whiskey always sharpened his wits and not a partner had ever suspected, least of all not little Dugan.

"If I weren't on duty, I'd join you," said Roy.

"Too bad," she said, not looking at him as she took a sip, grimaced, and took a larger one.

"If I were off duty I wouldn't let you drink alone," he said, and watched the glance she gave him and then she turned away and sipped the coffee again and did not answer.

"Might as well get the report started," said Dugan, coming back into the living room. "There's a jewelry box and a few other things in there that might have latent fingerprints on them. I've stacked them in the corner. The print man will be out tonight or tomorrow to dust the dresser and those items."

"I won't be here tomorrow. I work during the day."

"Maybe he can come tonight if he's not too busy," said Dugan.

"He'll come tonight. I'll make sure. I'll tell him you're a special friend of mine," said Roy, and she looked at him again and he saw no sign.

"Well, might as well get started on this report, ma'am," said Dugan. "Can I have your name?"

"Laura Hunt," she said, and this time Roy thought he saw in her eyes a sign.

As they were driving back to the station, Roy began to get jittery. It was not happening as often lately, he told himself. It was not nearly as bad now that he was back in the radio car. Those months of working the desk had been bad, though. He had periodic pain and his nerves were bothering him. He kept a bottle in the trunk of his car and made frequent trips to the parking lot. He worried that Lieutenant Crow, the watch commander, suspected something, but he had never been questioned. He never overdid it. He only drank enough to relax or to assuage the pain or to fight the depression. Only two times did he overdo it, unable to complete his tour of duty. He feigned sickness on those occasions, an attack of nausea he had said, and had gone to the lonely apartment, being careful to keep the speedometer needle pegged at thirty-five miles an hour and concentrating on the elusive white line in the highway. It was much better now that he was in the radio car again. Everything was better. And being back in the old apartment was good for him.

The months of living with his parents had been as damaging to his emotions as anything else. And Carl—with his fat little children and his impeccable wife Marjorie and his new car and his goddamn belly hanging over his belt even though he wasn't thirty years old—Carl was unbearable: "We can still find a spot for you, Roy. Of course, you couldn't expect to start as an *equal* partner, but eventually . . . after all, it *is* the family business and you *are* my brother . . . I always thought you could be a businessman if you just made up your mind to grow up and now I hope your brush with death has made you come to your senses and realize where you belong and abandon your whims you remember Roy when I was a child I wanted to be a policeman too and a fireman but I outgrew them and you've admitted that you don't really like your job and if you don't you can never expect to be a really successful policeman if there is such a thing and Roy you must realize by now that you're never going to get your degree in criminology. Roy, you haven't the desire to hit the books again and I don't blame you because why in the hell would you want to be a criminologist anyway and oh you don't want to be one anymore well Roy that's the best news I've heard from you in some time well we can make a place for you in the business and someday soon it can be changed to Fehler and Sons and someday Roy it will be Fehler Brothers and God knows Dad and

Mom would be so pleased and I'll do everything I can to bring you along and make you the kind of businessman worthy of the family name and you know it will be different than working for a boss who is an impersonal taskmaster because I know your faults and weaknesses Roy. God knows we all have them and I'll make allowances because after all you *are* my brother."

When Roy had at last decided to come back to duty and move to the apartment again it had been Carl who was the most bewildered by it all. Christ, I need to relax, Roy thought, looking at Dugan who was driving slowly checking license numbers against the hot sheet. Dugan checked thousands of license numbers against the hot sheet.

"Drive to Eighty-second and Hoover," said Roy.

"Okay, Roy. What for?"

"I want to use the call box."

"To call the station? I thought we were going in with the burglary report anyway."

"I want to call R & I. And I don't want to go in just yet. Let's patrol for a while."

"Okay. There's a call box just down the street."

"Doesn't work."

"Sure it does. I just used it the other night."

"Look, Dugan. Take me to Eighty-second and Hoover. You know that's the call box I always use. It works all the time and I like to use it."

"Okay, Roy," Dugan laughed. "I guess I'll start developing habits too when I get a little more experience."

Roy's heart thumped as he stood behind the opened metal door of the call box and drank hopefully. He might only have to make one call to R & I tonight, he thought grimly. He'd have to be extremely careful with a rookie like Dugan. His throat and stomach were still burning but he drank again and again. He was very nervous tonight. Sometimes it happened like this. His hands would become clammy and he would feel light-headed and he had to relax. He screwed the lid back on the bourbon and replaced the bottle in the call box. Then he stood for a moment sucking and chewing on three breath mints and an enormous wad of chewing gum. He returned to the car where Dugan was impatiently tapping on the steering wheel.

"Let's go to the station now, Dugan my lad," said Roy, already more relaxed, knowing the depression would dissolve.

"Now? Okay, Roy. But I thought you said later."

"Got to go to the can," Roy grinned, lighting a cigarette and whistling a themeless tune as Dugan accelerated.

While Dugan was in the report room getting a DR number for his burglary report, Roy started, wavered, and started again for the parking lot. He debated with himself as he stood by the door of his yellow Chevrolet, but then he realized that another drink could not possibly do more than relax him a bit more and completely defeat the towering specter of depression that was the hardest thing to combat unassisted. He looked around, and seeing no one in the dark parking lot, unlocked the Chevrolet, removed the pint from the glove compartment and took a large fiery mouthful. He capped the bottle, hesitated, uncapped it and took another, then one more, and put the bottle away.

Dugan was ready when he walked back in the station.

"Ready to go, Roy?" Dugan smiled.

"Let's go, my boy," Roy chuckled, but before they had patrolled for half an hour, Roy had to call R & I from the call box at Eighty-second and Hoover.

At 11:00 P.M. Roy was feeling marvelous and he began thinking about the girl. He thought of her bottle too and wondered if she were feeling as fine as he was. He also thought of her smooth lithe body.

"That was a pretty nice-looking girl, that Laura Hunt," said Roy.

"Who?" asked Dugan.

"That broad. The burglary report. You know."

"Oh, yeah, pretty nice," said Dugan. "Wish I could write a ticket. I haven't got a mover yet this month. Trouble is, I haven't learned to spot them yet. Unless a guy blasts right through a red light three seconds late or something obvious like that."

"She was put together," said Roy. "I liked that, didn't you?"

"Yeah. Do you know a good spot to sit? Some good spot where we could get a sure ticket?"

"An apple orchard, huh? Yeah, drive down Broadway,

I'll show you an apple orchard, a stop sign that people hate to stop for. We'll get you six tickets if you want them."

"Just one will do. I think I should try to write one mover a day. What do you think?"

"One every other day is enough to keep the boss happy. We got more to do than write tickets in this goddamn division. Hadn't you noticed?"

"Yes," laughed Dugan, "I guess we're busy with more serious things down here."

"How old are you, Dugan?"

"Twenty-one, why?"

"Just wondering."

"I look young, don't I?"

"About eighteen. I knew you had to be twenty-one to get on the job, but you look about eighteen."

"I know. How old are you, Roy?"

"Twenty-six."

"Is that all? I thought you were older. I guess because I'm a rookie, everyone seems much older."

"Before we get that ticket, drive down Vermont."

"Any place in particular?"

"To the apartment. Where we took the burglary report."

"Any special reason?" asked Dugan, looking at Roy warily, exposing large portions of the whites of his large, slightly protruding eyes, and the eyes shining in the darkness made Roy laugh.

"I'm going to do a little pubic relations, Dugan my boy. I mean public relations."

Dugan drove silently and when they reached the apartment building he turned off on the first side street and shut his lights off.

"I'm still on probation, Roy. I don't want to get in trouble."

"Don't worry," Roy chuckled, dropping his flashlight on the street as he got out of the car.

"What should I do?"

"Wait right here, what else? I'm just going to try to set something up for later. I'll be back in two minutes for heaven's sake."

"Oh, that's good. It's just that I'm on probation," said Dugan as Roy strode unsteadily to the front of the building and almost laughed aloud as he stumbled on the first step.

"Hello," he grinned, before she had a chance to speak, while the door chime still echoed through the breezeway. "I'm almost off duty and I wondered if you were really going to get drunk. I plan to, and one sad drunk always seeks out another, doesn't he?"

"I'm not really surprised to see you," she said, holding a white robe at the bosom, not looking particularly friendly or unfriendly.

"I really *am* sad," he said, still standing in the doorway. "The only sadder face I've seen lately is yours. The way you were tonight. I thought we could have a few drinks and sympathize with each other."

"I have a head start on you," she said, unsmiling, pointing to the fifth on the breakfast bar that was no longer full.

"I can catch up," said Roy.

"I have to get up early and go to work tomorrow."

"I won't stay long. Just a drink or two and a friendly pair of eyes is all I need."

"Can't you find the drink and eyes at home?"

"Only the drink. My place is as lonely as this one."

"What time do you get off?"

"Before one. I'll be here before one."

"That's late as hell."

"Please."

"Alright," she said, and smiled a little for the first time and closed the door softly, as he crept down the stairway, holding the handrail in a tight grip.

"We got a call," said Dugan. "I was about to come and get you."

"What is it?"

"Go to the station, code two. Wonder what's up?"

"Who knows?" said Roy, lighting a cigarette, and opening a fresh stick of gum in case he would be talking to a sergeant at the station.

Sergeant Schumann was waiting in the parking lot when they arrived, along with two other radio car teams. Roy walked carefully when they parked their car and joined the others.

"Okay, everyone's here, I guess," said Schumann, a young sergeant with an imperious manner who annoyed Roy.

"What's up?" asked Roy, knowing that Schumann would make an adventure out of an assignment to write parking tickets.

"We're going to tour Watts," said Schumann. "We've gotten several letters in the last week from Councilman Gibbs' office and a couple from citizens groups complaining about the drunken loafers on the streets in Watts. We're going to clean them up tonight."

"You better rent a couple semi's then," said Betterton, a cigar-smoking veteran, "one little B wagon ain't going to hold the drunks that hang out on one corner."

Schumann cleared his throat and smiled self-consciously as the policemen laughed, all except Benson, a Negro who did not laugh, Roy noticed.

"Well, we're going to make some arrests, anyway," said Schumann. "You men know all the spots around a Hundred and Third and down around Imperial and maybe Ninety-second and Beach. Fehler, you and your partner take the wagon. You other men, take your cars. That'll make six policemen so you shouldn't have any trouble. Stick together. Fill the wagon first, then scoop up a few in your radio cars and bring them in. Not here, take them to Central Jail. I'll make sure it's okay at Central. That's all. Good hunting."

"Oh, sweet Jesus," Betterton groaned, as they walked to their cars. "Good hunting. Did you hear that? Oh, sweet Jesus. I'm glad I retire in a couple years. This is the new breed? Good hunting, men. Oh, Jesus."

"Want me to drive the wagon, Roy," asked Dugan eagerly.

"Of course. You're driving the car tonight, aren't you? You drive the wagon."

"You don't need a chauffeur's license, do you?"

"It's just a beat-up panel truck, Dugan," said Roy as they walked to the rear parking lot. Then Roy stopped, saying, "I just thought of something. I want to get a fresh pack of cigarettes from my car. Get the wagon and meet me in front of the station."

Roy could hear Dugan racing the engine of the wagon as he fumbled in the darkness for his car keys and at last was forced to use the flashlight, but this side of the parking lot was still and quiet and he knew he was worrying unnecessarily. He wouldn't do it if he weren't feeling a little depressed again. Finally he unlocked the car, held the button on the door post in so the overhead light stayed out as he opened the bottle one-handed, expertly, and sat with his legs out of the car ready to jump out in case he heard footsteps. He finished the pint in four or five swallows and felt in the glove compartment for the other but couldn't find it, and he realized there was no other. He had finished it this morning. Funny, he chuckled silently, that's pretty funny. Then he locked the car and walked woodenly to the wagon which Dugan was revving in front of the station. He chewed the mints as he walked and lit a cigarette he didn't really want.

"Might be kind of fun working a drunk wagon," said Dugan, "I've never done it before."

"Oh yeah," said Roy. "Soon as a drunk pukes on you or rubs his shit-covered pants against your uniform, let me know how you like it."

"Never thought of that," said Dugan. "Do you think I should get my gloves? I bought some."

"Leave them. We'll just hold the door open and let the other guys throw the drunks in."

The rattling bumping panel truck was making Roy slightly sick as he leaned his head out the window. The summer breeze felt good. He began to doze and awakened with a start when Dugan drove over the curb into the parking lot at Ninety-second and Beach and the arrests began.

"Maybe we'll find somebody with a little marijuana or something," said Dugan, jumping out of the wagon as Roy looked sleepily at the throng of Negroes, who had been drinking in the parked cars, shooting dice against the back wall of the liquor store, standing, sitting, reclining in discarded chairs, or on milk crates, or on hoods and bumpers of ancient cars which always seemed to be available in any vacant lot or field in Watts. There were even several women among them in the darkness and Roy wondered what the hell was the attraction in these loitering places amid the rubble and broken glass. But then he remembered what some of the houses were like inside and he guessed the smell outdoors was certainly an improvement, although it wasn't any too good because in the loitering places were always packs of prowling hungry dogs and lots of animal and human excrement and lots of winos with all the smells they brought with them. Roy walked carefully to the rear of the wagon and slid the steel bolt back and opened the double doors. He staggered as he stepped back and this annoyed him. Got to watch that, he thought, and then the thought of a drunken policeman loading drunks in the drunk wagon struck him as particularly funny. He began giggling and had to sit in the wagon for a few minutes until he could control his mirth.

They arrested four drunks, one of whom was a ragpicker, lying almost unnoticed against the wall behind three overflowing trash cans. He held a half-eaten brown apple in one bony yellow hand and they had to carry him and flip him into the wagon onto the floor. The other drunks sitting on the benches on each side of the wagon didn't seem to notice the foul bundle at their feet.

They patrolled One Hundred and Third and then drove down Wilmington. In less than a half hour the wagon was filled with sixteen men and each radio car held three more. Betterton waved to Roy and sped ahead toward the Harbor Freeway and downtown as the slower wagon rumbled and clunked along.

"Mustn't be too comfortable back there," said Dugan, "maybe I should drive slower."

"They can't feel anything," said Roy, and this struck him as very amusing. "Don't take the freeway," said Roy. "Let's go on the surface streets. But first go up Hoover."

"What for?"

"I want to call the station."

"We can go by the station, Roy," said Dugan.

"I want to call in. No sense going in. It's out of the way."

"Well, your favorite call box is out of the way, Roy. I think you can use another call box."

"Do as I ask you, please," said Roy deliberately. "I always use the same call box."

"I think I know why. I'm not completely stupid. I'm not driving to that call box."

"Do as I say, goddamnit!"

"Alright, but I don't want to work with you anymore. I'm afraid to work with you, Roy."

"Fine. Go tell Schumann tomorrow that you and me have a personality conflict. Or I'll tell him. Or tell him whatever you want."

"I won't tell him the truth. Don't worry about that. I'm no fink."

"Truth? What the hell is the truth? If you've got that figured out, let *me* know, not Schumann."

Roy sat silently as Dugan drove obediently to the call box and parked in the usual place. Roy went to the box and tried to put his car key in the lock, then he tried his house key, and finally used the call box key. This was very funny too and restored his good humor. He opened it and drank until he finished. He threw it behind the hedge as he always did after his last call of the evening, and he laughed aloud as he walked back to the wagon when he wondered what the resident there thought when he found an empty half-pint in his flower garden each morning.

"Drive up Central Avenue," said Roy. "I want to drive through Newton and see if I see any of the guys I used to know." He was talking slightly slurred now. But as long as he knew it he'd be alright. He was always very careful. He put three fresh sticks of gum in his mouth and smoked as Dugan drove silently.

"This was a good division to work," said Roy, looking at the hundreds of Negroes still on the streets at this hour. "People never go home in Newton Street. You can find thousands of people on the corners at five in the morning. I learned a lot here. I used to have a partner named Whitey Duncan. He taught me a lot. He came to see me when I was hurt. When not many other guys came, he came to see me. Four or five times Whitey came and brought me magazines and cigarettes. He died a few months ago. He was a goddamn drunk and died of cirrhosis of the liver just like a goddamn drunk. Poor old drunk. He liked people too. Really liked them. That's the worst kind of drunk to be. That'll kill you fast. Poor old fat bastard."

Roy began dozing again and checked his watch. After they got rid of the drunks and got back to the station it would be end of watch and he could change clothes and go see her. He didn't really still want her so much physically, but she had eyes he could talk to, and he wanted to talk. Then Roy saw the huge crowd at Twenty-second and Central.

"There's a place you can always get a load of drunks," said Roy, noticing that his face was becoming numb.

Dugan stopped for the pedestrians and Roy had a hilarious thought.

"Hey, Dugan, you know what this wagon reminds me of? An Italian huckster that used to peddle vegetables on our street when I was a kid. His panel truck was just like this one, smaller maybe, but it was blue and closed in like this one and he'd bang on the side and yell, 'Ap-ple, ra-dish, coo-cumbers for sale!' " Roy began laughing uproariously and Dugan's worried look made him laugh even harder. "Turn left quick and drive through the parking lot where all those assholes are standing around shuckin' and jivin'. Drive through there!"

"What for, Roy? Damn it, you're drunk!"

Roy reached across the cab and turned the wheel sharply to the left, still chuckling.

"Okay, let go," said Dugan, "I'll drive through, but I promise you I'm not working with you tomorrow night or ever!"

Roy waited until Dugan was halfway through the parking lot, parting the worried throngs of loiterers before him, moving slowly toward the other driveway and the street. Some of the more drunken ones scurried away from the wagon. Roy leaned out the window and slapped the side of the blue panel truck three times and shouted, "Nig-gers, nig-gers, niggers for sale!"

AUGUST 1965

19. The Queue

It was bad on Wednesday. The Hollenbeck policemen listened in disbelief to their police radios which broadcast a steady flow of help and assistance calls put out by the officers from Seventy-seventh Street Station.

"The riot is starting," said Blackburn as he and Serge patrolled nervously in the juvenile car but could not concentrate on anything but what was happening in the southeast part of the city.

"I don't think it'll be a real riot," said Serge.

"I tell you it's starting," said Blackburn, and Serge wondered if he could be right as he listened to the frantic operators sending cars from several divisions into Seventy-seventh Street where crowds apparently were forming at One Hundred Sixteenth Street and Avalon Boulevard. By ten o'clock a command post had been set up at Imperial and Avalon and a perimeter patrol was activated. It was obvious to Serge as he listened that there were insufficient police units to cope with a deteriorating situation.

"I tell you it's starting," said Blackburn. "It's L.A.'s turn. Burn, burn, burn. Let's get the hell to a restaurant and eat because we ain't going home tonight I tell you."

"I'm ready to eat," said Serge. "But I'm not going to worry too much yet."

"I tell you they're ready to rip loose," said Blackburn, and Serge could not determine if his partner was glad of it or not. Perhaps he's glad, thought Serge. After all, his life has been rather uneventful since his wife sued him for divorce and he was afraid to be caught in any more adulterous situations until the case was decided.

"Where do we want to eat?" asked Serge.

"Let's go to Rosales' place. We ain't ate there in a couple weeks. At least I haven't. Is it still on with you and the little waitress?"

"I see her once in a while," said Serge.

"Sure don't blame you," said Blackburn. "She's turned

out real nice. Wish I could see somebody. Anybody. Doesn't she have a cousin?"

"Nope."

"I can't see my own women. My goddamn wife got my notebook with every goddamn number in it. I'm afraid she's got the places staked out. I wish I had one she didn't know about."

"Can't you wait until your divorce goes to trial?"

"Wait? Goddamn. You know I'm a man that needs my pussy. I ain't had a goddamn thing for almost three months. By the way, your little girl friend ain't working as much as she used to, is she?"

"She's going to college," said Serge. "She still works some. I think she'll be working tonight."

"What's with your other girl friend? That blonde that picked you up that night at the station. It still on with her?"

"Paula? It's more or less on, I guess."

"Bet she wants to marry you, right? That's what all those cunts want. Don't do it, I'm telling you. You got the life now, boy. Don't change it."

Serge could never control his heartbeat when he was near her and that was the thing that most annoyed him. When they left their car parked at the curb and entered the restaurant only minutes before Mr. Rosales put up the closed sign, his heart galloped, and Mr. Rosales nodded his gray head and waved them to a booth. He had thought for months that Mr. Rosales had guessed how it was with him and Mariana, but there had been no indication, and at last, he decided it was only the tattered remnants of his conscience fluttering in the hot wind of his passion. He made it a point not to meet her more than once a week, sometimes less, and he always brought her home early and feigned perfect innocence even though they had just spent several hours in a tiny motel room which the management kept for Hollenbeck policemen who only had to show a badge in lieu of payment. He thought at first that it would be only a short time before the inevitable melodrama would begin and she would wail and weep that she couldn't go on like this in a cheap motel and that her tears would destroy the pleasure—but it hadn't happened yet. When he was making love to Mariana it was the same no matter where, and it seemed to be so with her also. She had never complained and there were never any serious promises made by either of them. He was glad it was so, and yet he waited anxiously for the melodrama. Surely it would come.

And making love with Mariana was something to analyze, he thought, but he had as yet been unable to understand how she alone had made it so different. It wasn't only because he had been her first, because he had felt like this with that dark-eyed little daughter of the bracero when he was fifteen, and he was certainly not the first with that one, and sometimes he was not the first on any given evening with that one. It was not only that he had been first, it was that he was purged each time when it was over. Her heat burned him from the inside out and he was at peace. She opened his pores and drained the impurities. That was why he kept coming back for more although it was difficult enough to single-handedly match the sexual prowess of Paula who was suspecting there was another girl and was demanding more and more of him until the ultimatum and melodrama was certainly overdue with Paula also. Paula had almost exploded in tears two nights before when they were watching an inane television movie and he had commented on the aging spinster in the story who was unhappily pursuing a fat little stockbroker who was not able to break the stranglehold of a domineering wife.

"Show a little pity!" she almost shouted when he snorted at the miserable woman. "Where's your compassion? She's scared to death of being alone. She needs love, damn it. Can't you see that she has no love?"

He decided to be careful after that, very careful about what he said because the end was very near. He would have to decide whether to marry Paula or not. And if he didn't, he decided he would probably never marry because the prospects would never again be this good.

He thought this as they waited for Mariana to come from the kitchen and take their order, but she didn't come. Mr. Rosales himself came to the table with coffee and a writing pad and Serge said, "Where is she?" and watched closely but detected nothing in the eyes or manner of the proprietor who said, "I thought she should study tonight. I told her to stay home and study. She does so well with her studies. I do not want her to become too tired or upset because of overwork or anything else." He glanced at Serge when he said "anything else," and it was not a malicious glance, but now Serge was positive the old man knew how it was, but Christ, anyone with any intelligence would know that he wasn't taking her out several times a month this past year just to hold her hand. Christ, he was almost twenty-nine years old and she was twenty. What the hell did anybody expect?

Serge toyed with his food, and Blackburn as usual devoured everything in sight and without much urging finished most of what Serge didn't eat.

"Worried about the riot?" asked Blackburn. "Don't blame you. Makes me a little queasy to think that they might do here what they did in the East."

"It'll never be like that here," said Serge. "We're not going to tolerate the bullshit as long as they did back East."

"Yeah, we're the best Department in the country," said Blackburn. "That's what our press notices say. But I want to know how a few hundred bluesuits are going to turn back a black ocean of people."

"It won't be like that, I'm sure it won't."

They were all held over in Hollenbeck that night. But at 3:00 A.M. they were permitted to secure, and Blackburn only shrugged when Serge told him that it was evidently quelled and that tomorrow things would be normal.

But on Thursday things were not normal and at 7:05 P.M. a crowd of two thousand again gathered at One Hundred Sixteenth and Avalon and units from Central, University, Newton and Hollenbeck were rushed to the trouble spot. At 10:00 P.M. Serge and Blackburn had given up all pretense of patrolling and sat in the station parking lot listening to the police radio in disbelief as did four of the uniformed officers who were preparing to leave for the Watts area.

Shots were fired at a police vehicle at Imperial Highway and Parmelee, and an hour later Serge heard a sergeant being denied a request for tear gas.

"I guess they don't think the sergeant knows what the fuck is going on out there," said Blackburn. "I guess they think he should reason with them instead of using gas on them."

The word came again a few hours past midnight that

they would not be sent to Watts and Serge and Blackburn were given permission to secure. Serge had called Mariana at the restaurant at ten-thirty and she had agreed to meet him in front of the Rosales house whenever he could get there. She often studied until late in the morning and Serge would come by when the Rosales family was asleep. He would park across the street in the shade of an elm and she would come out to the car and it would always be better than he remembered. He could not seem to hold the moment in his mind. Not the moment with Mariana. He could not remember the catharsis of her lovemaking. He could only remember that it was like bathing in a warm pool in the darkness and he felt refreshed and never at any time did he think it was not good for *him*. For *her*, he wondered.

He almost didn't stop because it was fifteen past two, but the light was burning and so he stopped, knowing that if she were awake she would hear. In a moment he saw her tiptoe out the front door wearing the soft blue robe and filmy pink nightgown he had come to know so well even though he had never seen it in the light. But he knew the feel of it well and his mouth became dry as he held a hand over the dome light and opened the door for her.

"I thought you would not come," she said when he stopped kissing her for a moment.

"I had to come. You know I can't stay away very long."

"It is the same with me, Sergio, but wait. Wait!" she said, pushing his hands away.

"What is it, little dove?"

"We should talk, Sergio. It is exactly one year since we went to the mountain and I saw my first lake. Do you remember?"

This is it, he thought almost triumphantly. I knew it would come. And though he dreaded the weeping, he was glad it would be finally ended. The waiting.

"I remember the mountain and the lake."

"I regret nothing, Sergio. You should know that."

"But?" he said, lighting a cigarette, preparing for an embarrassing scene. Paula will be next, he thought. After Mariana.

"But it is so much better if it should stop now while we both feel what we feel for each other."

"You're not pregnant, are you?" Serge said suddenly as the thought struck him that this was what she was preparing to tell him.

"Poor Sergio," she smiled sadly. "No, *querido*, I am not. I have learned all the ways of prevention well even though they shame me. Poor Sergio. And what if I was? Do you think I would go away with your baby in my stomach? To Guadalajara perhaps? And live my poor life out raising your child and yearning only for your arms? I have told you before, Sergio, you read too many books. I have my own life to live. It is as important to me as yours is to you."

"What the hell is this? What are you driving at?" He couldn't see her eyes in the darkness and he didn't like any of this. She had never talked like this before and it was unnerving him. He wanted to turn on the light to be sure it was her.

"I cannot pretend I can get over you easy, Sergio. I cannot pretend I do not love you enough to live like this. But it would not be forever. Sooner or later, you would marry your other one and please do not tell me there is not another one."

"I won't, but . . ."

"Please, Sergio, let me finish. If you can be a whole man by marrying your other one, then do it. Do something, Sergio. Find out what you must do. And I say this: if you find it is my kind of life you want to share, then come to this house. Come on a Sunday in the afternoon like you did the first time when we went to the lake in the mountain. Tell señor Rosales what you wish to say to me, because he is my father here. Then if he approves, come to me and say it. And then it will be announced in the church and we will not touch each other as we have done, until the night of the marriage. And I will marry you in a white dress, Sergio. But I will not wait for you forever."

Serge groped for the light switch, but she grabbed his hand and when he reached for her desperately she pulled away.

"Why do you talk like this with such a strange voice? My God, Mariana, what've I done?"

"Nothing, Sergio. You have done absolutely nothing. But it has been a year. I was a Catholic before. But since we had our love, I have not been to confession or Communion."

"So, that's it," he nodded. "The goddamn religion's got you all confused. Do you feel sinful when we make love? Is that it?"

"It is not only that, Sergio, but it is partly that. I went to confession last Saturday. I am again a child of God. But it is not only that. I want you, Sergio, but only if you are a complete man. I want Sergio Duran, a *complete* man. Do you understand?"

"Mariana," he said in bleak frustration, but when he reached for her she opened the door and was gliding barefoot across the shadowy street. "Mariana!"

"You must never return, Sergio," she whispered, her voice breaking for an instant, "unless you come as I have said." He squinted through the darkness and saw her standing for a moment straight and still, the long blue robe fluttering against her calves. Her chin was uplifted as always, and he felt the pain in his chest grow sharper and thought for one horrible moment that he was being ripped in two and only part of him sat there mute before this ghostly apparition whom he had thought he knew and understood.

"And if you come, I will wear white. Do you hear me? I will wear white, Sergio!"

On Friday, the thirteenth of August, Serge was awakened at noon by Sergeant Latham who shouted something in the phone as Serge sat up in bed and tried to make his brain function.

"Are you awake, Serge?" asked Latham.

"Yeah, yeah," he said, finally. "Now I am. What the hell did you say?"

"I said that you've got to come in right away. All the juvenile officers are being sent to Seventy-seventh Street Station. Do you have a uniform?"

"Yeah, Christ, I think so. I got it here somewhere."

"Are you sure you're awake?"

"Yeah, I'm awake."

"Okay, dig your blue suit out of mothballs and put it on. Take your baton, flashlight and helmet. Don't wear a necktie and don't bother taking your soft hat. You're going into combat, man."

"What's happening now?" asked Serge, his heart already beginning to advance its rhythm.

"Bad. It's bad. Just get the hell down to Seventy-seventh. I'll be there myself as soon as I get all our people there."

Serge cursed as he cut his face twice while shaving. His light-brown eyes were watery, the irises trapped in a web of scarlet. The toothpaste and mouthwash did not cleanse his mouth of the vile taste which the pint of scotch had left there. He had drunk and read until an hour past daybreak after Mariana had left him there babbling to himself in the darkness and he hadn't yet thought it all out. How could he have been so wrong about his little dove who was in fact a hunting hawk, strong and independent. Was he the predator or the prey? She didn't need him the way he had gleefully imagined. When the hell would he be right about someone or something? And now, with a brain-cracking headache and a stomach twisted with anxiety and seething alcohol, and perhaps two hours sleep, he was going into he knew not what, where he might need every bit of physical strength and mental alertness to save his very life.

When this insanity in the streets was over and things returned to normal he would marry Paula, he thought. He would accept as much of her father's dowry as was offered and play house and live as comfortably as he possibly could. He would stay away from Mariana because it was only her youth and virginity that had attracted him in the first place as it would have attracted any reasonably degenerate hedonist. Now he could see that stewing over that had been stupidly romantic because it appeared that she had taken more than he had. He doubted whether she were feeling as miserable as he was at this very moment and he suddenly thought, let them shoot me, let some black son of a bitch shoot me. I'm not capable of finding peace. Maybe there's no such thing. Maybe it exists only in books.

Serge found that he could not buckle the Sam Browne and had to let it out a notch. He had been drinking more lately and was not playing handball as much since he was trying to handle two women. The waistband of the blue woolen trousers was hard to button and he had to suck in his stomach to fasten both buttons. He still looked slim enough in the tight-fitting heavy woolen uniform, he thought, and decided to concentrate on such trivialities as his growing stomach because he could not afford at this moment to be caught in a swamp of depression. He was going into something that no policeman in this city had ever before been asked to face and his death wish might be happily granted by some fanatic. He knew himself well enough to know that he was definitely afraid to die and therefore probably did not really want to.

Serge saw the smoke before he was five miles from Watts and realized then what policemen had been saying for two days, that this conflagration would not remain on One Hundred and Sixteenth Street or even on One Hundred and Third, but that it would spread through the entire southern metropolitan area. The uniform was unbearable in the heat and even the sunglasses didn't stop the sun from cutting his eyes and boiling his brain. He looked at the helmet beside him on the seat and dreaded putting it on. He stayed on the Harbor Freeway to Florence Avenue then south on Broadway to Seventy-seventh Station which was as chaotic as he expected, with scores of police cars going and coming and newsmen roaming aimlessly about looking for escorts into the perimeter, and the scream of sirens from ambulances, fire trucks and radio cars. He parked on the street as close as he could get to the station and was waved wildly to the watch commander's office by the desk officer who was talking into two telephones, looking like he was feeling about as miserable as Serge. The watch commander's office was jammed with policemen and reporters who were being asked to remain outside by a perspiring sergeant with a face like a dried apple. The only one who seemed to have some idea of what was happening was a balding lieutenant with four service stripes on his sleeve. He sat calmly at a desk and puffed on a brown hooked pipe.

"I'm Duran from Hollenbeck Juvenile," said Serge.

"Okay, boy, what're your initials?" asked the lieutenant.

"S," said Serge.

"Serial number?"

"One o five eight three."

"Hollenbeck Juvenile, you say?"

"Yes."

"Okay, you'll be known as Twelve-Adam-Forty-five. You'll team up with Jenkins from Harbor and Peters from Central. They should be out in the parking lot."

"Three-man cars?"

"You'll wish it was six," said the lieutenant, making an entry in a logbook. "Pick up two boxes of thirty-eight ammo from the sergeant out by the jail. Make sure there's one shotgun in your car and an extra box of shotgun rounds. What division are you from, boy?" said the lieutenant to the small policeman in an oversized helmet who came in behind him. Serge then recognized him as Gus Plebesly from his academy class. He hadn't seen Plebesly in perhaps a year, but he didn't stop. Plebesly's eyes were round and blue as ever. Serge wondered if he looked as frightened as Plebesly.

"You drive," said Serge. "I don't know the division."

"Neither do I," said Jenkins. He had a bobbing Adam's apple and blinked his eyes often. Serge could see that he was not the only one who wished he were somewhere else.

"Do you know Peters?" asked Serge.

"Just met him," said Jenkins. "He ran inside to take a crap."

"Let's let him drive," said Serge.

"Suits me. You want the shotgun?"

"You can have it."

"I'd rather have my blanket and teddy bear right now," said Jenkins.

"This him?" asked Serge, pointing at the tall, loose-jointed man striding toward them. He seemed too long for his uniform pants which stopped three inches above the shoes, and the shirt cuffs were too short. He was pretty well built and Serge was glad. Jenkins didn't seem too impressive and they'd probably need lots of muscle before this tour of duty ended.

Serge and Peters shook hands and Serge said, "We've elected you driver, okay?"

"Okay," said Peters, who had two service stripes on his sleeve, making him senior officer in the car. "Either of you guys know the division?"

"Neither of us," said Jenkins.

"That makes it unanimous," said Peters. "Let's go before I talk myself into another bowel movement. I got eleven years on this job but I never saw what I saw here last night. Either of you here last night?"

"Not me," said Serge.

"I was on station defense at Harbor Station," said Jenkins, shaking his head.

"Well pucker up your asshole and get a good grip on the seat because I'm telling you you aren't going to believe this is America. I saw this in Korea, sure, but this is America."

"Cut it out, or you'll be loosening up *my* bowels," said Jenkins, laughing nervously.

"You'll be able to shit through a screen door without hitting the wire, before too long," said Peters.

Before driving three blocks south on Broadway, which was lined on both sides by roving crowds, a two-pound chunk of concrete crashed through the rear window of the car and thudded against the back of the front seat cushion. A cheer went up from forty or more people who were spilling from the corner of Eighty-first and Broadway as the Communications operator screamed: "Officer needs help, Manchester and Broadway! Officer needs assistance, One O Three and Grape! Officer needs assistance Avalon and Imperial!" And then it became difficult to become greatly concerned by the urgent calls that burst over the radio every few seconds, because when you sped toward one call another came out in the opposite direction. It seemed to Serge they were chasing in a mad S-shape configuration through Watts and back toward Manchester never accomplishing anything but making their car a target for rioters who pelted it three times with rocks and once with a bottle. It was incredible, and when Serge looked at the unbelieving stare of Jenkins he realized what he must look like. Nothing was said during the first forty-five minutes of chaotic driving through the littered streets which were filled with surging chanting crowds and careening fire engines. Thousands of felonies were being committed with impunity and the three of them stared and only once or twice did Peters slow the car down as a group of looters were busy at work smashing windows. Jenkins aimed the shotgun out the window, and as soon as the groups of Negroes broke from the path of the riot gun,

Peters would accelerate and drive to another location.

"What the hell are we doing?" asked Serge finally, at the end of the first hour in which few words were spoken. Each man seemed to be mastering his fear and incredulity at the bedlam in the streets and at the few, very few police cars they actually saw in the area.

"We're staying out of trouble until the National Guard gets here, that's what," said Peters. "This is nothing yet. Wait till tonight. You ain't seen nothing yet."

"Maybe we should do something," said Jenkins. "We're just driving around."

"Well, let's stop at a Hundred and Third," said Peters angrily. "I'll let you two out and you can try and stop five hundred niggers from carrying away the stores. You want to go down there? How about up on Central Avenue? Want to get out of the car up there? You saw it. How about on Broadway? We can clear the intersection at Manchester. There's not much looting there. They're only chunking rocks at every black and white that drives by. I'll let you boys clear the intersection there with your shotgun. But just watch out they don't stick that gun up your ass and fire all five rounds."

"Want to take a rest and let me drive?" asked Serge quietly.

"Sure, you can drive if you want to. Just wait till it gets dark. You'll get action soon enough."

When Serge took the wheel he checked his watch and saw it was ten minutes until 6:00 P.M. The sun was still high enough to intensify the heat that hung over the city from the fires which seemed to be surrounding them on the south and east but which Peters had avoided. Roving bands of Negroes, men, women and children, screamed and jeered and looted as they drove past. It was utterly useless, Serge thought, to attempt to answer calls on the radio which were being repeated by babbling female Communications operators, some of whom were choked with sobs and impossible to understand.

It was apparent that most of the activity was in Watts proper, and Serge headed for One Hundred and Third Street feeling an overwhelming desire to create some order. He had never felt he was a leader but if he could only gather a few pliable men like Jenkins who seemed willing to obey, and Peters who would submit to more apparent courage, Serge felt he *could* do something. Someone had to do something. They passed another careening police car every five minutes or so, manned by three helmeted officers who all seemed as disorganized and bewildered as themselves. If they were not pulled together soon, it could not be stopped at all, Serge thought. He sped south on Central Avenue and east to Watts substation where he found what he craved more than he had ever craved for a woman—a semblance of order.

"Let's join that group," said Serge, pointing to a squad of ten men who were milling around the entrance of the hotel two doors from the station. Serge saw there was a sergeant talking to them and his stomach uncoiled a little. Now he could abandon the wild scheme he was formulating which called for a grouping of men which he was somehow going to accomplish through sheer bravado because goddammit, someone had to do something. But they had a sergeant, and he could follow. He was glad.

Need some help?" asked Jenkins as they joined the group.

The sergeant turned and Serge saw a two-inch gash on his left cheekbone caked with dust and coagulation but there was no fear in his eyes. His sleeves were rolled up to the elbow, showing massive forearms and on closer examination Serge saw fury in the green eyes of the sergeant. He looked like he could do something.

"See what's left of those stores on the south side?" said the sergeant, whose voice was raspy, Serge thought, from screaming orders in the face of this black hurricane which must be repelled.

"See those fucking stores that aren't burning?" the sergeant repeated. "Well they're full of looters. I just drove past and lost every window in my fucking car before I reached Compton Avenue. I think there's about sixty looters or more in those three fucking stores on the south and I think there's at least a hundred in the back because they drove a truck right through the fucking rear walls and they're carrying the places away."

"What the hell can we do about it?" asked Peters, as Serge watched the building on the north side three blocks east burning to the ground while the firemen waited near the station apparently unable to go in because of sniper fire.

"I'm not ordering nobody to do nothing," said the sergeant, and Serge saw he was much older than he first appeared, but he was not afraid and he was a sergeant. "If you want to come with me, let's go in those stores and clean them out. Nobody's challenged these mother-fuckers here today. I tell you nobody's stood up to them. They been having it their own way."

"It might be ten to one in there," said Peters, and Serge felt his stomach writhing again, and deliberately starting to coil.

"Well I'm going in," said the sergeant. "You guys can suit yourselves."

They all followed dumbly, even Peters, and the sergeant started out at a walk, but soon they found themselves trotting and they would have run blindly if the sergeant had, but he was smart enough to keep the pace at a reasonably ordered trot to conserve energy. They advanced on the stores and a dozen looters struggled with the removal of heavy appliances through the shattered front windows and didn't even notice them coming.

The sergeant shattered his baton on the first swing at a looter, and the others watched for an instant as he dove through the store window, kicking a sweat-soaked shirtless teen-ager who was straining at the foot of a king-sized bed which he and another boy were attempting to carry away headboard and all. Then the ten policemen were among them swinging batons and shouting. As Serge was pushed to the glass-littered floor of the store by a huge mulatto in a bloody undershirt he saw perhaps ten men run in the rear door of the store hurling bottles as they ran, and Serge, as he lay in the litter of broken glass which was lacerating his hands, wondered about the volume of alcoholic beverage bottles which seemed to supply the mighty arsenal of missiles that seemed to be at the fingertips of every Negro in Watts. In that insane moment he thought that Mexicans do not drink so much and there wouldn't be this many bottles lying around Hollenbeck. Then a shot rang out and the mulatto who was by now on his feet began running and Jenkins shouldered the riot gun and fired four rounds toward the rear of the store. When Serge looked up, deafened from the explosions twelve inches from his ear, he saw the black reinforcements, all ten lying on the floor, but then one stood up and then another and another, and within a few seconds nine of them were streaking across the devastated parking lot. The looters in the street were shouting and dropping their booty and running.

"I must have shot high," said Jenkins and Serge saw the pellet pattern seven feet up on the rear wall. They heard screaming and saw a white-haired toothless Negro clutching his ankle which was bleeding freely. He tried to rise, fell, and crawled to a mutilated queen-sized gilded bed. He crawled under it and curled his feet under him.

"They're gone," said the sergeant in wonder. "One minute they were crawling over us like ants and now they're gone!"

"I didn't mean to shoot," said Jenkins. "One of them fired first. I saw the flash and I heard it. I just started shooting back."

"Don't worry about it," said the sergeant. "Goddamn! They're gone. Why the hell didn't we start shooting two nights ago? Goddamn! It really works!"

In ten minutes they were on their way to General Hospital and the moans of the old Negro were getting on Serge's nerves. He looked at Peters who was sitting against the door of the car, his helmet on the seat beside him, his thinning hair plastered down with sweat as he stared at the radio which had increased in intensity as they sped northbound on the Harbor Freeway. The sky was black now on three sides as the fires were leaping over farther north.

"We'll be there in a minute," said Serge. "Can't you stop groaning for a while?"

"Lord, it hurts," said the old man who rocked and squeezed the knee six inches above the wet wound which Jenkins seemed unwilling to look at.

"We'll be there in a minute," said Serge, and he was glad it was Jenkins who had shot him, because Jenkins was his partner and now they would book him at the prison ward of General Hospital and that meant they could leave the streets for an hour or two. He felt the need to escape and order his thinking which had begun to worry him because blind fury could certainly get him killed out there.

"Must have hit him with one pellet," said Peters dully. "Five rounds. Sixty pellets of double ought buck and one looter gets hit in the ankle by one little pellet. But I'll bet before this night's over some cop will get it from a single shot from a handgun fired at two hundred yards by some asshole that never shot a gun before. Some cop'll get it tonight. Maybe more than just one."

How did I get stuck with someone like him? Serge thought. I needed two strong partners today and look what I got.

Jenkins held the elbow of the scrawny old man as he limped into the hospital and up the elevator to the prison ward. After booking the prisoner they stopped at the emergency entrance where Serge had his cut hands treated and after they were washed he saw that the cuts were very superficial and a few Band-Aids did the trick. At nine o'clock they were driving slowly south on the Harbor Freeway and the Communications operators were reciting the calls perfunctorily—calls which, before this madness, would have sent a dozen police cars speeding from all directions but now had become as routine as a family dispute call. "Officer needs help! Four Nine and Central!" said the operator. "Officer needs help, Vernon and Central! Officer needs assistance, Vernon and Avalon! Officer needs assistance, One one five and Avalon! Looting, Vernon and Broadway! Looting, Five eight and Hoover! Looters, Four three and Main!" Then another operator would cut in and recite her list of emergencies which they had given up trying to assign to specific cars because it was obvious now to everyone that there weren't enough cars to even protect each other, let alone quell the looting and burning and sniping.

Serge blundered into a sniper's line of fire on Central Avenue, which was badly burned. They had to park across from a flaming two-story brick building and hide behind their car because two fire trucks had come in behind them and blocked the street and had then been abandoned when the sniping started. The sniping, for all but the combat veterans of Korea and World War II, was a terrible new experience. As Serge hid for forty minutes behind his car and fired a few wild shots at the windows of a sinister yellow apartment building where someone said the snipers were hiding, he thought this the most frightening part of all. He wondered if a police force could cope with snipers and remain a police force. He began thinking that something was going on here in this riot, something monumental for all the nation, perhaps an end of something. But he had better keep his wits about him and concentrate on that yellow building. Then the word was passed by a grimy young policeman in a torn uniform who crawled to their position on his stomach that the National Guard had arrived.

At five past midnight they responded to a help call at a furniture store on south Broadway where three officers had an unknown number of looters trapped inside. One officer swore that when a lookout had ducked inside after the police car drove up, he had seen a rifle in the looter's hands, and another policeman who worked this area said that the office of this particular furniture store contained a small arsenal because the owner was a nervous white man who had been robbed a dozen times.

Serge, without thinking, ordered Peters and one of the policemen from the other teams to the rear of the store where a blue-clad white helmeted figure was already crouched in the shadows, his shotgun leveled at the back door. They went without question, and then Serge realized he was giving commands and thought wryly, at last you are a leader of men and will probably get a slug in your big ass for your trouble. He looked around and several blocks south on Broadway he saw an overturned car still smoldering and the incessant crackling of pistol fire echoed through the night, but for five hundred yards in each direction it was surprisingly quiet. He felt that if he could do something in this gutted skeleton of a furniture store, then a vestige of sanity would be preserved and then he thought that that in itself was insane thinking.

"Well, what's next, Captain?" said the wrinkled grinning policeman who knelt next to him behind the cover of Serge's radio car. Jenkins had the riot gun resting across the deck lid of the car pointed at the store front with its gaping jagged opening where plate glass used to be.

"I guess I *am* giving orders," Serge smiled. "You can do what you want, of course, but somebody ought to take charge. And I make the biggest target."

"That's a good enough reason," said the policeman. "What do you want to do?"

"How many you think are in there?"

"A dozen, maybe."

"Maybe we should wait for more help."

"We've had them trapped for twenty minutes, and we put in maybe five requests for help. You guys are the only ones we've seen. I'd say offhand there isn't any help around right now."

"I think we ought to arrest everyone in that store," said Serge. "We've been racing around all night getting shot at and clubbing people and mostly chasing them from one store to another and one street to another. I think we ought to arrest everyone in that store right now."

"Good idea," said the wrinkled policeman. "I haven't actually made a pinch all night. I just been acting like a goddamn infantryman, crawling and running and sniping. This is Los Angeles not Iwo Jima."

"Let's book these assholes," Jenkins said angrily.

Serge stood up and ran in a crouch to a telephone pole a few feet to the side of the storefront.

"You people in there," Serge shouted, "come out with your hands on top of your head!" He waited for thirty seconds and looked toward Jenkins. He shook his head and pointed to the barrel of the riot gun.

"You people come out or we're going to kill every goddamn one of you," Serge shouted. "Come out! Now!"

Serge waited another silent half minute and felt the fury returning. He had only momentary seizures of anger tonight. Mostly it was fear, but occasionally the anger would prevail.

"Jenkins, give them a volley," Serge commanded. "This time aim low enough to hit somebody." Then Serge leveled his revolver on the store front and fired three rounds into the blackness and the flaming explosions of the riot gun split the immediate silence. He heard nothing for several seconds until the ringing echo ceased and then he heard a wail, shrill and ghostly. It sounded like an infant. Then a man cursed and shouted, "We comin' out. Don't shoot us. We comin' out."

The first looter to appear was about eight years old. He wept freely, his hands held high in the air, his dirty red short pants hanging to the knees, and the loose sole of his left shoe flip-flopped on the pavement as he crossed the sidewalk and stood wailing now in the beam of Jenkins' spotlight.

A woman, apparently the child's mother, came next holding one hand high while the other dragged along a hysterical girl of ten who babbled and held a hand over her eyes to ward off the white beam of light. The next two out were men, and one of them, an old one, was still repeating, "We comin', don't shoot," and the other had his hands clasped on top of his head staring sullenly into the beam of light. He muttered obscenities every few seconds.

"How many more in there?" Serge demanded.

"Oney one," said the old man. "God, they's oney one, Mabel Simms is in there, but I think you done killed her."

"Where's the one with the rifle?" asked Serge.

"They ain't no rifle," said the old man. "We was jist tryin' to git a few things before it was too late. Ain't none of us stole a thing these three days and ever'body else had all these new things and we jist decided to git us somethin'. We jist live across the street, Officer."

"There was a man with a rifle ducked in that fucking doorway when we drove up," said the wrinkled policeman. "Where is he?"

"That was me, Mister PO-liceman," said the old man. "It wan't no rifle. It was a shovel. I was jist bustin' all the glass out the window so my grandkids wouldn't git cut goin' in. I never stole in all my life befo' I swear."

"I'll take a look," said the wrinkled policeman, entering the blackened store carefully, and Jenkins followed, the twin beams of their flashlights crisscrossing in the darkness for more than three minutes. They came out of the store one on each side of an immense black woman whose ringlets hung in her eyes. She murmured, "Jesus, Jesus, Jesus." They half-carried her out to where the others were as she let out an awesome shriek of despair.

"Where's she hit?" asked Serge.

"I don't think she's hit," said the wrinkled policeman as he released her and let her bulk slide to the pavement where she pounded her hands on the concrete and moaned.

"Kin I look at her?" asked the old man. "I been knowin' her for ten years. She live next do' to me."

"Go ahead," said Serge, and watched while the old man labored to get the big woman sitting upright. He supported her with great effort and patted her shoulder while he talked too low for Serge to hear.

"She ain't hurt," said the old man. "She jist scared to death like the rest of us."

Like all of us, Serge thought, and then he thought that this was a very fitting end to the military campaign of Serge Duran, leader of men. It was about as he should have expected. Reality was always the opposite of what he at first anticipated. He knew this for certain now, therefore it was about as he should have expected.

"You going to book them?" asked the wrinkled policeman.

"You can have them," said Serge.

"Don't fight over us, you honky motherfuckers," said the surly muscled man whose hands were unclasped now and hung loosely at his sides.

"You get those hands on top of your head, or I'll open your belly," said the wrinkled policeman, as he stepped forward and jammed the muzzle of the shotgun in the man's stomach. Serge saw the finger tighten on the trigger when the Negro instinctively touched the barrel, but then the Negro looked in the wrinkled policeman's eyes and removed his hand as though the barrel was on fire. He clasped the hands on top of his head.

"Why didn't you try to pull it away?" the wrinkled policeman whispered. "I was going to make you let go."

"You can have them," said Serge. "We're leaving."

"We'll take this one," said the wrinkled policeman. "The rest of you people get your asses home and stay there."

Jenkins and Peters agreed that they should go to Seventy-seventh Station because they might get relieved since they had been on duty now twelve hours. It did seem that things had quieted down a bit even though

Watts substation was under some type of sniper siege, but there were apparently enough units there, so Serge drove to the station and thought he had not died like the heroes of his novels, even though he was at least as neurotic and confused as any of them. He suddenly remembered that last month during a two-day stretch of staying in the apartment and reading, he had read a book on T. E. Lawrence and maybe the romantic heroism of books had triggered his irresistible urge to surround and capture the furniture store which had ended in low comedy. Mariana said he read too many books. But it wasn't just that. It was that things were breaking apart. He was accustomed to the feeling lately that *he* was breaking apart, but now everything was fragmented—not in two reasonably neat sections but in jagged chaotic slivers and chunks, and he was one of society's orderers, as trite as it sounded. Even though he had never felt particularly idealistic before, now, surrounded by darkness and fire and noise and chaos, he, suddenly given the opportunity, had to create a tiny bit of order in that gutted store on south Broadway. But what good had it done? It had ended as all his attempts to do a worthy thing invariably ended. That was why marriage to Paula, and getting drunk occasionally and spending Paula's father's money seemed a most appropriate life for Serge Duran.

To the surprise of all three of them, they were relieved when they reached the station. They muttered a brief good-bye to each other and hurried to their cars before someone changed his mind and made them stay for the rest of the night. Serge drove home by the Harbor Freeway and the skies were still glowing red but it was apparent that the National Guard was making a difference. There were far fewer fires and after reaching Jefferson he turned around and saw no more fires. Instead of going straight to the apartment he stopped at an all night hamburger stand in Boyle Heights and for the first time in thirteen hours, now that he was back in Hollenbeck Division, he felt safe.

The night man knew Serge as a juvenile officer in plainclothes and he shook his head when Serge walked inside and sat down in the deserted diner.

"What's it like down there?" asked the night man.

"It's still pretty bad," said Serge running his fingers through his hair, sticky and matted from the helmet and soot and sweat. His hands were filthy, but there was no restroom for the customers and he decided to just have a cup of coffee and go home.

"I almost didn't know you in the uniform," said the night man. "You're always wearing a suit."

"We're all in uniform today," said Serge.

"I can understand," said the night man, and Serge thought his sparse moustache made him look like Cantinflas although he was a tall man.

"Good coffee," said Serge, and so was the cigarette, and his stomach unwound for the last time that night as the hot coffee splashed into it.

"I don't know why the boss wants me here," said the night man. "There have been few customers. Everyone's staying at home because of the *mallate*. But I shouldn't use that word. Nigger is a terrible word and *mallate* means the same thing but is even worse."

"Yes."

"I don't think the blacks would try to burn the east side. They don't get along with us Mexicans, but they respect us. They know we'd kill them if they tried to burn our homes. They don't fear the Anglo. No one fears the Anglo. Your people are growing weak."

"I wouldn't be surprised," said Serge.

"I've noticed that here in this country, the Mexican is forced to live close to black people because he's poor. When I first came here the Mexicans wanted to get away from the black who is exactly unlike a Mexican, and to live near the Anglo who is more nearly the same. But the things that've been happening, the softness of the Anglo, the way you tell the world you're sorry for feeding them, and the way you take away the Negro's self-respect by giving everything to him, I'm starting to think that the Mexican should avoid the Anglo. I can tell you these things? I won't offend you? I talk so much tonight. I'm sick to my heart because of the riot."

"I'm not an easily offended Anglo," said Serge. "You can talk to me like I was a Mexican."

"Some police officers who work in the *barrios* seem *muy Mexicano* to me," smiled the night man. "You, señor, even look a little *Mexicano*, mostly around the eyes, I think."

"You think so?"

"I meant that as a compliment."

"I know."

"When I came to this country twelve years ago, I thought it was bad that the Mexicans lived mostly in the east side here where the old ways were kept. I even thought we should not teach our children *la lengua* because they should completely learn to be Americans. I've looked closely and I believe that the Anglos in this place accept us almost like other Anglos. I used to feel very proud to be accepted like an Anglo because I know of the bad treatment of Mexicans not too long ago. But as I watched you grow weak and fearful that you wouldn't have the love of the world, then I thought: look, Armando—*Mira, hombre, los gabachos* are nothing to envy. You wouldn't be one of them if you could. If a man tried to burn your house or hold a knife at your belly you kill him and no matter his color. If he broke your laws you would prove to him that it's painful to do such a thing. Even a child learns that the burning coal hurts if you get close. Don't the gringos teach this to their children?"

"Not all of us."

"I agree. You seem to say, touch it six or five times and maybe it burns and maybe not. Then he grows to be a man and runs through your streets and it's not all his fault because he never learned the hot coal burns. I think I'm glad to live in your country, but only as a Mexican. Forgive me, señor, but I wouldn't be a gringo. And if your people continue to grow weak and corrupt I'll leave your comforts and return to Mexico because I don't wish to see your great nation fall."

"Maybe I'll go with you," said Serge. "Got any room down there?"

"In Mexico there's room for all," smiled the night man, carrying a fresh coffeepot to the counter. "Would you like me to tell you of Mexico? It always makes me glad to talk of Yucatán."

"I'd like that," said Serge. "Are you from Yucatán?"

"Yes. It's far, far. You know of the place?"

"Tell me about it. But first, can I use your bathroom? I've got to wash. And can you fix me something to eat?"

"Certainly, señor. Go through that door. What would you like to eat. Ham? Eggs? Bacon?"

"We're going to talk about Mexico. I should eat Mexican food. How about *menudo*? You'd be surprised how long it's been since I ate *menudo*."

"I have *menudo*," laughed the night man. "It's not excellent, but it passes."

"Do you have corn tortillas?"

"Of course."

"How about lemon? And oregano?"

"I have them, señor. You know about *menudo*. Now I'm ashamed to give you my poor *menudo*."

Serge saw that it was after four but he wasn't the least bit sleepy and he felt suddenly exhilarated yet relaxed. But mostly he was hungry. He laughed in the mirror at the grimy sweat-stained face and thought, God, how I'm hungry for *menudo*.

Suddenly Serge popped his head out the door, his hands still covered with suds. "Tell me, señor, have you traveled a lot in Mexico?"

"I know the country. *De veras*. I know my Mexico."

"Have you been to Guadalajara?"

"It's a beautiful city. I know it well. The people are wonderful, but all the people of Mexico are wonderful and will treat you very good."

"Will you tell me about Guadalajara too? I want to know about that city."

"A pleasure, señor," chuckled the night man. "To have someone to talk to at this lonely hour is a pleasure, especially someone who wants to hear about my country. I'd give you free *menudo* even if you were not a policeman."

It was seven o'clock when Serge was driving home, so full of *menudo* and tortillas he hoped he wouldn't get a stomachache. He wished he had some *yerba buena* like his mother used to fix. It never failed to help a stomachache and he couldn't afford to be ill because in exactly six hours he would have to get up and be ready for another night. The news on the car radio indicated that looting and burning was expected to resume heavily today.

Serge took Mission Road instead of the freeway and there on North Mission Road he saw something that made him brake sharply and slow to fifteen miles per hour and stare. Eight or ten men, one woman, and two small boys, were lined up at the door of a restaurant which was not yet open. They carried pots and pans of all shapes, but each pot was ample in size and Serge realized they were waiting for the restaurant to open so they could buy a pot of *menudo* and take it home because they were sick or someone in the house was sick from drinking too much on Friday night. There was not a Mexican who did not believe with all his soul that *menudo* cured hangovers and because they believed, it did in fact cure the hangover, and even though his stomach felt like a goatskin bag pumped full of the stuff, he would have stopped and bought some more to keep for later if he had a pot. Then he looked at his helmet, but the liner was too grimy from oil and soot to carry *menudo* in, and he accelerated the Corvette and headed for his bed.

He felt he would sleep better than he had in weeks even though he had seen the beginning of the end of things, because now that they had a taste of anarchy, and saw how easy it is to defeat the civil authority, there would be more and it would be the white revolutionary who would do it. This was the beginning, and the Anglos were neither strong enough nor realistic enough to stop it. They doubted everything, especially themselves. Perhaps they had lost the capacity to believe. They could never believe in the miracle in a pot of *menudo*.

As he looked in the rearview mirror, the queue of forlorn Mexicans with their *menudo* pots had disappeared, but in a few moments their spirits would be soaring he thought, because the *menudo* would make them well.

"They are not good Catholics," Father McCarthy had said, "but they are so respectful and they believe so well." *Ándale pues*, Serge thought. To bed.

20. The Chase

"Good thing they're too fucking dumb to make fire bombs out of wine bottles," said Silverson and Gus cringed as a rock skidded over the already dented deck lid and slammed against the already cracked rear window. A glass fragment struck the Negro policeman whose name Gus had already forgotten, or perhaps it was buried there among the ruins of his rational mind which had been annihilated by terror.

"Shoot that motherfucker that . . ." screamed Silverson to Gus, but then sped away from the mob before finishing the sentence.

"Yeah, those Coke bottles aren't breaking," said the Negro policeman. "If that last one would've broke, we'd have a lap full of flaming gasoline right now."

They had been out only thirty minutes, Gus thought. He knew it was only thirty because it was now five till eight and still it wasn't dark and it had been seven-twenty-five when they drove from the parking lot at Seventy-seventh Station because it was written here on his log. He could see it. It had only been thirty minutes ago. So how could they survive twelve hours of this? They had been told they would be relieved in twelve hours, but of course they would all be dead.

"Friday the thirteenth," muttered Silverson, slowing down now that they had run the gauntlet on Eighty-sixth Street where a mob of fifty young Negroes appeared from nowhere and a cocktail had bounced off the door but failed to burst. This happened after someone had cracked the side window with a rock. Now Gus stared at another rock which was lying on the floor at his feet and he thought, we've only been out thirty minutes. Isn't that incredible.

"Some organization we got," said Silverson, turning back east toward Watts where most of the radio calls seemed to be emanating at the moment. "I never worked this crummy division in my life. I don't know my ass from pork sausage."

"I never worked down here either," said the Negro policeman. "How about you, Plebesly? It is Plebesly, isn't it?"

"No, I don't know the streets," said Gus, holding the shotgun tightly against his belly and wondering if the paralysis would fade because he was sure he could not get out of the car, but then he supposed that if they succeeded in breaking a fire bomb inside, his instinct would get him out. Then he thought of himself on fire.

"They just tell you here's a box of thirty-eights and a shotgun and point out two other guys and say take a car and go out there. It's ridiculous," said Silverson. "None of us ever worked down here before. Hell, man, I worked Highland Park for twelve years. I don't know my ass from sliced salami down here."

"Some guys got called down here last night," said the soft-spoken Negro policeman. "I work Wilshire, but I didn't get called down here last night."

"The whole goddamn Department's here tonight," said Silverson. "Where in the hell's Central Avenue? There was an assistance call on Central Avenue."

"Don't worry about it," said the Negro policeman. "There'll be another one any minute."

"Look at that!" said Silverson, and aimed the radio car down the wrong side of San Pedro Street as he accelerated toward a market where a band of eight or ten men were systematically carrying out boxes of groceries.

"Those brazen assholes," said the Negro policeman and he was out and running toward the storefront after the already fleeing looters as soon as Silverson parked. To his surprise, Gus's body functioned and his arm opened the door and his legs carried him, unsteadily, but still carried him, at a straight-legged lope toward the storefront. The Negro policeman had a tall very black man by the shirt front and palmed him across the face with his gloved hands which were probably sap gloves because the man spun backward and fell through the yawning hole in the plate glass, screaming as his arm was raked and bloodied by the jagged edge.

The others scattered through back and side doors and in a few seconds only the three policemen and the bleeding looter stood in the gutted store.

"Lemme go," pleaded the looter to the Negro policeman. "We're both black. You're just like me."

"I'm not nothin' like you, bastard," said the Negro policeman, showing great strength by lifting the looter one-handed. "I am nothing whatever like you."

A peaceful hour passed while they took their looter to the station and engaged in what had to pass for booking, but which required only a skeleton of an arrest report and no booking slip at all. This hour passed much too quickly for Gus who found that hot coffee knotted his stomach even more. Before he could believe it they were back on the streets, only now, night had come. The small arms fire was crackling through the darkness. He had fooled them for five years, thought Gus. He had almost fooled himself, but tonight they would know, and he would know. He wondered if it would be as he always feared, himself trembling like a rabbit before the deadly eye at the last moment. This is how he always thought it would be at the instant when the great fear came, whatever that fear was, which irrevocably paralyzed his disciplined body and brought the final mutiny of body against mind.

"Listen to that gunfire," said Silverson as they were back on Broadway and the sky glowed from a dozen fires. He had to take several detours on their patrol to nowhere in particular, because of the fire engines blocking streets.

"This is crazy," said the Negro policeman, who Gus knew by now was named Clancy.

It is the natural tendency of things toward chaos, Gus thought. It's a very basic natural law Kilvinsky always said, and only the order makers could temporarily halt its march, but eventually there will certainly be darkness and chaos, Kilvinsky had said.

"Look at that asshole," said Clancy, and shined his spotlight on a lone looter who was reaching through a window of a liquor store feeling for a quart of clear liquid that rested there, miraculously whole among the broken glass. "We ought to give that bastard some sidewalk surgery. Wonder how he'd like a lobotomy by Dr. Smith and Dr. Wesson?"

Clancy was carrying the shotgun now and as Silverson stopped the car Clancy fired a blast into the air behind the man who did not turn but continued his probing, and when he reached the bottle he turned a scowling brown face to the naked light, and walked slowly away from the store with his prize.

"Son of a bitch, we're whipped," said Silverson and drove away from the lonely snarling figure who continued his inexorable pace in the darkness.

For another hour it was the same: speeding to calls only to arrive in time to chase fleeting shapes in the darkness as the Communications operators continued a barrage of help and assistance and looting calls until all calls were routine and they wisely decided that the main order of business would be protecting each other and surviving the night uninjured.

But at 11:00 P.M. as they were scattering a group intent on burning a large food market on Santa Barbara Avenue, Silverson said, "Let's catch a couple of these assholes. Can you run, Plebesly?"

"I can run," said Gus grimly, and he knew, somehow knew he could run. In fact, he had to run, and this time when Silverson squealed into the curb and fleeting shadows faded into darker shadow there was another shadow pursuing fleeter than the rest. The last looter hadn't gotten a hundred feet from the store when Gus overtook him and slammed the heel of his hand in the back of the looter's head. He heard him fall and grind along the sidewalk, and from the shouts he knew that Clancy and Silverson had grabbed him. Gus pursued the next shadow and within a minute he was streaking down Forty-seventh Street through the residential darkness after the second shadow and another shadow a half block ahead. Despite the Sam Browne and the strangeness of a helmet, and the baton clacking against the metal of his belt, he felt unencumbered, and swift, and free. He ran like he ran in the academy, like he still ran at least twice a week during his workouts, and he was doing the thing he did best in all the world. Suddenly he knew that none of them could stand up to him. And though he was afraid, he knew he would endure and his spirit ignited as the sweat boiled him and the warm wind fed the fire as he ran and ran.

He caught the second shadow near Avalon and saw that the man was huge with a triangular neck that sloped from ear to shoulder but he was easy to sidestep when he made two or three halfhearted lunges toward

Gus and then collapsed in a gasping heap without being struck by the baton that Gus held ready. He handcuffed the looter to the bumper bracket of a recently wrecked car that was squatting at the curb where the man fell.

Gus looked up and the third shadow hadn't made another three hundred feet but jogged painfully toward Avalon Boulevard, looking often over his shoulder and Gus was running again, easy striding, loose, letting his body run as the mind rested, which is the only way to run successfully. The shadow was getting larger and larger and was in the blue glow of the street lamp when Gus was on him. The looter's eyes blinked back in disbelief at the oncoming policeman. Gus was panting but bounded forward still strong when the exhausted man turned and stumbled toward a pile of litter beside a smoldering building and came up with a piece of two by four. He held it in both hands like a ball bat.

He was perhaps twenty, six feet two, and fierce. Gus was afraid, and though his mind told him to use his gun because that was the only sensible thing to do, he reached instead for his baton and circled the man who sucked and rattled at the air and Gus was sure he would cave in. But still the man held the two by four as Gus circled him. Drops of sweat plinked on the concrete sidewalk at his feet and his white shirt was completely transparent now and clung to him.

"Drop that," said Gus. "I don't want to hit you."

The looter continued to back away and the heavy wood wavered as more eye white showed than a moment before.

"Drop that or I'll smash you," said Gus. "I'm stronger than you."

The board slid from the looter's hands and clunked to the pavement and he caved and lay there gasping while Gus wondered what to do with him. He wished he had taken Silverson's handcuffs, but it had happened so fast. His body had just started the chase and left his mind behind, but now his mind had caught up with the body and was all together.

Then he saw a black and white roaring down Avalon. He stepped into the street and waved it down and in a few minutes he was back on Santa Barbara and reunited with Silverson and Clancy who were astonished by his feat. They took all three looters to the station where Silverson told the jailer how his "little partner" had caught the three looters, but Gus still found that his stomach rebelled at coffee and would accept only water, and forty-five minutes later when they went back on the streets he was still trembling and perspiring badly and told himself, what did you expect? That it would now all vanish like in a war movie? That you who feared everything for a lifetime now would dramatically know no fear? He completed the night as he had begun it, quivering, at moments near panic, but there was a difference: he knew the body would not fail him even if the mind would bolt and run with graceful antelope leaps until it vanished. The body would remain and function. It was his destiny to endure, and knowing it he would never truly panic. And this, he thought, would be a splendid discovery in any coward's life.

21. The Golden Knight

What the hell's going on? Roy thought, standing in the middle of the intersection of Manchester and Broadway gaping at the crowd of two hundred on the northeast corner and wondering if they would break in the bank. The sun was still bright and hot. Then he heard a crash and saw that the group of one hundred on the northwest corner had broken in the windows of the storefronts and were beginning to loot. What the hell's happening, thought Roy, and gained little solace from the faces of the policemen near him who seemed as bewildered as he. Then they smashed the windows at the southwest corner and Roy thought, my God, a hundred more gathered and I didn't even see them! Suddenly only the southeastern side of the intersection was clear and most of the policemen were retreating to this side of the street except one stocky policeman who charged a pocket of six or eight Negroes with their arms full of men's clothing who were strolling to a double-parked Buick. The policeman struck the first man in the back with the point of the baton and brought the second one to his knees with a skillful slashing blow across the leg, and then the policeman was hit full in the face with a milk crate thrown from the crowd and he was being kicked by eighteen or twenty men and women. Roy joined a squad of six rescuers who ran across Manchester. They dragged him away and were pelted by a hail of stones and bottles one of which struck Roy on the elbow and caused him to cry out.

"Where do the rocks come from?" asked a gray-haired, beefy policeman with a torn uniform shirt. "How in the hell do they find so many rocks lying around in a city street?"

After they got the injured man to a radio car, the dozen officers returned to the intersection through which all vehicle traffic had been diverted. Officers and mob watched each other amid the screams and taunts and laughter and blaring radios. Roy never knew who fired the first shot, but the gunfire erupted. He fell to his stomach and began to tremble and crawled into the doorway of a pawnshop holding both arms over his stomach. Then he thought of removing the white helmet and holding it over his stomach, but he realized how futile it would be. He saw three or four more radio cars roaring into the chaotic intersection as the crowds panicked and broke into and away from the confused policemen who were shouting conflicting orders to each other. No one knew where the gunfire was coming from.

Roy stayed in the doorway and protected his stomach as the rumors came of snipers on every roof and that they were firing from the crowd and then several policemen began firing at a house on the residential street just south of Manchester. Soon the house was riddled with shotgun and revolver fire, but Roy never saw the outcome because a frantic policeman waved them north again and when he ran a hundred yards he saw a dead Negro blocking the sidewalk, shot through the neck, and another dead in the middle of the street. This can't be true, Roy thought. It's broad daylight. This is America. Los Angeles. And then he fell to his stomach again because he saw the brick hurtling end over end toward him and it shattered the plate glass window behind him. A cheer went up from thirty Negroes who had appeared in the alley to the left and a young policeman ran up to Roy as he was getting up. The young policeman said, "The one in the red shirt threw the brick," and he aimed coolly at the running Negroes and fired the riot gun. The blast took two of the men down. The man in red held his leg screaming and another in a brown shirt limped to his feet and was pulled into a mob of cursing looters where he disappeared as the looters scurried away from the young policeman with the riot gun. Then Roy heard two small pops and saw a tiny flash in the midst of the retreating crowd and the car window next to Roy shattered.

"Show yourself, you bastard," the young policeman shouted to the invisible sniper and then turned his back on them and walked slowly away. "This isn't real," he muttered to Roy. "Is it?"

Then Roy saw something extraordinary: a young black with a full beard and a black beret and silk undershirt and huge natural under the beret, a fiercely militant-looking young man, stepped in front of a mob of fifty and told them to go home and that the police were not their enemies, and other things equally provocative. He had to be removed from the area in a car under guard when the mob turned on him and kicked him unconscious in less than a minute, before the policemen could drive them off.

The sirens shrieked and two ambulances and a police car containing six policemen drove up. Roy saw there was a sergeant with them. He was young and almost everyone ignored him as he tried in vain to create order at least among the squad of policemen, but it took almost an hour to get the dead and wounded to the hospital and the temporary morgue. The Watts riot had begun in earnest this Friday afternoon.

Roy was ordered by the sergeant to arrest a wounded man in a red shirt, and he was teamed with two other policemen. They took the man to the prison ward of the County Hospital in a radio car with a windshield and rear window completely destroyed by rocks. The paint on the white door was scorched from a fire bomb and Roy was glad to be taking the long drive to the hospital. He hoped his new partners would not be too anxious to return to the streets.

It was after dark when they were driving again toward Seventy-seventh Street Station and by now Roy and his partners knew each other. Each had started the afternoon with different partners until the chaos at Manchester and Broadway, but what the hell did it matter, they decided, who was working with whom. They made a pact to stay one with the other and to provide mutual protection, not to stray far from each other, because they had only one shotgun, Roy's, and it was not reassuring at all, not on this night, but at least it was something.

"It's not nine o'clock yet," said Barkley, a ten-year policeman from Harbor Division with a face like a bruised tomato who had, for their first two hours together, mumbled over and over that "it was unbelievable, all so unbelievable," until he was asked to please shut up by Winslow, a fifteen-year policeman from West Los Angeles Division who was the driver and a slow careful driver he was, Roy thought. Roy was thankful he had a veteran driving.

Roy sat alone in the back seat cradling the shotgun, a box of shotgun shells on the seat next to him. He had not fired the gun yet, but he had made the decision to fire at anyone who threw a rock or fire bomb at them, and at anyone who shot or aimed a gun at them or looked like he was aiming a gun at them. They were shooting looters. Everyone knew it. He decided he would not shoot looters, but he was glad some of the others were doing it. They had seen a semblance of order begin in the bursts of initial gunfire. Only deadly force could destroy this thing and he was glad they were shooting looters, but he decided he would not shoot looters. And he would try not to shoot anyone. And he would shoot no one in the stomach.

In one of my rare displays of humanity I will blow their heads off, he thought. Under no circumstance will I shoot a man in the stomach.

"Where you want to go, Fehler?" asked Winslow, rolling a cigar from side to side in his wide mouth. "You know the area best."

"Sounds like Central Avenue and Broadway and a Hundred and Third are getting hit the hardest," said Barkley.

"Let's try Central Avenue," said Roy, and at 9:10 P.M. when they were only two blocks from Central Avenue the fire department requested assistance because they were being fired on in a six-block stretch of Central Avenue.

Roy felt the heat when they were still a half block from Central and Winslow parked as close to the inferno as he could get. Roy was perspiring freely and by the time they jogged the five hundred feet to the first besieged fire truck they were all sweating and the night air was scorching Roy's lungs and the pop pop pop of gunfire was coming from several directions. Roy began to develop a fierce stomachache, one which could not be relieved by a bowel movement, and a ricochet pinged off the concrete sidewalk. The three policemen dived for the fire truck and huddled next to a filthy, yellow-helmeted, wide-eyed fireman.

It was not Central Avenue, Roy thought. It was not even possible that the signpost which pointed Forty-sixth Street east and west and Central Avenue north and south could be right. He had worked Newton Street. He had patrolled these streets with dozens of other partners, with partners now dead even, like Whitey Duncan. This street was a vivid part of his learning. He had been educated in southeast Los Angeles and Central Avenue had been a valuable schoolroom, but this hissing inferno was not Central Avenue. Then Roy for the first time noticed the two cars overturned and burning. He suddenly could not remember what kind of buildings had been there on Forty-seventh and Forty-sixth that were now sheets of flame two hundred feet high. If this had happened a year ago I would certainly not believe it, he thought. I would simply believe that it was a fantastic seizure of d.t.'s and I would take another drink. Then he thought of Laura, and he was astonished that now, even now, as he lay by the big wheel of the fire engine and the sounds of gunfire and sirens and growling flames were all around him, even now, he could get the empty ache within him that would be filled warmly when he thought of holding her, and how she stroked his hair as no one, not Dorothy, not his mother, no woman, had done. He had guessed he loved her when the yearning for drink began to wane, and he knew it when, three months after their affair began, he realized that she aroused the same feeling within him that Becky did, who was now talking clearly and was assuredly a brilliant child—not simply beautiful, but stunning. Roy ached again as he thought of Becky, ethereal, bright, and golden—and Laura, dusky and real, altogether real, who had begun to put him together, Laura, who was five months younger than he, but who seemed years older, who used pity and compassion and love and anger until he stopped drinking after he was suspended sixty days for being found drunk on duty, and who lived with him and kept him for those sixty days in her apartment, and who said nothing, but only watched him with those tawny tragic eyes when he began to resemble a man again and decided to return to his own apartment. She said nothing about that since, and he still came to her three or four nights a week because he still needed her badly. She watched him, always watched him with those liquid eyes. With Laura the sex made it perfect but was far, far from all of it, and that was another reason he knew he loved her. He had been on the verge of a decision about her for weeks and even months and he began to tremble as he thought that if it weren't for the ache and the warmth which always came when he thought of Becky or Laura, if it weren't for this feeling he could evoke in himself, then now, now in the blood and hate and fire and chaos, he would turn the riot gun around and look in the great black eye of the twelve gauge and jerk the trigger. Then he guessed he was far from healthy yet, despite Laura's reassurance, or he wouldn't think such thoughts. Suicide was madness, he had always been taught to believe, but what was this around him, if not madness? He began to get light-headed and decided to stop thinking so hard. His palms were dripping wet and leaving tiny drops of moisture on the receiver of the shotgun. Then he worried about the moisture rusting the piece. He wiped the receiver with his sleeve until he realized what he was doing and laughed aloud.

"You guys come with me!" shouted a sergeant, crouching as he ran past the fire engine. "We got to clean these snipers out and get the firemen working before the whole goddamn city burns down."

But though they walked along Central Avenue in groups of three for over an hour they never saw a sniper but only heard, and they chased and occasionally shot at shadowy figures who scurried in and out of gutted storefronts that were not in flames. Roy did not shoot because the conditions had not been met. Still, he was glad the others were shooting. When Central Avenue reached the point that it was burning more or less quietly and there was little left to steal, Winslow suggested they go elsewhere, but first they should stop at a restaurant and eat. When they asked which restaurant he had in mind, he waved an arm and they followed him to the car and found that the two remaining unbroken windows had been smashed out in their absence and the upholstery had been cut, but not the tires strangely enough, so Winslow drove to a restaurant on Florence Avenue that he said he had noticed earlier. They walked through a gigantic hole in the wall of the cafe where a car must have smashed through. Roy guessed the car had probably been driven by some terrified white man passing through the riot area who had been attacked by the mobs that were stopping traffic and beating whites earlier in the day when they owned the streets before the shooting started. Then again it could have been a looter's car which the police had chased until he crashed through the restaurant in spectacular fashion. What difference did it make? Roy thought.

"Shine your flashlight over here," said Winslow, removing six hamburger patties from the refrigerator which was not running. "They're still cold. It's okay," said Winslow. "See if you can find the buns in that drawer, Fehler. I think the mustard and stuff is behind you there on the little table."

"The gas still works," said Barkley, propping his flashlight on the counter with the beam directed on the griddle. "I'm a pretty good cook. Want me to get them started?"

"Go head on, brother," said Winslow in an affected Negro accent, as he squeezed a head of lettuce he found on the floor, peeling away the outer leaves and dropping them in a cardboard box. They ate and drank several bottles of soda pop which were not cold enough, but it wasn't at all bad there in the darkness and it was after midnight when they finished and sat smoking, looking at each other as the ceaseless crackling small arms fire and ubiquitous smell of smoke reminded them that they had to go back. Finally it was Barkley who said, "Might as well get back out there. But I wish they hadn't broke our windows out. You know, the one thing that scares me most is that a cocktail will come flying in the car and bust, and fry us. If we only had windows we could roll them up."

Roy was more impressed with Winslow as the night wore on. He drove through Watts and west and north through the rest of the gutted city as though he were on routine patrol. He seemed to be listening carefully to the garbled endless, breathless calls that were blaring out at them over the radio. Finally one of the operators with a girlish voice began sobbing hysterically as she was jabbering a string of twelve emergency calls to "any unit in the vicinity," and she and all of them must realize by now that there were no units in certain vicinities, and if there were they were hard pressed to save their own asses and to hell with anything else. But at 2:00 A.M. Winslow stopped the car on Normandie Avenue which was exceptionally dark except for a building burning in the distance and they watched a gang of perhaps thirty looters ransacking a clothing store and Winslow said, "There's too many of them for us to handle, wouldn't you say?"

"They might have guns," said Barkley.

"See the car out front, the green Lincoln?" said Winslow. "I'm going after them when they leave. We'll get some of them at least. It's about time we threw some looters in jail."

Three men got in the car and even from a half block away in the darkness, Roy could see that the back seat of the Lincoln was filled with suits and dresses. The Lincoln pulled away from the curb and Winslow said, "Dirty motherfuckers," and the radio car roared forward. Winslow turned on his headlights and red lights and they passed the clothing store and crossed Fifty-first Street at eighty miles per hour and the chase was on.

The driver of the Lincoln was a good driver but his brakes were not good and the police car had tremendous brakes and could corner better. Winslow ate up the ground which separated them and didn't listen to Barkley who was shouting directions at him. Roy sat silently in the rear seat and wished they had seat belts in the back seat too. He could see that Winslow was oblivious of both of them and would catch that Lincoln if it killed all of them and then they were going northbound on Vermont. Roy did not look at the speedometer but knew they were traveling in excess of one hundred and this was of course absolutely insane because there were thousands of looters, thousands! But Winslow wanted *these* looters and Barkley shouted, "Soldiers!" and Roy saw a National Guard roadblock two blocks north and the Lincoln's driver, a hundred feet ahead, saw it too and burned out the rest of his brakes trying to turn left before reaching the roadblock. A National Guardsman began firing a machine gun and Winslow jammed on his brakes when they saw the muzzle flashes and heard the clug-a-clug-a-clug-a-clug and saw the tracers explode on the asphalt closer to them than to the Lincoln. Roy was horrified to see that the Lincoln did not crash as he was sure it would. The driver made the turn and was speeding west on a narrow dark residential street and Winslow doggedly made the turn and Roy wondered if he could lean out the window and fire the riot gun, or perhaps his revolver because that Lincoln had to be stopped before Winslow killed them all. He was surprised to discover how badly he wanted to live now, and he saw Laura's face for an instant and was thrown against the door handle when Winslow made an impossible right turn and picked up two hundred feet on the Lincoln.

Winslow, trying to conserve power, wasn't using his siren and Roy had lost count of the other cars they had almost hit, but he was thankful that at this hour in this part of the city, there were few civilian autos on the street and Barkley uttered a joyful whoop when the Lincoln bounced over the curb turning left again, and slammed against a parked car. The Lincoln was still skidding in a tight circle when the three looters were leaping out, and Winslow, jaw set, was driving across the sidewalk at the fleeing driver, a slim Negro who was running down the middle of the sidewalk with an occasional terrified glance over his shoulder at the approaching headlights. Roy realized that Winslow was going to run him down as he drove the radio car down the residential sidewalk taking corners off fences and running over shrubbery with the radio car that was too wide for the sidewalk. They were less than thirty feet from the looter when he turned the last time and his mouth opened in a soundless shriek as he dived over a chain link fence. Winslow skidded past him, cursed, and leaped out of the car. Roy and Barkley were out in a second but Winslow, amazingly agile for his size and age, was already over the fence and crashing through the rear yard. Roy heard four shots and then two more as he threw the riot gun over the fence and scrambled after it, ripping his trousers, but in a moment Winslow came walking back reloading his revolver.

"He got away," said Winslow. "The motherfucking nigger got away. I'd give a thousand dollars for one more shot at him."

When they got back in the car Winslow circled the block and returned to the looter's green Lincoln which sat awkwardly in the middle of the street, steam hissing from the broken radiator.

Winslow stepped slowly from the radio car and asked Roy for the riot gun. Roy gave him the gun and shrugged at Barkley as Winslow stepped to the car and fired two flaming blasts at the rear tires. Then he stepped to the front of the car and smashed out the headlights with the butt of the gun and then broke the windshield. Then he circled the car, his shotgun ready like it was a dangerous wounded thing that might yet attack, and he slammed the gun butt into both side windows. Roy looked toward the houses on both sides of the street, but all were dark. The residents of southeast Los Angeles, who had always known how to mind their own business, were not curious at any sounds they heard *this* night.

"That's enough, Winslow," Barkley shouted. "Let's get the hell out of here."

But Winslow opened the car door and Roy could not see what he was doing. In a second he emerged with a large piece of fabric and Roy watched him in the beam of the headlights as he put his pocket knife away. He removed the gas cap and shoved the piece of material into the tank and dripped gasoline on the street beneath the tank.

"Winslow, are you nuts?" shouted Barkley. "Let's get the hell out of here!"

But Winslow ignored him and made his trickle of gasoline extend a safe distance from the Lincoln and then he shoved the soaked piece of cloth back into the tank except for two feet of it which hung to the ground. He ran to the mouth of the gasoline stream and lit it and there was a small smothered explosion almost instantly and the car was burning well as Winslow got back in the radio car and drove away in the relaxed careful manner of before.

"How can you fight them without getting just like them?" said Winslow finally to his silent partners. "I'm just a nigger now, and you know what? I feel pretty good."

Things became a little quieter after three, and at 4:00 A.M. they drove to Seventy-seventh Station, and after working a fifteen-hour watch, Roy was relieved. He was too tired to change into his civilian clothes, and was certainly too tired to drive to his apartment. And even if he weren't, he would not go home tonight. There was only one place in the world he would go tonight. It was exactly four-thirty when he parked in front of Laura's apartment. He could not hear the pop of gunfire now. This part of Vermont had been untouched by fire and almost untouched by looting. It was very dark and still. He only knocked twice when she opened the door.

"Roy! What time is it?" she asked, in a yellow night-gown and robe, and already he felt the pleasurable ache.

"I'm sorry to come so late. I had to, Laura."

"Well, come in. You look like you're about to fall on your face."

Roy entered and she switched on a lamp and held his arms as she watched him in her unique way. "You're a mess. You're really a filthy mess. Take your uniform off and I'll fill the bath. Are you hungry?"

Roy shook his head as he walked into the familiar comfortable bedroom and unhooked the Sam Browne, letting it fall to the floor. Then, remembering how tidy Laura was, he pushed it with his foot into the corner by the closet and sat heavily in a padded, hot pink and white bedroom chair. He took his shoes off and sat for a minute wanting a cigarette but too tired to light one.

"Want a drink, Roy?" asked Laura, leaving the bathroom as the tub filled with a sound of rushing restorative water.

"I don't need a drink, Laura. Not even tonight."

"One drink won't hurt you. Not anymore."

"I don't want one."

"Okay, baby," she said, picking up his shoes and putting them in the bottom of the closet.

"What the hell would I do without you?"

"I haven't seen you for four days. I guess you've been busy."

"I was going to come Wednesday night. That's when this thing started, but we had to work overtime. And yesterday too. And then tonight, Laura, tonight was the worst, but I had to come tonight. I couldn't stay away any longer."

"I'm very sorry about all this, Roy," she said, pulling off his damp black socks, as he thanked her silently for helping him.

"Sorry about what?"

"About the riot."

"Why? Did you start it?"

"I'm black."

"You're not black and I'm not white. We're lovers."

"I'm a Negro, Roy. Isn't that why you moved back home in your apartment? You knew I wanted you to stay with me."

"I think I'm too tired to talk about that, Laura," said Roy, standing up and kissing her and then he took off the dusty shirt which was sticking to him. She hung up the shirt and the trousers and he left his shorts and T-shirt on the bathroom floor. He glanced at the concave scar on his abdomen and stepped into the steaming suds-filled tub. Never had a bath felt better. He leaned back with his eyes closed and set his mind free and dozed for a moment, then felt her presence. She was sitting on the floor beside the tub watching him.

"Thank you, Laura," he said, loving the flecks in the light brown eyes, and the smooth brown skin and the graceful fingers she laid against his shoulder.

"What do you suppose I see in you?" she smiled, caressing his neck. "It must be the attraction of opposites, don't you think? Your golden hair and golden body. You're just the most beautiful man I know. Think that's it?"

"That's just gold plate," said Roy. "There's nothing but pot metal underneath."

"There's plenty underneath."

"If there's anything, you put it there. There was nothing when you found me last year."

"*I* was nothing," she corrected him.

"You're everything. You're beauty and love and kindness, but mostly you're order. I need order right now, Laura. I'm very scared, you know. There's chaos out there."

"I know."

"I haven't been this afraid since you dried me out and taught me not to be afraid. God, you should see what chaos looks like, Laura."

"I know. I know," she said, still stroking his neck.

"I can't stay away from you anymore," he said, staring at the faucet which dripped sporadically into the suds. "I didn't have the guts to stay with you, Laura. I need peace and tranquility and I knew we'd face hatred together and I didn't have the guts. But now that I've been back in that lonely apartment I don't have the guts to be away from you and now that I've been in that darkness and madness tonight, I could never make it without you and . . ."

"Don't talk anymore, Roy," she said getting up. "Wait until tomorrow. See how you feel tomorrow."

"No," he said, grabbing her arm with a wet, soapy hand. "You can't depend on tomorrow. I tell you the way it is out there, you mustn't depend on tomorrow. I live for you now. You can never get rid of me now. Never." Roy pulled her down and kissed her on the mouth and then kissed the palm of her hand, and she stroked his neck with the other hand, saying, "Baby, baby," as she always did and which never failed to soothe him.

They were still awake, lying naked on their backs with only a sheet over them when the sun rose in Los Angeles.

"You should go to sleep," she whispered. "You've got to go back to the street tonight."

"It won't be bad now," he said.

"Yes. Maybe the National Guard will have things under control."

"It doesn't matter if they don't. It still won't be bad now. My vacation begins September first. It'll surely be over by then. Do you mind getting married in Las Vegas? We can do it without waiting."

"We don't have to get married. It doesn't matter if we're married."

"I still have a conventional bone or two in my body, I guess. Do it for me."

"Alright. For you."

"Weren't you brought up to respect the institution of marriage?"

"My daddy was a Baptist preacher," she laughed.

"Well then it's settled. I was brought up a Lutheran, but we never went to church very much except when appearances demanded it, so I think we'll raise our children as Baptists."

"I'm nothing now. Not a Baptist. Nothing."

"You're everything."

"Do we have a right to have children?"

"You're goddamn right we do."

"The golden knight and his dark lady," she said. "But we'll suffer, you and me. I promise you. You don't know what a holy war is."

"We'll win."

"I've never seen you so happy."

"I've never been so happy."

"Do you want to know why I loved you from the first?"

"Why?"

"You weren't like other white men that flirted with me and that asked me out on dates to their apartments or maybe to some out of the way pretty nice place where lots of mixed couples go. I never really could trust a white man because I could see that they saw something in me that they wanted, but it wasn't me."

"What was it?"

"I don't know. Just lust maybe, for a little brown animal. Primitive vitality of a Negro, that sort of thing."

"My, you're intellectual tonight."

"It's morning."

"This morning then."

"Then there were white liberals who would've taken me to a governor's ball, but I think with people like that almost any Negro would do. I don't trust those people either."

"Then there was me."

"Then there was you."

"Old Roy the wino."

"Not anymore."

"Because I borrowed some of your guts."

"You're such a humble man that I get annoyed with you."

"I used to be arrogant and conceited."

"I can't believe that."

"Neither can I anymore. But it's true."

"You were different than any white man I ever met. You needed something from me, but it was something one human being could give another and it had nothing to do with my being Negro. You always looked at me as a woman and a person, do you know that?"

"Guess I'm just not the lusty type."

"You're very lusty," she laughed. "You're a marvelous lusty lover and right now you're too silly to talk to."

"Where'll we go for a honeymoon?"

"Do we have to have one of those too?"

"Of course," said Roy. "I'm conventional, remember?"

"San Francisco is a fine city. Have you ever been there?"

"No, let's go to San Francisco."

"It's also a very tolerant city. You've got to consider things like that now."

"It's so quiet," said Roy. "For a while last night when I was most afraid I thought the sound of the fire would never stop. I thought I'd always hear the fire roaring in my ears."

"I hear we're going back to almost normal deployment starting tomorrow," said Roy. It pleased him to say it because he and Laura had decided that as soon as the riot was completely finished and he could do it, he would ask for some special days off and they would go to San Francisco for a week after being married in Las Vegas where they might stay for a few days, but then again they might go from Vegas to Tahoe for a night . . . "Sure will be nice to get off the twelve-hour shifts," said Roy in a burst of exuberance at the thought of doing it, and now that he and Laura were going to do it all his doubts dissolved.

"I've had enough of it," said Serge Duran as he made a lazy U-turn on Crenshaw where they were on perimeter patrol and Roy liked the solid way Duran drove, in fact he liked Duran whom he had only seen a dozen times during these five years and whom he never bothered to get to know. But they had been together only two hours tonight and he liked him and was glad that when the perimeter patrols were set that Duran had told the sergeant, "Let me work with my two classmates Fehler and Plebesly." And Gus Plebesly seemed like a very decent sort and Roy hoped he might become good friends with both these men. He became acutely aware that he had no real friends among policemen, had never made any, but he was going to change that, he was changing lots of things.

"Now that the riot's just about done, it's hard to believe it happened," said Gus, and Roy thought that Plebesly had aged more than five years. He remembered Plebesly as a timid man, perhaps the smallest in their class but he seemed taller now and solider. Of course he remembered Plebesly's inhuman stamina and smiled as he thought of how his endurance had been a threat to their P.T. instructor, Officer Randolph.

"It's not hard to believe it happened when you drive

down Central Avenue or a Hundred and Third Street," said Serge. "Were you down there on Friday night, Roy?"

"I was there," said Roy.

"I think we were there too," said Gus, "but I was too scared to know for sure."

"Likewise, brother," said Roy.

"But I was so scared I can hardly remember most of the things that happened," said Gus, and Roy saw that the shy grin was the same, and so was the deprecatory manner that used to annoy Roy because he was too stupid in those days to see that it was thoroughly genuine.

"I was thinking the same thing just today," said Serge. "Friday night is already becoming a kind of mist in my mind. I can't remember big chunks of it. Except the fear, of course."

"You feel that way too, Serge?" said Gus. "How about you, Roy?"

"Sure, Gus," said Roy. "I was scared to death."

"Be damned," said Gus and was silent and Roy guessed that Gus felt reassured. It was comforting to talk with a policeman who, like himself, was obviously filled with doubts, and he pitied Gus now and felt the tug of friendship.

"Did you ever finish college, Roy?" asked Serge. "I remember talking to you in the academy about your degree in criminology. You were pretty close to it then."

"I never got any closer, Serge," laughed Roy and was surprised to discover no irony in the laugh and he guessed he was finally making peace with Roy Fehler.

"I never built up too many units myself," said Serge, nodding his understanding. "Sorry now that I didn't, with our first sergeant exam coming up. How about you, Gus? You go to school?"

"Off and on," said Gus. "I hope to have my bachelor's in business administration in about a year."

"Good for you, Gus," said Roy. "We'll be working for you one of these days."

"Oh, no," said Gus, apologetically. "I haven't really studied for the sergeant's exam, and besides, I freeze in test situations. I know I'll fail miserably."

"You'll be a great sergeant, Gus," said Serge, and he seemed to mean it. Roy felt drawn to both of them and he wanted them to know about his coming marriage—

wanted them to know about Laura, about a white policeman with a black wife and whether they thought he
was mad, because he was sure they were compassionate
men. But even if they thought him a fool and proved it
by polite embarrassment it wouldn't change a thing.

"It's getting dark, thank goodness," said Gus. "It was
so smoggy and hot today. I'd sure like to go for a swim.
I've got a neighbor with a pool. Maybe I'll ask him
tomorrow."

"How about tonight?" said Serge. "After we get off
I've got a pool in my apartment building. We might as
well take advantage of it because I'm moving in a few
weeks."

"Where you moving?" asked Gus.

"My girl and I have a pad picked out to buy. It'll be
lawn mowing and weed pulling instead of moonlight
swims, I guess."

"You're getting married?" asked Roy. "I'm getting
married as soon as I can get a week off."

"You're tumbling too?" smiled Serge. "That's reassuring."

"I thought you were already married, Roy," said Gus.

"I was when we were in the academy. I was divorced
not long after that."

"Have kids, Roy?" asked Gus.

"A little girl," said Roy, and then he thought of her
last Sunday when he had brought her to Laura's apartment. He thought of how Laura had played with her
and made Becky love her.

"You didn't go sour on marriage?" asked Serge.

"Nothing wrong with marriage," said Roy. "It gives
you children and Gus can tell you what children give
you."

"Couldn't make it without them," said Gus.

"How long you been married, Gus?" asked Serge.

"Nine years. All my life."

"How old are you?"

"Twenty-seven."

"What's your girl's name, Serge?" asked Roy as he
had an idea.

"Mariana."

"How about having that swim tomorrow?" said Roy.
"Maybe Gus and his wife and Laura and I could come
over to your place and meet your fiancée and we could

have a swim and a few beers before we go to work tomorrow afternoon." It was done, he thought. It would be the first test.

"Okay," said Serge, with enthusiasm. "Can you make it, Gus?"

"Well, my wife hasn't been feeling well lately, but maybe she'd like to come over even if she won't swim. I'd sure like to come."

"That's fine. I'll be expecting you," said Serge. "How about ten o'clock in the morning?"

"Fine," said Gus, and Roy thought this would be the best way for him to see. To just bring her and see. The hell with apologies and warnings. Let them see her, lots of her, long-legged and shapely and incomparable in a bathing suit. Then he'd know how it would be, what he could expect.

"Would it be too much . . ." Gus hesitated. "I mean, I hate to ask you . . . If your landlady wouldn't like it, or if maybe you don't want a bunch of noisy kids around . . . I could understand . . ."

"You want to bring your kids?" Serge smiled.

"I would."

"Bring them," said Serge. "Mariana loves kids. She wants six or eight."

"Thanks," said Gus. "My kids will be thrilled. That's a beautiful name your fiancée has—Mariana."

"Mariana Paloma," said Serge.

"That's Spanish, isn't it?" asked Gus.

"She's Mexican," said Serge. "From Guadalajara."

"Come to think of it, isn't Duran a Spanish name?"

"I'm Mexican too," said Serge.

"I'll be damned. That never occurred to me," said Roy, looking at Serge for some Mexican features and finding none, except perhaps something about the shape of his eyes.

"Are you of Mexican descent on both sides?" asked Gus. "You don't look it."

"One hundred percent," Serge laughed. "I guess I'm probably more Mexican than anyone I know."

"You speak Spanish then?" asked Gus.

"Hardly at all," Serge answered. "When I was a boy I did, but I've forgotten. I guess I'll learn again though. I went to Mariana's home Sunday afternoon, and after I got the blessing of Mr. Rosales, her *padrino,* I went to her and tried to ask her in Spanish. I think it ended up more in English than Spanish. I must've been a hell of a sight, a big stammering clown with an armload of white roses."

"I'll bet you were just smashing," Roy grinned, wondering if he looked as contented as Serge.

"Mariana's informed me we'll talk only Spanish in our house until my Spanish is at least as good as her English."

"That's very nice," said Gus, and Roy wondered if she had required courting in the old Mexican manner. He wondered if Serge had known her a long time before he kissed her. I'm getting corny, Roy smiled to himself.

"Usually Mexican men dominate their women," said Serge, "until they get old and then Mama is the boss and the old boys pay for their tyranny. But I'm afraid Mariana and I are starting out the other way around."

"Nothing wrong with a strong woman," said Roy. "A policeman needs one."

"Yes," said Gus, gazing at the blazing sunset. "Not many guys can do this job alone."

"Well, we're *veteranos,* now," said Serge. "Five years. We can sew a hash mark on our sleeves. I thought we were going to have a class reunion after five years."

"That would've been nice," said Gus. "We can have a small reunion party tomorrow afternoon. If they bring us all back to the command post maybe we can work together again tomorrow night."

"I really think we'll be going back to our divisions tomorrow," said Serge. "This riot is over."

"I wonder how long the experts will screw around with their cause theories?" said Roy.

"This is just the beginning," said Serge. "They'll appoint commissions, and intellectuals who know two or three Negroes will demonstrate their expertise in race relations and this will be only the beginning. Negroes are no better and no worse than whites. I think they'll do whatever they can get away with and whatever is expected of them, and from now on there'll be lots of Negroes living up to their angry black man press notices."

"Do you think blacks are the same as whites?" asked Roy to Gus, who was still watching the sunset.

"Yes," said Gus absently. "I learned it five years ago

from my first partner who was the best policeman I ever knew. Kilvinsky used to say that most people are like plankton that can't fight the currents but only drift with the waves and tides, and some are like benthos which can do it but have to crawl along the slimy ocean floor to do it. And then others are like nekton which can actually fight the currents but don't have to crawl on the bottom to do it but it's so hard on the nekton that they must be very strong. I guess he figured the best of us were like the nekton. Anyway, he always said that in the big dark sea, the shape or shade of the poor suffering little things didn't matter at all."

"Sounds like he was a philosopher," Roy smiled.

"Sometimes I think I made a mistake becoming a cop," said Serge. "I look back over these five years and the frustrations have been bad but I guess there's nothing I'd rather do."

"I saw an editorial today that said it was just deplorable that so many people had been shot and killed in the riot," said Gus. "The guy said, 'We must assume that police can shoot to *wound*. Therefore it follows that the police must be intentionally killing all these people.'"

"That's a screwed-up syllogism," said Serge. "But you can't blame the ignorant bastards. They've seen a thousand movies that prove you can wing a guy or shoot a gun out of his hands. What the hell, you can't blame them."

"Just a pile of plankton dumped in a sea of concrete, eh, Gus?" said Roy.

"I guess I don't really regret the job," said Gus. "I guess I think I know something that most people don't."

"All we can do is try to protect ourselves," said Roy. "We sure as hell can't change them."

"And we can't save them," said Gus. "Nor ourselves. Poor bastards."

"Hey, this conversation is getting too damned depressing," said Roy suddenly. "The riot's over. Better days are coming. We're having a swimming party tomorrow. Let's cheer up."

"Okay, let's try to catch a crook," said Serge. "A good felony pinch always lifts my spirits. You used to work this area, didn't you Gus?"

"Sure," said Gus, straightening up and smiling. "Drive west toward Crenshaw. I know where there's some drop-off spots for hot rollers. Maybe we can pick up a car thief."

Roy was the first to see the woman waving to them from the car parked near the phone booth on Rodeo Road.

"I think we got a citizen's call," said Roy.

"That's okay, I was getting tired driving around anyway," said Serge. "Maybe she has an insurmountable problem we can surmount."

"It got dark fast tonight," Gus observed. "A couple of minutes ago I was enjoying the sunset and now, bang, it's dark."

Serge parked beside the woman who squirmed out of the Volkswagen awkwardly and shuffled over to their car in her bedroom slippers and bathrobe which fought to conceal her expansive largeness.

"I was just going to the phone booth to call the cops," she puffed, and before he was out of the car Roy smelled the alcoholic breath and examined the red face and weedy dyed red hair.

"What's the problem, ma'am?" said Gus.

"My old man is nuts. He's been drinking and not going to work lately and not supporting me and my kids and beating hell out of me whenever he feels like it and tonight he's completely nuts and he kicked me right in the side. The bastard. I think he broke a rib." The woman writhed inside the bathrobe and touched her ribs.

"You live far from here?" asked Serge.

"Just down the street on Coliseum," said the woman. "How about coming home and throwing him out for me?"

"He your legal husband?" asked Serge.

"Yeah, but he's nuts."

"Okay, we'll follow you home and have a talk with him."

"You can't talk to him," the woman insisted, getting back inside the Volkswagen. "The bastard's crazy tonight."

"Okay, we'll follow you home," said Roy.

"Breaks the monotony, anyway," said Gus, as they drove behind the little car and Roy put the shotgun down on the floor in the back and wondered if they should lock it in the front when they went in the woman's residence or would it be alright here on the floor if the car doors were locked. He decided to leave it on the floor.

"Is this neighborhood mostly white?" asked Serge to Gus.

"It's mixed," said Gus. "It's mixed clear out to La Cienega and up into Hollywood."

"If this town has a ghetto it's the biggest goddamn ghetto in the world," said Serge. "Some ghetto. Look up there in Baldwin Hills."

"Fancy pads," said Gus. "That's a mixed neighborhood too."

"I think the broad in the VW is the best pinch we'll see tonight," said Roy. "She almost creamed that Ford when she turned."

"She's loaded," said Serge. "Tell you what, if she smashes into somebody we'll just take off like we don't know her. I figured she was too drunk to drive when she waddled out of that car and lit my cigarette with her breath."

"Must be that apartment house," said Gus, flashing the spotlight on the number over the door as Serge pulled in behind the Volkswagen which she parked four feet from the curb.

"Three-Z-Ninety-one, citizen's call, forty-one twenty-three, Coliseum Drive," said Gus into the mike.

"Don't forget to lock your door," said Roy. "I left the shotgun on the floor."

"I'm not going in," said the woman. "I'm afraid of him. He said he'd kill me if I called the cops on him."

"Your kids in there?" asked Serge.

"No," she breathed. "They ran next door when we started fighting. I guess I should tell you there's a gun in there and he's nuts as hell tonight."

"Where's the gun?" asked Gus.

"Bedroom closet," said the woman. "When you take him you can take that too."

"We don't know if we're taking anybody yet," said Roy. "We're going to talk to him first."

Serge started up the steps first as she said, "Number twelve. We live in number twelve."

They passed through a landscaped archway and into a court surrounded by apartments. There was a calm lighted swimming pool to their left and a sun deck with Ping-Pong tables to the right. Roy was surprised at the size of the apartment building after passing through the deceiving archway.

"Very nice," said Gus, obviously admiring the swimming pool.

"Twelve must be this way," said Roy, walking toward the tile staircase surrounded by face-high ferns. Roy thought he could still smell the woman's alcoholic breath when a frail chalky man in a damp undershirt stepped from behind a dwarfed twisted tree and lunged toward Roy who turned on the stairway. The man pointed the cheap .22 revolver at Roy's stomach and fired once and as Roy sat down on the stairway in amazement the sounds of shouts and gunfire and a deathless scream echoed through the vast patio. Then Roy realized he was lying at the foot of the staircase alone and it was quiet for a moment. Then he was aware that it was his stomach.

"Oh, not there," said Roy and he clamped his teeth on his tongue and fought the burst of hysteria. The shock. It can kill. The shock!

Then he pulled the shirt open and unbuckled the Sam Browne and looked at the tiny bubbling cavity in the pit of his stomach. He knew he could not survive another one. Not there. Not in the guts. He had no guts left!

Roy unclamped his teeth and had to swallow many times because of the blood from his ripped tongue. It didn't hurt so much this time, he thought, and he was astonished at his lucidity. He saw that Serge and Gus were kneeling beside him, ashen-faced. Serge crossed himself and kissed his thumbnail.

It was *much* easier this time. By God, it was! The pain was diminishing and an insidious warmth crept over him. But no, it was all wrong. It shouldn't happen now. Then he panicked as he realized that it shouldn't happen now because he was starting to know. Oh, please, not now, he thought. I'm starting to know.

"Know, know," said Roy. "Know, know, know, know." His voice sounded to him hollow and rhythmic like the tolling of a bell. And then he could no longer speak.

"*Santa María*," said Serge taking his hand. "*Santa María* . . . where's the goddamn ambulance? *Ay, Dios mío* . . . Gus, he's cold. *Sóbale las manos* . . ."

Then Roy heard Gus sob, "He's gone, Serge. Poor Roy, poor poor man. He's gone."

Then Roy heard Serge say, "We should cover him. Did you hear him? He was saying no to death. No, no, no, he said. *Santa María!*"

I am not dead, Roy thought. It is monstrous to say I am dead. And then he saw Becky walking primly through a grassy field and she looked so grownup he said Rebecca when he called her name and she came smiling to her father, the sun glistening off her hair, more golden than his had ever been.

"*Dios te salve María, llena de gracia, el Señor es contigo . . .*" said Serge.

"I'll cover him. I'll get a blanket from somebody," said Gus. "Please, somebody, give me a blanket."

Now Roy released himself to the billowy white sheets of darkness and the last thing he ever heard was Sergio Durán saying, "*Santa María,*" again and again.